ESSENCE AND RUNES

Essence and Runes

Book 1

TAYLOR LYNN

*To all who wish to see themselves in worlds of fantasy and
imagination. You belong.*

*So grab your sword, don your crown,
and let the adventure begin!*

TO VOLIRA
VALTAN
BRETKA
LABRYNTHIA
PORTON
CORATH
THESTRAS
RETLAS
ANOLIAN OCEAN
DEMILTSCH ISLANDS
GULF OF ANOLIA
FRALLIS
ANICA
VOLENTI
WESSEN
ULMANTA
PROMITHIA
BENEVIA
ARYA
ORENUS
SENNA
ACADIA
ALWILKE
N
W
E
S

AUTHOR'S NOTE

Thank you so much for taking a chance on *Essence and Runes*! I hope you enjoy this adventure as much as I have enjoyed creating this world.

Please keep in mind that this book contains mature language, themes, sexually explicit scenes (FF and FM), and content that may not be suitable for all readers.

Trigger warnings include: Grief, Death of parents both on and off the page, War/Gore, Anxiety/PTSD, Imprisonment/Torture, Sexism, Mention of difficult pregnancies/births.

I did my best to be as inclusive with this list as possible, but if there are any warnings I may have missed, please let me know via email at hello@taylorlynnwrites.com.

The Spirits descended upon the world with their powers of essence and runes.

In a fury of fire and destruction, Earth met its end. But from the ashes, it rose anew. The lives of humans forever changed for generations to come.

The Powers of Essence

Cosmic:	**Natures:**	**Shadows:**
Solas	Elemental	Reader
Asher	Stormning	Shifter
Maker	Healer	Empath

All humans who are strong enough to develop the power of essence can attain basic abilities including, but not limited to, Veil, Transporting, Telekinesis, etc.

The Powers of Runes:

Runes used as a main power source can only be accessed once one has mastered the ancient language of the spirits, Eldrian. Rune symbols can be woven into fabric or objects and used as natural enhancers for essence wielders. They can also be sold as charms to those in need of a boost.

CHAPTER

ONE

I've grown accustomed to the weight of silence just after a battle ends.

It's the friend that awaits with open arms, letting us know that we've made it through. That we're among the *lucky* who live to see another day.

Steam rolls off the battlefield in wafts and spindly tendrils as we count our dead, gathering their bodies to be prepared for their return home. Charred earth crunches under the fall of heavy boots, and pained screams fill the air. An exasperated grunt leaves my throat as I help heave the last of the fallen into a cart.

Footsteps approach, and a comforting shift in the air engulfs my senses, so at odds with the doom and gloom of our setting.

"We'll be ready to depart by nightfall, Raya," Dessaray's familiar voice calls. The sound a welcome reminder of home and peace and joy despite the death that surrounds us.

I nod. "How many are missing?"

"I counted six from my legion. Brant counted eight..."

1

"And I counted another nine," I finish before she can ask, sharing the piece of parchment with the list of names from my group with her. My script is nothing more than chicken scratch with my bulky gloves, but somehow, she manages to make out my scribbles and scrawls. "Who are among the missing from your count?"

"Of note? Daveed, Breena, and Jax," she replies.

My heart sinks to the depths of my being. For a moment, I'm far from a smoking battlefield and standing in formation on the grounds of Acadia, our country's military academy, in my home region, Senna. Breena stands to my left, Jax and Daveed to my right. We're in the mess hall having one of many meals and cracking jokes as if we had all the time in the world to do so. We stand at the front of our graduating class, the "best" we were called. Heads held high, shoulders back, as if we were on top of the world. As if we always would be.

But now? In the middle of this never-ending war, we are too often reminded of the reality of our lives and our futures that are so swiftly cut short.

No, I can't afford to think that way. They are alive. They have to be.

"All of our soldiers are *of note*, Dessaray," I say, barely able to contain my annoyance at her disregard.

I know she doesn't mean it, still learning the ropes of leadership herself, but I'm tired. We all are. The fighting ended a little more than a day ago, but we've been working nonstop to find the wounded, count our missing, and collect the dead.

"You know what I mean." She gives me a look that's somewhere between exasperation and utter fatigue. She continues, "I haven't been able to find Jace or Paulina either.

Bringing the count of our higher-ranking officers missing to five."

"Dammit." I kick a battle-stricken barrel. It splinters as it tumbles across the torn terrain.

A few years ago, the soldiers of Corath started taking ours and bringing them back to their country as prisoners of war.

Our sources informed us they were using our people in whatever ways they deemed fit. Torture, pleasure, as servants. With the numbers they'd taken, it seemed something more sinister was afoot, although we were never able to prove it. We haven't seen this habit of theirs for five years.

"Why start this again? Why now?" she asks.

"The King of Corath is bored, I suppose." The thought makes me sick.

"Lieutenant General!" a soft, breathless voice cries over the clanking armor of soldiers packing up the camp.

I look up to the sky, not wanting to face the person now approaching us, already anticipating the request they bring.

Rain threatens the cloudy day, but no droplets have made their claim. The humidity on top of the heat has made this summer weather unbearable. When the sun shines its brightest, my black armor just absorbs the heat.

I beg the spirits and the reigning Celestials for just one hour of rain. Something to break apart the thickness in the air. But it's only a few more days until we're back at court, and then a few more after that until we're back on another battlefield.

I could ask one of our Stormnings for some assistance. To summon a few rain clouds, allow the droplets to loosen the air around us. But all of us are completely drained. I can barely feel my own essence as it slumbers. Dormant and just out of reach.

"Lieutenant General!" they call again.

"You're being summoned," Dessaray says next to me with a grim smile.

I shoot her what should be a menacing glare, promising to continue our conversation later, but she knows better. She laughs before walking away toward her tent, her golden-brown curls billowing behind her.

"I have an urgent message from Her Majesty, the Queen," the disheveled squire says. He bows his head as he approaches.

"All messages from Her Majesty seem to be urgent these days," I say, starting toward my own tents. He matches my more relaxed pace with a sigh of relief. "What is it?"

"She is ordering an emergency meeting of the High Generals. She requests your return to court immediately."

"Oh? Is that all?"

"You must return at once."

With a sharp turn, I stare down the squire, who now cowers slightly under the heat of my gaze.

"Was there an order anywhere in that request, or just a strong urging?"

"N-n-not exactly." He fumbles over his words.

"Let me ask you this." I take a step closer, and he stumbles back. "If you fought for Her Majesty on the front lines and you were to lose your life, would you want us to leave your body to be ravaged by vultures and worms? Or would you want us to bring you home for a proper burial?"

He gulps and shakily responds, "Bring me home, ma'am."

"I thought so." I continue on my path toward my quarters. "You may tell our queen I will return to court as scheduled. Besides, I'm sure my father and the other generals have already begun their discussions." My addition won't be much. It never is when it comes to my father.

"But—"

"If she would like us to return faster, she is more than welcome to get her pretty little ass off her throne and help us bring our dead home." I glance over the young squire once more. Squeaky clean and eyes wide with shock at how unafraid I am to speak plainly.

He quickly shuts his mouth and nods. "Y-yes, Lieutenant."

Without another word, he heads back to his horse. Once mounted, he leaves down the path he came from, steadily galloping away.

Dessy steps beside me as I watch the squire retreat, my arms crossed against my chest and another bead of sweat dripping down my brow.

She stands with me in silence for a beat more before speaking again. "You have to return to court. Let Father and the rest of the generals know what is happening."

"I will, but first, I need to help everyone regroup. Escort our fallen home. I'll send a letter ahead to warn that it has begun again."

"You can leave me to it. Our troops will understand."

"Not you too." The words leave my lips with an exasperated huff. I repeat the words our father instilled in me time and time again. "We must lead by example. If our troops fight, we fight. If they escort our fallen home, we're—"

"Yeah, yeah, I know. We're right by their side." She finishes for me, shaking her head. "You know, Raya, you don't have to carry this burden all on your own."

"While that is a noble thought, dear sister, I am their leader. No one else should carry the weight of our dead. And if they do, then I must be there to support them."

"You are so stubborn." *Just like Father,* her eyes seem to say.

While mine mirror the general's, clear blue with flecks as dark as midnight, hers are a perfect reflection of our mothers. Green with golden streaks, like the sunshine that peeks through evergreen leaves.

I want to laugh at her amusement, but the truth of it all lies heavily on my soul. "With everything we face here, I have to be."

TWO

The Great Hall buzzes with courtiers. Voices old and new echo off the stone walls and massive archways. I'm greeted by many wanting to welcome *the heir of Senna* back after a long time away on the battlefield.

It's always an adjustment, balancing the warrior and my position as my father's heir. Not only to his title as general but also as Duchess of Senna—leader of the famed region.

"Well, if it isn't the Wielder of Death."

I wince at the words. I've never been a fan of the nickname bestowed upon me by our enemies. Forcing a smile, I turn toward General Leigh Sanat, my lifelong friend, his voice jubilant.

"It's about damn time you showed up," he says with a laugh.

"It's nice to see you too, General." I wrap my arms around him in an embrace of both joy and relief at his own safe return.

"I'm surprised you didn't just transport back from the barracks," he says.

Always so frivolous with his energy this one.

Thanks to many years of intensive training at home and at the military academy, my essence can do many things, more than many of my counterparts. But *transporting* is something all essence wielders can attain. Most can transport between small spaces—across the room, the other side of the estate or town, or as far as a few towns over. But those who are stronger can jump across larger distances.

Transporting is useful, I'll admit, but it takes too much of my damn energy, so I try to only use it when I need to. Besides, I don't mind riding Dahlia, and the peace I feel when doing so.

"You know me, I always like to take the scenic route," I reply. "How's the climate here at court?"

"The usual. Drama, gossip. Only it's tinged with a bit of restlessness as Her Majesty awaits your return."

"Then I guess it's a good thing I'm here now." We walk some ways down the hall, away from the rest of the courtiers scattered throughout. "How are your troops faring?"

"About as well as everyone else's. We've had a few weeks of a break to connect with loved ones and family, but I'm sure that will end after tomorrow's meetings." *I heard Corath is at it again taking prisoners,* he continues in a whisper into my mind.

Leigh is a Reader, a talent we both share. He uses his abilities to reach into my mind, a habit we have grown accustomed to since childhood. But he's on the stronger end of the scale for this ability, like my mother was. Able to control other's actions or rewrite memories with a simple thought. How he didn't become a spy is beyond me.

I solemnly nod. *Yes. Breena, Jax, and Daveed are among the missing.*

His eyes widen, the only clue to the shock he feels. Leigh

was a year ahead of us at the academy, but since we were practically inseparable growing up, he spent much of his time with my friends and me. This news no doubt pains him as much as it does me.

Continuing on, knowing we will have more time to discuss what is occurring in private, I sigh. "Indeed. We lost many great fighters in the last battle. Reason why I was delayed in answering the queen's *beckoning* call."

I look out the window, taking a deep breath. A pack of servants and workers flit around the grounds, setting up decorations and bringing boxes of floral arrangements into the wing that houses the ballroom. Tonight, the queen and her court celebrate the return of the Court of Generals, our council of each of the region's leaders. Although, I must admit, I'm in no mood for celebrations.

"Where did my dear sister run off to?" I ask.

"You know her, immediately off to the kitchen. No doubt already eating her heart's fill with your father."

I can't help but grimace at the mention of my father. If Leigh noticed, he doesn't say anything, and I'm not going to bring it up.

"At least one of us is." My stomach growls at the thought of a real meal. Not the gray slosh served in the trenches.

"I'm sure there is something else you can't wait to eat. Or someone else, if you catch my drift," he says, eyebrows waggling at the implication.

I shove his shoulder, and he laughs in response. But just as quickly as his smile appears, it's gone.

His body stands at attention as the chatter throughout the hall turns into hushed whispers and servants pause their work. Everyone turns and bows toward the other end of the hallway in a ripple. I follow their lead, turning to the sound of heels clicking, flanked by thudding boots.

Queen Sarana walks toward us, head held high, nodding every so often to the murmurs of respect around her. Her deep brown skin glows against her white beaded dress. A tri-point diamond crown sits atop her head, like stars shining bright. Her hair, a crown of ringlets as dark as the midnight sky, is perfectly styled in braids and twists. A small train of pooled tulle and crystals trails behind her.

Some call her the king since there is no one who holds a title higher than her own. She has a husband, but the highest title he bears is Prince Consort. A title with little to no power in this court.

Prince Davison thought he would be crowned king after marrying her, but she is the true ruler. Having him named king would diminish her ruling, and we couldn't have that.

Sarana's eyes lock onto mine, and my heart skips a beat. Time slows and stills as she makes her way to our corner.

Leigh and I bow and murmur "Your Majesty" in sync.

"General Sanat. Lieutenant General Ontaria." She nods at both of us, and we release ourselves from our bows. "So good to see both of you. Apologies for rushing you all back to court, but we have some urgent matters to discuss."

"We completely understand, Your Majesty," replies Leigh.

Sarana smiles in his direction. "I hope our discussions are brief enough tomorrow so you may return to your troops, but I want you both to enjoy yourselves at tonight's festivities."

"I have no doubt we will," I say.

"Lieutenant, do you have a moment? I'd like to hear how things fared after the last battle."

"Of course, Your Majesty."

She walks ahead, and I follow, sneaking a peek back at Leigh, who gives me a knowing smirk and conspiratorial wink.

Her guards flank us as we head toward her private study. Away from the courtiers. Away from the other visiting generals. It's just her and I.

The two guards standing outside her study open the door, and she leads the way inside.

"You may leave us," she says, dismissing the flanking soldiers.

They all bow and promptly leave us to our privacy.

As soon as the door clicks shut, Sarana closes the distance between us. Her lips meet mine, and our tongues dance to the rhythm of the fire crackling in the hearth. I cup the base of her head and wind her thick braids around my fingers. She tips her head back, exposing the column of her neck.

There is nothing sweet and sensual about these kisses or our embrace. They rarely ever are when I return from the front.

It's a release of passion, desire, yearning, anger, love. All the emotions we felt while apart clash together in harmonious discord, as if we may never get this moment again. And who knows, we might not.

These stolen moments are all she can give me, but they are a shining beacon of light between days of darkness and death.

I trail my lips down her jawline and kiss the spot where her neck meets her shoulder, grazing the edge of her skin with my teeth before biting softly. She lets out a small moan.

"I missed you," she manages to breathe out.

I unlace her dress and let the fabric pool at her feet. Finding the ribbon of her corset, I slowly pull the bow undone. The corset meets the dress where it lies on the floor.

I take her in, standing in front of me with nothing but the jeweled crown on her head. She steps forward, into me, and kisses me fiercely. I cup her breast in one hand, teasing her nipple with my thumb, and draw her closer with the other.

"How much?" I say into her mouth.

But she can't answer, not when I trail my lips down then slowly roll my tongue across the raised peak of her breast. After another quick flick of my tongue and nip of my teeth, I continue down to her waist and past her hips.

A gasp of a moan escapes her, and a devilish smile plays on her lips as she says, "What a beautiful image. Seeing you on your knees."

I playfully bite her inner thigh.

"I only kneel for you." I plant a kiss right where I bit her. "My Queen." I kiss her again, climbing a little higher. "My everything," I say before devouring her slick center with my lips and tongue.

She doesn't hold back as she moans with delight.

WE LIE on the floor atop blankets and rugs. Her dress and my battle leathers are balled into a mess of white and black by her desk. Her breathing and the crackling of the fireplace fill the silence in the room. My head rests on her shoulder, and I wrap my hand around her stomach as her fingers swirl up and down my arms. My eyes grow heavy, and a wave of peace that I haven't felt in months washes over me.

"So, my warrior, how are you?" she asks, and my peace slips away with the current as my mind snaps back to reality.

"As good as I can be." My eyes move to the fireplace, watching as pieces of the log burn and pop with the flames.

"I'm sorry my throne-rested ass couldn't help you deliver your soldiers home. But as long as you think it's pretty…"

A bark of a laugh escapes my lips. At least her squire had the guts to tell her the truth of what I said. What I would have given to see the look on her face when he did.

"Apologies, my Queen." I kiss her shoulder where my head lies and take a deep breath. "This war. It needs to end."

"Every time." She rolls her eyes, saying the words more to herself than to me. "Can't we just have one conversation that's not about the bloody war?"

"What do you expect from me, Sarana? I'm a soldier, and we're at war. I have nothing else to talk about."

"Nothing at all? You may be a soldier, Raya, but is there truly nothing else in your life that you wish to entertain? Do you even know who you would be if you weren't a soldier?" I open my lips to speak, but she holds up a finger. "Don't you dare say that you'd be a *leader* because that will just prove my point."

"And what point might that be?"

"That you have lost yourself in the image your father has pressed upon you."

I rise at that, hoping to hide my burning cheeks. Because what she's saying just isn't true. My line dates back millennia. At one point in time, we were great rulers before Sarana's ancestors made their moves to unite the seven kingdoms into one.

My father is proud of that lineage, and so am I. We would do anything to ensure its survival, to be the guiding leaders of our lands and people.

Crossing my arms over my chest, I let my anger stew as realization and resentment settle deep within. Realization that maybe, just maybe, what Sarana says has an inkling of truth, and resentment for even considering that truth when my father has given me so much. Has given this country and our region so, so much.

"As if your mother never pressed upon you her vision for your future," I bite back.

Sarana rises behind me and wraps her arms around my torso, planting the softest of kisses upon my shoulder. As if kisses could take back the words she said and the questions now flooding my mind. As if kisses could wash away the death. The pain. The nightmares of killing.

"My mother only ever wanted the best for me. Any decision that was made for me was made with my input. Even when I was young. She knew that as a ruler, I would need to learn the lessons of choices and that in order to be my own person, even with a path laid out before me, I needed to be comfortable making decisions for myself."

"You're just saying these things because you don't truly understand the toll this war has taken on our people," I say, mainly out of spite and anger. Anger from her words and the bit of truth in them. "You don't feel the weight of battle the way we do."

"While part of that might be true, I understand well enough."

"Do you, Sarana?" I turn myself to look into her brown eyes. "Look at Senna. Crop output has severely decreased. Port towns that were once prosperous are beginning to run dry. Businesses are being forced to close. Families have been obliterated. Our people are struggling."

I used to be able to look into her eyes and feel her warmth. It was as if all of Mother Nature lived within them, and I could feel the dirt and the trees and the sun in the sky. Now, I'm starting to see the dirt from the battlegrounds she has yet to touch.

Not that I want her anywhere near a battlefield. Fuck no.

But it makes me wonder if she truly understands what it means to give pieces of your soul away to the destruction that war brings.

"Yes, Raya, I do." A tinge of hurt laces her voice, and I snap at myself internally. "It pains me not to be there with my people. It's not what's engrained in me, to do anything less."

It's the truth. Her mother—Queen Solange—taught Sarana the ways of war. No one could keep the late queen from fighting, and it eventually led to her downfall.

Soon after her death, the Court of Generals and parliament agreed to restrict the amount of fighting a reigning monarch could engage in. Now, Sarana is only allowed to grace the battlefield during times of great import or when morale is low. Even then, she doesn't *really* fight, just observes from the background and joins when it seems safe enough to do so.

"I feel the effects this war has brought on our land, our people." She continues, "For centuries, Corath and their king have wanted nothing to do with peace. They only want to claim our land as their own. All we can do is fight and protect it."

"This war has lasted for three hundred years, before you or I were born. How much longer can we go on?" I ask, slightly defeated.

Silence is her only response. A pained look crosses her face, telling me all I need to know.

Not much longer.

THREE

Of all the things I miss while on the battlefield—like Sarana, wine, and food—corsets do not make the list. While this gown from Sarana is a delight with the gold damask embroidery, sheer sleeves, and a rippling chiffon skirt cut with a high slit, the corset digs into my sides with every step I take.

I recognized the pattern of the fabric as soon as I saw it hanging on my wardrobe. She had the dress made from one of her favorites, and my heart warms knowing I am wearing something of hers. *If only it didn't have this wretched corset.*

In the ballroom, a black marble floor rests in the sea of perfectly decorated tables and glittering patrons. Vines of roses and shimmering starblooms overflow from their vases and over archways. Gilded chandeliers of runelight hang high above the space, suspended midair on invisible tethers. Tables line the room, filled to the brim with a decadent meal. Where people shovel mounds onto their plates, runes quickly work to replace the meals from the stores of prepared food waiting in the kitchens below.

Barely noticing the bustling crowd and flaring dresses that spin around, I scan the room. When I finally spot my sister's bouncing curls, I head straight to her, not bothering to wait for the greeter to finish announcing my arrival. Countless eyes skate their gaze toward me. Eyes that stare with intrigue, lust, envy, and contempt.

At first, Sarana and I acted with discretion. But now? Everyone knows our relationship. The agreement she made with her trophy husband. While most courtiers don't seem to care, the gossip starts as soon as the doors close and their backs are turned. I'll add court gossip to the list of things I didn't miss. But to hell with them all and whatever opinions they may carry.

I smile and nod at those I pass until I finally reach my destination.

Greeting my sister with a warm hug and a kiss on her cheek, I ask, "Have you seen Father yet?"

"Too busy being welcomed home by you-know-who to see him sooner?" she asks, lifting her eyebrows suggestively. Grimacing through a smile, I elbow her playfully in the gut, and she coughs out a sputtering laugh. "General Petrus just pulled him aside. He should be free in an hour or so."

It doesn't take me long to find my father tucked away in the back corner of the room, lips tight and brows furrowed as he listens to the overbearing general from Anica, one of the northern regions.

My father is dressed in his formal attire, a tan doublet with crystal-blue details reminding me of the sands and waters of Senna. His piercing blue eyes that match my own shine bright with a warmth I haven't seen in a while, and his long brown locs twisted with gray are pulled back and tied at the nape of his neck.

"Well, that dress looks gorgeous on you, my lady." Leigh

approaches from the dance floor, giving a mocking bow once he reaches us.

"Oh, shut up," I say playfully, grabbing a glass of champagne from a passing butler.

"No, I mean it. Her Majesty has really outdone herself this time." His voice lilts in friendly teasing.

"Do you hear that?" He looks at me confused, and Dessy does as well. "I think that's Lady Scarlett calling you. She seems to have left her whip in your bedroom."

Dessy's light smile slips ever so slightly into an unenthused grimace. But her lips tip back up so quickly I don't have enough time to ponder why.

"As a matter of fact, I believe she did leave it there, along with her shackles," he responds with a smug smirk.

"You sadistic prick." I give him a small shove before taking a sip of my drink. The bubbles dance their way down my throat.

"It *is* a pretty dress. Too bad a corset is involved. Which is why I go for gowns that don't require one," Dessaray says, spinning around in a playful twirl. Her skirt flows around her with the motion.

"Smart girl." I peer at my sister with loving eyes, wishing we could go back to a time when we were just two girls by the sea. Not two sisters in the midst of a war and court drama.

"They don't call me the best for nothing."

Leigh scoffs. "They don't call you the best. Period."

"Raya's right, you are a prick."

We clink our glasses in solidarity.

"You forgot the sadistic part," he says, wiggling his eyebrows. "Speaking of pricks, Lord Greva was asking about you earlier. I still can't believe you and him..." Leigh shakes his head at the thought.

"What do you mean?" Dessaray interjects, any notion of a frown completely washed away. "He's attractive, and Raya was only looking for a bit of fun."

"While that's true, Leigh has a point. I've encountered bulls with better personalities than him." I take another sip of champagne. "To be honest, I probably would've said yes to his proposal if he wasn't such an ass." But with my success on the rise and Father passing off more and more responsibilities to me, I didn't want to be a wife and produce heirs just yet. I have a long life ahead of me to do that, and I am going to push that off for as long as I can.

"He proposed?" Leigh asks in shock.

"Yes, and he still does," Dessy chimes in with a snort. "Remember the dovelings that didn't fly on cue?" she says to me, and I can't help the obnoxious laugh that bubbles in my throat.

"Or how about the orchestra he staged on our entry drive? Father had to shoo them all away just so he could enter the house," I add, shaking my head from laughter. "I'm willing to bet he'll shoot his shot again tonight. Probably why he was asking for me."

"I'm always down for a bet." Leigh's eyes burn bright. "What are we talking here?"

I take a moment to mull over what I could offer him, knowing full well I shouldn't be catering to his habits.

"My rooms here at court overlooking the northern gardens and city," I say. They *are* the best in the palace, aside from Sarana's.

"I'll wager my best armor and sword."

"The ones made in Volira?" Dessy asks, eyes wide as if she's the one who might win them. "You both are mad."

When he came back from that trip, he wouldn't shut up about that set he had the blacksmith forge. It *is* an exquisite piece. The hilt of the sword and body of the armor are inlaid with gold and accented with glittering diamonds. Better suited as decorative pieces than for fighting, but damn, they are beautiful.

He nods in response.

"You better have them polished for me by the time I come to claim them."

With a smile, we shake on it.

A few moments later, Leigh turns to my ear. "Speak of the devil."

If he asks, I'll wink, I whisper in his mind before turning to find Lord Greva walking toward us, a wide smile on his face.

He steals more than a glance my way, barely hiding his desire, and I shudder in displeasure, all while keeping a cool and calm demeanor.

When he reaches me, he bows. "Would you care to dance, my lady?"

I force a smile, then nod and take his outstretched hand. We make our way to the dance floor, and he spins me to the rhythm of the music.

"You have been making enemies left and right," he says, voice low so only I can hear.

I turn to face his amused expression. This is not how I was expecting this conversation to start.

"It comes with the territory, Greva. Unless there's someone new I should worry about?"

"I planned on sharing an update with Her Majesty tomorrow, but I wanted to let you know first."

"Well, out with it," I spit out through gritted teeth.

He spins me to the beat of the song, then reels me back into his arms with the grace of a swift lover.

"General Tyrannis has it in his head that he will capture

you. And when he does, he plans to present you as a gift to King Mattias."

These Corathians always aim so high.

I scoff. "I'd like to see him try."

"This is not a game, Raya." He gazes at me imploringly with red-rimmed green eyes, working his jaw.

"Did I say it was? No. I just don't believe a man like Tyrannis would actually be able to pull off something like that."

"And why not? Because you are just so skilled and spectacular that you won't be fooled by the likes of him?"

"Well, yes," I say matter-of-factly.

"That's rich, Raya. Even coming from you."

"It's the truth."

His eyes turn soft as he speaks. "You are a magnificent force, but not even you can stop what's to come."

"Why do I feel a 'but' coming on?" I ask.

He simply cocks his head to the side, setting his lips in a firm line.

I roll my eyes. "Not this again, Greva."

"Please don't make me beg," he says through gritted teeth, but a hint of amusement flashes in his red-rimmed eyes, secretly relishing the idea.

"But begging is your favorite pastime," I say, mind far away from silly bets.

"I know you look at me with disdain, but you do have to admit that we had our fun." His wicked smile takes me back to some of our many long nights, reminding me just how much fun those lips can be. "With Tyrannis on your trail, let me help you. Let me protect you."

"You protect me?" I laugh at the thought. "I have a whole army at my back."

"Then have your army and my Nightspies behind you, protecting you from what's to come."

"How can you be so certain what is to pass?"

He levels me with a flat stare, no hint of jest in his voice. "The wisdoms do not lie."

"The wisdoms? You mean to tell me you found them and are seeking their counsel." The wisdoms haven't been seen since the last of the spirits were driven from our land all those millennia ago.

"No, but they have spoken to me. In a dream."

My breath hitches and a chill crawls down my spine.

Greva's dreams are not to be easily disregarded. While the future is unwritten and many paths might lie before us, this warning means he believes the future he has seen may come true, and that should not be taken lightly. There are many reasons he is the master of the Nightspies—this rare ability to predict the future is one of them.

"Be mine, Raya. Be my wife, and I swear I will do everything in my power to make sure no harm comes your way."

No matter how sincere, no matter how true his words may be, I can't bring myself to do it. To say yes.

After some time, I finally answer, "When the spirits decide to cascade upon the earth again."

With a growl, he spins me out to my new temporary partner. I smile at the young man who grabs hold of my waist, bracing for the lift. All too soon, I'm spun back into Greva's arms.

"How long do you think your relationship with our queen will last? It's not like she can just leave her husband. And what about heirs?"

I scoff at his remark. As if there aren't plenty of children in this country who need a good home. But I know what he's inferring. We wouldn't be able to procreate naturally. I'm not above adopting and passing everything I am to *my child,* no matter their biological origins.

I'm not one of those scheming royals, always looking for a way to ensure my own genetics. And if I decide not to have children or adopt, my sister will remain next in line.

But there's another truth behind his words that I have no interest in entertaining, at least not at this moment. *Where will this relationship go?* I practically hear the silent words. *She will never leave her husband, no matter their arrangement to see other people. Heartbreak is the only thing that awaits you both.*

"Just think about it. Between my wealth and your power, we would be a formidable force."

With every word from his lips, silent and audible, the more I look forward to the end of this song and dance.

"Believe me, I do not need your wealth."

His face flushes red.

Good, he's angry. Let him be. Maybe the more he grows angry, the more he will tire of this ridiculous chase. I'm not sure how his ego has handled all of my rejections over the years.

As if sensing the power thrumming under the surface of my skin, readying a deadly blow just for Greva, Sarana steps in between us. She wears a dress that is the perfect opposite of mine. A parallel color scheme with a golden base and black designs. The only difference is the bodice. It flows down to the floor in an A-line skirt, and her collar stands up at the base of her neck. She looks as radiant as the golden sun.

"Mind if I cut in?" she asks as Greva bows, and I dip in a curtsy.

"Of course not, Your Majesty." He saunters off, lips

pressed into a thin line, essence of Shadow swimming in the air after him.

The music changes to a slow waltz, and a path in the center clears for us.

"This dress looks marvelous on you, I'm glad you wore it tonight." She smiles, and as I survey the wrinkles of happiness forming around her eyes, the glow of gold radiating off her, I melt in her warmth.

"How would it look if I refused a gift from my queen?"

"Exactly, you can't." She laughs in jest, and the sound sends ripples of happiness down my spine. She pulls me to the side and grabs a glass of wine from a passing butler. "So, will I be seeing you again tonight?"

"I'm not sure," I say and take a sip of the blue liquid. "You know, Greva's offer may hold some weight this time. I think I may consider it." I can barely hold in my laughter.

The intense glow of gold once glaring in her eyes—effects of her powers from the sun and stars—has faded to a softer hue, relaxed and happy. We both laugh, and for a moment, while looking at her, I forget about all the other people in the room.

I forget about Lord Greva, the courtiers, the gossip, and the drama. I only see her and her beauty. *My* beauty.

"He'd have a pretty hard time getting an approval from me." A deep voice rings in my ear. My father steps toward us, extending a bow to Sarana, looking dashingly perfect as always. "Your Majesty."

"Lovely seeing you, Your Grace," Sarana quips with a gleam in her eyes, sensing my obvious disdain for being near my father right now. "I'm sure you and your daughter have much to discuss, I will leave you to it."

"Thank you, Your Majesty," he says, extending an arm to me.

Shooting a glare at Sarana, who simply sends a playful smirk my way before making her way through the parting crowd, I reluctantly take my father's elbow. He can't allow me one night of peace?

The silence hangs heavily between us as we walk to an unoccupied corner of the room. I brace myself for the questions. His need for all the information about the battles he's missed, no matter the time. No matter the place. But instead...

"Do you ever tire of toying with that man's heart?" he asks, his stern jaw adorned with an amused smile as I scoff at his words—in both surprise and relief.

"I'm not sure he even has one, Father. He only wants me for our money, title, and lands," I say.

"Although he would make a decent match, bringing the strength of the Nightspies with him, I would never approve. Unless, of course, it was what you wished." He grabs a glass of wine for himself from a nearby tray.

Sure, Nightspies are great with their Shadow abilities. They can slip behind enemy lines without being noticed, and having a whole legion of them at my disposal would only strengthen my position, but considering our region is already the strongest with the largest ground forces in Promithia, that wouldn't entice me to spend the rest of my life with him.

"Hmmmm." I hum, feigning true contemplation on the matter.

Despite myself, I can barely hold in my laughter, and it's not long until his own bark of laughter erupts from his lips.

Too soon, his expression turns pressing and urgent, like there is something resting at the tip of his tongue. Words begging to be free.

"Is everything all right, Dida?" I don't know why I just

called him that. I stopped calling my parents Dida and Mima when I was ten, proclaiming I was too old to continue using the "childish" nicknames. But his expression reminds me of the same one he would wear when he was about to tell me something important. A father imparting wisdom...or sharing a grave warning.

As quickly as the expression forms on his face, he shakes it away.

"It's nothing, it's...Nothing for you to worry about, *mun'lil Duchesse*. I'm just happy to see you," he says with a smile.

I survey the wrinkles of happiness forming around his eyes and melt in his warmth. Between the unrelenting war and the passing of my mother, I can count on one hand the number of times he's laughed or smiled this year.

Instead of spending time with Dessy or me beyond the training rings and battlefield, he's thrust himself into war strategy and council meetings, handing off much of the on-the-ground logistics of battle to me.

So despite the nagging in the back of my mind that I should dig a little deeper, I bask in what little joy he may share and cherish this rare moment between us.

FOUR

Fourteen of us sit around the long table, the seven High Generals and their lieutenants.

Since the earliest recordings of Promithian history, the Court of Generals, also known as The Seven, has been comprised of the highest-ranking warriors—typically each of the seven regions' leaders—to act as a consulting body to the crown on matters of maintaining peace and warfare among each other and our neighboring countries.

Queen Sarana is seated at the head of the table, one finger drumming in consternation on her temple. I eye her from where I sit a few chairs away. The heat of her frustration practically billows into me, even from across the room, growing as she listens to the two older generals argue over whose troops are best to tackle this specific mission.

They've been at it for nearly forty-five minutes. An argument going nowhere, just like usual. If it's not them, then it's another pair. All leaders here, no matter how old or young, feel they need to defend their pride.

Across from me, Leigh begins to nod off. With an

inconspicuous kick to his legs under the table, he jolts awake, straightening his posture and pretending to look intrigued, as if he's been following along the entire time.

Finally having had enough, Sarana clears her throat, and the two leaders immediately end their feud.

"Generals, while I know your soldiers are fearsome warriors, both of your forces are in critical positions on our borders. We can't risk moving them for this battle, nor can we afford another forty-five minutes arguing when our soldiers are being kidnapped and tortured by our enemy."

The two generals bow their heads, then settle back into their seats.

"Now, I have asked Greva to relinquish some of his Nightspies to join each of your armies in battle. They're tasked with retrieving any information they can on our enemy's dealings. Hopefully, they'll shed some light on what exactly Corath is doing with our people."

"Do we plan on sending anyone else across the borders? Into the heart of Corath itself?" Petrus asks from my left, his voice gruff in my ear.

Greva responds this time, all business as he relays his part. "Since Corath started taking prisoners again, the king has closed ranks, making it increasingly difficult for our informants to send any information from the inside. We can assume they have nothing useful to share or they're dead. We'll keep trying to contact our sources, but as soon as it's safe to do so, we'll send another in."

"Beyond that, does anyone have any suggestions on how we may regain control of our port in the north?" Sarana asks, leaning her elbow on the armrest of her chair.

Leigh shifts in his seat, his chair creaking ever so slightly with the movement, and sends a whisper into my mind. *Your plan is insane, but it could work. Speak up.*

My conversation with Greva ran circles in my mind long after the ball had ended. I couldn't stop thinking about the Corathian general's whims to have me captured… and how we might use them to our advantage. As soon as the idea popped into my head, I sought out Leigh and Dessy. Both of whom were less than pleased at my interruption, given Leigh's company and Dessy's love for sleep.

She will never allow it, I whisper back.

She won't, or your father won't?

I glance over to the right, where my father sits next to me. A vein pulses at his temple, his jaw working as he clenches the muscle while he mulls over a potential strategy in his mind. Every strategy aside from mine, no doubt. He was livid when I presented the idea to him this morning.

What will happen if I share this plan? There's a chance everyone won't agree. But if they do and we succeed, then this could be the fight we need to change the tide of the war in our favor. All while proving to my father that I am ready to lead in more ways than one.

If I don't, then everything will stay the same. His view of me and our place in this war. And currently, we're drowning. If we suffer another lost battle, I fear we will truly descend into defeat, one there is no return from.

Luckily for you, all of the generals' opinions matter, not just his own. Once the vote is cast, he can't stop it, Leigh continues.

"General Ontaria," Sarana booms, interrupting our whispers. "You are our best strategist. Anything you or your lieutenant would like to share?"

My father quickly looks to me with a stone-cold expression, the joy from the night before completely dissolved.

Before I lose all nerve, I clear my throat. "I believe I might have a plan."

My father goes rigid in his seat beside me.

"By all means, do share," she says.

I sit a bit straighter in my seat, ignoring my father's rage simmering toward an explosion.

"It has been brought to my attention that General Tyrannis means to take me as prisoner. Deluded with the idea that I would be a great trophy for his king." I mutter, "Whatever that means." Rising from my seat, I point down toward the map of Frallis and the surrounding forest. "According to our reports, Tyrannis is due to return to Frallis in the next few days. I suggest my father's army and I take the lead and meet him there. We'll be the first on the battlefield. While his armies are busy fighting us, another troop will march in under a veil of protection from around the mountain ridge, flanking on either side of the field. We can use his ambition against him, distracting him with a fight his arrogance won't be able to refuse."

"And which force do you have in mind to assist you?" Sarana asks, voice tinged with an anger that matches my father's.

"That is for the rest of the generals to decide. Whoever here feels their soldiers can handle this attack."

The generals murmur and whisper to each other around the table.

General Faria of Wessen is the first to speak up. "This plan is risky. Especially because it involves the possibility of losing you. You may be young, but you are one of the best warriors Promithia has seen." Her sincere voice is met with murmurs of agreement from around the table. "But if we were to win back the northern port, that would mark a monumental turning point in the war for us."

Young. The word echoes in my mind. And I guess I am despite my sixty years on this earth. But sixty compared to some of the older generals' nearly three hundred years of living? My mind scoffs at the thought. *Young indeed.*

We age differently compared to our distant human ancestors. All thanks to the mingling lines of spirits and humans through procreation. Essence helped too, rejuvenating the earth and stretching human lifespans over the years. Our people could live as long as seven hundred years. At least, that was the case before the war between Promithia and Corath.

Now we're lucky if our people live to be as old as four hundred, but even that's pushing it.

"Is there anyone here who does not agree with this plan?" Sarana waits for someone to disagree or oppose, jaw ticking as she attempts to swallow her rising temper. When no one speaks up, she reluctantly does. "Then I suppose I am in agreeance as well."

"I would like to initiate the vote of the Court of Generals as the first one in support of the lieutenant general's strategy," Faria starts.

"Very well then," says the queen, boiling flames tipping the corners of her tone. "All those in favor, say 'aye.'"

The majority of the table erupts in scattered "ayes" of agreement.

"Then, it's settled. The Ontarias will lead. I will leave it to you all to decide which forces will be joining them."

We all rise and bow as she stands from her seat. Just before she leaves the room, our eyes lock. I see no love in hers. All that is present is silent, unrelenting fury.

Even my father beside me stews in his anger, and I anticipate the lashing of words I will likely receive later this evening. I know this plan is risky, that I'm exposing myself in more ways than one. But if what Greva says is true, and it more than likely is, then we must strike quickly before

Tyrannis has a chance to conceive a plan of his own. This is what must be done. For my people, for everyone I love, for Promithia.

"So it's settled then," my father says next to me. He lifts the carafe from the table, and water trickles into his glass. "Leigh and his troops will be joining us in battle along with a small company led by Captain Noren."

It's nearly midnight, and we only stopped once to eat dinner in the Great Hall before reconvening. All our faces are streaked with exhaustion, ready for sleep to take us before beginning our days anew.

With the approval of the rest of the generals, we adjourn our meeting. Chairs slide against the stone floors with creaks and squeaks as we all take our leave.

My father remains seated as he speaks in a menacing growl, stopping me in my tracks. "A word, *Lieutenant.*"

I turn to face him, then move to stand closer to the edge of the long table, putting as much distance between us as possible. I know that voice. The intimidation and authority it reinforces.

I stand at attention. "Yes, General."

"What did I say when we spoke this morning?" he asks, then remains quiet, his only indication this isn't a rhetorical question and he wants me to respond.

"That my plan would not be presented," I say, willing away the tremor in my voice.

I'm not usually nervous in front of my father. But he's

angry, has been since I spoke up earlier today, and rightfully so. I defied his order.

"So why, pray tell, is it that you did exactly that?" He swirls his glass between two large fingers, still refusing to look my way.

"No one else had a plan, and while you do not agree with me, mine was the best option we had," I say, unwavering in my resolve.

"It might've been the best option in your mind, but it is reckless and foolish," he says, rising from his seat and finally locking eyes with mine.

"Of course you think it's reckless. If it doesn't come from your perfectly crafted mind, it's foolish." I scoff.

"Mind your tongue, Raya. I am still your general." I can't help the laugh that escapes my throat, but he ignores me and presses on. "I only wish to protect you and our troops. Greva's premonition only gives us a piece of the larger puzzle. If something goes wrong, Senna could be without a leader and the land without an heir."

"You are forgetting you have another daughter," I say through gritted teeth.

My blood boils at his blatant disregard for Dessy. She may not be ready to lead, not completely, but it's not like he's helped guide her on the matter. I have been doing that.

My knuckles go white as I clench my fists, nails digging into my palms as I say, "but let's be honest, Senna has been without its true leader since mother died."

I dig low. All that has gone unsaid these past few months comes brimming to the surface.

"You may sit behind and plot and plan with the generals, but I am on the battlefield. Dessy is there beside me," I continue, "We're the ones leading the troops or in Senna managing our lands and leading our people. When was the last time you were even home?"

He's silent and deathly still. But his breathing grows more shallow and clipped as rage fills his core. Despite his menacing voice that has the ability to be so tender and soft, I see him—really see him—for the first time in a while.

The usual vibrancy of his dark brown skin has dulled, more gray strands have taken root in his twisting locs, and his eyes—once the brightest of blues—are now gray and sunken. He has become a distant shadow of the exuberant and lively person I once knew. The one who would look at me and Dessy as if we held the future in our palms. When Mother died, she carried his soul with her to the afterlife.

I shouldn't blame him for the grief he feels. And deep down, I know I don't. But part of me is so angry with him for not even trying. Not for himself, not even for us.

"Save your righteous bullshit for someone else, Father. Don't claim you care about the good of our people, or whether I live or die, when you have barely shown an inkling that you do," I say and swiftly turn on my heels to walk out of the room.

In one quick motion, he steps through space and time. One second, sitting at the table, and the next, blocking my path to the door.

"I was a fool to think you were ready, a fool to think you could listen to reason," he says, voice low. "All you are is this legacy I leave you. You will do well to remember that."

Just like that, the final memory of his smiling charm from last night disappears, leaving behind the formidable general in his wake... and the thoughts swimming around in my mind that he's right.

CHAPTER

FIVE

I should be making my way to my rooms to rest. Instead, I walk down the other end of my hall to the heavily guarded gold gilded doors.

Sarana's rooms are bright and light, and if I didn't know any better, I would think it was still the middle of the day.

My parents named me after the sun and the light it shines over the shores of Senna. So I guess it makes sense that I would be drawn to Sarana and her essence, the power of the sun itself—power that descends from the spirits of the Cosmos, Ach'tella and Dane'er.

Sarana can use the power of the sun to conjure small items and objects from nothing, but she can't create much more than that. It's her ability to ash, to turn any living creature into a pile of dust before your eyes, that truly makes her a force to behold. A frightening, rare power that many who possess even an inkling of are unable to fully master without fear of burning themselves up from the inside out. Sarana can only use it sparingly, and when she fought, she had to reserve the power for only the most dire situations.

I head straight for her sleeping chambers only to find her sitting on the adjoining balcony instead. She left the doors open, allowing the summer air to waft through the room. Leaning against the doorframe, I watch as she stares out into the sea of darkness.

"Sarana," I say, unsure if I should be apologizing or defending myself.

"It's Your Majesty to you."

A little bit of both, I suppose.

I walk over to the balcony and prop myself against the railing in her line of sight. She doesn't care to look in my direction, keeping her gaze straight ahead. I roll my eyes. A fight with my father, and now her? This isn't how I want to spend this night with her.

"So we're doing this again, are we?" I cross my arms. "Sarana, you know what this position entails. You know the risks that come with battle."

"But why would you offer yourself up like that? Practically serving yourself on a platter to our enemy."

"Why wouldn't I, Sarana? This is our country we are talking about. Why wouldn't—why shouldn't—I do what I can to protect it?" I walk over to where she sits, kneeling beside her. I take her hands in mine, kissing her palms. "To protect you?"

She finally meets my gaze, eyes glaring into my soul. The fury is gone, overshadowed by dread and fear.

"I can order you to stay," she says. The strength of a queen laces her voice.

"Even you, Your Majesty, cannot overrule the vote of the High Generals. You know the consequences if you try."

"I'd like to see *them* try to stop me." The energy of her power swirls around us.

I know she hates this, feeling as though she is powerless

when she is the epitome of power herself. Ruler of a great nation. Wielder of devastating abilities. Yet her power cannot overrule the collective.

In turn, for their allegiance, the leaders of the regions that make The Seven, who were once powerful countries on their own, have a say in how the greater nation is run. If a monarch goes against the will of The Seven, that's cause enough for the regions to revolt against the crown.

"A civil war is not something we can afford. Especially for my sake."

She hisses with contempt. "We could have come up with another way. Had another general take your place."

I shake my head at the notion. "You know as well as any of us that wouldn't be enough to lure Tyrannis into the fight. He wants me, my blood on his hands. The ability to bring me to his king if he doesn't kill me first."

She rests her forehead against mine.

"If they take you or worse…" she says, unable to finish the thought. "What will Promithia do without you? What will *I* do without you?" She asks the last question in a near-inaudible whisper.

I crack a half smile before pressing my lips to her forehead.

"If we succeed and regain our foothold in the north… regain our lands? Corath won't stop, but Promithia will stand a chance in finally putting an end to this war." I sit next to her on the bench.

She scoots over, giving me more room, and I pick up her legs to rest them on my knees. I place my index finger under her chin, lifting her gaze to mine again.

"Promise me," she says, her eyes filled with stone-cold determination. "Promise me that you will come home. No matter what happens out there." She sits up straight, taking my face in her hands. Lips moments away from my own. "Promise me that you will come home to me."

I place my hands on her hips and bring her as close to me as possible. "I promise I will do everything in my power to return to you."

Just as the words leave my mouth, she crashes her lips onto mine. Her tongue glides against the seam of my lips, and I part for her, granting her silent wish. She tastes like the sweetest honey and fills me with warmth as smooth as sunshine.

We stumble our way to her bed. Her fingers fumble over buckles as I shrug off my coat and pants.

With the last of my clothing pried away, I stand before her, reveling as her eyes take their fill of me.

With her scent—citrus, vanilla, and cloves—and the hum of her essence in the air around her, she's as captivating as the night sky and as radiant as the rising sun.

She takes a step closer, and her lips are back on mine. She trails painfully slow along my jawline, to my ear, then down my neck.

A ragged breath shudders through me.

"Last night, you catered to me," she says, her voice purring through my soul as she pushes me playfully onto her bed.

Hovering over me, she traces her lips down my body from my neck, over my breasts, and past my navel. She drags her nails across my chest until the rounded tip of one slowly circles my nipple. She pinches the peak between her fingers, and a soft moan leaves my lips.

I'm writhing beneath her, aching for her mouth to touch my skin.

"Tonight, I will worship you," she whispers from where she's settled between my thighs.

With nothing but a thought, I summon a gust of wind, closing the doors to her balcony and dimming the lights around the room.

She flicks her tongue up my center, peering up through her long, dark lashes.

Another shudder of pleasure courses through me, and my back arches in response, driving my hips up toward her mouth.

Dragging her hands slowly along my inner legs, she separates my thighs, spreading me so I'm on display before her. She hisses in delight at the view.

Another flick along my bundle of nerves, and I can't help the groan that escapes me.

As if my pleasure was a signal for her to let go of all restraint, her licks and bites and sucks come in full force. She brings me to the edge with her tongue, and as I'm about to find my release, she slows. Taking her time, she teases me with every motion.

She slides a finger inside me. Then another. Coaxing and gliding in a come-hither motion.

My body writhes, and she places her other hand on my stomach, as if that could subdue the intensity of the release I crave.

Finally letting go, her tongue dances and plays in perfect rhythm to the pounding of her fingers until I see nothing but shooting stars.

CHAPTER
SIX

The trek to the encampment in the Arrabican Forest is long and arduous, but we make it by nightfall. Our only reprieve was a short break to rest and regroup with Noren at Fort Umbria.

Much to my dismay, I was not able to evade my father for long. He managed to catch up to us shortly after we left. I had been hanging back for most of the journey, chatting with our soldiers and riding alongside Leigh while my father led at the head of the group.

When I finally dismount from Dahlia, my ass feels like it's been rammed by a bull, and I can almost hear my cot calling me like a siren from inside the general's tent. One of the soldiers takes our horses and guides them into the makeshift stable next to our temporary lodgings.

The crackling of fire pits weaves through the laughter and chatter of soldiers as they take in this last night of peace. That peace is abruptly broken when a booming cheer roars some distance away.

Leigh and I give each other a sideways glance, a vicious

smile on his face as the promise of betting crosses his mind. I swear, if he didn't have people helping manage his estate, lords and ladies to help govern the region, all his wealth and belongings would be gone.

I cock my head to the sound of the roaring, then turn toward it. He follows at my heels.

"So, are we joining or breaking it up?" he asks, eyes wide with excitement.

I shoot him a serious glare. "What do you think?"

"You're no fun," he says with a playful pout.

"We have a battle to win tomorrow. The last thing we need is for our soldiers to waste their energy and give up our location with how loud they are."

"Thanks to our wards, no one can hear or see us in these woods."

I eye him, making it clear that we will not allow this to continue.

"Fine, you're right. Let's show them who's in charge."

"Like we have to show them," I say, my lips turning up into a smirk as my essence emboldens the flames of the torches and runelights around us. Just a small taste of the ruinous blaze it could very easily become with my Elemental gifts.

Like my father, I possess the skill to tap into the natural elements. Gifts descended from the spirits of Nature, Artemis and Senta. Air. Water. Earth. Fire. I wasn't gifted with Stormning abilities—the power to manipulate the weather—or Healer abilities like Dessy.

I've inherited the bare minimum of my mother's Reader abilities, a power that derives from the spirits of Shadows. But the third gift bestowed upon me by the spirits is the one I've grown to hate most of all. Empath, another Shadow ability. Being a soldier and constantly surrounded by death, having the ability to feel the emotions and pain of others is not one I enjoy.

For the most part I can ignore it. Except when I'm on the battlefield, where emotions are charged and death and dying is all around. Then I move my mind to a distant place that's cool, calm, honed for killing. Where I can feel and not feel. Be present but, at the same time, completely detached from the world around me.

But the Empath ability has its benefits. Like taking away pain or allowing others to feel something completely different. It's useful for the Nightspies, for them to make people feel calm when they should be frightened or cause panic at just the right time.

We finally reach the tent where the crowd bellows. Some soldiers—who are on their way to either join in on the betting or spectate—swiftly turn the way they came once they spot us. Others don't know what to do, so they just stand there dumbfounded as they gaze upon their leaders.

We enter the tent to a large crowd gathered around a ring. Two soldiers fight in the center. Both are men I don't recognize, but I do spot some familiar faces in the crowd of spectators.

Focusing my energy on the space around the two fighters, I ball my hand into a fist. Air wraps tightly around them, holding them in place. One is trapped in a headlock; the other is being elbowed in the groin. Their eyes the only part of their bodies that can move, and fear coats their gaze as they lock onto mine.

These two are mine, Leigh speaks into my mind. *I will deal with them later.*

"You all know why we are here, do you not?" I address the spectators in the tent.

They all look at me without saying a word. Leigh shakes his head.

"Have I frozen all of you or just the two idiots fighting? Do you all know why you are here?" I ask again, voice rattling through to their bones.

The ground and tent shake as I show them the power of my essence.

They all nod, and some yeses mumble throughout the crowd.

"Good, then you all know that this battle and the soldiers of Corath we will face tomorrow will make or break our position. And you all thought that spending your hard-earned coin on fights within our own ranks would help that?"

I don't wait for their response before continuing. "Spend what could be your last night alive the way you want to. Sing, dance, tell stories, have a drink or two. But what is one rule we have across all our armies?"

"Not to waste our energy before a battle," a few say in unison.

"And yet here you all are. We need every able-bodied soldier fighting tomorrow at the best of their ability. We can't win if even one of you steps onto the battlefield anywhere below your best." I finally release the two fighters from my grasp, and they fall with a thud into the dirt.

"I suggest you all get some rest. We have a long and painful day tomorrow," Leigh says, but they all stay where they are.

"Go," I boom.

The ground shakes once more, and they all scatter.

"You know, you are a fearsome woman," Leigh says through a chuckle while we walk back to our tent.

"My father didn't train me to be anything less," I respond

in kind with a small laugh of my own, kicking a rock in my path.

My false bravado is convincing enough, but my father's words from the night before still echo in my mind.

I was a fool to think you were ready… All you are is this legacy I leave you.

Leigh glances my way, seeing right through me. He knows me and my tells better than anyone. Probably even better than Dessy and definitely better than myself.

"You know, Raya, there is more to life than just honor and duty, right?"

"What's that supposed to mean?"

"It means that you need to live a little every now and then. Find what you're passionate about. Have fun."

I scoff. "I have fun."

"Sex is great and all," he says, eyes squinting at me. "But Sarana shouldn't be your only source of fun. You shouldn't put all your happiness into one person. To rely on them so heavily to bring you joy? It's unhealthy."

"And gambling away your fortune isn't?" I shoot without a thought.

Leigh's expression darkens as he recedes into his mind. I've hit a nerve, just as tender as the one he struck in me.

"That comment was uncalled for."

"I'm sorry," I say, face heating, cheeks no doubt turning red. "I shouldn't have said that."

"I know you didn't mean it. That you're putting the attention on me and my own faults because you're uncomfortable."

Shame swallows me whole for stooping so low. He knows I would never mean him harm, but being his friend doesn't absolve me from my hurtful words. Especially when he's right.

After swallowing, he continues, "All I'm saying is that I know your father has instilled the highest of standards in you, but there's more to life than just leading armies and governing your region."

"How can I *live* when I have people who depend on me to support them, serve them, protect them? Living up to my family name? My life will be fulfilled if my people are happy and protected."

"Is that what you want or what your father wants?" he says as we approach the tent. "That life might be fulfilling, but will it be truly yours?"

I move my lips to answer, but no words come through. Doubt fills my core as I realize I have no answers to the questions he poses, at least not ones I'm ready to admit.

TWO SOLDIERS HOLD open the entry flaps for us as we duck inside the tent.

The space is large. Four separate sleeping areas are tucked away around an open center. A sitting area greets us, with chairs and wide cushions atop woven rugs. Noren rests comfortably on blankets in front of a small fire. He swirls a glass of red wine in his hand. The ruby liquid dances with the motion.

In the middle of the room is a large table, where my father sits and studies the map of the battlefield spread atop. He barely acknowledges our arrival. His only welcome is a curt grunt thrown our way.

Noren rises from where he sat against the throw pillows

on the ground to shake both of our hands. We corral around the table next to my father.

"General, Captain," Leigh starts. "Apologies for the delay. Some of the soldiers were having a bit too much fun, and we had to disband their merriment."

Noren laughs, shaking his head. He's taller than I imagined, with hair cropped short on top of his head. His skin is dark and battle worn. But despite the evidence of battle on his body, his eyes are a piercing chestnut and filled with life. With hope.

"Yes, I heard about that. I was about to disband them myself when I felt the ground shake." He smiles approvingly in my direction, which I return in kind.

I walk over to the small cart behind me and pour Leigh and myself a glass of wine before rejoining the men at the table.

"How are you feeling about tomorrow?" I ask, taking a sip of the dark blue nectar.

"Ready," Leigh says affirmatively. "It won't be easy, but the plan is solid. As long as we stick to it, I think we will be successful."

"How about you, Noren?"

"You're asking *me* how I'm feeling?" Noren laughs and leans against the table. "I feel useless, to be honest. Just sitting around and waiting for a call that may never come. I wish there was more we could do."

Just then, a thought pops into my mind. One that will change the plan we've set in place. Only slightly, but definitely for the better.

"Noren, you're familiar with Frallis and its defenses, right?"

"Very. I was stationed here for a few years before the siege. Why do you ask?" He tilts his head, observing me. It's like he can see the gears churning in my mind.

"What are you thinking, Raya?" Leigh asks, moving to stand on the other side of the table.

We both look down at the map splayed across the strained wood. I drag my finger along the drawing of the stone walls that surround our beautiful port city.

"Is there a way to get to the docks from outside the wall?"

"Not through the wall, but there is an old cave system that can take you from just outside the Fields of Frallis to the cliffside. From there, you're a quick walk to the beach and the dock. Why?"

Leigh and I lock eyes, immediately in sync with our thoughts. A wide smile stretches on both of our faces.

"You know, Noren," I say, glancing his way, "I find it peculiar how a person who grew up on the water has a special affinity for fire."

His eyes spark to life as he finally catches on. "I like where your mind goes."

Dessaray walks in a few moments later, along with some of our remaining higher-ranking officers, followed by Leigh and Noren's officers as well.

As the highest-ranking and most experienced soldier in the room, everyone naturally gravitates toward my father. A twinge of envy pulses in my center, and I try my hardest to push the feeling away.

It's always difficult for me when my father makes his gallant return. As soon as he does, the respect I've garnered after months of being the commander on the field is reduced to ashes. But I understand the strength and pull my father has. The way he's able to command a room with just a lift of his brow or twitch of his lip. This power isn't given just by his experience or title. It comes from the respect he has earned from his people, our soldiers, and fellow generals on the council. A respect I hope to continue to earn as well.

Without hesitation, he shifts his attention toward where I stand, allowing me the space to relay the plan. He locks eyes with mine, giving a small nod of encouragement. The anger that emanated from him is replaced with confidence… in me. A stark shift from his stance the night before, but it's all I need to turn and address those gathered in the space.

"Tomorrow marks an important battle for us. Tyrannis is known for sending his troops out in waves, and we will match him step by step. And then some," I start, giving a conspiratorial grin to Noren. "If we are successful, we should be able to reclaim our territory by nightfall."

And with those words, we dive into the strategy, ensuring every piece of the puzzle is in place.

ONE BY ONE, the officers leave the tent, off to carry out their orders to their directives. Dessaray stays behind, standing with my father and me around the table. Leigh and Noren slink off to the other corner of the tent, talking in hushed tones.

"How would you like me to assist you in your fight against Tyrannis?" she asks, not waiting another moment.

I eye her quizzically. Obviously, our father didn't disclose to her why she was here. After months of us governing from afar, I had suggested she be sent home. Especially since everything could go very wrong in the blink of an eye.

"Dessaray, your task will be to stay here in the camp. You will aid the wounded and await our word. With Father and me both on the battlefield, we can't risk you being there too. Should anything happen to us, we need to ensure you are safe." I take a sip of wine and lean against the table, inspecting the map once more.

She looks between the two of us, eyes wide and incredulous, as if she doesn't believe the words that left my mouth.

"Then task me to lead the second wave and have Father stay behind." She says "Father" as if he isn't the general or the duke.

If I weren't in the middle of asserting an order, I swear I would surely be laughing at that comment. Others would be too.

"Tyrannis's forces are not like the others we have faced these past few months. We need as much strength as we can out there. We need Father's abilities. And we need you to stay here. To help heal the wounded."

"As if all I'm good for is healing. It seems you always forget I can be of more assistance with my storm." As if to make a point, a whipping wind flaps against the canvas walls of the tent and thunder rumbles in the distance. "And Raya, what if they take you? What then?"

"If they take me, then I can rest easy knowing there is another heir of Senna, safe and sound and far away from battle."

"But Raya!"

My voice is stern when I reply. "The fight between Tyrannis and I will remain between Tyrannis and I. I need him fully distracted and concerned with me, not the battle, for this plan to work. No one else is to engage. No one else is to interfere. No matter what happens."

"You can't expect me to sit here doing nothing while you are both out there fighting!" Her voice rises with anger.

Leigh and Noren shift in the corner, their hushed conversation stopping abruptly before picking up even quieter than before.

I try to respond, but Father asserts his authority. "We can, and you will. Tomorrow is not about you or what you wish to do. It is about the greater good of our family and our people. We cannot leave Senna or our troops without a leader." Finality rings in the air, hanging on every word he speaks.

"You are dismissed," I say, eyes as stern as they can be. "Please ensure the officers have relayed the plan to our soldiers."

My sister leaves the tent, worry and fear for tomorrow lingering in the air behind her as she struggles to keep the tears from falling from her eyes. Leigh follows her like a silent shadow.

SEVEN

A shift in the air tingles up my spine, jolting me awake from my less than restful slumber. I jump from my cot, dagger in hand.

A shadow moves swiftly through the tent.

Slinking out of my sectioned-off room and through the shadows, I silently follow the intruder into the common area. The figure sits, hunched over the large table in the center of the space.

I summon the power of my essence, and a ball of fire dances to life in my palm, ready to be used as I see fit. Before I can second-guess myself, I aim the blast toward the unsuspecting shadow.

The figure rises from his seat and spins, mouth agape in shock and eyes wide. Eyes that are an exact mirror of my own. My father's.

Without a second to spare, the towering man whips a wave of water over the blade of fire, extinguishing the flames with a hiss. Steam billows in the air between us.

"You're lucky I didn't kill you," I say, shoulders sagging in relief as I slump into the seat across from him.

He follows suit, his chair creaking from the shift of his weight as he takes his seat once more.

I wait for him to impart his wisdom, the lesson I must take away for not inspecting before I attacked. The silence hangs between us heavy like a weight.

But instead, he just sighs deeply and asks, "Couldn't sleep?"

"Kind of hard to do that when you think your enemy is stealing your plans and getting ready to kill you," I say.

Then he does something that takes me utterly and completely by surprise.

He laughs.

Between the other night at the ball and now, this is the most I've heard him do so in the past few months, and I can't help but join him. I'm not sure if this is his reaction to me almost barbecuing him alive or the dread of anticipation for what's to come tomorrow.

When our laughter subsides and silence returns, he clears his throat, then speaks in a voice much lower than before. "I'm sorry," he says. He fixes his gaze squarely on me, locking his eyes on mine. "I'm sorry I haven't been the father you and Dessy have needed. Your mother was… still is… the love of my life, and when she died, I couldn't see anything beyond my own grief. Instead of being there and being strong for the both of you, I locked myself away at court."

A stray tear falls and crawls down my cheek, landing on the wooden table.

"We didn't need your strength, Father. We just needed you. Dessy and I had each other, but we wanted to be there for you too. We lost our mother, and since then, it has felt like we lost you as well."

"I know that, and I promise you, things will be different.

We will be a family again, and I won't run away from my grief, or from you. But, Raya." Reaching across the wooden table and taking my hand, he continues, "I am so proud of you. For stepping up and leading when I could not. I'm proud of you and Dessy both."

"Even if my leadership results in me making reckless plans?" I ask, a hint of a smile lifting the corners of my mouth despite the tears running down my face.

In the moonlight, I can see his cheeks are tear stricken too.

His eyes grow somber as he takes in my words. He rises from his chair, then rounds the table to kneel at my side.

For a moment, I'm not sitting in a tent on the eve of battle. I'm in a training ring in Senna, and he's comforting my young and selfish mind as he prepares to leave for war. Even now, he still looks as massive as he did when I was younger.

His eyes flicker to the gold chain hanging on my neck. The pendant is a reminder of my duty to our region and the responsibility that comes with my abilities.

"Being a leader means making difficult decisions for the greater good of your people. As your father, I am frightened for what tomorrow brings and what might happen to you as a result. As your general, I have never been more in awe of your determination. I know I won't be here when it's time for you to take my place. But when I leave this world, I will go with a peace of mind, knowing my legacy is in the best of hands."

My father is an unyielding man of strength and will. But no matter how fearsome he may seem, his voice is gentle and his thumb is featherlight as he lifts his hand to my cheek and swipes away the tears.

I ring my arms around his neck, bringing him into a

warm and loving embrace. He places a kiss at my temple as he wraps his arms around me.

"Your destiny, your future, lies beyond this war." He pulls back, eyes intense and boring into my own.

At first, I think he's referring to my duty as leader of the region, carrying the torch of our ancestors when the time comes. But his intense gaze flips something deep inside me. A roiling shift I don't fully understand.

"Remember that mun'lil Duchesse." *My little Duchess.*

TOO SOON, a restless night meets dawn, and I find myself readying for battle.

My armor isn't much, but it doesn't need to be. With the way I can protect myself with my essence, more armor and clothing on my body would just slow me down. My leather pants tuck under the long-sleeved black bodice. Boots are laced knee high. Chainmail lays over my chest, cinching high on my neck. Black metal pads protect my shoulders, connecting to long black gloves. Circles of runes on my palms amplify my essence—stitched perfectly by our elders who imbued the fabric with the power of runes.

When I finish getting dressed, I head straight to Dahlia.

She whinnies as she senses me near, nudging my shoulder when I'm finally close enough to smooth my palm down her mane.

"You're antsy today, aren't you?" She takes a few more steps toward me, ready to lead the way as if she knows what's to come. "I know, Dahlia. I am too."

I pick up the brush hanging on the post and glide the

bristles against her coat. With each passing stroke, she nuzzles her muzzle into the crook of my arm. Just as she is soothed by the brushing, I'm soothed as well. Through the branches and tree trunks, I see the glimmer of sunlight deep in the horizon. The campground quickly comes to life around me, and I swallow down the lump in my throat.

Something feels… different about today. A warm wind picks up behind me, and although it's the middle of summer and the humidity feels as though it could suffocate me at any moment, a chill crawls up my spine.

Come home to me, the wind whispers in my ear, an echoing memory of Sarana's final command. *Come home to me.*

But the voice is far from her luring charm. It's urgent, desperate. Pulling me toward the battlefield.

A pit settles at the bottom of my stomach, and for the first time in a very long while, I'm frightened of what's to come.

Gravel shifts under heavy boots behind me, Leigh coming to tell me what I already know. "It's time."

With my sword at my hip and knives hidden in my armor, we set off.

Leigh and I ride at the front, leading our troops to take our places for battle. My father hangs back, waiting for my legion of troops to pass so he can follow along with his own. A mile before we reach the peak of the hill, Leigh glances over.

"I will see you again," he says, a sad smile forming on his lips.

"Oh, you can bet on it. I still need to claim my winning prize from you," I reply with a smirk.

A laugh escapes him. He pounds his fist against his chest twice, the symbol of respect among parting soldiers.

"May we meet again," he says.

"And may the spirits guide us home," I respond, returning the gesture.

In the blink of an eye, he and his soldiers are gone, veiled in the forest, even from us, to take their places.

We finally make it to the peak, and we peer beyond at the Corathian army scrambling into formation below. Our troops traveled in plain sight to this point, knowing their sentries would spot us and send word to Tyrannis.

Frallis, our beautiful city, sprawls behind them. What was once a bustling port town is now eerily silent, the glow from the city lights reflecting on the water diminished.

I bring Dahlia to a halt as my officers take their formation.

Reaching into my saddle pack, I fish around until I find what I'm looking for. Atop my gloves, I slide metal claws on my fingers, each one razor sharp like mini daggers at the tips. If I lose my sword and my knives, at least I'll have these.

I turn Dahlia to address my cascading army behind me. Although our numbers are large, we, alone, are no match against the forces below. But with Leigh, Noren, and their troops, this day will be successful. I'm sure Tyrannis will fall for the trap. He has to.

"I won't bore you with a long speech. You all know I'm not one for the theatrics," I start. My voice booms and carries over the troops before me, and a couple chuckle at my opening remarks. "For over three hundred years, we have fought countless battles. We've made great strides and suffered many defeats. But today? Today, we stare down our enemy on the battlefield and change the tide of this war. Today, we take back Frallis." A roar erupts among the soldiers, echoing down the hillside.

War drums beat softly in the distance beyond, slowly growing faster in pace. The battle is about to begin.

EIGHT

The rules of war are few—stay alive and win. Everything else is fair game in a world of essence and runes.

I try to spot Tyrannis, but from this distance, I know I shouldn't bother.

The drums stop beating.

The world holds a collective breath.

An eternity passes before we finally hear the horns blow.

"Veils up!" I shout.

With a thought, I activate my veil, as does the rest of the front line, cascading a shield around our army. Runes on the back of my gloves glow in response.

"Hold!" I yell as we watch our enemy's lines begin their march forward.

Their archers send a shower of arrows into the sky. We watch as they bounce right off the invisible wall of protection, tumbling down the hillside.

They continue forward.

"Hold!" I bellow again, unsheathing my sword from my back.

A trickle of sweat rolls down my temple. I pay the strain no mind as I hold the veil above. I want to draw their armies out as much as I can. Draw them as far away from the city as possible.

Another shower of arrows comes hurling toward us, to no avail.

With a cry and a rise of my sword in the air, we begin our descent onto the battlefield. Hooves thud against dirt. Voices rise above the sound of clanking metal.

The front line reinforces the veil as the arrows keep coming, until both sides clash against each other.

Blood splatters. Dirt sprays. Both sides collide like a tidal wave.

Pain echoes through me as friend and foe meet their end. But before the pain becomes all-consuming, I tunnel down. The world around me fades away; the sounds of screaming soldiers grow ever more distant as my mind zeroes in on the task at hand: Become the killing calm. Find Tyrannis. Stay alive.

As I cut down every enemy soldier in my way, blitzes of essence whirl in the air as each soldier does their best to defend themselves.

Before long, Tyrannis's second wave comes teaming out in a roar onto the battlefield. Shortly after, my father and his troops do the same.

I'm surrounded by opposing soldiers, and in an instant, my father is at my side. I reach out to the elements, calling to the heat trapped within and around us. In a thought, sparks turn to flames as I direct the blast toward the group of Corathian soldiers.

My father steps right in without a word, using a gust of

air to spread the flame. I love fighting with Dessy because she always seems to be there when I need her, but fighting with my father is different. We work as one; our abilities and use of the elements bleed into each other like extensions. We are essence and nature, brute strength and elegance of the spirits all wrapped into one pair.

Using his swell of air, I pull on the cords of the element. With a squeeze of my hand, I suck the breath from the soldiers' lungs. They clutch their throats, gasping for air. One by one, deprived of oxygen and succumbing to the pain of the flame, they drop to the ground.

A pathway clears, and I lock eyes with my target.

"Tyrannis," I grumble low and deep. Like a lion, purring as it stalks its prey.

"Go!" my father roars, finishing off the rest of the enemy warriors.

I dig my heels into Dahlia's sides, pressing her to a swift gallop. Without warning, a blast of wind blows me clean off my horse. Throwing out my hands, I transport Dahlia away to the safety of her pen in the camp, praying I will see her soon.

I scramble to my feet, picking up my sword before continuing my pursuit. From my peripheral, I see soldiers running toward me. Closing my hand into a fist, they all stop in their tracks as I steal the breath from their lungs. I release my hand, and the soldiers fall. Carrying on, I continue down my path of destruction toward Tyrannis, dropping soldiers around me like flies. He's doing the same, using the power behind his runes to cut down my soldiers, closing the distance between us.

I pick up my pace and throw a blast of fire toward him. He deflects the flames easily, swinging his sword toward my head. Using the force from my run, I slide on my knees in the mud and blood, sword still in hand. He tries to spin out of the way, but my blade catches onto his calf, giving him a fine slice to his leg. He roars in pain as I hop back onto my feet. Our swords clash with fear and fury.

We continue for some time like this. Essence wafting toward each other in deadly blows. Swords and knives slicing here and there. With every blow of my sword, I'm closer and closer to overpowering the fearsome Corathian general.

I knock his sword from his fist and use his shock to steal the breath from his lungs. Triumph erupts within me as I feel his life slipping from him.

That is, until the air around me shifts again, just as it did this morning.

Come home to me, the voice on the wind beckons.

Time slows and stills. The voice with hands of fate barrels into me like a sucker punch to the gut. The ground gives way beneath my feet, and I release my death grip on Tyrannis as I stumble.

In my second of distraction, he regains his stance and sends a blast of runefire my way. I tumble out of its path, but not without injury. The edge of the blast catches my arm. Blinded by searing pain, I do my best to ignore my pulsing bicep. I regain my stance and turn, sinking my sword into a soldier who attempts to use my fumble to his advantage. But the voice lingers in my head—one that I now realize is far from Sarana's enchanting tone—pushing me forward. Toward something that has yet to be seen.

…Come home to me…

Once again, the voice on the wind consumes me, rocking me on unsteady feet. Tyrannis knocks a shockwave of power into me. I roll back before popping up onto my feet, blocking his sword's blow with a wall of wind. Summoning a blast of fire, I put some distance between us. When the flames extinguish, Tyrannis is gone.

Not gone, no. Mist-traveling. Concealed from my sight in a place owned by the mists and Shadows.

But I realize this too late. As I'm about to join him in the plane between worlds, he reappears, landing a blow with a bone-crunching *crack* against my temple.

Head whipped by the force, I lock eyes with my father some distance away, looking every bit the fearsome general he is.

As I take another punch to the cheek and the gut, his eyes grow wide with fear. His love as my father overpowers any resolve the general typically keeps in check. In a split-moment decision, distracted by my pain, he changes gears—beelining right to my position.

What the hell is he doing?

With another burst of power, I'm brought to the ground again. Tyrannis towers over me, grabbing me by the hair.

"The Wielder of Death doesn't look so deadly to me," he growls, cracked lips just inches away from my ear.

His face is covered in splatters of blood and grime, just as I'm sure mine is as well. I attempt to free myself from his grasp, but it's no use. Invisible chains wrap around my body. He locks me in place with the work of his runes.

My father's roars cascade across the field as he continues to force his way to me. Before I can warn him away—to regain focus on the battle and to abandon me—he disappears from sight.

Shit.... I think, partly out loud but only to myself.

Tyrannis tilts his head to his left as if he can hear someone approaching.

Shit, shit, shit.

As soon as my father ripples into view, Tyrannis leaves

me frozen in place to spin and face the furious general, greeting him with a long sword in his belly. My father's eyes go wide, this time in shock and pain as the sword tears away from his flesh.

My father falls to the ground with a heavy thud, and if I weren't frozen in place, I would've fallen with him. The life quickly drains from his warm brown skin.

Tyrannis leans down, grabbing my father's face between his thumb and first finger. "How sweet, the love a father has for his daughter," he sings almost like a serenade. "But there is no room for that love on a battlefield." His voice turns brutal and devoid of emotion as he takes my father's sword out of his hand and drives it through his chest, into his heart and deep into the ground below.

My father does his best to turn his head toward me, blood sputtering out of his mouth. "Remember," he says.

But before he can finish the thought, the last bit of light fades from his eyes.

I try to scream, to lash away at my invisible bonds, but it's futile. Tears, hot and flooded with anger, stream down my cheeks.

Tyrannis whips back around to face me. "I think my king would like to keep you."

His words echo, dinging around the confines of my mind.

Knowing the fate that awaits me, I pull in the rest of my essence, storing it in the depths of my being, silohing it away for later use.

Tyrannis grabs my wrist and smiles, revealing his sharpened fangs and two rows of black teeth. With ease, he drags me away from my father.

Just as he thinks he can throw me onto his horse and ride out of the battlefield, smoke rises from beyond the fortified city.

Your ships are burning, Tyrannis. There's nowhere else to go, I whisper into his mind, still unable to move my lips.

A low, menacing growl sounds from deep within his chest.

With the signal of the ships roiling in flames at the docks, Leigh's forces sound their horns and come riding out onto the battlefield, closing in on the Corathian forces.

A few of Tyrannis's men are able to escape and make it back to the city walls before Leigh's army traps them on the battlefield. Nothing Noren's soldiers can't handle.

With a roar of anger, the world around us fades away as Tyrannis transports us far from clashing swords and essence.

When I can finally see light again, I don't recognize my surroundings. The sounds of battle are nowhere to be heard. *He transported us back to Corath.* I'm not sure where in Corath, but by the look of the men around me, this is the rest of his command.

He drags me to the back of a horse-drawn, iron wagon. A slit is carved in the domed top, meant to allow in the smallest bit of sun. It's not a wagon but a cage. My cage.

"General Tyrannis, we weren't expecting you back so soon," a short man says, belly round and cheeks red from the ale I suspect they've been enjoying.

Tyrannis takes off his helmet and slams it onto the ground. His inky black hair is slick with sweat. "Frallis is falling. It will be back under Promithian control by nightfall."

"Should we send more troops?"

"At this point, let it fall. By the time we can transport

more soldiers to the front, it will be too late." Tyrannis runs his fingers through his hair.

He grabs a canteen and drinks up the lot. Most of it runs down his face rather than his throat, soaking the tunic under his armor.

The pudgy man's eyes slink to me. "What the hell is she doing here?" He nods in my direction, anger and fear lace his expression. "His majesty said we're not to collect anyone else. That we have enough subjects to te—"

Tyrannis lunges for the man, wrapping his grimy hands tightly around the column of his neck. The man claws and scratches at Tyrannis's hands to no avail.

Through gritted, jagged teeth, he hisses, "Mind your tongue, Smith. She may appear to be an impotent little thing, but she is a viper." In a lower voice, barely more than a whisper, he continues, "And one wrong slip of the tongue will have us all killed."

He releases the man, Smith, with a sharp push, and he tumbles to the ground. Tyrannis turns in my direction.

I try to gather as much strength as I can to overpower the freeze on my body, if only to spit in his face, but all my efforts fail. I'm too weak, drained from battle and the power from the voice on the wind.

One of the men hands a band of some sort to Tyrannis, and with an insidious smile, he ties the cuff around my wrist, chanting words of the ancient language. As the runes activate, I become empty as a void. The hum of my essence that usually flows freely is subdued.

The band is a diminishing cuff. Impossible to remove on my own, it prevents the use of essence or runewielding by the person wearing it.

A part of me gone, just like that. Emotionless. Lifeless like my father lying cold on the ground.

But the siloh worked. I can feel the slightest flickering of my abilities that I've tucked away, ready for use when my strength returns. I could overpower the runes for a moment if, and only if, I use all my silohed essence. So I must save it for the right time. Whenever that should be.

If that time should ever come.

"Ready the horses," he says with a rotten smile, leaning down to meet my gaze. "I'd like to bring His Majesty his gift."

Tyrannis has brought me to the court of King Mattias, just outside the capital city, Labrynthia, so named for the maze its shifting streets create.

A full guard detail leads me into the enormous structure of pristine marble, towering steeples, and magnificent buttresses. I've never seen this place in person, but it seems as though I'm peering into the picture my great-grandfather painted for me as a child. He relayed his memories of the Corathian palace from a time long before the start of the war. When Corath and Promithia were allies instead of foes.

As we step into the entryway, we are met with marble floors. The castle is ornate, too ornate and well-kept for a country that's been at war for three hundred years. Not that ours in Promithia are decrepit, but they certainly don't look like *this*. New and fresh as if they were built yesterday.

Golden chandeliers line the ceiling, crystals dangling and dancing in the glow of runelight. Tableaux of battle, coronations, and celebrations decorate the walls in vibrant colors.

I lock eyes with an artist at the end of the hall preparing to paint a new scene over whatever was there before.

Perhaps he'll capture this moment. The image of a battle-stained warrior being dragged through pristine halls.

I'm finally led into the Great Hall where the king and queen greet their guests, enemies, and citizens in the presence of their court. Gold carvings protrude from the beams, corners, and ceiling. But aside from the golden decor, the rest of the room is rather plain, with more marble floors and a few flags and banners hanging on the walls around us.

The king and queen are the only truly decadent fixtures in the room with their embroidered robes of crimson red and sparkling jewels. The room is intended to focus solely on them. A reminder of what they own, what they rule. Everything. Their reign upheld by the blood of the youth they force to serve.

They sit on their golden thrones atop the dais. King Mattias's expression is stricken with malice, but his eyes... they glisten with opportunity. He sits up straighter, nearing the edge of his seat. His wife is quiet, sitting in silent indifference, eyeing my appearance. She looks more concerned about me potentially dirtying the floors than my ability to kill her, her husband, and her entire court.

"Do we really have who we think we have? Queen Sarana's whore?" King Mattias lets out a snarling laugh that echoes throughout the room. A few of his courtiers laugh along with him. Anger riles within me when he utters her name. "Oh, the fun we will have with you. Tell me, did you ever imagine you would go from being a whore to a pet? Your dear queen let you rise in stature just because of your powers of seduction."

The lies he's willing to tell in order to sully my reputation.

Despite feeling as though I'll cave at any moment as my

mind replays the past day's events, I find my footing, standing tall and straight next to the guards who dragged me in. The diminishing cuff casts a groggy shadow over me, but I ignore the effect.

My tone is unnerving as I speak. "My position in the Promithian Army is well deserved."

"Is that what your father told you?"

"That's what your death toll clearly shows," I say through gritted teeth.

A guard's metal-covered fist meets my cheek. Blood pools in my mouth, and I spit just before the ruler's feet.

The crimson color is vibrant against the white stone.

Queen Corra gasps in disgust as she moves the gilded hem of her gown away from the splattered blood. I eye her as she squirms and notice a young man standing to her right, a few inches behind her throne. He's dressed just as ornately as the two royals sitting in front of me, in a vest and robe of gold, and if he sat on the throne, I swear he would blend right into it. A ruby jeweled collar of state decorates his chest from shoulder to shoulder.

Perhaps it's the prince? I've only ever seen the prince once, and even then, I was too far away to get a good glimpse. We were in the middle of a battle, and his small legion of guards never strayed far from his side, ensuring his safety even at a time when safety can never be ensured.

Just before I can really take in the features of his face, he turns and steps off the dais to approach a blond-haired guard at the bottom of the steps. His whispers are inaudible.

"Why have you come here?" asks the king, face turning red as his blood boils beneath his cheeks.

Fire burns in my core. *He thinks I wanted this?*

Swallowing my pride and rage, I maintain an air of

indifference, matching the queen's. "I just wanted to see the view," I respond, scoffing at his question.

"Don't be smart." His words slip through his upturned lips. But his eyes show no joy, no amusement. Only desolate darkness.

"I'm not being anything, *Majesty*. As you can clearly see, I didn't have much choice in the matter." I raise my shackled hands, keeping my tone cool and steady.

"Neither did your father when I shoved his sword through his chest," Tyrannis sneers as his lips turn up into a snakelike smile.

Any restraint I think I have is lost as my indifferent disposition quickly turns venomous, and a shrieking scream rips through my throat. I lunge for Tyrannis, nails like claws aiming for his eyes. But I barely make it an inch before I'm knocked to the ground. Guards grip either side of my head, pressing it sharply into the marble floor. Tears spring in the corners of my eyes as blaring pain cracks through my skull and neck. Someone's knee digs into my back.

"Everybody *out*!" Mattias shouts. His courtiers scurry out of the room with barely more than a hushed whisper. "Guards, leave us."

The guards holding me down hesitate, pressing me deeper into the hard stone. A squeal of pain escapes me before they finally release their hold.

Mattias nods to his wife, dismissing her too.

With everyone gone, I sit up on my knees and press my eyes closed with the heels of my hands, ignoring the pulsing ache at my temples.

All I needed to do was stick to my plan. I could have defeated Tyrannis if I wasn't so easily distracted. But instead, I'm trapped here with no plan and too weak to conjure my saved abilities. My father is dead because of me, and now Dessy… Oh, Dessy. She's alone.

Father was right. I was foolish to believe I was ready.

Tears sting as they attempt to erupt, but I do my best to keep my composure.

How could I be so stupid? So careless? So…

No. Not here. Not now. Not when there's nothing between me and my enemy. I must remain strong.

When I open my eyes with newfound resolve, the king is standing right in front of me, his cold eyes glaring down at me. I hadn't even heard him approach.

The power of his essence and runes thrums all around him, vibrating the air between us. The power of the King of Corath. Just inches away from me.

He places his index finger underneath my chin, forcing my head back to return his gaze. His touch is hot with sickening malice.

"I suppose congratulations are in order. Raya Ontaria, *Duchess* of Senna, the newest High General to join The Seven." His voice caresses my name and titles as though I'm merely an object he can control. "Now that we are alone, away from my gossiping court and others I don't necessarily trust, I must know, how were *you* captured? *Why* were you captured?"

Who doesn't he trust? I think to myself. *Tyrannis? His son?* If that were even his son.

"Maybe I have found my better," I rasp out.

"Perhaps, if he was able to take down someone as formidable as your father." I grimace at his words. "Even so, Tyrannis is good, but he's not you. You can easily take down hundreds of soldiers on your own. So I don't buy it. Why are you here?"

"If you don't buy it, then why not kill me?" I test him.

A wicked smile lifts the corner of his lips, but his eyes are hauntingly lifeless.

"Oh, dear Raya, you're only of use to me if you're alive," he says, running his finger down the length of my neck. Bile rises within me, but I swallow it down. "I can tell, even with the grime, that you are a treasure. No wonder why Sarana claimed you."

"You keep her name out of your filthy mouth," I snap. "And I am not to be claimed."

"And powerful. Even with the diminisher." His eyes glint, the closest thing to joy I've seen emanate from them since stepping foot into this hellhole.

"Why are you toying with me?" Pulling away from his lingering touch, I stumble to my feet, keeping my distance.

I'm sure, at one time, he was an attractive man. Before the taxing weight of war turned him into this shell before me today. The only thing that shows me his strength is the muscle that appears to be under his jacket. His dark eyes are sunken with circles underneath them. Cheeks gaunt. Skin ashen. His eyes, a deep, pitch black, look as though they could capture your soul if you stare too long. A deep scar runs from the bridge of his nose to his jaw, just missing his thin lips, upturned at the corner.

His sure and stable hands are deciding whether they want to strangle or caress me.

Pig.

"Can we not have a simple conversation?"

"I'm not sure why you'd want to speak with your enemy, especially after my forces destroyed your hold in Frallis. A vital position, isn't it?" I press.

Something is hidden in his eyes. The air grows thick with hatred as he circles me until he rests his hand on my shoulders, then snakes them up to my throat. He squeezes tightly as he brings his lips to my ear.

Clawing at his grip, I fight to draw in the slightest bit of air I can, but it's no use. His hands around my throat keep me where I am, trapped in his iron grasp.

"By the time I'm done with you, Raya Ontaria, you're going to wish you used your power to destroy Tyrannis, just as he did your precious father. You're going to beg for death."

With a shove, he releases his grip, and I let out a sputtering cough, sucking sharp breaths of air back into my lungs. The doors to the throne room swing open with a crash, guards returning to bring me to my cell.

TEN

Darkness. Complete and utter darkness surrounds me. Engulfs me. Becomes me. To the point where I don't know where my body begins and ends.

But I can feel them. The eyes.

They see me. They stare and peer into my soul. They caress my bared body, cleanse my wounds while I relinquish myself to the black abyss. In this void of nothingness, grief cannot find me. The pain from whatever torturous activity the king conjures up cannot reach me.

Come home to me, a voice in the darkness whispers.

The same voice from the wind. From before. But before what? I cannot remember.

Who are you? I respond. *What do you want from me?*

I only want to keep you safe and alive. The words hiss around and through me.

How do you know me?

How do I not? We are one. Connected by the spirits. Have been and always will be. I led you to this moment and will continue to lead you closer to me.

The words echo. Coming from the side, behind, and all around. Everywhere and nowhere all at once.

What the hell is that supposed to mean?! I shout into the void, panic setting into my voice.

The time to rise is near. Your destiny lies ahead of you, all you need to do is reach out and grab it.

My eyes shoot open, and I sigh in disdain to find I'm still in my damp and decrepit cell. It's dark, but nothing like the darkness of the abyss.

I still feel the eyes peering into my soul, but there's no one else present in my lonely quarters. Looking down, I find a fresh tray of food untouched by the vermin that live in this tower. With a kick of my grime-covered boot, I shove it away, convincing myself that I'm not hungry despite the way my stomach churns at the smell of the freshly baked bread.

My ventures through the dark abyss have been a common occurrence the past few weeks—although I'm not sure how long it's been exactly since my capture—but more frequently now as the torture becomes more severe. I wonder if it's a nightmare conjured up by the king. A way to make me suffer during the moments I've earned a reprieve. Making me believe my purpose in this life was to end up here in this never-ending cycle of pain and misery and grief. I wonder, even, if they've brought me back to my cell on the brink of death—that, I have no doubt—and the abyss is my travel back to the living world.

How long will this last? How long can this king and his guards continue to break me, then heal me, just so I feel the same pain over and over and over again? They're not trying to get information out of me. They know I will never break. So they put me through this pain for no other reason aside from their enjoyment of it.

The king enjoys it most of all. I'm his little distraction from the war. A distraction and a reminder all at once. When he's done tearing me apart, he sends his healers in to put me back together again.

On and on the cycle goes. But I suppose this is what I deserve. My punishment for my mistakes. For the deaths I've wrought, my father's included.

I close my eyes and focus on the beating of my heart, steadying my breath.

Just as I'm about to fall asleep, my cell door opens with a creak, and I'm pried from my resting place. I barely have the strength to walk as they drag me down the stairs.

Down we descend through back passageways and caves, depriving me of a scenic route to my destination. But I still count the steps we take, making note of the turns and pivots, even if it's no use. Thanks to the mirage they've cast, distorting my view of what I see in the castle, all the stones and passageways look the same. Nothing present to mark the way.

We finally reach a wooden door, the only one we've come across so far, at least from what I could tell. They knock on the door with four syncopated raps. The internal mechanisms slide and churn as the door clicks open to a bathing chamber.

Before I have a chance to question the guards, they leave the way we came, and two maids swiftly take their place.

They don't even ask as they begin undressing me out of my very muddied and bloodied battle uniform.

"Does the king plan to boil me alive tonight?" I ask, hoping they might give some inkling as to what I might endure.

But they ignore me, continuing to strip me bare, then motion for me to get into the already filled tub. Not sure if I'm relieved or disappointed to find the water lukewarm.

The maids provide me with the soap and sponge I need to clean myself—*at least they let me do that on my own*—then, when I'm finished, they come back and help me out of the basin.

I stand in front of the mirror, barely able to recognize the image reflected before me. My typically golden skin is tinged with gray, and my full lips have lost their lively hue. My high cheekbones are gaunt. Bruises paint my body, and the lines of my ribs peek through my skin. I no longer look like the feared warrior. Certainly no Duchess of Senna.

They start dressing me in my clothes—no sign of dirt or blood on them—and leave my curly hair down.

The shorter of the two maids eyes my body up and down. She hovers her small, bony hands over the exposed bruises on my arms, chest, and face. Her power thrums in the air between us.

The way she uses her essence reminds me of how we train our new recruits. The technique used to summon and deliver the magic is identical: Extending the tendrils of our essence around us like phantom limbs. Asking the world for permission to use her power, instead of just taking it.

"Are you from Promithia?" I whisper.

She doesn't respond, but her gaze into my eyes is confirmation enough.

I take her hands in mine, imploring, "How can I help you?"

Her lips part as if to respond, but no words leave her mouth. A guttural groan sounds from the back of her throat as she attempts to form a string of words. A thick scar and an empty bed lie where her tongue should be.

"I'm so sorry," I say, voice low and despondent. I'm not even sure why I asked, when there's absolutely nothing I can do.

I fight back tears as she works her essence on my wounds that weren't entirely healed.

Thin white scars freckle her cheek, bubbling burns cover her shoulder, and a branded *M* is on full display on the back of her hand. A prisoner of war turned slave. A clarity to the unanswered questions we've had of our missing soldiers, or at least a partial clarity.

Is this what lies ahead for me?

When they finally finish with me, my guards return. They shackle my wrists together, a long chain connecting to cuffs at my ankles. The metal presses and digs the diminishing bracelet deep into skin and bone.

They lead me through the passageways again, leading me down, down, down, until we reach our destination. Another wooden door appears, and a large corridor welcomes us. The lights are bright, and my eyes work to adjust to the change. At least the lights were dim in the bathing chamber. Here it's as bright as the middle of the day.

At the entrance of the banquet hall, all guests stop and stare at their new partygoer. The sea of twirling couples part, clearing the path for the prisoner they've been told to fear. I can see their smirks. They seem to question why they ever feared me to begin with. And in this state, I would too, if I were them.

The king rises from his seat at the head table, set for five with one empty chair. I wonder who it's intended for.

The prince?

According to our reports, he rarely stays at court. He has a residence a few hours away where he lives full time and only comes here when summoned. Was he summoned tonight and disobeyed his father?

Mattias claps with glee, excited to see his pet out to join them. To his left, two royal guests accompany him. They look familiar, but I can't put a name to their glowing faces.

"Bring her here," he says to the guards.

They obey, chaining me to the side of the room near the head table. Close enough for the king to taunt me and within perfect view for all the attendees to gawk at my state.

"I can't believe it," says the man next to the king in an all too familiar tongue. *That accent... I know that accent.* "How did you manage to capture her?"

Their guests are the rulers of the Voliran empire. Volira is a neutral party in the war, still engaging in trade with both Promithia and Corath. Their country lies to the west of both of our nations, beyond the Anglian Ocean.

Mattias is parading me in front of them like a trophy. An obvious attempt to persuade them to join Corath as an ally and break their neutrality.

"That is a story Tyrannis should tell when he returns tomorrow," replies Mattias before downing the rest of the wine in his goblet.

He motions for a servant to come and refill his cup.

The Voliran emperors glance over every now and then. I'm unsure if that's intrigue, pity, or scheming in their eyes. They may be neutral now, but seeing me here, seeing one of Sarana's greatest warriors captured? That might just tip the scale.

My gut riles and rips, and it's not from the king who now eyes me like the plaything he sees me as. The feeling caresses something deep in my core, reminding me of the eyes that watch while I'm in the abyss, their gaze snaking over my skin.

I do my best to block the effects of the prying eyes, for fear of what may happen if I give in to the stare. But a familiar face catches my gaze ever so swiftly. His deception falters, revealing red-rimmed eyes before he melts back into his disguise.

Greva.

THE LORD of Deception walks around the room surveying, chatting, and flirting with the guests. As he sips his wine, he glances over to me, only for a second.

He uses his abilities, and his voice glides straight into my mind.

Our queen is adamant about bringing you home. I will be at your cell tonight. We only have one window of opportunity, so be ready.

I scoff at his words, but before I can push back or protest, he disappears, melting back into the crowd. His abilities allow him to blend into his surroundings, be everywhere and nowhere all at once. To turn himself into anyone, anything. A Shifter and a Reader, essence derived from the spirits of the Shadows—Ekkheim and Idris. The only thing he's missing are Empath abilities. To be able to control the emotions of the people around him? That would make him a truly formidable force.

I often wonder why the spirits didn't bless him with the gift? To make him a child of the Shadows. They aren't common, no. But sometimes, when children are born with their parents' Shadow gifts, the spirits will bless the child with the missing piece of Shadow essence. It's why so many Shadows marry. To try their hand at creating some of the most feared and revered beings. For they are the right hands and spies of royalty, they are power.

But no matter how great he may be, he can't rescue someone who doesn't want to be saved... who doesn't deserve to be saved. His plan is doomed.

CHAPTER

ELEVEN

Silence. That's all I hear as I fall.

With a thud, I crash into the dirt and rocks below. Bones and muscles ache from the impact.

"Again, Raya," my father calls with a gravelly voice.

That's impossible. I jolt up, unable to believe my ears. But there he is, as sure as stone, standing on the other side of the training ring. There's no missing the blue of his irises swimming with flecks of black. Eyes that match my own. Eyes that say "again" without him needing to even whisper the word.

"When you're on the battlefield, do you think the soldiers of Corath will hesitate to kill you? No. They will cut you down mercilessly because this is war," he says coldly. "Now. Get. *Up.*"

The past comes crashing into me as realization finally hits. This isn't some mere fever dream but a memory from my first training session with my father when I was eight. But why am I dreaming of this now? This holds no importance…

Without tearing my gaze away from his, I rise from the ground, gathering the energy from the elements around me. I reel in what I can with the tendrils of my essence. The dirt, the air, the fire of runelight, the little particles of water flowing on the tides of the wind from the sea. I picture what I want them to do for me in my mind's eye, matching my pulse with the vibration of the elements, grasping its form, and shaping it to my own will.

I pull the droplets in the air together. A cloud of swirling dust takes shape between us. Using a gust of cool air, I freeze the droplets into long shards. Pointed and sharp. With a push and all the force I can muster, I aim my power toward him. The dust gives way, and in its wake, the shards slice through the air.

Before they even have a chance to hit him, he holds his hand up. The blades of ice pause for a moment before they fall to the ground, melting back into the earth.

The snarl on my father's face disappears as soft thuds enter our training ring from the path that leads to the estate. A massive structure built of sandstone and sea glass. My home. *Our home.*

"General Ontaria, Lady Raya," Orlo says, bowing slightly to the both of us, clearly in a hurry to deliver whatever message he has received.

He hands my father a neatly folded square of paper, the royal seal on display in the center.

My father's eyes grow wide but only for a second as he reads the words on the page. The pulsing vein near the corner of his eye is the only clue that gives away the severity of the situation on the rise. No one else would notice, except perhaps Orlo, his adviser and lifelong friend, but I do.

I inspect his face and decipher the hidden meanings of

those expressions and ticks of his muscles. The only visible marker of the weight he carries.

"Dida, no!" I scream. My heart rips into two as I run toward him, hurling my body into his and wrapping my arms tightly around his waist. "You can't go! You just came back." I sob into him, his warmth cocooning around me as he wraps me in his arms. "Please don't leave us again. Don't leave *me*." I continue my whispered plea.

The ground shudders underneath us, matching the pace of my tears and rippling heart.

The rock-solid form in my grasp slowly kneels, his face eye level with mine. Even on one knee, he still looks massive. Despite his force and strength, his touch is gentle and calming as he wipes away the tears that stream down my face.

"I wish I could, my young warrior, mun'lil duchesse." He says the words with a voice as soft as distant thunder.

Tears threaten to escape his own eyes as he pierces through my soul with his gaze.

He kisses my forehead before rising, carrying me in his arms to our home's foyer, where my mother is waiting with a young Dessy fast asleep in her arms.

Reluctantly, my father sets me down on the marble tile as he pulls my mother into a warm embrace.

If I were in control of this memory-charged dream state, I would have tightened my grip around his neck and never let go. Instead, I follow along with the memory as if I was reliving it.

"Kellen," my mother says in a hushed tone. "We still haven't told her. Can't you wait to leave until the morning? If not for another hour?"

I don't think they meant for me to hear them. But that's

the thing about children, we hear and see much more than parents like to believe.

"Why can't we let her be a child before placing the weight of the world on her shoulders?" he asks.

"As if you are not doing exactly that by starting her training?" she asks with narrowed eyes, setting her lips in a thin line.

"This is her birthright, Leonora," he says, pulling her to walk with him toward the door.

"Yes, but it's not her only one." My mother stands her ground, refusing to walk.

Instead, she turns to me. Father does too.

I take a step back, stumbling over my feet.

This isn't part of the memory.

The corners of my vision begin to blur as pieces of the dream chip and break away like glass.

"Remember," Father says, taking a step toward me and gripping my arm.

Except the man before me is no longer the glowing version from this dream but the defeated general on the battlefield. And we aren't standing in the foyer of our oceanside home but kneeling in the smoking dirt of a battlefield, his leathers dripping with his own blood.

"Remember," he repeats.

His words glide upon a shifting wind just as the rest of the dream fades away.

GUARDS DRAG me out of the cell and through the maze of passageways, ripping me out of my dreams. Just when I think

I'm going to be thrown into another torture chamber, I'm blinded by the light of the sun. My eyes burn, struggling to adjust to the harsh rays, and I furiously blink away the sting.

We're going outside?

They walk me through the labyrinth of gardens, footpaths appearing and disappearing around us. They know precisely which paths to take and which to avoid to not be swallowed by the hedges.

Finally, a path opens to reveal a wide oval of sand and dirt. Concrete risers surround the clearing, with benches carved into them. Members of the court fill the seats, looking on with excitement glinting in their cold eyes.

Something deep inside roils as the guards walk me into the arena. They nudge me forward, pressing me to continue. But they don't follow.

I walk to the middle of the arena, directly in line with the king and queen sitting in the center of the stands. Their son sits to the left of his mother, while the Voliran rulers sit to the right of the king.

This is the first time I've seen the prince since my arrival. A black doublet hugs broad shoulders. His lips are pressed into a tight line, either from discontent or boredom, and his nose flares with every breath he takes. His eyes, however, are covered by the shadow cast by the royal canopy. I can't see anything above his upturned nose.

But that stare, the one from the abyss, I feel it again. And for some strange reason, I think it's coming from the prince.

That's impossible.

Behind me, leaves and branches rustle. I turn, and the entrance I walked through is gone, blended seamlessly into the tall hedge once more. My guards are nowhere to be found.

What game does the king intend for me to play?

The king clears his throat, hushing his courtiers. "We bless the harvest and welcome our guests here at court with The Giving, and who better to perform for us than our *lovely* guest, Raya. The Wielder of Death."

The crowd in the stands boo at the mention of my name. Some cheer, but I believe they are just cheering on my demise.

Realization settles in. This is a celebration of the harvest, which means it's the start of autumn. I've been here for a little over a month. Maybe a bit longer. While it hasn't seemed that long, the days are blending into one.

"The Giving," continues the king, "is a time to give thanks to the spirits for the bounty they will provide by giving back the essence and power they have so graciously given us."

Confusion spreads across my face as he claps his hands. I spin around when a cage appears behind me in the center of the ring. Eyes of molten lava stare into mine.

No, I think to myself as a breath escapes my lips. *No, no, no, no.*

Greva. Inside the cage. Bruises paint his eyes and cheeks. Dried blood covers his chin, just below his split lip.

It's been days since the banquet. Painless days of quiet and dreaming of distorted memories long since passed. Because they were too busy torturing him.

I do my best to hide the swell of anger roiling inside as my mind plays out the scenarios of what is to come. Yet another person damned because of *me.*

For the way they replenish the spirits and give thanks is through blood. Where prisoners fight to the death. Allowing their blood to seep back into the earth. I didn't think this was something Mattias still did, not with a war still raging on. But here we are.

Sick, twisted monsters. Every last one of them, I think to myself as my veins boil and my breath quickens.

The cage disappears, leaving Greva in the open, eyeing me with anger in his eyes.

Not eyeing *me*, I realize. Eyeing the king.

I look at his wrist and see the bracelet of runes now diminishing his abilities too.

Greva walks forward until he's standing at my side. A slight limp here and there, but I'm sure he'll be able to fight through it.

I grind my teeth together, jaw clenching as my fingers curl into fists. My eyes darken as I face the king once more, locking my death glare onto his.

From the corner of my eye, Volira's emperors betray no emotion as they look ahead with stone-cold expressions.

Lips pressed into a hard line, I keep my emotions in check.

The king looks amused, and with a snap of his fingers, a bow and arrow, a set of throwing knives, two swords, a spear, and five daggers appear on the far wall of the ring.

Other prisoners appear behind us. I don't dare look, but given the crowd's reactions, I assume they're fearsome. Probably well fed and strong.

I could do it, I think to myself. *I could use my silohed power to transport myself to safety. I could go home.* With just enough of my abilities tucked away, I would be able to escape.

But there won't be enough for me to carry Greva with me, and my departure would only ensure his death. That is something I cannot allow... my freedom at the cost of his suffering. I scowl at the thought.

As best as I can, I harden my anger into stone-hard resolve. Focused solely on the task at hand.

With a bellowing voice, the king rumbles, "Begin."

TWELVE

The ground trembles and quakes beneath our feet. The sand shifts as buildings of stone and decrepit monuments emerge from the terrain.

I run, trying to keep myself steady while also keeping an eye on my opponents. Indeed, the other three are tall and strong, solid masses of muscle. But they're uncoordinated, unable to keep steady atop the shifting ground.

I nimbly leap between the conjured formations, then find my cover as I watch the ring transform into a cascading forest of toppled buildings, an ancient city in ruin.

The weapons are no longer strapped to the wall of the ring. A dagger rests on my hip. The bow and arrows are strapped to my back.

Of course, I'm stuck with the bow. I scoff at the thought. I'm a decent shot, but I prefer a sword at my fingertips.

My ears perk as I listen beyond the stone post providing me cover, nocking an arrow into the bow in defense. I peer around the side, surveying the area around me.

If I can end this quickly, then maybe I can go back to my cell, I think to myself, revolting at the thought that the dark, decrepit place is my safe haven.

An enemy knife comes flying past my face, and I dodge out of the way. I'm quick, but not quick enough. I hiss in pain as it slices across my cheek. I take refuge once more behind the stone column as my enemy's approaching footsteps thud closer and closer. Their pace sure. Trained. Strong.

Swallowing hard, I ready myself and aim in the direction I sense him approaching. Taking a deep breath, I round the corner. With a controlled exhale, I let the arrow fly, and it pierces his neck. He falls to the ground with a thud.

One down, two to go.

I check my surroundings before picking up his dagger. Greva is taunting his opponent in the distance of the arena, but I see no sign of the other fighter.

I dart to a nearby covering and crouch behind what might have been a storefront. The large frame and broken glass of a window are my only clue.

A howling sound behind me draws nearer. I turn to find one of the fighters hurling toward me, a sword in hand. I take aim and fire, but the arrow narrowly misses his head as he dodges out of the way. Just as he's about to strike me down, I drop my bow and roll. The blade hisses against the bricks where my torso once stood. His moves are sloppy, like he's not entirely sure how to use the instrument of destruction in his hands, so they should be easy enough to maneuver around.

Freeing a dagger from its scabbard, I pop back onto my feet. He brings down his sword and, before I have a chance to think, I bend back. Ducking underneath his blade and spinning out of the way. Landing behind him, I stab my dagger deep into his shoulder then rip it free, severing the tendon as he releases a snarling cry.

Arm hanging at a grotesque angle, he holds the sword in his other hand and takes an unsteady lunge forward. I evade his advance again, then sink my dagger into the soft flesh of his belly. The sword clatters to the ground as he drops to his knees, awaiting my killing blow. Before I have a moment to reconsider my actions, I slice his throat, leaving him to bleed out where he falls.

That's two.

Another yell sounds from somewhere in the arena, but this time I recognize the voice. *Greva.*

Grabbing the sword from my felled opponent, I rush to Greva's aid. When I finally reach him, he's on the ground, blood running down his leg. The other fighter steps toward him, sword raised.

"Hey!" I yell to where they stand, grabbing their attention.

In that split second, Greva stabs the other with his dagger, up into his heart. He falls onto the blade, and Greva shoves him to the side.

I walk toward him, keeping my new sword up in defense, just in case.

Greva shakily rises to his feet and does the same. Until we're mere feet apart from each other. Sword and dagger drawn. Fury and fear on our muddied faces.

But Greva's typical determined expression shifts to one of... defeat. His eyes show nothing but admiration and acceptance as he drops his dagger and raises his palms to the sky.

With tears in my eyes, I drop the sword from my hand then plunge the blade into his abdomen.

Greva's red-rimmed eyes go wide in shock.

The crowd erupts in a ravenous applause, roiling the bile in my belly.

But Greva still breathes, and our spectators are none the wiser.

All I really did was nick the side of his torso. A slice that will do no harm. The shock on his face from not meeting death helps make this act a bit more believable.

I gently place a kiss on his forehead.

"Tell the queen not to send anyone else after me. I will not kill her best warriors and spies for *him*," I say, low enough for only his ears.

"Raya, you are not a spy," he whispers. "I know you are hurting. But what good are you here?"

"It's not about what I'm good for, it's what I deserve."

His eyes grow somber in understanding of the grief I feel. He knows there are no words to help ease my pain, nor is there any way of dissuading my conviction.

"*She* will not be happy."

"She's going to have to live with it," I reply. "And so are you."

Before he can protest any further, I summon all my silohed essence, tearing through the diminishing runes tied to my wrist, through the wards protecting the palace grounds.

In an instant, he's gone. He is home. Safe in Promithia. In the queen's capital, Arya. Our runewielders there can ensure his diminishing cuff is removed.

I fall back as the last of my essence drains from my body. The deafening wave of silence returns. As I fade into unconsciousness, I see the prince glaring at me with shadow-covered eyes just as the corners of his mouth tug up into a satisfied smile.

THIRTEEN

The surface below me is cool like the rest of the room. I try to rise from where I lie, only to be forced back down by the restraints at my wrists and ankles. I twist and pound against the straps to no avail.

I ease my breathing, finding a steady rhythm while looking inward. Digging deep, I search for any drop or morsel of my essence. It's there, silenced by the runes tied to my wrist. Just out of reach, like smoke billowing against glass that I'm too weak to break.

I used everything I had to send Greva home.

Home.

How I miss home. My sister. My bed. Sarana. Father…

My father.

My heart rips and cracks in two as the vision of Tyrannis plunging the sword into his chest invades my mind. I will it away, but it's no use. As soon as it's there, it plays on repeat.

My body shudders with thundering sobs. With every heave of my lungs, my ribs ache and moan, signaling a few broken bones. With every thrash of my arms, my wrists pull against their restraints, and a sharp twinge shoots up my arm. My sobs morph into barks of pain as I strain to see the blood pooling at my wrists. The leather bonds slice deep into my skin, to the bone.

The doors to the room barge open, and in walks the king. A twinkle gleams in his devilish eyes.

"Oh good, you're awake. Resting well?" He chides as if I'm simply laughing instead of crying in pain.

He dismisses his guards and trails a finger along the edge of the stone table I'm lying on, eyes traveling up and down my body.

I don't respond. I refuse to.

"Raya, you know it's disrespectful to ignore royalty."

"You are nothing to me," I spit through gritted teeth.

He brings his head down to my level, lips grazing the tip of my ear. "Darling, I am *everything*."

A bit of a grandiose sense of self, but I guess he needs this to feel important. To feel powerful. The title of king not nearly enough.

"Now, Raya, tell me. If you could have whisked yourself away at any moment, as you did your friend, why didn't you do so sooner?"

I stay silent, keeping my gaze fixed on the sparkling flecks of stone that adorn the ceiling. Divots caress the surface, and edges meet in jagged form as though rugged hands carved this room out of the earth's rocky terrain.

A cave built to muffle screams with stone.

"Answer me," he booms.

His words rattle deep in my core. Broken bones scrape against each other and the muscles that surround them. I grimace in pain and struggle to catch my breath.

"I didn't know it was there," I cry. "Whatever strength I had to summon my essence over the runes is gone."

He lowers himself to my ear once more. "I don't buy it," he sings.

"Then kill me!" I scream despite the protesting pain, my voice cracking with despair. Tears well and overflow, sending a steady stream down my cheeks. "Just get it over with and kill me."

"I imagine that death would be a reprieve right about now," he says. "But no, I don't want to kill you. I need you completely broken so I can bring out your true potential."

"Am I not broken enough?" I whimper softly.

"Close, but not quite." His lips spread into a gut-roiling smile as he places his hands on either side of my head, flat against the solid surface.

He speaks the old language, and his words activate the hidden runes underneath me. One by one, they glow a deep red and orange hue, flickering like waves. No… Like flames.

A searing pain courses through me as the flaming runes run their fingertips over my body. I can't help but release a blood-curdling shriek that reverberates off the stone walls of the cavern.

Burning. That's what it feels like. I look down, and that's exactly what I see. Flames climb over the barely there scrap of cloth that covers my body, licking my bruised and battered skin. Only it's not melting. My skin is still intact, and my bones aren't being reduced to ash. It's only the heat that tortures me. And the pain.

My screams echo off the stone walls as my body fights unconsciousness. As much as I want to beg and cry out for him to make it stop, a thought digs its way into my mind. *That's exactly what he wants. For me to cave.* Whatever he has planned for me is a fate worse than death.

But isn't that what I deserve for all the pain and destruction I caused in the first place?

THE WEATHER HAS STARTED to turn. The cold is finally seeping into this new cell of mine, turning it into a numbing pit. And that's how I feel, despite the fiery torture. Cold and numb and frozen in place.

I close my eyes, trying my best to fall asleep as the air in the room grows colder, picturing myself back home.

The dark corners of my mind quickly melt into green shrubbery and vines of flowers growing over marble statues.

Sarana's ahead of me, running and laughing through the garden maze. By the time I catch up to her, she's lying in a field of starblooms. During the day, while the sun is in the sky, the petals are a dazzling, crystal blue. But once the moon in the night sky reaches its peak, the blooms come to life in a glittering starlight.

She pats the patch of grass next to her, motioning for me to join her. The grass and flowers tickle my feet and ankles with every step I take. When I fall into the grass beside her, her warmth wraps me in a comforting cocoon. She curls into my chest, her arm tucks around my torso.

"We've missed you here," she says, breaking the silence.

As I look around, I'm not really sure where *here* is. There is a meadow near my home in Senna, so close to the ocean you can hear the waves as they crash against the shore. But all I hear now is the rustling of leaves in the treetops, and I can't shake this feeling that I've been here before.

"Where are we?" I ask.

"You'll find out soon enough," Sarana says, taking my hand in hers. "Come home to me," she whispers.

I look up above in the sky and find the sun growing. Its rays become more blinding as they stretch across the sky.

"Wake up," she says this time, pushing against my body.

The sun grows even wider now. The sky above is no longer blue and speckled with clouds but pure white light. It seems to bleed onto the green trees and grass that surround us, washing the color out with its rays.

… Wake up…

I look at her and find that it's no longer Sarana pleading. It's Greva and his shocked expression as I use the last of my essence to transport him to safety. It's my father looking back at me just before the sword impales his heart. It's my sister's pained expression as I tell her she must stay behind. And they're all yelling. Telling me to come home, telling me to wake up. They're pushing me, shaking me. But all I can do is lie there.

Light washes over each of their faces, and my breath comes out in staggering, painful huffs.

"I'll meet you in the meadow."

The words glide along the edges of a whispering wind, but the voice is not Sarana's. It's deep and ancient, and it somehow pulls me out of this nightmare before the light has a chance to claim me too.

A stabbing pain prickles along every inch of my skin, and my breathing seems to worsen with every second. Someone stands next to me, but they block the glow from the runelight above, casting their face in darkness. I can't make out the person's figure, but I can feel their eyes. The intense gaze that forces bile to rise. The gaze that seeps into the depths of my soul.

I want to scream, but I can't. There's nothing left.

"Just let me go," I let out in a whisper so gruff from the cold I barely recognize the voice as my own.

Death. I just want death. Unfortunately, the stranger does not comply.

Instead, the figure uses their essence to heal my broken bones and soothe my nearly frozen skin. Slowly, I feel my body healing and repairing itself. The pain subsides. My breathing comes easier.

They untie the bonds at my hands and feet, then work to repair the damage done from my resistance and thrashing. The wounds close, but my skin is still raw where the diminishing band rests.

"I'm sorry I can't heal you any more than this," he says.

Although I can't see this stranger's face, his voice is soft, sincere, and filled with sorrow.

I'm not sure what to make of it. Should I be thankful? For this person to save me just to be tortured all over again tomorrow. Or should I be wary? And rightfully so.

He presses something to my lips, and the smell of freshly baked bread wafts up my nose.

I refuse to take it, unsure if I can trust this act of kindness.

"You need to eat," he says sternly, pressing the roll into my hands.

The warmth spreads through me, and despite my protestations, the delicious smell intensifies. I take a bite and let the sweetness of the dough satiate my tastebuds.

"Why are you doing this?" I ask between bites.

I should really ask him who the hell he is, but I'm pretty sure this isn't real.

"Why wouldn't I?" he says plainly.

"I can think of a thousand reasons." I scoff in reply.

His gaze is no longer a pressing weight in my core but now a comforting warmth cascading over me.

It feels familiar, almost peaceful. Like a comforting

continuation of the path I've been set on, pulling me forward to follow along.

"I'm nothing like the king or most of his men here. They are blinded by revenge, hate, and greed. I see you as nothing more than a person. And if I were in your shoes, I would want someone to care enough to help me."

I take the last bite of bread, savoring the final taste.

"Thank you for your help." Caution laces my tone.

"Don't thank me too soon. I do have to put you back in those shackles." Pain fills his voice as he says the last few words. As if he truly regrets having to put me back in them.

Resigned, I lie back down.

He tethers my ankles and wrists back to the table underneath me, looser than before.

"Hold on, Raya," he says. "The end is near."

The end?

Before I can question him, he's gone. The door behind him shutters closed, the lock clicking into place, and the room returns to its freezing state.

No sign of his warmth or kindness in his wake.

FOURTEEN

"Rise and shine, Duchess," a voice shouts into this stone torture chamber as the door slams open.

I brace myself for what's to come, but the king's maniacal gloating doesn't follow. Just the sneering guard peering down at me with crossed arms and the shuffling of small feet into the chamber.

A familiar maid stands over me, looking over my body with confusion for only a moment before shaking her head and continuing on. She quickly moves her frail hands over me, her essence healing whatever gashes and bruises the stranger didn't fix.

As soon as she finishes, the guards unshackle my wrists and ankles from the table and pull me to my feet.

Through the castle's back passages we go, the maid attempting to keep up as I'm pulled along, until we stop in front of a wooden door.

"Make her presentable," the guard says, throwing me into the bathing chamber. "She looks too much like a rat for our guests."

The maid wastes no time, quickly undressing me, the tub already filled with warm water. The scent of lavender and eucalyptus fills the air around us. I don't protest when she starts washing my hair. Her steady hands work quickly to ready me for whatever awaits me in the royal court.

"I hope I'm being prepared for my funeral," I say as I step out of the tub.

Death is surely what waits for me now, right? What the man alluded to last night when he said "The end is near"? My end.

With a wave of her hand over the bath, the water inside disappears. She summons a gust of wind to dry my hair before motioning for me to step inside a dress.

If that's what I can even call this thing.

This scrap of fabric is a midnight-blue, almost black, satin that falls loosely on my body. The halter top swoops deep down my chest, leaving my back completely bare. Two high slits trail from the bottom of the skirt up to my hips. My legs peek through with every step I take.

Mattias has painted me as nothing more than Sarana's whore to his court. This is the image he wants them to see. Not a woman who has trained her entire life to lead thousands of soldiers. Nor the noble destined to lead her region as duchess. And certainly not the warrior who can withstand his deadly torture.

She paints my lips red, lines my eyes with kohl, and sweeps my hair into a low updo, ensuring my back is visible for all to see. Strands of curls are pulled out to frame my face, and she decorates my hair with glittering jewels.

I step into the slippers she places before me. *Thank goodness they're not heels.*

And almost as if on cue, the guards arrive to escort me to

the banquet hall, shackling my wrists in chains before heading back into the passageways.

King Mattias and Queen Cora sit at the head of the room with an empty seat next to the king. A seat for the prince, no doubt. A band plays on a small stage in front of the open ballroom floor, and a small group of courtiers dance in a circle. They spin and twirl to the rhythm in sync. As soon as I enter the room, they all stop to stare, but the musicians play on.

I recognize some of the faces in the room. General Tyrannis and emissaries from Volira and Valtan. Valtan's presence is no surprise as they have been longtime allies of Corath. But what does surprise me is the presence of Alwilke representatives.

Alwilke has been an ally of Promithia since the start of the war. Has the news of my capture and my father's death swayed them to take Corath's side?

Scanning the crowd with my chin held high as I walk toward the dais, I dig my eyes into each person who dares to meet my gaze, and it isn't long before they look away. General Tyrannis is the only one who challenges my glare.

Despite how I felt last night, staring into the eyes of Tyrannis sparks something deep within me. Perhaps I was saved for a reason. To redeem myself, restore honor to my title… and ensure my father's death is avenged.

With that realization, my expression darkens and the corners of my lips rise the slightest bit. Tyrannis's grim grin falters as if he can read my mind.

I will take my time killing this one, I vow. *If I somehow make it through this, I'll make him pay.*

Then I feel it. It pummels into me like a ton of bricks.

The stare from those moments in the abyss, from the first time in this room and the arena. The stare that saved me last night. I prepare myself for the bout of nausea that usually follows, but it doesn't come. This stare is now comfort, just as it had turned to comfort last night. Comfort from knowing someone here may actually care about my well-being, even if it is for their own benefit.

Unless they saved me just so I could be here in this moment. Paraded around like some plaything for men to ogle and fondle.

I follow the trail of the stare through the stream of once-dancing courtiers and past a woman who eyes me with daggers until I find whose eyes have been boring into my soul.

I lose my footing, catching myself on the arm of the guard in front of me.

The person on the other end of the heated gaze is not some mere stranger.

The pair of eyes staring at me with such wonder belong to none other than the Prince of Corath himself.

Orion Elias Valor.

Tonight, his face isn't concealed by shadows or darkness, and I wonder if he kept himself just on the edge of light, just beyond my field of view, so I could see him in full here and now. So I can meet his gaze and know that he is the one who has been piecing me back together all along.

He's dressed in all black. Doublet detailed with golden swirls and patterns, reminiscent of the dress I wore the last time at court in Arya, the dress Sarana had given me. That same collar of state hangs proudly from his shoulders. The ruby medallion dripping like thick crimson blood down the center of his chest.

His curled hair falls in dark brown waves on top of his head. He wears no crown, but he doesn't have to. It's as if he is the center of gravity and the world is pulling toward his force. The power of an heir.

His eyes do not leave mine as he steps away from his dancing partner, whose dagger-like stare has turned even more murderous, and makes his way to the dais. They follow me as I am led from the entrance to the table he shares with his parents.

When we reach the dais, I stay firmly planted in my stance, unwilling to cave. Not again.

Frustrated, a guard elbows me in the gut, ordering me to bow. In a move of defiance, I stand taller, more rigid in my place. I purse my lips into an indifferent smirk.

Mattias seethes in his seat, and the runes embedded in his coat begin to glow with his anger.

Sick of my games, a guard kicks the backs of my legs. I fall to my knees, pain searing up my thigh. Taking a deep breath, I lower my head. But not before glancing over at the prince. His face gives no indication that he cares. Lips still pressed into that fine line. But his eyes... Is that rage I see nestled within?

King Mattias slides his chair back and raises his goblet in the air. "Ladies and gentlemen of the court, my esteemed friends and guests, our lovely visitor from Promithia has finally arrived. And might I say, she is looking particularly lovely tonight. Much better than the state I left her in, that's for sure." He laughs, and the crowd behind me laughs with him. "Tonight, however, is not about pain and destruction. Something Raya knows all too well. Tonight is about love and joy. Tonight, we celebrate Prince Orion. Will you all do me the honor of raising your glasses and wishing my son a very joyous birthday?"

"Hear! Hear!" the guests cheer, the hall echoing with boisterous applause.

King Mattias turns and looks at me. "Raya, I'm afraid I didn't hear you. Don't you have any well-wishes for the prince on this special occasion? It's only polite as you are a guest here tonight."

His eyes glow at the same time a rune activates on my bracelet. In an instant, invisible talons dig into my mind. My body caves in, straining against the blaring pain in my head in soundless agony.

When the pain subsides, the talons unlatched from my mind, I comply. "May this year bring you happiness, Your Highness," I grit out. A tear crawls down my cheek as I lock my gaze with the prince.

A spark of fire ignites within his eyes.

"Good girl," the king says, satisfied, before returning his attention to his guests. "Enjoy!"

My guards lift me off my knees and guide me toward a large birdcage that sits to the right of the table.

I'm nothing but an animal. A pet in a cage. How fitting.

Partygoers and guests gawk at me throughout the night. Some are daring enough to try to stick their fingers through the slits of metal. When they do, I snap my teeth at them. A little closer every time.

A guard saunters over and pokes me with the sharpened end of his sword. Just enough to slightly nick my skin.

I jump back, glaring at him in the process.

Tyrannis makes his way over to my cage, a smug look of victory on his face. His inky black hair falls over his forehead. "You know, this look suits you much better than your armor."

"I didn't ask for your opinion, Tyrann-ass."

"*Your Grace*," he taunts. "A person of your stature should have a cleaner mouth than that. Must be all the time spent with your queen. Having her lead is a disgrace. Forces women to forget their place."

"A woman's place is wherever she wishes it to be. It's a concept people here aren't familiar with because men like you have too fragile egos. Can't stand having a woman be better than you."

"Just as you are better than me?"

"I am," I say confidently, despite my current predicament.

He scoffs, stepping closer to the cage. "Look at where you are. How can you even think you are better than me?"

A dark grin and sinister laugh escapes me. "You seem to think, *General*, that you made the decision to capture me." A lie, but an effective one.

Anger flashes across his face as he tries not to consider the possibility.

"I think I'll ask the king if he'll allow me to show you your place tonight. I'm sure he won't have an issue with that." He takes a step closer to my gilded cage. "I will make you sing, little canary."

My pulse quickens at his implication, and I swallow the lump in my throat at the vile thought.

Before I can respond, the king rises from his seat once more. "The Birthrite," he starts, "our ongoing tradition that fulfills the royal heirs one wish. Each year on his birthday, the heir apparent can ask for one thing. It can be whatever he desires, aside from the crown itself or my death, of course." Chuckles murmur throughout the room. "Prince Orion, what do you claim?"

A beat of silence hushes over the room.

The prince rises from his seat. Dark curls fall gracefully over his forehead as he approaches the king at the edge of the dais. "Raya Ontaria, High General of Promithia, Duchess of Senna. I have claimed my Birthrite, and the Rite shall be granted."

Shock and confusion flit and flurry around the hall.

My eyes widen as he locks his gaze squarely on me, his eyes digging into his target, like a predator finally capturing its prey.

"You can't be serious?" the queen says, disgust lacing her words.

"Absolutely not." The king's voice is low, too low.

"The prince's request on his birthday must be fulfilled," Orion says coolly. "Besides, I've been bored in Thestras. I'd like to put your pet to use."

The flash of rage I thought I saw before is gone, completely cooled. Now he shows nothing but what he thinks is a simple request. Easy to fulfill. *Required* to fulfill.

"Very well," the king says through gritted teeth. He walks over to his son's side, patting him on the back. "Some instances I fear you are more like your mother, but perhaps you have more of my fire in you than I thought." I'd roll my eyes at the comment if I weren't still locked in surprise by the prince's actions. "The Birthrite is fulfilled. The pet, Raya, is yours."

A slow grin spreads across the prince's face as he returns his gaze to me. Eyes flat and distant.

Then something pulls at my center. An invisible wire connecting us, tugging and pulling with each of our movements. An invisible tether locks between us.

A claim, a rite, takes hold.

FIFTEEN

I'm left in the cage for hours. Long after the king and queen retired to their bedchambers.

Without their presence, the party's atmosphere changes from hesitant foolery to outright debaucherous. The music becomes livelier and more intense, matching the emotions and rhythm of the guests dancing and laughing throughout the room.

A steady stream of courtiers and guests make their way to my cage throughout the evening, pressing their faces between the bars to peer inside. To catch a glimpse of the prince's new possession.

Hands and fingers creep through the slots and gaps of metal. I quit trying to threaten them off. Now I just let them point and jeer at what I fear I have officially become, an animal on display.

With steps of ease and swagger, Orion walks toward my new cell, waving his hand in front of the lock. Runes stitched on his sleeves glow bright, and the cage unlocks with a click, the door swinging wide open. He extends his hand to me.

I eye him skeptically.

"I don't bite," he says, then steps a bit closer, nearly climbing into the cage himself. "Unless you want me to."

He smiles, and dimples form at the corners of his mouth. But it's not a real smile. Those lines that should appear around his eyes, the light that appears as a result of joy, aren't there. Not at all.

What game is he trying to play here?

I roll my eyes, clearly unimpressed, but take his hand. Anywhere else is better than here.

I half expect the guests in the crowd to stop and stare, but they're all too drunk or absorbed in their partners to notice. Many of them have wandered off and escaped to different parts of the room. Partners devour each other without a care in the world. Lips trailing along necks. Hands groping breasts. Bodies grinding with abandon.

Now that no one is poking or taunting me, I notice the outskirts of the room are lined with canopied squares of pillows and couches. Drapes of red velvet can be pulled down for privacy.

At Sarana's court, I know parties such as these take place. But that is usually in the privacy of personal apartments or parlors that rest deeper in the palace. Not that there's anything wrong with them, but they never occur so outright and openly. It takes me aback.

Orion stills in the middle of the dance floor, and the music slows to a sultry rhythm. He wraps his arm around my waist, pulling us closer together. I grit my teeth in response, and he... laughs? He's *laughing* at my disgust? What about my distaste for him is so amusing?

I push down the urge to punch him in the face and allow him to lead me along the beat of the music.

"My father's courtiers have a *different* idea of entertainment."

"You say that as if you don't enjoy the pleasure of these gatherings."

He smirks as he responds, "Sometimes I do, but I'm not in the mood today."

"Then why did you stay for this party?"

"It is for me. It'd be rude to leave early when everyone here traveled a long way to wish me well."

"I think everyone else is a bit too preoccupied to really care if you left early."

He lifts me in the air as the music tilts upward, making a short spin before placing me back on the floor.

"True, but it's not like we can go back home at this time of night anyway. Too dangerous."

"We? *Home?*" I peer up at him, brows raised.

"Did you think I would leave you here with my father after claiming you?"

My belly roils at the truth, the realization that the kind soul from yesterday, the man before me now, only saved me to stake a claim on my body and soul. No, I can't accept that.

When I look into his eyes, something flashes deep within. Something so far from the air of cold detachment he exudes. There has to be another reason.

"I am *not* to be claimed."

"The second you were captured, my little Duchess, you gave up that right of freedom."

His pet name for me stings, and instead of his voice, I hear my father's.

My little Duchess... Mun'lil Duchesse.

"Don't call me that," I say, unable to help the hostility in my voice, resisting the urge to knee him in the balls.

We lock eyes, and I'm sure he sees all the venom in

mine. But he just quirks a brow. A flash of concern crosses his expression before melting back into his indifferent mask.

He leans in ever so slightly, and my spine stiffens. "I can call you whatever I wish," he whispers in my ear, his warm breath grazing the edge of my skin.

His words are cold but tinged with a slight panic. A hint of concern rests on the edge of his voice.

He gazes into my eyes as if staring straight into my soul. The usual way, I suppose. But instead of panicking, I feel my anger die. My tension releases. All I see is him, and the oddities of the court around us disappear.

"We're leaving," the prince says as soon as I've swallowed the last bite of my meal. Nothing as elaborate as the feast his guests had tonight, but just enough to fill my empty stomach without overindulging.

He takes my hand, shaking his head at the guards who attempt to put me back in chains, and leads me away from the ballroom, guests dwindling.

It's early morning now, the sun just beginning its ascent into the sky. Prince Orion's all black carriage awaits us.

I stifle back a laugh as I realize he and his carriage match. Gold filigree decorates the corners of the carriage like vines creeping up a wall. Four black horses lead the front. They remind me of Dahlia.

A pang of guilt pierces my chest, but I'm pulled back to reality when I hear another guard addressing the prince.

"Your Highness." He bows his head. "Would you like a

cage detail to transport your…" He doesn't know what to call me, so he just gestures in my direction.

"That won't be necessary. I'd like to test out my new prize on the way," the prince replies, pulling me closer to him.

He drags his nose along the tip of my ear.

A surge of repulsion courses through me. *He can't be serious.*

He stares at me with that lifeless smile again before motioning for me to step inside.

Servants load up the back of the carriage with trunks of gifts and trinkets he was given the night before. As soon as the last trunk is loaded and secured, he climbs inside, sitting directly across from me.

I watch out the window as the cascading castle of nightmares steadily shrinks with every inch, foot, and yard the horses trot along.

A sigh of relief escapes my chest once the last spire disappears from view.

Orion's face seems to relax too, his lips no longer pressed into a hard line. His eyes are lighter and shining with a bit more life. A mask he had been wearing has been lifted, as if the prospect of leaving court is a blessing he counts down to every time he arrives.

He watches me intently. Eyes grazing over me from my head to my slippered feet. As if he's analyzing me, ensuring I am truly safe and unmarred.

Out of that wretched place, he looks… normal. As normal as a prince can be, at least. He glows in the light of the rising sun peering in through the small windows of the carriage.

In the light, I notice the details of his doublet. The golden runes that line the hem of the fabric. I never really understood the magic of runes, probably because I never grasped Eldrian, the old language of the spirits. I only ever needed to know enough to help enhance my own essence. But I've always admired the detail of their craft.

A small chuckle escapes him, and I realize it appears that I've been staring at his arms, chest, and hands. His eyes continue their gaze, but I can't bear to return the favor. Instead, I move my line of sight to the window.

I'm not sure when I fell asleep, but the sudden stop of the carriage and the neighing of horses wakes me. A heavy blanket lays atop my body, and something cool presses against my cheek.

Peering down, I notice a metal clasp. This isn't a blanket, it's his cloak.

He helps me out of the carriage onto the steady ground below. I give him back his cloak, but instead of wrapping it around his shoulders, he wraps it back around mine. He secures the clasp under my chin, his fingers lingering just a second longer than they should. His eyes grow distant as he peers down at me.

"Thank you," I say, clearing my throat.

He nods slightly, then turns toward the entrance of his home.

I gape at the sprawling castle in front of me. Stained glass windows of varying hues rest within the walls of brick and mortar. Darker, rich colors engulf the windows closer to the ground, and the colors fade lighter to pastels the farther up they go, until they melt into the sky.

Another castle, another court. No matter how beautiful this structure may be, I dread the idea of being a spectacle for others. *Again.*

Guards open the front doors as he approaches, but I stand in my place, expecting someone to escort me to whatever new cell he has prepared.

But they don't come.

He stops when he realizes I'm not following. "Would you rather freeze?" he asks coldly.

Right back to the frigid prince from Labrynthia I've come to observe.

Hesitantly, I follow behind him.

Marble floors sweep the hallway of the foyer, and when I look above, my eyes meet a large chandelier hanging from the ceiling. Thousands of tiny teardrop crystals dangle from each tier. Skylights in the tall ceiling welcome in the rays of the sun. The light cascades off the crystals in beautiful rainbows around the room.

A fountain of beasts and spirits rests in the center, the sound of bubbling water fills the room. Guards stand by doors lining the walls on either side of the foyer. Behind the fountain, two grand staircases curve up to the second floor. The golden banister shines in the light.

In between the staircases, a wide hallway with walls of gilded mirrors leads to the gardens and the rest of the palace grounds beyond. The large double doors are propped open, allowing a cool breeze to sweep in. I can just make out the large lake resting in the distance.

This place is so different from where we were a few hours ago. His father's castle is dark despite the white marble he loves to decorate with. His presence taints the crisp decor with shadows and despair.

Every inch of this castle, however, is an homage to the sun, to light, to nature itself.

Orion walks up the staircase, and I quickly follow. At the top, we are met with another set of stairs and a hallway that extends from left to right, but instead of going either way, we continue up to the third floor. We walk in silence down the hall, passing painting after painting of previous monarchs and members of the royal family I have never heard of, until he stops at a guarded door.

The guard nods his head in respect before allowing us to enter.

The room is spacious and moderately decorated. A chaise and two chairs face the fireplace in the center of the left wall. A black marble hearth and mantel decorated with baubles from around the world remains the focal point of the room. Resting by the window is a rounded ebony table with four chairs.

The door clicks shut behind me, and I turn to find the prince standing awkwardly by the entryway, not daring to step any closer.

"You will be staying here for the time being. This wing is reserved for myself and immediate family members, but it's just me here so you'll have your privacy." He points to the back right of the room where a door is nestled in the corner. "Through that door is a study, and on the other side are the sleeping and bathing chambers. Your wardrobe is already filled."

"Why are you doing this?" He doesn't answer, so I ask again. "Why?"

"The least you can do is be grateful." His words bite. "If you don't appreciate my kindness, I can take you back to my father."

"Kindness? You think this is kindness?!" I can't help but laugh at that, the sound maniacal. "Binding me to you with the Birthrite? Forcing me to come with you to a place I do not know? While this cage is gilded luxury, it is still a cage."

He's stunned silent as my words continue to flow out. I'm unable to stop the flood now that it has already been unleashed.

"*He* speaks of kindness, of all people," I say more to myself than to him, shaking my head. In a flash, I close the distance between us, shoving the tip of my finger into his chest. "You cannot speak of such a thing. *You* are the crimson prince, tainted by the blood of children forced into a war they do not know how to fight."

Slowly, he closes his hand around my finger still pressed against his chest. Not once does he remove his eyes from the heat of my gaze. Despite the anger I feel, the intensity of his eyes locked on mine sends a prickling wave down my spine.

"Well then, Duchess," he starts, voice as smooth as silk, "if I am the crimson prince, then you are the crimson heir, for you have just as much blood on your hands as I."

Without another word, he turns and leaves the way we entered, leaving me in this new cell of velvet and gold.

CHAPTER
SIXTEEN

I've spent the past few days in my room, taking my meals in solitude and getting some much-needed rest, which is easy to do with a bed so plush it feels like heaven. Then again, any bed would feel like heaven after months of sleeping on stone and straw.

Right on cue, a note comes sliding underneath the door to my chambers. I reluctantly rise from my spot on the chaise and pick up the piece of paper with Orion's swirling script. Without so much as a glance, I toss it onto the table with the rest of the short notes I've received from him, all asking the same thing: to join him for a meal.

Instead, I traipse into the study, hoping to find a book that might pique my interest.

The study is larger than I thought it would be. A massive mahogany desk sits in front of the bookshelves that rise as high as the ceiling. A small sitting area is situated invitingly by the fireplace.

I walk along the shelves behind the desk, dragging my fingers and tracing invisible paths along the stiff spines.

Particles of dust fly as they pass over the titles. Works of fiction, nonfiction, and collected journals rest like skeletons on these shelves. Works that have long been forgotten.

History of Corath and Her Territories

Castles of the House of Valor

Corath: Legends of Warriors

Why, why, why, why? The word swirls around in my head as I pace around the small library. *Why did the prince want to save me?*

There has to be an ulterior motive as to why my enemy's son—my *enemy*—would want *me* of all people. It's clear he was prepared for my arrival here. Was I a part of his plans all along?

A groan rumbles from within as realization settles of what I must do.

There's only one way to uncover the answers. Go to the source.

He won't give information away freely, so I'll have to befriend him. Get him to trust me. If his distaste for his father is real, not just an act to gain my trust, then that shouldn't be too difficult. But I'm not naïve. That trust will only come if I trust him, or at least make it appear that I do. Share small details of my life, my truth.

Abandoning my stubborn resolve, I head straight to the closet nestled in the far wall of my sleeping chambers.

The prince wasn't kidding when he said I'd find everything I needed. I was in here for all of five seconds the other day to grab a nightgown and haven't been back in since. Now that I care to really have a look around, I find it's filled to the brim with gowns, tunics, vests, and more pieces of jewelry than I need as a prisoner in my enemy's land.

Shrugging out of the nightgown, I examine my body in the tall mirror. Although Orion and the maid healed me of the larger, more visible wounds—I'm still covered in scars from before my capture—I barely recognize myself.

My face is gaunt, with dark circles under my eyes. Places once filled with muscle and fat, are now slimmed from malnutrition. My curves are still here, but not as they once were.

Forcing myself away from useless examination, I pull clothes from their hangers and rush to the bathing chambers.

I THINK my guard enjoys watching me huff and puff my way around the palace. With every twist and turn, I fear I will never find the dining hall.

But does he guide me or tell me which way to go? No. Not even a head nod.

He just quietly follows as I walk aimlessly through the halls. Perhaps he thinks I'm just giving myself a tour? Maybe he's just an ass.

We've been walking around for twenty minutes when I think I've finally found the right destination.

A long ebony table rests in the center of the room. Matching chairs with red velvet cushions sit around empty place settings. Gold platters and trays line the middle of the table, all as empty as the plates before them. The room is silent, save for a butler cleaning silverware in the corner. No visitors. No advisers. No prince.

Frustration boils over as a maid brushes past me with a cart of clean dishes. She glances over and seems to recognize who I am.

"You'll want to head down the hall, make a left, and then the first door on the right is the private dining room."

She doesn't wait for my response, just keeps walking until she meets the man in the corner who's been polishing the same fork since I walked into this room.

"Thank you," I say, glaring at my guard and his idiotic smirk before making my way out the room.

I've finally made it to our destination. The prince sits at a round table and glances in our direction as we enter the small and intimate room. The seat across from him is the only one set.

I walk forward, ready to take my place, when my guard pulls out his sword, stopping me in my tracks.

"Bow in front of His Highness," he says coolly.

With a growl I didn't entirely mean to release, I reluctantly dip into a curtsy, then take my seat.

A few moments later, a few servants bring out trays of food, and I'm overcome by the sweet perfume of the small banquet in front of me.

Eggs, fruit, ham, potatoes, chicken, breads, muffins—all here for the taking.

I wait for the prince to serve himself, but he doesn't move. He just eyes me from across the table, so I return the stare. We sit there for a moment, too long for comfort, but I don't dare look away. Whatever challenge this might be to him, I won't be the first to give in.

"I didn't know what you would like," he starts, also refusing to look away from my gaze. "So I had them make a little bit of everything. Please dig in."

His voice is much different from before. Relaxed. The ice that he seemed to carry has melted away.

I hesitate, then lift my arm and fill my plate.

We eat in silence for a while until he breaks it first.

"I'm sorry about your father," he says.

Well, I wasn't expecting that.

"From all accounts I've read, he was a magnificent warrior and leader. Considering he spent his last moments trying to save you, I can only assume he was also a loving father."

Tears threaten to surface, but I push them down, clearing my throat. While that might have been true at one point, this past year was not a shining example of it. But he had told me he would try to be better, to be there for us, before everything went horribly wrong.

"Thank you." My voice is low. This is the first time someone has sincerely offered any sort of condolences.

"I'm sure his will be pretty big shoes to fill," he adds, and I still.

"Yeah, no kidding," I murmur under my breath. "I'm clearly off to a less than impressive start."

I cut my muffin in quarters before stuffing a piece in my mouth. The sweetness from the blueberries bursts in my mouth, my tastebuds savoring the flavor.

He grimaces, then thankfully changes course. "That man, the spy you saved during The Giving, who is he?"

A strange change in conversation, but if it brings us further away from the topic of my father, then I welcome it.

"Someone I used to share a bed with before the queen and I started seeing each other."

Unprepared for that answer, he stifles a laugh as he takes a bite out of his fruit, nearly choking on the pieces.

Imagine the report back to Sarana: *'Raya Ontaria manages to kill the prince and only heir of King Mattias of Corath by making him choke on his own laughter.'*

But unfortunately, he still lives, eyeing me with a raised brow from across the table.

"What?" I ask.

He stumbles over his words. "Nothing, I just... I..."

"You didn't think I was attracted to men?" I say, taking a sip of water from my too-obviously royal gauntlet. "I know things are different here, so maybe I can help familiarize you with how love works." I sigh, taking another sip before continuing. "For me, I appreciate the person, the way that person makes me feel, no matter their gender."

"Actually, I was just going to say I wasn't expecting your bluntness. It might come as a shock to you, considering the laws my father has in place here, but I fully support all ways of loving and being," he says with a smug smirk on his face, one I'd like to smack.

"If only the rest of your country had more of *your* ideals," I say.

His expression is curious, but his eyes seem to say *they will soon enough.*

I shake off the prickling of pins that crawls over my skin.

"Why did your relationship end?"

Why the hell is he asking me this? I have half a mind to throw my fruit, or my knife, at his pretty, princeling head. But I'm reminded of my thoughts from earlier. *Befriend him, make him trust you.*

"We were together during a particularly rough stretch during the war. We had lost many great soldiers, and he pulled me through my darkest of days. And while we had our fun, distracting each other from the pain of war, he was ambitious. It was clear he was only really interested in me for my wealth and status."

"And now that you are with the queen, how do you feel?"

A sting courses through me as I reflect on my stolen moments with Sarana.

"What about you?" I ask, shirking his inquisition. "Anyone here that makes you feel alive or carefree?"

"Ah, so Sarana makes you feel alive?" He throws my deflection back into my face, lifting his lips triumphantly at the corners.

"Avoiding the question, I see."

"I believe I asked you the question first, dear Raya." He says my name with a lilt. A hint of affectionate jest in his tone that's too familiar.

"Fine, if you must know, Sarana does make me feel alive. Like I have something to fight for. After my mother died, she was someone other than my sister who cared that I came back from the battlefield alive. Made me feel something other than grief."

He purses his lips. "She cares for your well-being, yet I still can't wrap my head around why she would let you be taken away so easily."

"If you're implying that she meant for this to happen, then please mind your tongue." My words are clipped. "She has no control over what happens on the battlefield, and neither do I, for that matter. I'm not really sure why we're even having this discussion."

The guards in the corner shift, hands on the hilts of their swords.

The prince shakes his head, and they release their tensed arms.

I can't help but let out a scoff. They're afraid of me because I dared to raise my voice at His Highness? *Please.*

"Apologies if I offended you."

Lies, I'm sure he just wanted to see if he could strike a nerve. And to my dismay, he did.

But just like that, he changes course. "This castle is yours to roam. A guard will accompany you at all times. I keep a limited staff here, so if there's anything urgent you may need, let me or Samson know." He nods toward the guard who escorted me here. "I will call for maids to come to help you dress and—"

"No need, I can dress and bathe myself, thank you very much."

"Then I will make sure you have someone for when we have guests, as this attire will not be appropriate for some of the dignitaries I may host."

I glance down at the black chiffon set I have on. The long-sleeved bodice is decorated with a belt of dark rubies at my waist. Black pants meet the belt while the vested overdress flows to the floor. When I'm not moving, it looks like I'm wearing a dress, but when I walk, you see the pants that hide underneath. Honestly, I'm not really sure what the problem is.

"Then why is it in my closet?"

"I'm familiar with the style in Promithia and yours."

I suck my teeth. "Dare I say, Prince, it appears you have been anticipating my arrival." I take a sip of the water I wish was wine. In a voice I hope is every bit as charming as it can be, I use this moment to strike. "I have to ask. Why are you helping me?"

At first, I fear he'll brush me off as he did the other day. But this time, the gears in his mind churn, debating.

"What my father was doing to you wasn't right. I saw an opening to grant you safety and protection, so I took it."

"Does this mean you will let me go back to Promithia?"

He gives me a knowing look. "You know I can't do that. But when the time is right, you will be able to leave here and return home."

"Then can I at least send a letter to my sister? Let her know I'm alive?"

His lips thin into a grim line. "As much as I want to allow that, I can't. My father will be watching my every move now that you're in my custody. If he suspects I'm sending letters to the enemy, then we will both be taken prisoner."

"But—" I start.

"No, Raya." His words cut me off. "The answer is no, and that is the last I will hear of it."

I drop my utensils, and they clatter onto the plate. "I don't know why I thought saving me meant you would actually be able to show some compassion. My sister is the only family I have left, and she deserves to know I'm okay."

"Trust me, I'm sure your past lover told your sister all she needs to know."

"I'd hardly call that proof of life. If anything, that might solidify their belief of my death. A Promithian soldier captured with silohed essence? A warrior who could have escaped at any time?"

"Then why didn't you?!" Orion's voice is no longer calm and smooth, his temper shining through. "We all saw how you sent him back to your country and broke through every single ward. You could have left at any moment before then, despite the torture you had endured, so why didn't you save yourself?"

I'm stunned into silence, mouth agape in a soundless gasp as I try to come up with the words to respond. But Orion does that for me.

"Let me guess. You feel responsible for your father's death? You felt that you didn't deserve your freedom? That the Promithian forces could end the war without you? Well, *Duchess*, your absence from this war only prolonged it. That much is certain."

His jaw twitches as he clenches and unclenches the

muscles. There seems to be something more grinding away in his thoughts, but this time he stays quiet.

The silence between us is thick and writhing.

Despite the pressure building inside me and the roaring thoughts that compel me to respond with a fist to his perfectly chiseled jaw, I fold my napkin, place it on the wooden surface of the table, and dismiss myself from his presence.

I walk away in disbelief at the prince's harsh words, ignoring my stinging eyes as I race back to my quarters.

SEVENTEEN

Light pours in through the windows, cascading across the desk in front of me. Towers of books and pages of notes clutter the surface. I clamp the bridge of my nose with my index finger and thumb, unsure what to read next.

I've spent my time scouring through all the books I could find on the history of Corath in my personal library, but the only ones remotely close to useful are the texts on the building of the palaces. I studied the outlines and drafts front and back, memorizing all the passageways, secret doors, and layouts of each floor. Even the maze of the gardens.

After our conversation ended on a very bitter tone last week, we've been avoiding each other like the plague. Well, I suppose I'm avoiding him. He's been sending me short letters. Every. Single. Day.

Reminder: You are free to roam the grounds and gardens. You aren't locked in your room.

I do roam the grounds and gardens when I'm certain he isn't around to see me.

I'm out for the day to survey land in the region. I won't be long.

I dined with the servants that night and laughed more than I have in who knows how long.

I've been called to Labrynthia to meet with my father. I'll return tomorrow.

I groan at the thought of his presence back in these halls. My freedom slipping away by the second.

A few quick raps at my door capture my attention.

I swing the door open wide, and the prince stands in the hall awkwardly, my guard dismissed. My spine stiffens.

When he said he'd be back tomorrow, I thought he meant in the evening. I'm surprised to see him back so early from his travels—to see him at all, really.

Well, there goes my extra day of freedom.

"I'm sorry to disturb you," he says, shifting from one foot to the other before pulling his hands behind his back. "I was wondering if you would accompany me for a walk in the gardens."

I stare at him as if he's grown five heads. "It's freezing outside."

In Corath, the end of autumn brings colder weather, welcomed by the occasional snowstorm. I'm used to snow well into the depths of winter, but apparently, autumnal snow and even more frigid winters are a norm this far north in this region.

"I have runes in place that keep the palace grounds warm."

I squint my eyes. Not because I don't believe him, but because I would much rather stay in the safety of my room.

"If you don't believe me, then grab a coat if you wish."

We stare at each other for some time, but I feel he won't take no for an answer.

"Fine." I walk over to my closet and find a black coat lined with gray fur. *This will have to do.*

I stuff a matching pair of gloves in the pockets in case he decides to leave me in the forest and test my survival skills.

When I return to the living area, he stifles a laugh.

"What?" I ask.

"You're going to be sweating in that thing."

"If I'm too warm, I'll leave it in the bushes."

He shakes his head, holding the door open as I step across the threshold.

Outside, the air is warm and soothing despite the snow on the treetops in the distance. Orion was right, this coat is too much. But in an act of stubbornness, I keep it on.

"I'm sorry," he starts, finally breaking the silence between us. "It was wrong of me to speak to you the way I did. I was out of line, and I apologize."

I look into his eyes and find all the sincerity in the world, his expression set into a soft gaze. What he said to me was certainly uncalled for, but there was a bit of truth to his words, though I will never admit that to him.

As much as I want to tell him off, toss him into a bush, and storm away, I can't help but trust that he means what he says.

"Thank you. I appreciate your apology, even if it is a week

late. I don't think I necessarily accept it, but I appreciate it nonetheless."

"I would've apologized sooner if you weren't avoiding me at every turn." He seems a bit hurt by my statement. "I wouldn't expect you to accept it. But hopefully, with time, I will earn your respect and trust."

He extends his hand out to me, and hesitantly, I take it.

With a firm shake of our clasped hands, the bitterness in the air around us softens and melts away into something warm and inviting, an understanding forming that neither of us expected. A jolt zaps through me, leading from his fingertips to my core, a warmth that spreads to an undeniable heat.

I instinctively step forward, his feet doing the same, when a scream sounds in the distance.

Releasing our grip on each other's hands, we're pulled back to reality.

Guards rush past us, toward the grotesque screams growing louder and louder by the second.

Without another thought, I discard the thick coat and set into a run.

"Raya!" Orion yells after me but quickly matches my pace, which isn't that difficult.

Out of shape and lacking training, I'm nowhere near the condition I was in before my capture, but it's enough.

"Raya, please," he shouts again. "You must get to safety!"

Someone's hand grips my arm, but the touch lacks the warmth of Orion's. This hand is cold and distant and filled with dread.

I'm not surprised to find Samson's cool blue eyes staring squarely into mine, filling me with an uneasiness I can't quite describe. My body wants to run... away from *him.* I rip my arm out of his grip, putting some much-warranted distance between us.

"Return to your quarters at once." His voice is gruff. "We will take care of it."

"You mean for me to sit back and do nothing?!" I'm frantic, energy coursing through my veins. "Absolutely not!"

"That was an order, Duchess. Now go!"

Orion steps up to me then, eyes set with determination and tinged with a softness I don't understand. "Please, Raya, go."

"In the time we've been standing here arguing, who knows how many more of your people have been injured or, worse, killed," I say, looking between them both. "Now stop wasting time."

I return to my pace, and luckily, the two thick-headed Corathians behind me fall in step. Together we run, chasing the piercing cries until we find the source of the mayhem unfolding.

A slew of royal guards and a few servants lie across the garden pathway, many injured and slain. Body parts strewn across the pristine gardens.

At the end of the path, a large beast rears his head and releases a searing cry. Its body is covered in black, iridescent scales, and its mouth is filled with long, razor-sharp teeth. It stands on its hind legs, almost humanlike in its position, limbs lanky but muscular.

I watch in sheer horror as it swipes its giant paws, tipped with curved blades for claws, at its opponent, cutting the guard clean in half. He falls to the ground in pieces, the beast kicking the body into the bushes.

"What the hell is that?!" I ask as softly as I can to Orion and Samson, careful not to snag the monster's attention.

"I have no fucking clue," Samson answers, just as dumbfounded as I am.

Looking to Orion, I search his eyes for any hesitation. A prince is the last person who should be anywhere near that thing. But all he does is nod in confirmation. If he's ready, then so am I.

Clearing my head, I lift a sword off the ground from a fallen guard and rush the beast as it flings another guard away. His body slams into the ground with a sickening thud.

Without the use of my essence, this will be difficult. But the foundations of my training focused on sheer might without my powers. To master the art of the blade and hand-to-hand combat before adding the threads of essence into our forms.

Letting out a warrior's cry, I capture the beast's attention. With the hissing of claws scraping against a blade, I strike the beast head-on. I do all I can to be the distraction Samson and Orion need to transport and attack from behind. As if sensing their movement through space and time, the monster simply deflects my attack, then whips its bladed tail just as Orion ripples into view.

"No!" I scream and run to Orion's side with just enough time to block most of the beast's swipe with my sword.

The beast presses down on the blade with its sharp claws, and I stumble to my knee.

Lifting my other hand, I grab hold of the sharp edge and push with all my strength. "Now would be a good time, Samson!"

Daring a glance behind the beast, I watch as Samson brings his blade onto its tail.

A piercing shriek bellows from the monster, and just as it removes its pressure from my blade, I push and slice through its fingers, and the claws clatter to the ground. Another shrieking cry fills the air, but we don't let up.

Samson swipes across the beast's hind legs. It loses its footing and falls to the ground with an earth-shattering thud. Before it has a moment to heal, if it can even do such a thing, I bring my sword down onto its neck. The beast's dark blood splatters across the ground, as its shrieks turn into gurgling cries of pain.

Until… silence.

Quickly, I turn back to Orion, Samson already at his side.

"We need to get you to a Healer," I say, my voice in a slight panic as I examine his wounds.

"Please don't fuss, I'm fine," he says through a wince.

He's managed to sit himself upright, but the gashes on his abdomen ooze crimson.

"The hell you are." Samson's voice is unamused and unfazed.

In an instant, the world around us blurs into darkness. When color returns, we're inside the castle.

"I'll go get Heren," says Samson briskly.

"Don't bother them, Samson, I'll be fine." Orion tries to stop him, but it's no use.

Samson slips away, leaving Orion and me alone.

The rooms we're in are dark. Swords of varying sizes hang on the ruby velvet walls, and books are piled high on the coffee table. Through two large doors is an enormous study that puts my small library to shame. Papers litter the desk that rests in the center.

I quickly realize this is Orion's chamber.

Moments later, Samson returns with who I assume is Heren, the Healer, in tow. They carry a basket of supplies. Wordlessly, Orion sits on the lounge, and they immediately get to work cutting open his tunic, inspecting and cleaning the wound, then using their abilities to close it. The gashes are still visible when Orion finally stops them.

"Please, don't waste all your energy on me when there are others who need it more, Heren."

"But, Your Highness—"

Orion raises his hand to stop them, promptly finishing their thought.

Without another word, the healer leaves the room, off to help the trove of injured awaiting downstairs.

"You should have let them finish," Samson says in a frustrated huff.

"I'll be fine. Just need a few stitches." Orion winces as he shifts, lifting the scraps of fabric still clinging to his body.

The muscles in his arm ripple with the movement. Scars dance across his chest and shoulder, and it takes more effort than I care to admit to stop myself from reaching out to touch each one.

"I've got this, Samson," I say, having tended to enough wounds on the battlefield to know the basics of healing without the use of essence.

Samson hesitates, unsure if he should leave me with his prince.

"Samson, I may not be a Healer, but I can at least do this. Now go help the others."

Orion nods, giving the approval the brooding guard needs to relent.

Finally alone, I take a moment to wash my hands in his bathing chambers, only to be reminded of the deep gash on my palm. I wince as the tear pulls but wrap my hand in a small towel before making my way back to Orion.

I start unraveling the tools from the healing kit when he stops me in my tracks, his hand slowly taking hold of my wrist and pulling me to him.

That heat from before returns, coursing through my body with one simple touch.

Orion eyes my hand. "Let me heal you," he says, voice soft and comforting as it echoes around us.

Unable to form words, I nod.

He removes the towel and covers my palm with his free hand, the other still gripping my wrist, his eyes never leaving mine as heat radiates from his healing touch. The skin knits itself together, slightly burning in the wake of his healing essence working its magic. When he releases my hand, the wound is gone. Only a small scar stands as evidence of the monster we just fought.

"If only Healers could just heal themselves," I manage to squeak out with a chuckle. "Now it's your turn." He almost looks amused as he lies down on the chair, tucking his arm behind his head to give me better access.

After threading the needle with care, I begin stitching the first gash.

"You're lucky there are no courtiers here," I say, filling the silence between us. "Today's attack was already awful, but add the panic of a court and it could've been so much worse."

He chuckles. "Indeed. This is probably the first and only time anyone would say I'm lucky for not hosting a full court."

"Why don't you?" I ask. "I appreciate the solitude, but I'd be lying if I said I wasn't shocked when I arrived to find no one else living here."

"Unlike my father, I've never enjoyed sharing company with scheming and gossiping royals. That's why I live here, where there's peace and quiet. I only go to the *king's* court when needed." The way he says "king" is laced with fire. "There's too much drama."

"The drama is what keeps it entertaining. What was this place before you made it your home?"

I already know the answer from my research of Corath's royal family over the years, but I'm hoping the conversation distracts him from the pain. Tying off the last stitch, I move on to the next gash. He winces as the needle pushes through his skin.

"My family's old summer palace. My father stopped coming here a long time ago. It was practically abandoned until a few years ago. Birthrite made it mine."

"Must be nice to get whatever you desire," I scoff.

"And what would you desire?" He shifts his head so he can look at me.

"Right now? To go home. Be with Dessy and Sarana. Be the leader I was meant to be for my people and warriors."

The deep timbre of my father's voice echoes in my mind, reminding me of my years of training, instilling in me the very words I just said. The reasons for my existence.

"Too obvious. If you weren't here, if you were safe at home, leading your people with your sister at your side, or in the comforting embrace of your lover, what would you ask for?"

I would wish for my parents to be returned to the land of the living, but that kind of essence is forbidden. So I go with the next best thing. "For the war to end. For your king and my queen to come to an agreement so we can all lay down our weapons." He looks at me, blinking as if he's surprised by my response. "Were you expecting another answer?"

"Given your strength, your abilities, and your power on the battlefield, I would assume you enjoyed it. Or at least wish for the death of your enemies."

My hand trembles, blood boiling at his ignorant statement, but I do my best to cool my temper, taking a deep breath before making the next stitch. "Oh, believe me, the day will come when Tyrannis will meet his end, and it will be done by my hand. But I have watched hundreds of my soldiers die. I have killed to stay alive, but that doesn't mean I enjoy it. This needs to end. *Three hundred years* of bloodshed. If this doesn't end soon, I fear there will be a hundred more."

We're quiet for a moment as I tie this stitch, then move onto the final gash.

When he speaks again, there's a new sense of solemnity in his voice. "Our forces fought once, you know."

"I remember seeing you," I say.

My memory from that battle is foggy, bogged down by the blur of smattering rain and spraying of mud. But I still remember him on the field, surrounded by his personal legion of guards. Doing their best to protect their prince in battle.

"I watched you fight, wielding your essence like an art form and engaging in hand-to-hand combat. Weaving between the two like it was natural." He shivers. "Struck the fear of the spirits in me, but it was incredible to watch you."

Tingles ripple across the surface of my skin, longing for the feeling of that power flowing through my veins. These past few months, all I've felt was numb, thanks to the rune bracelet. What I would give to have my magic returned to me, truly returned.

"Thank you, I think," I say.

He laughs for a moment, then winces as I tug the stitch through.

"Sorry." I grimace

"Honestly, makes me wonder how you lost to Tyrannis," he says, more to himself than to me.

All I can do is grunt in response.

"Do you miss it?" he asks.

"My essence or the adrenaline of battle?"

"Both, I suppose," he clarifies.

"Well, I think it's obvious what my answer is about my essence. I feel empty and incomplete without it. Like a piece of my soul is missing. But the fighting?"

Blasts of essence dance across my vision. Tyrannis's face as he held me still, the devilish smile plastered on his rancid mouth while my father lay bleeding behind him.

"No," I finally answer, shaking the memories from my mind. Then I continue, voice faint, "But there were times in between battles when I felt the need to go back. To be on the field again fighting alongside my people." *Because being alone with my thoughts and replaying death-filled battles in my mind would become too much.* My expression and eyes grow dark from my silent admission.

He watches me, concerned, and I barely notice his hand that crept from resting behind his head to lightly brushing the curve of my cheek. We lock eyes for a moment, his gaze heating my core for the second time today.

I swallow, unable to tear away from his stare, and pray to the reigning Celestials above that he doesn't sense the effect his eyes have on me.

As if remembering himself, he tucks his hand back behind his head.

I finish the last stitch in silence, and he rises from the seat to grab a fresh tunic off the back of a chair.

He slowly pulls the fabric over his head, then returns to sit beside me.

Forging on, I shift the focus back to him. "Why has your father pulled you from fighting? Isn't it like a prince's right to lead on the battlefield?"

"I almost died." *That's news to me.* "It was during the battle that originally won us Frallis. One of my guards was wounded. I went in to save him. I thought I put enough power behind the veil rune, but it wasn't enough. A blast crashed nearby and sent both of us tumbling. He died on impact, and I shattered almost every bone in my body. It took months for our healers to put me back together. It was excruciating. Bones that healed incorrectly needed to be rebroken in order to be reset properly. It was like I relived the explosion over and over again."

"That pain must have been unimaginable." I shudder. "At least you're alive today."

"I'm surprised you're not wishing I was dead."

"In any normal situation, I would, but you're the one who took me away from your wretched father, so I'm grateful," I say, then rise. "We should probably head back down, see if they need any help. I'm sure your gift of healing will be useful."

"Yes, Heren might have an apprentice, but I'm certain they'd appreciate some assistance."

"What was that thing anyway?" I ask as we exit his room and head toward the stairs.

"I'm not sure, but I'll employ a team to do some research on the specimen. See if there were any other reports of attacks in the neighboring town."

We walk in silence, but when we reach the first landing, he stops and takes my hand in his. He caresses the back of my hand with calloused fingers, rough and impossibly smooth at the same time.

"You asked me whether or not I was expecting a different answer from you, regarding your desires. In truth, I was."

"And what exactly were you expecting?" I ask, releasing a huff of breath. *Had I not answered honestly?*

"I was expecting the truth." *Apparently not honest enough.* "One that doesn't stem from the destiny of your birthright."

My eyes widen in response. Who is he to speak of birthright when he claimed me as his own?

He takes a cautious step forward, closing the distance between us.

Instinctively, I shuffle back, bumping right into the wall behind me.

Slowly, he raises his hand, and my body goes still. His soft fingers delicately tuck a stray curl behind my ear, leaving a trickle of warmth from my ear to the top of my neck in his wake.

Any other person and I would have had their head for touching my hair without my permission, but for some reason, it takes all my strength to prevent my body from curling into his touch. This close, he smells like teakwood and summer rain and all the bits of nature that remind me of my own essence.

And while all that is true, there is a part of me that cowers at his touch. My stomach roiling at his proximity. My mind terribly flustered by the shock of his actions.

He seems to notice this too. His eyes sharpen in alarm as he takes a step back.

"What do you want, Raya? Not for your people or your country, but for yourself?" he asks before walking down the stairs ahead of me.

It takes me a moment to collect myself after that and follow him down. But long after I finish helping clear the dead from the gardens and collect the beast for inspection, when the sky beyond my window melts from soft yellows and pinks to the darkest midnight blue, my answer to his question, one that apparently everyone wishes to know the answer to, swims in circles in my mind.

What do I want?

I used to be so sure. But now? *I don't know.*

EIGHTEEN

Tap. Tap. Tap.

My fingertips tap against the metal table on my balcony, in time with the clock tick, tick, ticking away in the far corner of the room. A spoon rests in my other hand as I mindlessly stir the honey into my cup of tea. By now, the honey has surely dissolved, but I'm lost in intrigue as I watch the soldiers, who arrived days before, sparring in the open field beyond the garden. Soldiers who are barely men. *Boys. They're just boys.*

Apparently, this is a tradition held here in Corath. Each year, before groups of newly trained soldiers enter the battlefield, they stop here in Thestras to complete their training with the prince. Leaders from the region and a few high-ranking officers are here with them.

I suppose it's a way for Orion to still give what he can to his soldiers when he can't fight with them.

Because of our *lovely* visitors, I've made myself scarce. Taking meals in my room and going on walks early in the morning or late in the evening to avoid any interaction with the very people who surely want me dead. Some have been walking through the gardens below my balcony, but none have noticed me yet.

I continue to watch the young soldiers' clumsy sparring. Their inability to stave off an attack. My stomach roils with nausea at the thought of these sad excuses for soldiers going off to battle by the end of next week.

It's not their fault, I remind myself. The king makes the orders, the prince assists in carrying them out, the boys abide. The vicious cycle in this horrific country.

The soldiers are staying in the barracks that surround the outer border of the palace while the generals and officers have been granted rooms in the castle.

Nowhere near mine, thank the spirits.

Nevertheless, I've holed myself away in my room, reading the rest of the books I could find on the runes that power these castles—the king's and the prince's—and the land that surrounds them. While the runes make escape that much harder, knowing these details will help me better prepare for one.

But now, the solace of my solitude has become maddeningly dull. The ache of boredom creeps into my soul. I can only keep myself occupied for so long before my thoughts turn truly dark.

With a grimace, I set down my cup and saucer. "Samson!" I call, sounding a bit more panicked than I intended.

"Raya?!" He rushes into my apartments.

"Out here!"

Finally, his clunking form graces my terrace, sword at the ready and ability-enhancing runes activated on the chest plate of his armor. With a huff, he sheaths his sword and removes his helmet.

His long blond hair is a bit disheveled, and his face is

worn with frustration as he peers down to where I sit in my chair. He holds his helmet in the crook of his arm, his golden waves flat against his head from wearing the damn thing for hours on end.

"I thought you were hurt," he says unamused.

"And now that you know I'm not, you can join me," I respond, kicking out the chair across from me with my foot.

The metal legs of the chair scrape painfully against the stone. The few soldiers walking in the gardens glance up in our direction, sharing confused looks with one another.

Reluctantly, he considers taking the seat and finally concedes. He's about to sit but hesitates, unsure how to position himself in his inflexible armor. It feels as though a decade passes until he finally figures out the best way to sit, creaking into the chair.

We rest there a moment in silence until his voice cuts through the air. "Is this what you've been doing every day?"

"You really think I would've been able to sit here for days doing nothing without going mad?"

"Not sure what else you could be doing."

"This is coming from the man whose job it is to stand outside my door for hours on end." I eye him through slitted lids.

"Touché," he says before we slip into silence once more.

This time, I'm the one to break it. "So...how long have you been in the service of the prince?"

He glances my way, probably wondering if I really just want to make small talk, to which I just shrug.

"About fifty years. As soon as I came of age, I was assigned as his personal guard. Then followed him here when he established his own house and staff."

"Did you know him before you went into service, or was the assignment random?" I ask, feigning innocent curiosity.

A stray strand falls over his sky-blue eyes, angled cheek, and aquiline nose. In the sunlight, his fair skin glows, illuminating the spattering of freckles across his cheeks.

Despite the overwhelming sense of dread I typically feel in his presence, there's something oddly familiar about him. A stirring sensation curls within me, and I know it's telling me to run. But that's madness. I've never met him before.

He tilts his chiseled chin as he considers my question, wondering if he should continue entertaining this discussion.

Whatever internal struggle he wages, he decides it's not a threat to divulge. "He and I have been best friends since we were children. I grew up in the castle, taken there at a young age to begin my training. As soon as we saw each other…"

"Was it love at first sight?" I ask, resting my elbows on the table and leaning my chin on my hands as I bat my eyes.

"No, smart-ass." He rolls his eyes. "We just… knew we'd be fast friends. Always having fun, getting each other out of and into trouble." He smiles at the memories that play in his mind. "We've been inseparable ever since."

"Sounds like true love to me."

"While my destiny lies in the service of the prince, our friendship is a bond unlike any other." His eyes gleam.

True love indeed.

"And now he's entrusted you to protect me," I say. "How *kind.*"

"Who says I'm here to protect you?"

"The way you barged in here like a gallant knight said just enough." I smile at the brooding guard, who fights the tug at the corner of his mouth.

THE BUTLERS OPEN the doors to the banquet hall, the old wood creaking as they swing wide.

I didn't receive a note saying I shouldn't eat here today, so I decided to make my presence known. When Samson didn't stop me as I made my way here, I half expected the room to be empty.

I was sorely mistaken.

The men at the table stop midbite and midsentence to see who will be joining them. Fury swells in the air as I lock eyes with several high-ranking officers and a surly general.

I curtsy toward the prince, who sits at the head of the table. He nods my way, almost as if he's been expecting my arrival, and motions for a butler to set a place beside him for me.

My long lace overdress ripples behind me as I walk past the leaders of Corath. I decided to wear my usual pants and bodice combo. The fabric is cinched at my waist with a ruby belt, and the matching jewels set in my hair make it look like I'm wearing a small crown.

I can feel the men at the table staring, burning a hole deep into my soul. Refusing to return their gazes, I walk with my chin held high.

Why is he allowing me to join him and his guests, especially when I have very clearly intruded? Leaders of his armies, lords of his lands?

I take my place at his side, a butler tucking my chair in before returning with a pitcher of wine to fill my glass.

Whatever conversation they were in the middle of is not

resumed. I take my napkin from my place setting, and another butler comes around to start filling my plate.

They continue eating while I finally start digging into my own meal, but a few hold their angry stares. I glance up at one of the men and immediately recognize him from one of our battles.

His eyes glare into mine with the heat of contempt. One that I'm all too familiar with.

"Is there something you'd like to say to me, General Mavre?"

He blinks, surprised. Either from my bluntness or the fact I know his name.

"Did you think I do not know who any of you are?" They all just stare in confusion, but I continue, "While I do not know all of you, there are a number of you I remember. Like you, Kassius, from the Battle of Frallis, the first one. Mavre, you attempted to take my region, Senna, but failed. And you, Lamarc, from the Battle of Katan? I make a point to find out which armies I'm fighting, where they're from, who their leaders are. We all do, as I'm sure you do too."

"Why do you even bother?" spits Mavre.

"Well, it is my job to know my enemy as it is yours. But despite what you've been told about me, or any of the other leaders from Promithia, I still believe we are all people. And we all deserve the same respect we would give our own fallen soldiers, regardless of which side we are on," I say, the words similar to the prince's when he saved me that last night in the king's care.

When I find the prince's gaze, I hold it for only a moment. There's nothing but confidence and pride in his eyes.

"We see each other as enemies," I continue. "But the truth is we are just pawns being played by our rulers."

"Pawns?" Kassius interjects. "Do you really think *you* are a pawn being played by your queen? You get her protection."

I scoff. "Where is her protection now?" I take a sip from my wine glass.

The prince just eyes me cautiously.

My guard has his hand on his hilt. There goes *his* protection.

Why are they so afraid of me? I'm helpless in my current predicament.

"I've seen you on the battlefield, *Duchess*," starts Lamarc. My rightful title sounds like a mockery coming from his lips. "You're merciless, you kill whoever is in your path."

"Do I? And what do *you* do? Would you stand there and let your enemies kill you? How many of my soldiers have you or your men killed? How many lives have you taken?" Nothing but deep silence follows my question. "You look at me with disgust, yet we are no different. The only difference is who we serve. So don't sit here and chastise me for my dealings on the battlefield when you are just as guilty of the same."

My muffled essence boils under the surface. The prince's unbearable gaze sears in my core again. A buzzing sensation tingles at my wrist as the runes holding my essence at bay falter. My Empath abilities are *miraculously* restored. Around the room, the bubbling of emotions wraps around my being, suffocatingly so.

I eye Orion suspiciously. His expression gives nothing away.

"I don't know why you let this monster sit with us, Your Highness," Lamarc spews. "Tyrannis should have speared her, just as he did her father."

Slamming my fists down, I rise, towering over the table. The guards unsheathe their swords and step toward our seats, toward me, but Orion holds a hand in the air, halting their approach.

I let my rage consume me as I aim all my fiery will toward the spineless man across from me. "My father was more of a warrior than you will ever be. You think you're so high and mighty because of the company you keep, taunting me with words because I have no way to retaliate. Well, *my lord,* one day I will have these runes removed, and I bet you will have far less to say then."

Lamarc cowers in his seat, and the others go silent. Mavre just stares at me intently. His rage, hot and thick, surrounds his being, then he turns his gaze to Orion.

"You expect me to work with this bitch after everything she's done? She killed my son!" he says, pain etched on the edge of his words. "I watched as she drove a spear through his heart instead of showing mercy or attempting to save him. Lamarc is right, we should leave her to rot in a cell and be ravaged by vermin."

My brows furrow at his words, and I'm about to question what he means by "work" with me when a thrum of power hums in the room, silencing us all as a bubbling fury wraps around us. Everyone in the room goes deathly still.

"If any of you continue to question my judgment, it will be the last thing you do." Orion's voice twists.

There's no hint of fire or anger in his eyes, just cold detachment as he turns into something wicked. Someone completely different from the warm prince I've come to know.

"General Duchess Raya is a guest in this home, *my* home, just like all of you. You have all taken the lives of Promithian warriors, heirs of their leaders, keepers of their lands. So save your hypocrisy, shut your mouths, and remember your place."

I never knew he was capable of that. Then again, I don't know him at all.

Mavre pushes back a snarl but concedes. The guards in the room slacken their tensed muscles, replacing their swords in their sheaths.

"At my Stabilit, the spirits gave me the gift of Empath. I feel it all. Emotions. Pain. Everything. More of a curse than a gift, really." I say that last bit more to myself than to everyone else. I shudder as every conquest plays in hyperspeed in my mind, as I remember the pain of every bone-shattering blow and twist of essence at my fingertips. "So, you may see me as a monster, and in many of the battles I have fought, I have seen myself as one too. But I don't take killing lightly because I know those deaths."

I shift my gaze to Mavre. "By the time I got to Johnson that day, he was close to the end." At the sound of his son's name, Mavre finally meets my eyes, his own wide in shock. "He begged me to end his life. Our healers were too far away, and I was too weak to transport. I knew he wouldn't have made it if I carried him, so I granted his wish and made sure he felt no pain. He only felt peace in the end."

"You can do that? Take pain away?" One of the leaders on the opposite end of the table asks.

I simply nod.

"But why? We're your enemies."

"I do it because although I know someone else may not find it in their hearts to spare me of the pain, it is still the right thing to do." I echo Orion's words once more.

With that revelation, I reclaim, my seat and the table returns to their meal. The stares my way cease.

I've learned how to drown out the emotions and pain from others, so feeling death doesn't faze me as much as it used to. I have experienced it so many times that I'm numb to it now.

Samson finally relaxes behind me. Even Orion seems to ease as the tension flows out of the room.

But when our gazes meet again, a new understanding passes between us, and the slightest bit of trust.

WAKE UP.

Wake up.

WAKE UP.

I shoot out of bed in a panic, sweat dripping down my brow. The curtains billow from the howling wind. A storm passing through.

The wind... it was just the wind. I assure myself. But even I know the voices that whisper on the waves of wind often mean so much more.

With sleepy steps, I make my way to the windows and close them tight. My tongue scrapes against the roof of my mouth like sandpaper, but when I go to pour myself a glass of water, the carafe is bone dry. Not even a drop left.

With a sigh, I pull on my satin robe hanging off the edge of the bed and head to the kitchen.

When I open the door to my room, I'm met with a gasp and sharp *zing* of a sword being unsheathed.

I'm surprised to find Samson guarding my room so late. Usually it's one of the others. Samson is obviously just as shocked as I am.

He slides his blade back into its place at his hip as I

swiftly exit my room and walk down the hall toward the staircase.

An exasperated groan sounds from behind me, followed by the quick thud of his boots.

"You shouldn't be out this late," he grumbles, grabbing me by the arm and turning me to face him.

Perhaps I woke him from a nap of his own.

"You look a little disheveled, *Captain*. Sleeping on the job?" He narrows his eyes and furrows his brows in annoyance. "I don't think Orion would be pleased to hear about that. Think of all the mayhem I could have caused if I slipped past you while you took your beauty rest."

With a huff and another disapproving groan, he releases my arm. "What do you need? Surely you don't want to go for a stroll dressed like... *that*."

"Have you never seen a woman in a robe before?" I gesture down to the silken fabric that flows to the floor. A sash is tied tightly at my waist.

He purses his lips, unamused.

I simply shrug and continue my descent, rounding the corner to the final staircase.

These Corathian men... So uptight. They don't have any comments to make about rolling around shirtless in the mud with each other, but as soon as I step out in pants or, spirits forbid, a full-length robe, then all hell breaks loose.

"Oh, lighten up, Samson. I just want some water, and then I'll be back in my pretty little cage in no time."

"We do have maids for that, you know."

"Why would I wake someone up in the middle of the night when I am perfectly capable of fetching myself a glass of water?"

He looks at me dumbfounded as if he expected me to do the very thing I was questioning.

"Or perhaps you're just angry that I interrupted *your* sleep?" With that, I carry on, finally making it to the grand foyer. My slipper-covered feet pad softly across the marble floor.

Voices echo down the open space from the entryway as a few soldiers reconvene after their rounds about the grounds. Their voices become hushed when they notice our presence, then one jogs over swiftly.

He salutes Samson, eyeing me skeptically before speaking. "Good evening, Captain. May we have a word with you?"

Although his expression gives away nothing, a slick murmuring of panic surrounds him.

Samson nods, then turns to me. "Stay here, I will accompany you in a moment."

"I can find my way myself, you know."

"Stay here," he repeats through gritted teeth, like I'm a child he's quickly losing patience with.

"I would think saving your prince from a monster attack would garner some privileges!" I shout behind him, but he just grunts in response.

I throw my hands up in surrender as he turns to walk with the young guard toward the group.

Such a grump, I think to myself as I inspect the art on the walls. Scenes of rolling hills, blazing suns, bright round moons, and creatures that walk both day and night.

Each painting seems to come to life as I pass, trees blowing in the wind, clouds rolling past the moon. The work of animator runes, no doubt, allowing the painting to come alive with repetitious motion.

I make it halfway down the hall when the sound of voices speaking urgently back and forth floats beyond the wall. I glance toward the captain and his men. Samson still has his back to me, listening to whatever the guards are sharing with him.

Keeping my interest on the art, I move closer to the hidden conversation. Their words are muffled by the thick walls, but I can hear well enough.

"I agree with the prince," says a voice I don't recognize. "Having her here will only aid us in our efforts."

"How will *she* aid us in anything?" Kassius's deep timbre rumbles. "All she is good for is death and destruction."

I roll my eyes at the statement. Mattias really did a number on my reputation here.

"Need I remind you she helped save us from the attack on the grounds last week, saving my life in the process. You are blinded by war and rage, Kassius." Orion sounds as though he hasn't slept in ages. Despite his weariness, his words still carry those rich tones, filled with power and precision. A leader through and through. "Think of the future we are looking to build here. My hope is to one day put this nasty war aside, to be at peace, and Raya may be the only one who can help us given her stature and position in her court."

Well, well, well... Do we have a scheming prince on our hands?

That explains what Mavre meant when he mentioned "working" with me.

"And you really believe her? Believe that she will help us achieve our goals?" Kassius asks.

"I do. She helped us when she could've easily sat behind, and she did it all without a drop of her essence. She is a force without her abilities, but with them? We know the devastating effect all too well. The power she possesses is one we should look to ally with. When the time comes, I know she will do what is right."

Before I can glean any more information from their

conversation, Samson's thudding footsteps make their way toward me.

I continue inspecting the artwork farther down the hall.

"I thought I told you to stay put," he says, grumbling his annoyance once more.

"I'm still technically in your vicinity, aren't I?" I pull my eyes away from the wall, facing him. "Anything I might be able to assist with?"

He shakes his head. "Don't you worry, *Duchess*. The men can handle it."

"Yes, and if they had tails, they'd be pressed between their legs," I grumble under my breath.

"What was that?" he asks, a flash of amusement coursing through his eyes.

"Nothing, just that I hope that monster doesn't have vengeful friends," I say, and his face blanches in response. A pit drops in my stomach.

"Was there another attack?" I ask, voice low.

"Yes," he says roughly. His eyes grow distant.

Two attacks in a matter of weeks? I wonder if there have been more.

"Is there anything I can do to help?" I know what his answer will likely be, but I have to ask.

He gives a firm shake of his head, his gaze turning cold. "His Highness has everything under control."

Clearly, I think with a scoff, but I don't press any further.

"Fine," I say resigned, my fingers curling into a fist at my side. "If you all insist on keeping me in the dark, then can we please get some water before I die of thirst?"

"If that's the case, then why not take our time." Despite his sentiment, he leads me to the kitchen below.

Aw, he doesn't actually want me dead.

As we descend, I push the thought of monsters far away

from my mind. If the prince wants my help, then he will ask for it. Besides, it's not like I'm an expert in mythical monsters and beasts.

But I can't stop my mind from wandering back to the conversation happening right above my head. I had a feeling Orion was hiding something. I mean, why go to the lengths of saving me?

But this? Treason? The wheels in my mind start churning, trying to decipher what plot the prince is brewing.

NINETEEN

A knock sounds at the front door of my apartments. Instead of answering, I roll over in my bed, hiding my head under one of my pillows.

Perhaps if I ignore the noise, the visitor will just go away?

Much to my dismay, the knocking only grows more incessant until whoever it is takes it upon themselves to enter my rooms.

Heavy boots thud their way into my bedchamber, drawing the curtains apart to let in the gray winter morning.

"Is there a reason you have decided to wake me before the sun has even fully risen?" I say, sitting up to see who my intruder is.

Standing at attention at the foot of my bed is Samson in his training leathers instead of his typical armor. Mouth agape and cheeks growing bright red, he turns away from me… and the lace sleeping garments I wear.

Clearing his throat, he says, "You have been invited to train with His Royal Highness and the soldiers. You are to be escorted there at once."

Hating being summoned, I groan in contempt. Not to mention, I'm probably only invited so I can be a punching bag, but I don't refuse. Training with them is better than not training at all… or being cooped up in here all day.

"Do you ever get any sleep?" I ask, but he ignores me. Considering he's been at my door all night, I'm not sure how he's still standing. "Thank you for waking me, Samson. I will get dressed and meet you at my door."

He simply nods, still turned away from me, before sauntering back out to the hall.

I quickly jump out of bed and run to my closet. After pulling on pants and a black square-neck bodice with full sleeves—the material flexible for training—I braid my unruly curls down the middle of my head, slip on a pair of over-the-knee boots and a black coat before meeting Samson in the hall.

When we reach the gardens, he starts a brisk jog, motioning for me to follow. I didn't realize that when he said I'd been invited to train, he meant I would be *training* as rigorously as one of their soldiers.

With a growl, I jog after him.

My hands shake at my sides, eager to finally get back in the ring. Essence or no essence. Eager to train, to fight. We run through the gardens, around the lake in the back of the grounds, and through a short trail in the nearby wood, stopping every so often to catch my breath. Samson silently follows along. Runs when I run, stops when I stop. By the time we finally make it to the training grounds, I'm a heaving disaster.

If Dessy were here, she would force me to sprint laps around the training ring and consider that the rest of the warm-up.

Dessy.

My heart pulls in my chest at the thought of my sister. I wonder what she's doing, how she's fared these past few months, having to pull herself together to lead and mourn our father on her own. I hate that I'm not there with her. That she can't lean on me, nor I her. We've always kept each other grounded, and it's odd not having her by my side now.

Samson leads me toward a table to the left of the fields. Some of the other officers are here, and they turn away as I enter. Soldiers are sparring, some with dull blades, others in hand-to-hand combat. In one corner, runewielders practice their craft.

Considering their customs, a woman would never be allowed to step foot in the training rings, to visit or otherwise. They believe it is a man's job to fight and a woman's to tend to the home and family.

One boy looks at me with brows furrowed in confusion.

I doubt he's gone through the Stabilit yet. The process is different for everyone. Mine occurred at twenty-one. Dessy's at twenty-three. But I can tell, by the innocent gleam in his eyes and the way his gangly limbs are awkward and uncoordinated, he still has a couple years until he reaches his.

Another older soldier whispers something in his ear. The boy's eyes grow wide with recognition, then fear and rage power his rigid stance.

My reputation precedes me.

Samson leaves me at a table lined with carafes of water and drinking glasses. Without wasting time, I pour myself a glass of water, and the cool liquid satiates my dry throat. I look around the training field, wondering why on earth I was invited in the first place. Obviously, weapons are out of the question. Surely no one will want to spar with me, the villain in their stories, even if I did save their prince from a beast.

The prince stands beside me, grabbing a glass of water for himself. "I'm surprised you actually came."

"I'm a warrior who has not been allowed to train or use my essence. And fighting that beast was harder than I'd like to admit. Is it so hard to believe I would take you up on your offer?" I ask, eyes sweeping over the soldiers on varying points of the field. "Though it didn't really seem like I had a choice."

"Well, it looks like everyone is either too afraid of you or may use this as an opportunity to kill you." He leans against the solid table next to me.

I give him a look that says, *I'd like to see them try.*

I would like to see that as well, his stare back seems to say.

"Speaking of the beast, any update on where they might have come from?" I ask, and his eyes go wide in shock. Clearly, he wasn't informed of my knowledge regarding last night's attack. "Samson was escorting me to the kitchen's last night when he was briefed. I put the pieces together."

He nods, though shifts uncomfortably on his feet.

"There's no update, yet," he says, shaking his head. "There's no history of any animal or monster like it."

"So strange," I mutter, taking a sip of water.

"Don't worry," he says, squeezing my shoulder. "We won't stop looking for answers."

The prince takes off his cloak and lays it on the back of a lone chair next to the table. He's wearing a black tunic. It's loosely tied at the top, the muscles of his chest poking through.

For a moment, and I swear only a moment, my fingers

itch to trail along the solid and firm mounds of his pecs, over the ridges and valleys of his abs, across the sculpted muscles of his arms.

He smiles, seeing where my gaze has fallen.

Heat rises in my cheeks, and I quickly divert my gaze back to the field in front of us.

"Why don't we see how you fare against me?" he asks, pointing toward an empty section of the training field.

"You're joking, right?" His face is unmoving as stone. No hint of laughter or joking in his eyes. "Oh, you're serious?"

"You'll come to find, Raya, that I am usually always serious. And right now, I'd like to see what the fabled Wielder of Death can do… or should we call you the General of Death now?"

I ignore his use of the nickname, suppressing an eye roll. "The Giving wasn't enough for you?"

"I'd like to see firsthand." He's determined.

I purse my lips but concede.

"Fine, what are the rules?" I say, placing my glass back on the table.

"Fight and win. The first one to have the potential to land a deadly blow is the victor."

"What weapons are we using?"

He eyes me, a flash of amusement dancing across his face.

"Raya, we *are* weapons." His eyes grow bright as his power flares.

All I can do is laugh. "You seem to forget my rune bracelet is still very much active and dampening my abilities." I wave my arm in front of his face.

He takes my hand in his, and his calluses caress my palms. Although he says he doesn't fight in battles, the calluses on his fingers tell me he trains like he does.

I look into his eyes and shudder as a strange sense of comfort washes over me. Mindlessly, my feet shuffle forward ever so slightly, my body instinctively leaning into his, but I stop myself, preventing my limbs from any further betrayal.

He waves his other hand over my bracelet, gaze never leaving mine as he works to relieve the dampening powers of the runes.

My essence returns to me in a rush. Not all of it, but enough to scrimmage. My skin tingles as my power cascades through me, glittering between my fingers. A sigh of relief washes over my being.

"There," he says, eyes finally releasing my own. "You will be able to use your power, but the Rite will prevent us from being able to truly land deadly blows to one another."

Well, that's news to me.

I'm relieved to know there are some protections in place, but I know full well that if he needed me dead, he could make it so.

"With that said," he continues. "I do hope you won't go easy on me."

"I haven't trained in months. I doubt I'll be able to do much damage at all."

His eyes run over me once more as I remove my jacket and place it over his. We stand there, matching in all black. Perfect opponents.

"Is there something wrong?" I ask.

"Will you be able to fight in *that*?" He says, referring to my black leather bodice, long sleeves stopping at my wrists.

"Corathian men," I mumble. Ignoring the question, I make my way to the empty ring of dirt.

THE PRINCE FOLLOWS me into the center of the ring. We bow to each other before taking our stances. A guard to the side whistles, signaling the beginning of our duel.

We circle around each other, unsure who will make the first move. Before I can blink, he lunges forward, but I—just short of gracefully—spin out of the way, avoiding his punch. Using his force, I manage to pull him down. Unfortunately, he takes me down with him, but I roll out of his grasp and back onto my feet. He quickly clambers back up to a stand, a devilish grin spreading from cheek to cheek.

Before I can brace myself, a squalling wind takes me off my feet. I roll backward sloppily, then land in a kneeling crouch. Palms on the ground, I use my essence to feel every piece of dirt and gravel underneath me.

The ground rumbles, and blocks of dirt shoot up toward the prince. He's knocked back a few feet as the earth tumbles down into place. Before he has a chance to get up, I run toward him.

He flips himself upright and attempts to land a roundhouse kick. I duck and punch him in his back near his ribs. He fumbles slightly, but not enough. Using the momentum from my punch, he spins back around to face me. His fist meets my jaw as the ground rumbles again.

He uses my own trick against me, raising blocks of dirt. I jump and dodge out of the way. Using air as a propeller, I lift myself on top of the blocks, running toward the prince.

He releases his hold of the rising blocks, but he's not

quick enough. I'm one step ahead, jumping off each block to the next before they tumble back to the ground.

I leap off the final block before it disappears from below me. In midair, I blast wind under his feet, and he tumbles onto his back. As soon as he's down, I land on top of him, pinning him to the ground with shackles of dirt around his ankles and wrists. My hand hovers over his heart.

My lips curl up in victory. If this were a real fight on the battlefield, this would be a killing blow.

We stay that way for a few fleeting moments. My thighs grip his waist. Our chests so close we can feel every rise and fall of our breaths. The world around us fades away, going still and silent as though we are the only two that exist. His eyes gleam as they gaze into mine with a sparkle of excitement. But that sparkle quickly turns into a spark of burning intensity. Like a flame, yearning to be set ablaze. The space between us has its own gravitational pull, as if we are two stars destined to collide.

His head slightly lifts toward me, eyes darting to my lips. Before I can even register the action, mine does the same.

Until someone moves, metal armor clanking with the action. The bubble around us bursts, and I'm all too aware of just how close we are. Of the heat emanating from him and settling a little too nicely deep in my core.

I'm about to move when that devilish smile of his returns and cracks of thunder sound high in the sky. The shackles holding him down burst, and I'm knocked off him. A bolt of lightning crashes down into the dirt, but before it has a chance to strike true, I tumble out of the way.

Like me, the prince is an Elemental, so he possesses the essence to control the elements of the earth. But unlike me, the elements are not where his strengths lie. He's also a very strong Stormning.

While my power is limited to the elements—air, water, fire, earth—Stormnings can manipulate the weather. Summon hurricanes and rainstorms. Wield streaks of lightning from the heavens.

We continue fighting, round after round, taking turns getting each other into deadly positions that would mean defeat until we're both out of breath. Muscles and bodies sore from exertion, both covered in dirt from head to toe.

He reaches down to help me stand, and I'm surprised when I see all the soldiers looking on. They're probably simultaneously enthralled by our practice, interested in seeing us both in action, and worried I might actually kill their prince, completely unaware of the bind the Rite has on us both.

He's incredibly talented—I'll give him that. His power, combined with his ability to runewield, makes me wonder why his father insists on keeping him off the battlefield while also thanking the spirits he is no longer allowed to fight against my forces.

"What are all of you staring at? Back to training," he says, voice forceful yet understanding.

They all scurry back to their sparring partners, a couple others drawing swords and practicing stances.

I walk to the table and grab the first carafe of water I see, Orion following close behind me.

"I see why they say you wield death," he says breathlessly as I hand him the carafe after I fill my glass.

"Trust me, *that's* not why," I say. "It's a good thing your father doesn't let you back on the battlefield," I continue with a chuckle, gearing the conversation away from my ability to steal the breath from my opponents before they even realize what's happening. "Although, his forces could use more fighters like you."

"Perhaps it's for the best. I'm his only son. If I died on the battlefield, that would be the end of his line."

"Your mother could have more," I say plainly, leaning against the stone table.

A pained look crosses his face. "Unfortunately, that's not possible." He swallows down whatever painful memories begin to resurface. "My mother had a miscarriage many years ago. She suffered major complications from the ordeal. Healers say that if she tries to conceive again, it would mean her death."

"I'm sorry to hear that," I say, swallowing down my own painful memories. "My mother died while giving birth last year. Both she and the babe were lost. A time that should have been joyous was filled with devastation. If the healers suggest against it, then it's best they don't try. No one should ever lose a person in that way."

"No, one should not." His eyes are somber as they gaze upon me. "I'm sorry for your loss. For your loss of both of them."

I give a small, sad smile in response.

We stand there in silence for a few moments more, watching the soldiers as they fight one another, before I grab my coat and push off the table to head back to the palace. I can almost smell the scent of lavender and honey soaps that await me in my tub.

Before leaving, I turn back to the prince. "Thank you for not allowing your soldiers to kill me."

His face turns hard again. "I would never do that to you."

I furrow my brows. "Do what exactly? Because I know if you needed to have me killed, you would."

"Break your trust. You trusted me not to stab you in the back. I would *never* do that to you." He reiterates the words like a solemn vow.

"Now, Prince, there's no sense in making promises you can't keep." I bow before leaving, my guard in tow.

A few generals glance my way as I exit, and this time they don't look away.

I could have sworn I overheard the prince muttering, "I think I've met my match."

TWENTY

The soldiers keep me busy on the training field for the next week and a half. A little too busy, but it's a much-appreciated change to the monotony of life at a quiet court. When I enter the dining hall in something other than slacks and a tunic for breakfast, the mud from the training ring washed out of my hair, I'm shocked to see the surprise in their eyes. Even the prince holds his stare a bit longer than he probably intended.

My dress, a gauzy silver thing made of starlight and dreams with long billowing sleeves and ribbons that tie at the waist, glides across the floor in a mini train.

I bow to Orion and nod in greeting to the rest before I make my way to my seat. Aside from the initial gazes, the generals and officials don't acknowledge my presence.

We sit in silence for some time, eating our meals and carrying on small conversations, until the prince clears his throat to speak.

"Tomorrow is the winter solstice. I can hardly believe two

weeks have passed since your arrival, but I hope you and all your troops will join us for the annual Solstice Feast and celebration tomorrow."

A buzz of excitement seems to flit around the table. One by one, the generals and officers depart. No doubt to let their men know they will be attending "a feast beyond proportion," to quote one of the officers.

Only a handful of us are left when I rise from my seat and bow to the prince before making my exit.

I barely make it out the door when someone steps behind me.

"Would you accompany me for a walk in the gardens?" Orion asks, holding his arm out for me.

I smile and nod, avoiding his gaze.

To be honest, I would much rather be digging into a few books I found in my study yesterday about Corathian traditions and runebinding, but I don't let my disappointment show.

"You look nice," he says once we're outside, farther away from prying ears and eyes. The words come out awkwardly, like he's unsure if he should be complimenting me.

"Thank you?"

"I mean, you look nice every day, but today you look different. Still nice, just different." He fumbles over his words, kicking a small rock in frustration over his rambling.

"Honestly, I just didn't feel like wearing pants."

He laughs at my confession, though a darkness crosses his eyes, puzzling me. I'm about to ask him what plagues his thoughts, but the darkness clears as though it was never there to begin with. Perhaps it never was.

"I'm sorry I've been indisposed in meetings these past few weeks."

I eye him, taken aback by his apology. "No need to apologize, Your Highness. You have your duties to fulfill."

"Please, just call me Ori."

I smile at the thought of being able to call him by a nickname. It means he trusts me. *Good.*

"How many people have the liberty of calling you Ori?"

"Not many. Only Samson and a friend I met while traveling abroad. So, including you, only three people."

"Well, I'm honored," I say, placing my hand over my heart in mock flattery.

He nudges me lightly with his elbow, a soft laugh leaving his lips.

We're silent for a bit as we walk along the garden's path.

We pass by a patch of dead roses. They're in a spot that doesn't receive the gift of sunlight like the others do. I separate from his arm only for a moment and touch the rose buds, giving them new life.

He stops as I use my essence on the once wilting roses and watches as life and color return to each one. I turn back to him and loop my arm through his. I take this as my chance to finally approach him about a certain conversation I overheard.

"Can I ask you something?"

"Anything," he says.

Air fills my lungs, chest expanding as I take a deep breath.

"I overheard a conversation between you and your friends about how my abilities can aid your cause. I'd like to know what *cause* I might be aiding."

"Ah yes," he says expectantly, as if he has been waiting for me to bring up the subject.

"Was I meant to overhear that conversation?" I ask, confused once more.

He sends me an infuriating smirk but doesn't answer my

question. Motioning his fingers toward the ground, he casts a circle of silencing runes around us.

"The friends who are visiting are not here merely to see our soldiers off. We have been devising a plan to put an end to this war. It wasn't always our intention to have you as part of those plans, but your capture changed things."

"That is why you claimed me? Not to save me from your father, but to use me for your own gain?" I ask, a twinge of pain lancing from deep within my chest, although I'm not sure why I'm hurt by that. If I were in his shoes, I would've done the same thing.

His eyes darken ever so slightly, "Would you believe me if I told you both were my goal? To get you to safety, away from my father, *and* to leverage your position."

"And how exactly am I to aid your cause, *Ori*?" I cross my arms over my chest as I quickly lose patience. I don't like the idea of being used.

"Would your queen ever be open to discussing the terms of a cease-fire? One that could lead to peace negotiations and even a treaty?"

I purse my lips.

"I'll take that as a no."

"I've tried talking to her about it, her excuse was that Mattias would never agree or would betray her at the meeting."

"Both probable outcomes...Unless..." He thinks out loud, shifting his stance.

He fumbles over his words, unsure how to put his thoughts into complete sentences.

"Well, out with it!" I practically shout.

"What if we arrange a meeting with Queen Sarana?"

I shoot him a look, unsure if he realizes what he's saying, the word "we" echoing in my mind.

"I think madness truly runs in the family. Why on Earth would you want me to go with you?"

"Because Sarana trusts you. If you can be the party in between, the voice of reason for both sides, it may make it easier. We can worry about my father after."

So *this* was his plan? I gnaw at my lip, working through the possible outcomes of this mission in my mind. It's madness.

"You realize that if Sarana knows I'm there, she would come with an army, right?"

I can't believe he's even suggesting this.

"I suspected as much, which is why I didn't mention you would be in attendance," he says, his voice matter of fact.

I freeze, unsure what he means. "You say that as if you already sent a letter out."

"That's because I did."

My eyes grow wide. "You did what?!" I say, clenching my fingers into a ball, nails digging into my palms.

The ground trembles as my blood begins to boil. Grabbing a hold of my hands, he attempts to calm me with his touch. It works well enough, although the earth beneath us still trembles with the aftershock.

"I wish you would have consulted with me first."

"I'm sorry, I didn't think it would be an issue. This is for the sake of diplomacy and a brighter future for both of our countries."

His hand lingers, thumb grazing over my wrist. My anger washes away just by his soothing touch.

"Why didn't you tell me about this plan when you first brought me here?"

"I needed to make sure I could trust you. And I wanted to see where your interests in this war truly lay. If you wanted the war to end in peace, or if you were just as determined to see Corath fall as my father is ready to have Promithia submit to him."

"And I suspect that is why he began taking prisoners again? A way to slowly weaken our forces until Promithia falls?" The words seethe with anger.

"What are you talking about, Raya?" His brows knit together in utter confusion.

"You can't tell me you haven't a clue about this? Before I was captured, many of my soldiers went missing after a battle. A good number of them high-ranking officers too."

His jaw clenches, and his knuckles turn white as his confusion quickly spins into rage.

He takes a deep breath, attempting to calm down before responding. "Raya, I hope you believe me when I say I had no idea this was going on. But I promise you, I will do everything I can to get to the bottom of this. You have my word."

I purse my lips, sensing the sincerity in his tone. But then something dawns on me that riles my anger once again.

"Wait one moment... you sent *Sarana* a letter, but I couldn't send a peaceful note to *my sister* letting her know I'm safe?! You are the one who actually committed treason!" My nostrils flare as heat skates over my cheeks.

"It's because I sent that letter to Sarana that I couldn't let you send one to your sister," he says, eyes pleading. "It would have been too risky. I was already worried that my father was going to find out somehow."

As much as I want to stay angry with him, anger being the simplest emotion to surface, I can't.

With a nod, I relent. But the look on his face tells me there's something more he wants to say.

Glancing around the garden, he takes my hand. "Come here."

He pulls me to the side of the path where a bushel of starblooms grow.

He plucks a brilliant, crystal-blue flower, offering it to me. "Hold this bloom in your palms and think of the message you wish to share. Repeat it in your mind until I say stop."

I cup my hands, holding the bloom as instructed, then he places his hands underneath mine. In my mind, I repeat the words I wish I could share with my sister right now.

I love you. I'm safe. I will see you soon. I love you. I'm safe. I will see you soon.

He speaks the old language, and the space between us hums as he weaves together the power of runes all around us. He locks his eyes onto mine with the intensity of a thousand stars, heat lancing around me, through me, settling deep in my core. All I want is to allow myself to be carried away by this undeniable pull that seems to always be between us.

Piece by piece, the starbloom turns to dust in my hands, the specks flying on a phantom wind up into the sky.

"There," he says, a bit winded from the use of energy. "Your sister will find the bloom, and when she touches it, she'll hear your message."

The glittering specks of the starbloom rise high into the air, then fade through space and time. On their way to find my sister.

Tears well in my eyes, and a stray drop falls down my cheek, but I race to wipe it away.

"Thank you." My words are barely more than a whisper.

Orion gives a small smile before we continue our walk through the gardens.

"So, is there anything else you need me to help you with? Aside from being there to moderate your discussion with Sarana?" I ask, voice breaking our silence.

"Now that you mention it, I know you've been doing some research." My eyes widen at his confession. "All part of your survival so I understand, but I need your help finding two journals. They were my grandfather's."

"Any idea what they look like?" I ask, unsure what good these journals will do us now.

His head moves side to side. "Unfortunately, no, but my father said he documented everything about the start of the war. I was hoping they might have some information that could help us."

"All right, I'll help you find them."

"Excellent. I have a few meetings today, but we can begin searching the library this afternoon if that's all right with you?"

"I'm not sure. My schedule is *so* busy." I laugh and lift a brow his way. His cheeks and the tips of his ears turn pink. "But yes, I think I can pencil you in."

"I'll meet you in the main library at the fifteenth hour then," he says, seeming to walk with a lighter step now that the truth is off his chest. "Thank you, by the way."

"I'm just happy I can be of use and try to end this war, even if it feels like I don't really have a choice," I say, watching our feet as they step in sync.

"Raya, you do have a choice in the matter, whether it seems you do or not. You just say the word, and I will leave you out of all this," he says, and I hold back a scoff, knowing full well if he needed to, he would force my hand.

Of course I don't have a choice here. Quite frankly, my life has been a series of choices made for me. My destiny was decided at birth. My training was decided by my father. The hands of fate even decided my journey now. So why would that change?

"But that's not why I'm thanking you," he says, stopping

us in our path. His dark eyes stare into mine with a fervor I've only ever seen in Sarana's. "Thank you for training with my soldiers. You didn't have to, but you did. By doing so, you may have saved a few of those kids' lives."

I wave a hand, brushing him off. "It felt good to be training again. I usually spend some time at the beginning of the year training our recruits at the military academy in Senna. I just wanted to make sure the younger ones had a fighting chance to see another day."

"You helped them in more ways than they can ever repay you."

The more I helped the soldiers, shared better ways to use their enhancing runes in battle and gave tips on stances, strikes, and maneuvers, the death glares receded, and more asked to work with me. But the pangs of guilt in my chest only grew worse day by day from helping my enemy.

Most of the soldiers here are young. Too young. It's better to give them a fighting chance than to let them be slaughtered by wolves. If my father were here…

Father would have never gotten himself into this mess, my subconscious sneers.

A shiver crawls up my spine, and I shake my head to clear away all thoughts of my father and his untimely demise.

"I don't need them to repay me." I bite out the words, knowing if I was a monster who expected repayment, it would never come.

"Of course you don't," he says, brows furrowed in frustration with himself. "I meant no offense."

"Your Highness," a butler calls from the top of the stairs of the patio. "The lords and officers are waiting for you."

Orion pries his eyes away from the heat of my own. Looking at the butler, he nods. With a huff, he returns his attention to me, a cold facade locking into place as he prepares for the meetings to come.

"Thank you again for your help and for the company." He nods in a bow, then jogs up the stairs. "Don't forget, Duchess. Three o'clock!"

TWENTY-ONE

Boredom consumed me before the day even had a chance. It wasn't long after Orion left that I found myself making my way to the massive library.

A staircase winds in circles in the middle of the room, surrounded by shelves lined with an endless number of books that fill the main floor and upper levels of the rotunda, several stories high. A rounded glass ceiling tops the room. The rune veil shines with a shimmering glow in the air just beneath the dome, set to protect and preserve the collection.

A small podium rests at the front of the room, and a piece of parchment lies on the surface with the directory.

The main floor houses all the journals, memoirs, and biographies. All other nonfiction works can be found on the two floors above, and fiction on the rest. Anything older than a millennium is stored below.

Walking past the rows of long tables and loungers, I make my way to the first shelf, the hem of my gown trailing along the wooden floorboards.

I should've changed before beginning this task, but there

was no use wasting time traipsing all the way across the castle. Instead, I tie the long skirts up by my waist and get to work, searching through the first floor's autobiography section. Collections of journals and texts collect dust on the shelves.

Gathering a slow swell of air around me, I get to work. Carrying each text on a soft wind, I search through them, to no avail. Nothing that denotes it belonged to the late King of Corath.

Hours pass by in a blur, and just as I finish searching through the last of the units in the middle of the floor, the double doors creak open.

"You've been busy, I see." Orion's voice echoes throughout the space.

I peek around the corner of the bookshelves and find him walking toward the stacks, eyes wide as he takes in the piles of books littering the surface of each table.

"It's about time you showed up," I say as I lift my hands, summoning the wind once more to carry the books carefully back to their rightful places.

As the last book slides into its spot, Orion rounds the corner.

"Apologies," he says, leaning against the case, voice weary. "Our meetings took longer than expected."

His black tunic is untied at the top, revealing a bit of his bare chest. The sleeves are rolled, and his crossed forearms tense as he flexes the muscles. Some of his longer waves fall onto his forehead.

A part of me wants to step forward, swipe the strands away from his eyes, and trail the pads of my fingers down the front of his chest and over his strong arms. His eyes trail me in a similar way that sends a shiver down my spine.

Whoa, I think to myself. I know he's attractive—anyone

with eyes can see that. And while I've felt the tug that pulls every now and then between us, I can't *act* on it.

No, no, no. I shake the thoughts away.

"Not like I couldn't use a hobby to fill my time." I hum as I step past him, careful not to touch him as I head straight for the first unit on the wall.

"Any luck?" He pushes off the shelf and turns toward me as I walk away.

"Not yet," I say. "I just finished searching the stacks in the middle of the floor, only have the walls to look through now."

That last push took all the essence I could muster, thanks to the diminishing cuff. It'll take some rest and a few meals to replenish my store before I can use my power again. How I long for the day when this cuff will be removed. For my power to restore to its full strength. Closing my eyes, I remember the rush of my abilities as they were. The vibrating energy that emanated from me. The brightness of life around me that nearly sang with vibrancy.

I'm about to start the next section when his footsteps click closer my way, until he's standing beside me. All I have to do is stretch out my pinkie, and it would graze against the back of his hand.

"Find anything interesting?" he asks, his breath warm against my cheek.

"Just that your family really loved to keep journals, and your great-aunt, Princess Tessaia, details accounts of her life that belong in the romance section above instead of here."

He chuckles at that. "Aunt Tessy was an interesting soul."

I turn to look at him with wide eyes. "Please, don't tell me you've read it?"

"Oh, stars above, of course not." This warrants a heartier laugh from deep within his chest. "I just happened across the book one day, took a look at page one, and immediately put it back. She was always a free bird. Sharing her strange theories and debating with the lords who visited. Adventurous with her lovers too, a new one on her arm every time I saw her, up until she passed."

"Good for her," I say in triumph, as if her conquests were my own. "I'm sure it wasn't easy with your grandfather as her brother."

"Indeed," he sighs in agreement, but the corners of his lips pull up into a small smile. "Full of life she was, with so much love to give too."

His eyes collide with mine as he says that last part, and I can't help the stirring that erupts within me, prickling over my skin and nestling in my core, causing heat to pool low... too low.

Spirits, is it hot in here, or is it just me?

Distance. I need distance between me and the prince. I turn, reaching up to the top of the shelf to begin my search, but I can't quite reach.

Orion steps close behind me, grabbing the book with ease from the shelf, his strong arm caging me against him and the bookcase.

His warmth pulls me into a trance, and out of instinct, I lean back against his chest, his muscles a steady brace. Before I truly register what I've just done, we both still. His arm is suspended in the air above me, book in hand, as his warm breath grazes across the most sensitive spot on my neck, just below my ear. I can't help the shiver that runs through my body at the sensation.

Slowly, I turn to face him, ready to give us both some much-needed space, but I'm stopped by the intensity in his eyes. This close, I can see streaks of green within his striking blue irises and the barely there smattering of freckles that softly dust his cheeks and nose.

Instead of moving away, like I know I should, I lift my fingers to trace the length of his jaw, completely obliterating my "don't act" rule.

Beside me, something falls to the ground. The book. He dropped the book, I realize, as one of his hands braces my waist and the other reaches under my chin.

With a hooked finger, he tips my head back.

There's a question in his eyes, and I know I shouldn't give in, but I have a history of doing the exact opposite of what I should.

Without a second thought, I nod.

His lips are on mine in an instant, and while the thick air between us screams of hunger, the kiss is soft. Our tongues glide against each other, exploratory. The sensation sends a thrill through me, heating my core. He steps into me, one of his legs between mine, and it takes all my willpower not to press against him and chase the satisfaction, the release, that sweet friction would provide.

He tastes of the cosmos. Of possibility and hope and... freedom.

But I'm not free. Not yet. Might never be free again if this war doesn't end amicably or with Promithia on top. I am still a captive in enemy care. The only difference between the evil king and his prince is that Orion shows kindness, whereas Mattias inflicts pain.

But knowing that doesn't stop the warmth of Orion's lips from turning cold against mine. Doesn't stop Orion's hands from twisting into the nightmare of blinding pain from Mattias's sinister touch.

I jump back, but with such little space around us, I end up knocking into the bookshelves behind me. The surprise in

Orion's eyes is the only thing that reminds me I'm in Thestras with the prince and not in the king's torture chamber.

Something dark and brewing flashes in Orion's gaze, and before I have a chance to attempt to ease his mind, to promise that kiss would never happen again, his stance goes rigid. His hands that were about to reach out to me ball into fists as he wars with whatever thoughts wrap around his mind.

"I'm sorry," he says, the only words left between us as he swiftly turns and disappears up the stairs.

Taking a moment to catch my breath, I squeeze my eyes shut. I want to chalk it up to the lack of comforting physical interaction these past few months. Perhaps our close proximity is forcing lines to be blurred. But spirits above, that was... unlike anything I've ever experienced... until it turned dark and *wrong*.

Come on, Raya, keep it together.

Releasing the air from my lungs, I wheel over the gliding ladder, pick up the book Orion dropped from the floor, and begin searching the tomes on the shelves.

Shelf by shelf, I continue to check, still nowhere closer to finding this damn journal than I was before. But when I near the end of the row, I notice a door in the corner between the two walls.

I push gently, and the large wooden door carved with runes opens with a long creak. Like a moth drawn to flame, something in my chest pulls me to the passageway that leads to the floors of ancient texts below.

There's no way the journal is down here, but perhaps...

Taking a deep breath, I step through the doorway and start down the stairs. Runelights flicker to life with every few steps I take until I finally reach the first landing.

As if on cue, the door swings open, runelights inside the room blinking awake with the action.

Inside the room, more shelves are covered with books seemingly older than the structure itself, older than time if that were even possible. Cobwebs lace every object and dust clouds swirl with the stirring of stale air.

I don't want to touch anything in here because every tome looks like it might crumble if I do.

I scan each shelf and tabletop, but nothing looks particularly out of place. Most of the texts in here are written in Eldrian from the age of the spirits, when Dane'er and Ach'tella ruled over the world. Before Ach'tella rose against her malevolent partner.

Some date back to a time before the ancient beings, when humans alone walked the earth. The only clues are the strange letters and symbols on the covers. Languages long since forgotten.

I'm about to give up as I make it back to the front of the room when I notice an unmarked book lying on top of the central table that I didn't notice before. The black leather still shines, compared to the rest of the tomes in here, which are all faded with time.

Slowly, I pull the book off the surface, sure not to rip the delicate binding. The spine and cover bear no title. A small clasp keeps the book sealed from prying eyes.

Carefully, I flip the book open. The first page only bears a name and its title:

Hester A. Valor
~~*Crown Prince of Corath*~~
King of Corath

"Son of the spirits," I say with a release of breath.

I found it! Well, at least I found one of them, I think to myself as I peruse through the book and scan over hundreds of pages of King Hesten's handwritten notes.

All the entries seem to be short. Just quick transcriptions of thoughts, dreams, and memories.

How the hell did one of King Hesten's journals end up down here?

I skim through the first few entries, all dated 2825 AGR (After the Great Rift)—about eight years before the war started—and finally find one that seems interesting.

December 25th, 2825 AGR

They came to me last night.

The Spirits.

They told me I will be destined for great things and that I will pave the way for greatness and strength here in Corath. That I will be the catalyst for the union of Promithia and Corath, uniting the two powerhouses of this earth.

Imagine that. King Hesten and Queen Solange joined together, leading and ruling this world, like Dane'er and Ach'tella. Well, before she turned her back on the great Spirit. If someone told me, before this, that Solange and I would marry, I would tell them they're crazy. But now? If the Spirits say it, then it must be so.

I can almost taste it. The crown. The throne.

My crown. MY throne.

I crossed my current title out at the beginning of this journal and wrote my true title in. King of Corath. An affirmation set that I will one day fulfill.

I know I haven't taken my studies or training seriously, but starting today, that all changes. Because when the day comes that I claim the throne from my father—and believe me, that day will come—I need to be ready for whichever path he chooses.

King Hesten's rise to power was not merely of whim but of planning. Planning and precision by a rambling man who believed the spirits talked to him. Who revered the spirits as gods instead of what they truly were, tyrants and conquerors.

I continue to read through the pages, flipping through entry after entry and skipping over the parts I already know. His first attempt at a proposal to the late Queen-King Solange is something not spoken about often as it is overshadowed by his second, even more disastrous attempt.

He had been invited to the Fall Harvest Festival in Promithia and decided to propose again there. Instead of it being the happy celebration he thought it would result in, he was denied and then forced to witness the announcement of her engagement to Prince Solomon of Alwilke.

He was devastated, and from reading a bit of his journal entry from that day, it seems he never fully recovered from the embarrassment:

They will rue the day they made a mockery of me. King Stefanus should have put his foot down, pressed his daughter to make the right decision. But no matter. The Spirits say I will bring the union of Corath and Promithia. If it's not through marriage, it shall be by force.

I shake my head in disbelief.

All of this bloodshed because a man's ego was bruised? I scoff before continuing on to another entry.

October 5th, 2833 ASR

Today, I signed the proclamation. In order to allow women the freedom to care for the home and truly focus on their families, they will no longer carry the burden of essence or runewielding. As we have seen, women having this privilege and the ability to make decisions of their own gets in the way of the will of the Spirits. We should have learned from Ach'tella's betrayal, setting the world against Dane'er, that women have no business handling the power of the Earth.

With this proclamation, they will no longer need to worry about the complexities of these abilities, nor do they need to make decisions far beyond their comprehension.

The only women who will need to know the skills of runewielding or essence will be maids. They will be taught the basics, only what they need to know for their assignments.

But the proclamation isn't the only thing I accomplished today. The Spirits said I will unite

Corath and Promithia, so I set in motion a plan that will help me accomplish that vision.

Marseille and his band of mercenaries will intercept Promithia's delivery of our agreed-upon goods for the winter. Corathian's may perish, I understand this, but it will be for a good cause. To fulfill our destiny.

I slam the journal closed, no longer caring if I bend or break the delicate leather worn from time.

This bastard planned his own demise and destined two countries to remain in an endless war because of pure pettiness. And because what? *"The spirits"* said he would conjoin the two nations and he didn't get his way?!

This man was no king. He was a tyrant who passed his tyranny to his kin.

And what was his obsession with Dane'er? If it weren't for Ach'tella and Ekkheim, humans would have remained slaves, and *we* would have been seen as little more than spirit-human mutts by Dane'er and his supporters.

The only one in his bloodline who seems to be morally aligned is Orion.

Does he know about the origins of the conflict? If I bring this up, will he even care?

There's only one way to find out, I think to myself as I gather my notes and the journal and storm back upstairs.

"Orion!" I call as I close the door behind me and race to one of the long tables in the center of the library. "Orion!"

His boots thudding against the floorboards echo around the rotunda as he flies down the stairs.

I turn to greet him as he reaches the table, holding out the journal toward him.

His eyes glisten as he takes in the long-lost piece of his family history, as damning as it is.

"You found it?! Where?" he asks, taking a seat at the table and flipping through the pages of the book.

"Downstairs with the ancient texts," I say, sitting across from him.

He looks up at me then, raising a brow in confusion. "How did you get down there?"

"The door at the back corner of the room?" I point behind me.

"What door, Raya?"

"Orion, the door that's right—" I turn around in my seat only to find that the door has vanished, and another bookshelf has taken up the space where it once stood. "I swear it was there a moment ago."

"I believe you. This library, the entire castle, has a mind of its own. Something to do with the essence laced within the grounds. How did you get it to appear?"

"I don't know, but it was there. Runes carved into its surface and all." A chill creeps up my spine at the thought.

He simply nods, then goes back to reading the entries before him. After some time, he closes the journal, having had enough of what was written inside.

"These were ramblings of a madman. One who should have never led this country." He pinches the bridge of his nose.

"Can't you bring this to your father? Make him see this

war was started out of pure pettiness and greed?" I ask, leaning forward in my seat.

Orion shakes his head. "You've met my father. He will destroy the evidence, destroy the both of us, and continue down this path."

Already knowing the answer to my question, I ask anyway. "And there is no way he would react agreeably if Sarana is willing to meet and discuss an amicable end?"

"You think the man who hates women with and in power will want to yield to Sarana?" He scoffs. "In his mind, the only way this war is going to end is when one side is defeated. It's why we are approaching the queen *without* him."

"It's not *yielding*. It's a... pause. To meet and discuss a *potential* end to the war," I say, hoping he will see what I see. The potential of peace. But I know my pleading is useless. It's not him I need to plead with.

"My father won't see it that way, no matter if it makes sense or would be good for our people. He will see it as a sign of weakness. He wants to crush Promithia, and at this point, he won't stop until he rules over it."

"Just like his father," I mutter, shaking my head. "That's not Sarana's thought process. Speaking of Sarana, have we heard from her yet?" I ask.

He shakes his head.

As I tap my finger across the leather-bound journal, another question comes to mind. "Why do you want to find these journals? This one doesn't seem to be of any use."

"My grandfather liked to ... *experiment*. He also liked to hunt for essence-powered oddities. I was hoping he had something we could use for when we eventually have to face my father."

"Why would you need that kind of power to face your father?" I ask, clearly not following.

He looks up at me from the journal, his eyes betraying a battle waging in his mind as he determines whether or not he should tell me. Eventually, he does. "Because when we sit down with Sarana, we will be drafting a treaty to present to my father in front of his people."

"You're joking, right?" I ask, half disbelieving and completely taken by surprise. "You just said he would never *yield* to Sarana, so why do you think this approach would be any different?"

"I have support from half of the military, and I plan to present the treaty not just to him but with his court in attendance…"

"By appealing to the people, you might just force his hand." I finish his thought for him, as a question bubbles up in my mind. "But what if it doesn't?"

As I ask the question, his words finally click. My eyes go wide in realization, and all he does is nod, leaning an elbow against the wooden table.

If this doesn't force his hand, it will mean war between the king and his heir.

TWENTY-TWO

The commotion outside my window wakes me before the sun can even do the job. Checking the time, I find it's well past noon.

I leap out of bed and peer out the windows to the grounds below, where members of the royal staff buzz around. In the distance, stable hands run from the storage house beyond, carrying additional equipment to handle the influx of carriages that will arrive later today. Tables are being carried to their places throughout the gardens, a makeshift stage is built in the middle of the open pasture, and tents are being set reminiscent of the red velvet canopies from Orion's birthday celebration.

What a great way to send off their youth to be slaughtered.

I know this feast is for the solstice, but with the soldiers leaving tomorrow, I can't stop my mind from the negative thoughts.

A knock sounds at the door, but when I go to welcome my visitor, no one is there. A box with a large satin bow rests on the floor.

I'm bubbling with excitement at this surprise as I bring the gift into my bedchambers. After pulling the ribbon loose, I find a beautiful crimson gown inside the box that perfectly matches the party's decor.

A note written in delicate script rests atop the fabric.

You may be known in these lands as the Wielder of Death, but the Duchess will still hearts tonight.

Despite my dislike of the nickname, my cheeks burn and heat. My stomach flutters as I smile and place the card on my end table.

The gown is beautiful, made of lace and jewels. Buttons bring the back together along the spine. While the sleeves are sheer, lace caps the shoulders, and more jewels wrap around the wrist.

When I lift the gown out of the box, I find a white fur shawl. I have half a mind to send a quick thank-you note to the prince, but before I have the chance to do so, a bickering group of people burst into my bedchambers.

The three maids quickly bow, saying "Your Grace" before the tallest one steps forward. Her red hair is vibrant against her olive complexion, with the strands pulled into a high bun on top of her head.

"Good afternoon, Your Grace. My name is Ayn. This is Brien"—she points to the short, stocky woman on her right—"and Frey." She points to the other woman on her left with piercing brown eyes and a healed scar that stretches from the corner of her left eye down to her neck.

I nod at all three of them.

"We do apologize for barging in, Your Grace, but the

guests will start arriving within the hour, and we must get you ready for the ball."

"It's lovely to make your acquaintance, ladies, but I have told the prince before that I have no need for maids. I can dress and get ready myself."

"With all due respect, the prince insisted and ordered us to not accept 'no' as an answer from you. Our orders exceed yours."

I let out a snarl in exasperation. "Surely it doesn't matter if I'm on time, does it?"

"Actually, it does," Ayn says, a tinge of annoyance in her tone.

"And why is that?"

"Because the prince wants you there at his side."

Ayn and I stare at each other in a standoff of wills.

"And I suppose what the prince says goes." I cave, fuming.

"Exactly, Your Grace." Ayn gives a curt smile.

"Please don't call me that. Raya will do."

With a fierce nod in understanding, the ladies get to work, and the hour passes in a blur.

I really did not miss this. All the fuss, the heavy jewels, and the corsets.

But as I take one last look at myself in front of the full-length mirror, the woman before me looks regal, especially with the diadem of gold and rubies atop my head.

No longer am I the starved, caged bird. Gaunt cheeks filled in, the circles under my eyes disappeared, curves almost restored to their former glory, and muscles taking their shape once more. Now I look more like the duchess I'm supposed to be. Caged, yes, but at least it's better than where I was before.

Despite the beauty of this gown, the deep garnet of the fabric only bolsters the truth of my nature. The crimson heir incarnate, wearing the color of the blood on her hands. The color of the blood that builds the foundation of both Promithia and Corath.

I shake the thought away and smooth out the front of the skirts.

A chorus of sounds sweep into the room on a wind through my open balcony door, the murmuring of a crowd, music playing from a band, and a butler announcing guests of prominence as they enter.

I peek outside one of the windows to find the gardens bustling with partygoers and waiters.

The cotton-candy sky is vibrant with the softest pinks, brushed blues, and intense corals as the sun makes its descent. Guards stand at every entrance and exit while others walk through the crowd, monitoring as people meander about. The young soldiers in their formal dress mingle with the attendees.

My maids hurry me along out of my apartment and toward the grand staircase. The railing is cool underneath my fingers, calming my nerves. But as I take sight of who is waiting to greet me at the bottom of the stairs, my breath hitches.

Orion's dark eyes gaze up at me. They're wide with pride as he scans me from hem to crown.

He stretches his hand, and I take it gladly, allowing his firm grip to steady me as I step onto the foyer's marble floor.

Orion's dressed in all gold, with ruby designs weaved into the fabric. He glows. Golden as the sun to brighten the longest night. He's dressed to match me, with accents of red.

Total opposites, yet perfectly in sync.

"You look absolutely breathtaking," he says in an astonished whisper.

"You do too." My cheeks warm as he folds my arm under his.

We walk in comfortable silence down the hall of mirrors toward the large doors that lead to the sprawling lawns and garden.

After a moment, the greeter bellows, slicing through the quiet between us. "Now presenting, Her Grace, High General of Promithia and Duchess of Senna, Raya Ontaria, and His Royal Highness, Prince Orion Elias Valor."

CONVERSATIONS still as guests peer around shoulders, hats, and bodies to get a better glimpse of the prince... and me. The General of Death. The enemy queen's lover. Prince Orion's Birthrite.

Bile rises in my stomach at the thought. That they see me as nothing more than property and possession. As someone who belongs to another rather than herself.

But isn't that what you are? You've made your name on the battlefield because of your father. You belong to the queen, to Promithia, and now to your enemy. You will never belong to yourself, a voice from deep within jeers.

I ignore the words and concentrate on my descent.

Everyone stares at me, some in awe that they get to see the prince's prize, others in disgust and fear. No doubt my army or I killed loved ones of those here. Their gazes send shivers up my spine. I do my best to control my breathing, my true emotions hidden behind a mask of strength.

As if sensing my discomfort, Orion gently squeezes my hand.

I'm here, I have you, that simple action conveys.

We finally make it to his table, at the head of all the others, as everyone else makes their way to their seats.

"You'll be sitting here with me," he says, ignoring the butler and pulling out the chair for me.

"Really?" I ask, confused.

"Of course. You belong at my side," he whispers in my ear, his lips slightly grazing over my skin.

A chill runs down my spine. But that chill quickly turns to something else. Something… *other*.

His lips are no longer soft and smooth. *They're rough.*

His voice is no longer enticing and warm. *It's cold.*

His whisper is no longer charming. *It bites.*

The man at my side is no longer Orion. *It's Mattias.*

I jump, ready to bolt, heart racing as I pull away from him.

When I turn to face the owner of the voice, I find Orion still there. His face is twisted into the same bit of pain I saw yesterday. Darkness hangs on the edge of his features as if he's fighting it off… trying to keep it at bay.

That darkness is swiftly overshadowed by concern once he sees my worried expression. He wraps his hand around mine and asks in a low voice, "Are you all right?"

Taking a deep breath, I smile through a grimace. "I'm fine, I didn't mean to alarm you."

He nods his head, brows still knit together. I will my hands to stop shaking as he turns to address his people, who all eagerly await his word.

The musicians stop playing their music as they wait for their cue to begin again.

"Please raise your glasses in a toast," he says, and they all obey, the sounds of clinking and clanking of glassware echoing throughout the gardens. "Tonight, we celebrate the winter solstice, the longest night, in hopes that the sun will grow stronger and shine brighter with the passing of the days to come. A night that marks the official start of winter, with the hope that the warmth of spring will be chipping at its frigid heels. Not only do we celebrate the solstice, but tomorrow, we send off our soldiers to take their place with the rest of the army. Tonight, we hope to show them our appreciation with a feast they can remember for years to come.

"Our men have been fighting, some would say, for too long. But I'm hopeful, as even on the longest of nights, I see the light at the end of the tunnel." He looks at me for only a brief second.

To others, it appears as though he's scanning the crowd, talking to every single person in his captivated audience. But the moment he locks eyes with mine, I see a gleam in his eyes I have seen before, but now that I know the truth, it all makes sense.

"To my soldiers, thank you for your service. I pray to the spirits for your safe return. To everyone here, I wish you all a joyous winter solstice. May you find the light in this dark night. Cheers."

"Hear! Hear!" echoes from the crowd, and the band strums up again.

Following the prince's lead, we all take our seats as the feast begins.

We eat together in silence, the music loud enough to drown out my thoughts.

After some time, guests rise from their seats to enjoy the spectacles around them. Some begin dancing on the raised stage ahead in the clearing, and other partygoers crowd around to watch the entertainers scattered around the gardens on platforms.

Eventually the prince is whisked away by some lords, their daughters in tow. Orion grimaces as they clearly attempt to offer up their daughters as potential wives… or mistresses.

Having had enough of watching the parading presentation for the prince, I rise from my seat. Samson shifts where he stands but surprisingly doesn't follow me as I walk away.

A butler passes with a tray of champagne flutes, and I stop him, taking a glass. The sweet nectar tingles as it makes its way down my throat. It's been a while since I've been to a celebration like this or had more than one glass of wine at meals. A bubbling sensation rushes to my head as I down the rest of the liquid then replace my empty flute with a new one.

That creeping sensation finds its way into the pit of my core again.

I turn to find the prince's gaze locked on me, clearly not interested in whatever the beautiful blonde in front of him is saying. She places her hand on his bicep, and a flare shoots through me. But certainly not from jealousy. I just find it sad that the girl can't sense when someone's not interested.

I raise an eyebrow and lift my glass toward him; amusement plays on his lips.

Continuing down the main path of the gardens, I walk past the makeshift stage in front of the band and toward the flame throwers.

I watch as the flames dance in the moonlight, mesmerized by the shimmering light of their craft. These are very skilled Elementals who hone their gifts into art.

Fire comes to life from their palms. Serpents made of flame slither through the crowd, which garner a few giddy squeals. Then each flame thrower creates their own fiery dragons. They fly just above the crowd, the heat blazing down around us, before soaring high into the sky and crashing into each other in an explosion of fireworks. Exclamations of delight from the crowd reverberate around me.

As my eyes wander around the party, I spy Mavre cautiously scanning his surroundings before making his way down one of the garden pathways.

Without a thought, I follow him, keeping enough distance between us.

In the silence, leaves rustle, but the sound doesn't come from this path. I move closer to the wall of brush and vines and peer through a small opening. In between the other row of bushes is Mavre, whispering urgently with a man I don't recognize.

They're speaking too low for me to hear, so I concentrate on the small flow of essence in my grasp and feel the tendrils of the air moving through the earth. I search until I find the space that surrounds Mavre and his companion, and the air sings to me as though I were standing right between them.

"What you're saying is preposterous," the other man says. His voice is deep yet calm, like a soothing wave.

"Is it? He will never win, not with this army. More like a band of misfits than anything else," Mavre retorts.

"You brought me on as your second, as a person you trust. Are you telling me now that I must abandon that goal?"

"You sacrificed a lot to join me, and I thank you for your belief in me, in this cause. But I have seen the reality of this situation, and I realize now those goals of his, those foolish and reckless dreams he clings to, will never come to fruition."

The other man hisses at Mavre's words, but just as he's

about to respond, I lose my balance, shifting my weight, and a twig snaps with a crack under my foot.

They immediately halt their discussion, but before they can find the snooping ears listening in on their conversation, I make a run for it and slip through the twisting pathways of the garden.

TWENTY-THREE

ould they be talking about the king? My mind tumbles through thought after thought as I race through the pathways. *So what Orion said is true, though I didn't have cause not to believe him, I suppose. The Corathian people are finally seeing how mad their ruler actually is.*

In my hurry, I nearly stumble into a wandering guest. "By the spirits, my apologies," I say, steadying myself.

I recognize this man as one of the lords who pulled Orion aside before. He's drunk. Very drunk, stumbling toward me.

"Well, well, well," he slurs. "What is the prince's prize doing out in these parts of the gardens alone?"

I look around. Spirits be damned… where is Samson when I need him?

"Please excuse me," I say, trying to step around him.

He blocks my path. "I support my prince, as I support the crown in all their endeavors, but surely you'd like to see what a real man can do."

His breath reeks of sparkling wine and dark liquor as he grips his half-hard arousal through the fabric of his trousers.

I hold back a gag while my feet take a cautious step back. "Sir, I suggest you continue walking."

"What are you going to do to me?" He takes another jagged step toward me and snakes his hand around my wrist, the diminishing bracelet digging into skin and bone with the force of his grip. "You are powerless against me."

"Funny you should say that." With my essence, I urge the brush around us to grow, and arms of vines reach out and slither around this arrogant ass's body. "You thought the prince would leave me without the ability to protect myself with the likes of you around? That this would be your chance to take advantage? *You* are the one who is powerless against *me*."

Surprise turns to fear as his eyes trail behind me. "Your Highness, thank goodness you're here," he cries. "I was just walking down the path when your pet unleashed her terror on me."

I don't turn to meet the prince's gaze. Instead, I hold this *lord* in his stance, tightening my grip before finally releasing him. My vines creep back into the shapes of the bushes they once were, but the lord stays locked in place, completely unmoving.

The prince steps forward next to me, eyes glaring as red as the rubies in my crown. Hidden runes along the inside of his coat light in activation, and I recognize the signs. They're associated with the Reader ability, allowing him to control the actions of others.

Anger and rage paint his face. The lord would cower in fear if he could, but the prince holds him in place with the power of his runes. All color leaches from the lord's face.

"Talet, you pompous ass," he starts. "I can smell the lies pouring out of you just as I smell the stench of alcohol on your breath. You are blinded by your privilege. If you so much as touch her or anyone else again against their wishes, I will take much more than your title. Do you understand?" Lord Talet stays still in the prince's grip. "I said, do you understand me?!" The prince's voice booms, shaking the ground beneath us.

"Yes, Your Highness," Talet says, voice strained under Orion's pressure.

The prince releases his grip, and Talet falls to the ground, gasping for air.

"Good. My guards will escort your wife and daughter off the premises immediately. But you..." Orion steps closer to Lord Talet, bending down so he's eye level with the trembling man. "We have a special place here at the palace for people like you."

"Where are you taking me, Your Highness?" Tears stream down his cheeks, and his eyes widen at Orion's words, but the prince ignores him, standing tall.

"Guards!" he shouts, and his trailing protectors step forward. "Please escort Lord Talet to a cell. Treat him like the vermin he has shown himself to be, and don't let him out until I say so. I want to make sure he learns his lesson."

A wicked smile lifts the corner of Orion's lips as he holds out his arm.

I gladly take it, and we step around the shaking lord. As we pass, I'm sure to give him a menacing look, and delight in seeing the little color that reappeared on his cheeks wash away once again.

When we're in a secluded area of the gardens, still protected by guards, he turns to me, worry washing over him. "Are you all right? I shouldn't have told Samson to leave you be tonight. I was foolish to believe no one would try anything."

"I'm fine. Essence or no essence, I would've been able to handle him."

"Believe me, I know, but that doesn't mean I shouldn't try to stop behavior like that when I can, especially in my own home," he says, cheeks flushing red with anger despite the sense of relief that seems to course through him. "How are you enjoying the festivities otherwise?"

"It's fun. A bit grand for my taste, but still very fun."

"Grand? How do you celebrate the winter solstice back in Promithia?"

"Every region in Promithia celebrates differently, but in Senna, we all take to the beach. Light bonfires, prepare feasts, tell stories, and perform sacred rituals," I say in a playfully ominous tone.

Despite my joking, my mind takes me back to the beaches of Senna and the last solstice celebrated with both of my parents. The bonfire raged in the pit on the sand, one of many. My father gathered all who cared to listen as he told one of the many stories of the re-creation of this earth.

How the spirits came to the planet just as it was on the brink of destruction from pollution and overpopulation. With their arrival and their abilities, they leveled Earth, destroying most of the world. The tectonic plates shifted, reforming the continents into the world we know today.

Orlo, my father's right hand and the man who helped train my sister and me, would beat the drum to the rhythm of his story.

"Sounds more or less the same to me," he says through a smile.

I can't help but chuckle at the gleam in his eyes. "Our festivities are far less glamorous. It's all very traditional and *family* oriented." I nod my head back in the direction of the red tents.

"Those red tents do not make an occurrence at every ball, I assure you."

I shrug. "Who am I to judge? People want to live a little. No harm in hosting a more *tantalizing* affair."

"Well, I do have a reputation to uphold. If only for my father's sake. Let him believe I'm nothing more than a scoundrel. When he does, he leaves me alone."

I want to question him about the relationship between him and his father. I wonder what he means by that last bit, but the look in his eyes indicates he wants to stay away from that topic.

So I continue, "Honestly, as morbid as it is, I understand. Many of these soldiers probably have never experienced something like this. So it's a chance for them to live and have fun before being marched off to their deaths."

"You must think we're monsters," he says, shame riding the edges of his words.

I sigh and reach for his hand, although I'm not entirely sure why. "War is difficult. I may disagree with a lot of your customs and traditions, but I don't see *you* as a monster. Your father, well, he's another story. But I have a feeling that when you become king, things will be different. Until then, your *father* will continue to do what he does."

We walk back through the maze and into the party, guards following a good distance behind. Guests nod and bow to him as we pass. One of the young girls who was swooning over him earlier now stares sadistically at me, eyeing my arm in his. I nestle a little closer to him and smirk to myself as the girl's sadistic stare turns murderous.

He checks his pocket watch, and I peer over to see the hands turn to midnight. *How has the time passed so quickly?*

"I think I'll watch the show from my balcony," I say. Then,

words I don't expect come tumbling from my mouth. "Care to join me?"

"I would love to." He smiles and leads me to my chambers, away from the crowded garden.

THE BOATS BEGIN to drift out into the lake beyond the gardens while the remaining guests move to claim their spots closer to the water's edge.

Without a moment's notice, sparks fly high into the sky, then burst into cascading ribbons of red and gold. This high up on my balcony, a chill fills the air, and I shiver as I watch the splendor in the distance.

"You didn't wear your shawl," he says, commenting on my shudder.

"I didn't need it for most of the night," I respond.

Instead of retrieving it like I expected, he places an arm around me, pulling me close to his chest. The heat radiating from him instantly warms my core. My body sinks into his, and I'm reminded of yesterday. His comforting embrace of support, the heated kiss in the library, and the way it almost feels natural to be in his arms. *Almost.*

"There's something I've been meaning to ask you about the Rite."

"Ask away, I have nothing to hide from you," he says.

"What does this *bond* created by the Birthrite do? Has this even been done before?"

He nods. "Yes, once before, a very long time ago, between my great-great-grandfather and his wife. Think of the bond like a rope that connects us together. This connection allows us to sense each other, for instance, our overactive emotions or if we're in danger. But if I tug on that rope, then that activates the bond and sends a command through the connection. It also allows us to tap into each other's powers."

Stepping away from him, I furrow my brows in contempt. "That is incredibly intrusive."

I knew the Birthrite is another claim of ownership, but hearing the confirmation doesn't put my mind at ease.

"I swear to you, that's not how I will use this bond," he says, shaking his head, sincerity lacing his words.

But I know how easily sincerity can be faked. A person can sincerely want to mean their words, but that's not the same as being honest and truthful.

"When your cuff is fully deactivated, you will be able to tap into that connection as well."

"So I can have the power to control you and take your powers if needed?" I ask before quickly adding, "I wouldn't do that either, but it just seems like a risky thing to put in place."

No wonder why his father was furious.

"It's risky, but I knew it was the only way to get you away from *him*." With the amount of vitriol that laces his words, I know he's talking about his father.

"So when *will* my diminishing cuff be deactivated?" I ask, but the pained look on his face tells me all I need to know. "Figures."

"I want to give you all your power back, I do. But I need to know that I can trust you first."

"Have I not proven my trust? Protect you from unidentified monsters? Check. Train your young soldiers before they enter the killing fields? Check. Help you find your grandfather's long-lost journals? Check. Allow myself to be dressed up and paraded around in front of your people? Check." Frustration bubbles over with every word I speak. "I have no choice but to trust your word that you will never use the bond on me. What's to stop you from unleashing my abilities on my own people? From using me to end this war in even more vile and despicable ways?"

He flinches at my words. But he doesn't push. Doesn't press. He only nods in understanding, taking my hands in his.

"I would never violate your trust that way or misuse this bond."

Heat flares at my wrist, and I look down at my rune cuff to find it glowing. A few more of the runes are erased as the glowing fades and dims. He's allowing me to feel the connection, the path between us. The comforting warmth of honesty flows through. Along that path, the pulse of his Stormning abilities is just beyond reach. It would take one thought for me to grab hold of the current and unleash it on the people below. But I don't.

"Your customs make no sense to me," I say, resigned.

He simply laughs, and I may break in two at the sound of delight that escapes his lips. It's the first time I've heard him laugh, really laugh, since I met him. The wrinkles around his eyes barely move, not used to the action.

He wraps his arms back around me, pulling me against his rigid form, and we settle back into our embrace.

His lips press against my forehead in a featherlight kiss, so quickly I almost believe I imagined the simple action. But once again, just as they did before, his soft lips turn rough.

I jerk my head away, forcing Orion to step back, face twisted in pain from the blatant rejection.

He looks as if he might step toward me, palms reaching and mouth ready to ask me what's wrong.

Before he has a chance to utter one word, I retreat to my

living area, heart whirring uncontrollably in my chest. Gripping the back of the upholstered armchair, I squeeze my eyes closed. With every second that passes, my racing breath calms, and my galloping heart slows.

Behind me, Orion steps closer and closer until he stands a perfectly respectable distance away. From the air between us, I can sense his hesitation. His confusion.

"Sometimes I get the sense that you're comfortable around me. But then you pull away," he says, words delicate and soft as if his voice is enough to scare me away. "Have I done something to upset you?"

"I don't mean to, truly, I don't. In fact, I wish I didn't," I start, mustering up all the courage I can manage. I take a deep breath, turning to face him. A stray curl finds its way out of the perfectly placed pin in my updo. "But there are times when my mind can't separate the reality of you from the torturous memories of your father."

I expect his expression to contort into something akin to pain from insult, but instead, he remains stoic. The only indication of his true feelings is left in the unsteady shifting of the air around him. The way the shadows of his face grow darker, and he seems to retreat within himself. He clenches his jaw and balls his hands into fists at his side.

"I'm sorry," he says, voice etched in pain despite the control over his emotions he so desperately tries to hold on to.

"It's not your place to apologize for him," I snap. "You did nothing wrong."

He moves his hand as if he's about to push the stray lock away from my face, then sharply pulls away.

"I might not have, but he's still my father," he says. "What can I do to help you?"

"There's nothing you can do." I take a step closer to him,

and his eyes lock on to mine. "When it happens, I just need to remind myself that you are not your father."

Slowly, I lift my hand and press my palm to his cheek. He leans into my touch until his lips are close enough for his breath to graze over my own.

He pulls my hand from his cheek and lifts it up to his lips. But with the fabric of my dress covering most of my hand, he kisses my palm.

This time, his lips don't turn rough. They are soft and lush and warm against my skin, sending a wave of yearning through me, surprising me. A yearning to discover what those lips may feel like elsewhere. On my neck. Trailing down my torso, my thighs, in between my legs.

Before I can pull away, he pulls me to him, slowly, carefully, as if the moment could shatter us like glass. He releases my hand and brings his up to my cheek while the other finds its place at my hip.

In one breath, he closes the distance between us. In another, he trails the tip of his nose along my jawline, tipping my head back. He grazes his lips over the skin of my exposed neck, sending tickling waves through me. My body is clearly ready for a repeat of our interaction in the library, but my mind isn't. We can't cross that line again… Can we?

"Ori," I whisper, and he all but melts into me at the sound. "This can't happen," I say, lacking the strength I hoped to convey. The words sound weak as they escape my lips.

I look up through my lashes into his eyes and see my own reflection. It's clear my words don't match my desire, as my eyes echo the longing in his.

Without thinking, I step forward, pressing my body into him, and he hardens against me. A soft moan escapes his lips, and the sound courses through me like a tidal wave as he walks me back against the wall.

I feel it all.

His desire, want, need. And a hint of something else. Caring? Admiration? Love? *Impossible.*

I close my eyes, listening to his heartbeat in the silence of the room—my own matching his rhythm.

I want nothing more than to reclaim my body's reaction. But the questions remain: *How do I know this is what I truly want? That this isn't him using the bond to get what he wants?*

"Will you let me?" he asks.

My eyes flutter open. "Let you what?"

"Will you let me erase your haunted memories and doubts?" Not once does he let go of my gaze. "When you hear my voice, I want you to only hear the echoes of my yearning for you. When you feel my breath on your skin, I want you to remember how it left the sensation of desire in its wake."

My body shivers at his words, and something flips deep within me.

"Do you feel that fluttering in the pit of your stomach? The racing of your heart? That desire that's pooled low and deep in your core. Desire can *not* be faked by the bond."

His words answer the questions floating in my mind. His lips graze the edge of my ear, before sliding across my skin as he positions his mouth a hair's breadth away from mine.

"So," he says in a low rumble. "Will you let me?"

A part of me wants to push him away, to stay strong in the face of his growing desire, and my own for that matter. But another piece of me is ready to give in, to cave under the weight of his affection.

I lace my arms around his shoulders and trail my fingers through his raven waves.

Locking my gaze onto his, I hand myself over to the latter. "Yes."

All restraint gone and inhibition released, our lips meet in a crashing force. Our bodies melt into the kiss, and he glides his tongue across the seam of my lips, begging for me to let him in, and I grant his wish. With each stroke of his tongue against mine and each swipe of his wandering hands as they trail along my hips, over the curve of my breasts, I find myself coming a bit more undone. My fingers explore his chest, up to the nape of his neck, and dive into the silky strands of waves and curls atop his head.

I tug slightly, exploring what he likes, what he doesn't. The press of his body harder against mine tells me he likes that, so I do it again, and he releases a low growl, his hips bucking, grinding his arousal against me.

I can't help but smile against his lips.

Our moment in the library was pure whim and exploration. But this? This is all need. His need to finally give in to desire. My need to ground myself in the feeling of him and to realize that he is not the cause of my dark memories. That in his arms, I can be safe.

He nips my chin, then trails his lips down my jaw, toward the nape of my neck, then over the swell of my breast. He peels back the top layer of my dress with his teeth, never once tearing his gaze from mine. A hiss escapes me as cool air kisses my freshly exposed skin. His hand fumbles over the skirt of my dress, making its way under the hem. The tips of his fingers travel up, up, up in between my legs until they finally stop at my hips, just at the surface of my apex.

I arch my back, my chest lifting toward his face, and that smug smirk plasters on his lips. I practically whimper, begging for him to do as I wish without speaking a word.

Sparks blaze in his eyes as he takes in my frenzied state.

"Now, Raya," he purrs, his lips grazing feather-soft kisses against my nipple, and another ripple of desire courses through me. "If you want something, you're going to have to use your words."

He trails the tips of his fingers closer to my apex.

He's so close to where I need him, want him, the most. And all I need to do is ask?

I give another tug at the roots of his soft strands, forcing his eyes to look into mine once more.

"Touch me," I command.

But his smile turns teasing.

"Where?" he asks innocently. "Here?" He flicks his tongue against the pebbled peak of my breast, sending a chill over me. "Or here?" He glides his thumb across my lacy underwear and down my slick center, drawing a gasping moan from my lips.

"Both," I whimper.

His lips curve up into a seductive smile. "Your wish is my command."

He closes his mouth around my nipple, alternating between sucking and swiping his tongue across the peak as he swiftly pushes aside the lace fabric.

Another sigh of pleasure escapes me as he gently rubs my clit. My hips chase the sensation of his fingertips, shifting to align him perfectly with my aching bud.

With his other hand, he lifts my leg and skirt, holding me steady against him as his fingers work their magic. He slips one finger inside me, but it's not nearly enough.

"More." My voice is nothing more than a breathy moan, but with a heady groan, he complies.

His one finger is accompanied by two more. He fills me, the sensation more than I could imagine, as they slide in and out. His fingers move with ease as he coaxes pleasure from my very core, massaging my swollen bundle of nerves with his thumb. Each thrust of his hand is met with an ever-intensifying moan.

He pulls back to see the pleasure on my face and smiles, dimples and all. Our lips crash together again, following the rhythm of the beating strikes of fireworks beyond the lake.

"Raya," he moans into my mouth, and the world melts away.

I crumble into him as he muffles my cries of pleasure with his lips, tasting each moan until he's had his fill.

I want to lose myself in the warmth of his embrace, in *him*. To see what his hands, his lips, his body can really do.

Tearing away from the kiss, I look into his eyes. I can feel the fire burning in mine, but for some reason, it's not burning in his.

But then I realize it's not his eyes staring back at me. Instead of his bluish-green orbs, I find Sarana's brown gaze.

Sarana and I had agreed from the start that our relationship would be open. We always knew there would be others. Lovers, partners, and a future spouse for me—one that I intend to marry for more than just political gains. We knew there was a stamped time that marked our end. So why does giving into this—giving myself a taste of pleasure and happiness in this sea of darkness—feel so much like betrayal?

What am I doing?

This isn't right. He isn't *home*.

But he can be, my mind seems to purr.

Reluctantly—with a mental kicking of my own ass—I slide my hand out from the depths of his soft strands and press my palm against his chest, fingers splayed.

We stand there for a few more silent moments, foreheads resting against each other.

I have no clue what is running through my mind, my

thoughts a frenzied mess, but I force myself to stand straight nonetheless, gazing at him with what I only hope is a determined and stern expression. He takes a reluctant step back.

"This, whatever *this* is, can't happen again, Your Highness." I return to an air of formality that seems to have never been present between us in the first place.

Shadows flash across his face once more. They stretch, his features turning dark and gaunt. He seems to cave inward, an internal fight between what he desires and his restraint.

Fear pulses through me, unease settling at the sight of the darkness that has quickly taken root, just as it did in the library.

But as quickly as the shadows grow, they disappear. Life brightens his face, melting his features into a replica of my own expression, and in that moment, I fear we may both give in. But our resilience wins over as he loosens his breath and disappears into the hall.

TWENTY-FOUR

I barely slept last night. Guilt and shame continue to creep into my soul as my mind replays my... *interaction*...with Orion.

I keep trying to tell myself there is nothing I am guilty of. I am a person with needs and whims. I can do what I please. I can seek pleasure with whomever I please. My only commitment to Sarana is one of duty. An oath of a soldier, not the vow of a betrothed. Yes, we love each other. That love and our stolen moments are all we can give each other, nothing more.

But it's no use. The guilt is still there, lurking in the background, and something else entirely has also taken center stage. Something I don't quite understand. Something I don't think I'm completely in control of.

Whatever happened last night will likely happen again. I *want* it to happen again. And next time, I fear I won't have the strength to stop it. Neither will Orion. It feels like something greater than any being on this earth is pulling, no, *forcing* us together.

With the last curl pinned into place, my hands grow clammy with the realization that I can't escape the prince's presence. Not when we're expected to send off the visiting soldiers to war.

Samson greets me at the door, then escorts me to take my place next to the prince. Orion nods my way as I fall into a curtsy, refusing to meet his gaze.

We stand there in silence, where the cobblestone meets the marble steps of the front drive.

"How did you sleep last night?" he asks, still facing forward.

"I didn't," I say plainly.

Stomping boots against cobblestone echo down the drive as the group of young soldiers begin to make their way from the barracks to the main entrance.

"And why not?"

I turn to look at him—because that's what it seems I do around him, I give in—but he keeps his gaze forward.

"Guilt," I say, matter of fact. His desire-tinged remorse surges in the air between us. "And how did you sleep?"

"I didn't," he says, still refusing to look at me.

Unsure of what else to say, I turn and make my way toward the soldiers. I go down the line, shaking their hands, finding the ones I trained with, and sharing some parting wisdom to each of them. I know the armies they're fighting, and they don't stand a chance. I share whatever I can to bolster their confidence, doing my best to share my well-wishes with each and every one of them until there is no one left.

Horses' hooves on cobblestone slowly turn to hooves on gravel, then quiet, moving farther and farther away.

These soldiers are so young. They should have their whole lives ahead of them, but instead, they were ripped from their families, from their homes, to fight in this war because their king is so set in his ways. Because he can't see past his own desires. Won't listen to reason to try to end this war with peace.

I clench my fists, my whole being shifting with anger. The ground around me starts to tremble at the thought of these young lives meeting death too soon.

The prince stands by my side as the last of the visiting soldiers crosses the palace gates. Without saying a word or so much as glancing my way, he takes my hand in his and squeezes in agreement. In agreement of my anger, my fury, and my hatred for his father and this war.

THE LIGHT of the setting sun shines through the large bay windows of the study, illuminating the once dust-covered shelves.

For the past few weeks, Orion and I have been scouring the books in all the personal studies throughout the palace, to no avail. Separately, thank the spirits. I don't have the capacity to deal with his mood, not when our heightened tensions could so easily turn into something... *more*. That's the last thing either of us needs. To continue to muddy the waters any more than they already are.

Now, I'm in my own study, pulling every leather-bound book off the dusted shelves, hoping to find something even remotely close to the late ruler's second journal. The only break I took today was when Orion came to inform me that half of the boys I helped train had already perished on the battlefield.

If half of them have met their end in a matter of weeks, how much longer will the rest last?

I push away the treacherous thought and focus on the task at hand: find the last journal. If this one is our key to ending the war, I have to find it.

Piles of books surround me on the floor as I rest my head against the soft couch behind me. I've searched this room a hundred times, on top of scouring the other studies, and the second damn journal is nowhere to be found. I fear it may be lost forever.

With a huff of breath, I look over the books in front of me and one of the titles snags my attention. *Corathian Rulers: Traditions Through the Ages.*

I flip through the pages, hoping this book can enlighten me on their strange customs. Namely, how to reverse bonds made by the Birthrite. Looking down at the page, I trace the swirling lines of the runes inscribed on the borders. I'm about to start reading the text when two knocks sound at the door.

Ayn enters with a tray of food, her red hair tied at the nape of her neck.

"Raya, you should really get out, enjoy the day. Some fresh air would do you good." She places the tray on the coffee table, pushing aside the stack of books, and takes a seat in the armchair. "What are you looking for anyway?"

"I'm trying to find a way to break this bloody curse." Taking a piece of bread off my plate while she digs into hers, I plop the warm, fluffy dough into my mouth.

Our daily lunches have become our little ritual, something I can look forward to in between the solitude among the stacks of books.

"Unfortunately, Raya, those answers won't be found in a book. Only on your journey to meet the spirits."

I stop chewing. "So if either of us dies, then the bond of Rite is broken? What a load of shit." She eyes me cautiously. "Don't worry, Ayn, I'm not going to do anything foolish." *I couldn't even if I wanted to.*

She smirks, partly satisfied, and looks to see what page I'm on. "The Stalemate? Why are you reading about that?"

"I randomly flipped to this page when you walked in," I say, shrugging. "Why, what is it?"

"That book can give you more information on the subject than I ever could." She shifts in her chair.

"Try explaining anyway, I can always read about it later." I scoot a bit closer to the small table and start digging into the meal.

"Very well," she says with a sigh. "The Stalemate is what kings and their heirs enter when the heir makes a challenge to claim the throne. This can be for a number of reasons, like the heir finds the king unfit to lead or simply because they want to rule. But there are two paths that can be taken once the heir claims the throne, and they can only be declared by the current king.

"The king can either choose to fight to the death—neither party can demand a champion—or enter the Stalemate. When the Stalemate has been declared, the king and the heir enter a battle of the minds in a place that I can only describe as the abyss."

I look up at her at that last word and swallow down a nervous lump as the memories of my own darkness lurk to consume me.

"What's the abyss?" I ask.

"It's a place that can only be inhabited by the king and his heir for this reason. They enter each other's minds and alter the other's realities. Whoever defeats the other is named the victor and declared king. The other is trapped in the abyss for all time."

"This sounds like a practice of our own called *Ashreda*. The Promithian heir can declare the current ruler to be deposed, but only with proper justification. There are checks and balances in place, although I don't remember the specifics. How many times has this happened in Corath?"

"The last Stalemate happened a little over three centuries ago. Orion's grandfather, King Hesten, claimed the throne from his father prematurely. He was always an ambitious man. Believed the spirits chose him to be the next savior. And here we are."

Ah, so that's what he meant, I think to myself, remembering the words I read in the late king's journal: *I crossed my current title out at the beginning of this journal and wrote my true title in... An affirmation set that I will one day fulfill.* Although he never meant to fulfill it through the natural progression of life, but by his own will.

Does Orion intend to do the same if his father doesn't agree with the treaty? I assumed he just meant to stage a good old-fashioned coup... but this? It's a huge risk.

"Well, I must be off. Good luck with your studies, Raya." She smooths out her skirts before heading toward the door. "Just keep looking. I'm sure you'll find what you're searching for."

"Thank you for the food, Ayn, and for the company."

She smiles before sauntering out of the room.

Rising from my spot on the floor, I take the text on Corathian traditions and make my way to the desk. I have every intention of reading through and learning all I can about this *Stalemate*, but when I plop down onto the leather chair, my knee hits the underside of the desk, and a rattling sounds from beneath.

"Shit!" I hiss, rubbing my stinging knee. There will definitely be a bruise there later. I swipe my hand on the underbelly of the desk and notice there's something there. "What the hell?"

Slipping down to the floor, I inspect the desk, and sure enough, attached to the bottom is a hidden box. At first glance, it looks like it could be a drawer. Sliding my finger across the side, I find a latch and gently pull, afraid I might break it. The box swings down, still attached to the desk, and out slides a black leather-bound book, identical to the journal I found just a few days before.

"What the hell?" I say again, officially incapable of forming any other words.

My suspicions are confirmed once I open the strap and stare at King Hesten's swirling handwriting on the first page. Although I want nothing to do with this man and his delusions, I still find myself flipping through the pages, wondering if I can even believe the outlandish words written.

Thestras is complete, and she is absolutely breathtaking. The entire structure is an homage to the nature that surrounds it, and I look forward to spending my time exploring the world outside its doors. But there's a reason I chose this place to build the palace. Many moons ago, the voice shared his secrets from a time that has long since passed. An object of great power has been lost to the Shifting Wood for millennia, and he believes I am the one who can find it. The object is said to give any who possesses it the power of the Celestials. One that can help change the hands of destiny.

Well, it has been months, and I still can't find the bloody source. Those damn Shifting Woods always rearranging themselves makes it difficult to find my way in the forest. The more time I spend in there, the more I fear that one day I may never return. But one day, I will find the symbol I'm looking for, the one that marks the object's resting place. The power that will lead me to true greatness.

Underneath the entry, Hesten drew the symbol he mentioned. It looks like two sideways *V*s overlapping with a line down the center. Below the symbol, a hand-drawn map is sketched, detailing the path and the general area where he believed the treasured item is buried.

Are these the ramblings of a madman? Most likely.

But...

For some strange reason, I can't help but wonder... What if this is real? I mean, he did build a whole palace near the forest where the mysterious power source supposedly resides, so he must have believed the legend.

Could this be the item Orion is looking for?

Before I have a chance to dissuade my resolve, I quickly trace the map and symbol he drew, find the warmest clothes I can, and leave behind the comfort of my chamber to embark on this wild treasure hunt.

TWENTY-FIVE

After the solstice, Orion relinquished my guard detail, which works pleasantly in my favor. At least, that's what I thought when I started this journey hours ago.

I left the palace soon after I read the entry with a bundle of croissants tied to my belt, a flask of water in my coat pocket, an old compass from my fireplace mantel, and a short dagger I stole that was on display in the hall. Not my weapon of choice, but better than nothing.

At least if I still had a guard detail, someone would know where I was. The note I left behind only shared "Went out for a walk." This is clearly the last place anyone would expect me to be, so the chances of me being found are slim to none.

With every hour that passes, the path ahead changes ever so slightly. A fork in the trail appears where one had not been before. The sprouting of dense trees where a clearing once peeked through bushes. Even the sun seems to be creeping across the sky at a faster rate.

Only three hours have passed, but the position of the sun

and the velvety pink hue of the sky signals we're getting closer to sundown rather than afternoon. So either I've been here for much longer than I thought, or time is faster in these woods.

The frigid air turns biting cold as I continue my walk through the forest, my map a useless scrap of paper, teeth clattering from the plunging temperature. I'm tempted to abandon all hope and turn back around when an opening of trees clears ahead.

The small clearing is silent save for the rustling of leaves and branches from the blowing wind. A sea of starblooms dance in the bitter breeze. I imagine this space is filled with buzzing bees in the spring and summertime. A beautiful meadow made from dreams.

But not just any dreams… my fever dreams. The place my mind traveled to while I was still a prisoner in Mattias's cell.

A warmth pulls in my chest, urging me to enter the meadow.

This can't be possible.

I have never stepped foot into this place before now, yet my dream was exactly the same. More a memory than a dream.

In the center, a formation of moss-covered rocks juts from the ground in a perfect ring. Too perfect. Resting in the center of the formation is a short stump of stone.

On the whisper of the wind, a lulling hum calls to me. It awakens something sleeping deep within my core. In recognition and welcome.

With a mind not all my own, I step a little closer to the formation, inspecting the stones. From far away, the surfaces seemed to be weathered by time, but at a closer look, I realize the notches are perfectly crafted swirls and symbols of runes I don't recognize.

"This must be it," I whisper through my chattering teeth.

In the center of the boulder is the symbol from the journal. The two overlapping arrowheads, a line cutting through its middle, the image stamped into the rock's face. An insatiable urge to place my hands upon the structures overcomes me until it's all I can think of.

Reaching closer and closer, my hand is a breath away from the surface of the rocks when a shrieking cry sounds in the distance, pulling me out of the trance.

Around me, the starblooms come alive, glittering like fallen constellations. The silver moon hangs high in the sky, shining a light on the snowflakes dusting the ground as they tumble down from the heavens in troves.

The shrieking cry comes again, much, much closer. Through the circlet of stones, a pair of golden eyes peek into my soul.

Woodhounds. This escapade has certainly taken a turn for the worse.

Out of the corners of my eyes, more golden and silver pairs blink to life around me. Without breaking eye contact with the creature in front of me, I carefully take a few steps back, slowly reaching for the dagger at my belt.

Another blood-curdling howl sounds from behind, directly at my ear. Hot breath grazes the side of my face as I whip around to face the giant hound that greets me.

Shit.

The pack begins to close its ranks. About a dozen surround me, but woodhounds are known to settle in droves. If I don't run now, I will surely be their next meal.

So that's exactly what I do.

As quickly as I can, I make a run for it. A rippling of howls sound throughout the forest, followed by the pounding of enormous paws against snow-covered ground.

Orion may have alleviated some of the runes on my diminishing cuff, but it's not enough to transport back to the safety of the palace. Even using the veil would drain too much of my energy.

In other words, I'm royally fucked.

Every few steps, I send a blast of fire behind me. A few shrieks from the beasts are the only confirmation I have that my aim struck true.

The brush along the path rustles, and before I can change course, a hound comes crashing into my side, sending us tumbling.

Long, sharp teeth tear into my forearm, and a cry of pain rumbles from my belly. I sink my dagger into its thick neck, and with a gurgled yelp, the hound goes still. I toss the body to the side and immediately jump back to my feet. Ignoring the excruciating pain in my arm, I continue running east.

At least, I think it's east.

With every racing step forward, I feel the hounds closing in. But where there was darkness, the wood shifts again to reveal light from the palace shining in through the trees.

Just a bit faster, Raya, I think to myself and silently thank the wood for working in my favor, willing my legs to carry me swiftly.

As I'm about to reach the forest's edge, another hound pounces. Its claws slice from my shoulder down my back, eliciting another guttural cry from me. The pain is blinding as I slam into the ground, my head hitting the dirt with a disconcerting *crack*. The hound attempts to pounce again, but I less than gracefully roll out of the way.

Too disoriented to stand, my mind spinning from the impact, I drag my hands across the forest floor, feeling for the roots nestled deep within the ground. I urge them to grow and soar until they spear the wolf nipping at my heels.

One after one, the hounds come. When one falls by my piercing vines, another swiftly takes its place.

There are too many.

Blood drips down my arm and back, soaking through my clothes. I need to do something before they finish me off.

Taking a deep breath, I rise onto unsteady feet and gather the air around me, funneling the winds until they're whipping. Snow is sucked into the cyclone, the freezing winds turning them from harmless flakes to pelts of ice. Around us, the branches whip in the air and leaves get trapped in the force.

I tunnel down into the little bit of power I have access to until I reach the surface that blocks me from the rest. I blast the funnel forward with a battle cry toward the remainder of the pack. Shrieking and yelping and crying, they fall to the ground with earth-stilling thuds as pellets of ice pierce through their bodies. The rest, finally frightened by their foe, run off with whimpering cries.

My body wants to crash along with the fallen hounds. Shaking, I will myself not to give in to the pain, the poison from the hounds' fangs, and blood loss. I need to make it back to the palace.

Rising onto my trembling legs, I step out of the line of trees and onto the path. The gravel shifts ahead. In the darkness, two figures appear. As they walk closer, I can just make out Samson's brooding frame and Orion's glower. Both are furious.

"About time you two showed up," I say as I reach them, my voice sounding more pained than sarcastic.

"What the hell were you thinking?" Orion panics in fury, looking between me and the Shifting Wood that towers at my back.

"I was thinking I needed some fresh air and a walk," I say

nonchalantly, swaying in the breeze. *Is it just me or did the wind pick up?*

He instinctively reaches out to steady me but is met with my cries of pain as his fingers dig into the open slices on my shoulders. I fall to my knees, then face-first into the thin layer of snow.

Orion and his four legs dip low to the ground…

Wait, that isn't right. He should only have two.

As carefully as he can, he picks me up into his arms, but it doesn't stop my wailing cries from the pain.

One moment, we're standing on the snow-dusted path, tinged crimson red where I fell. In the next, the world is fading away as Orion transports us. His arms wrap tightly around my body, and I fight to keep control as my mind begins to slip into darkness.

When we emerge, we're back in the palace. Orion gently lays me down on a plush, velvet-covered surface. Whispers sound from somewhere deep within the space, and I attempt to rise, if only to go back to the comfort of my own chambers. Just the simple act sends the room spinning again, and a blood-curdling shriek erupts from my throat. Moving on my own is out of the question.

Orion comes rushing back to my side, urging me to lie down on my belly once more, and I don't protest. As soon as he's sure I won't attempt to walk out of here again—wherever here is—he turns away, speaking to who I assume is Samson.

"Go alert Ayn, let her know we'll need a change of clothes from her chambers," he says, worry coating his tone. "And grab Heren as well. We'll need their expertise with expelling poison."

He quickly returns to my side and attempts to remove my clothing.

I swipe his hands away. "Mm—what're yadooing?" I ask… although I'm not sure how clear my voice is.

"My dear Raya." I can hear the smile in his voice, trying to sound more positive despite the shaky undertone. "It's nothing I haven't seen before."

I'm not sure if I should be grateful for his nonchalance at seeing my naked body or offended at the implication that *I* am nothing special.

Too weak to argue over his choice of words, I concede, letting him undress me so he can better tend to my wounds. I have no energy to form a crafty comeback as unconsciousness threatens once more.

He swears under his breath. "Come on, Raya, you need to stay with me," he says.

My cries drown out the whispering of unfamiliar voices as healing hands work on my wounds. The slices of pain quickly recede to a tingly warmth as my skin knits back together. Carefully, I'm rolled over, allowing them to heal the wounds on the front of my body.

When they're finished, covers wrap around me, though I'm not sure by whom. The pain from teeth and claws vanishes, only to be replaced by an intense shivering that nestles deep into my bones.

"Oh dear," another voice says with grave concern.

That voice… can it be?

"Dessy?" I ask, eyes fluttering open to see who arrived but to no avail. My vision is little more than a blurred mess.

"Thank you for bringing this," Orion says, voice just as much a dismissal as it is a tone of sincere gratitude.

"Do you need help?"

Must be Ayn, Dessy would have rushed to my side if it were her.

A chuckle sounds in response to my not-so-silent thought.

"No, thank you. I can take it from here." Orion turns back to me, helping me into whatever clothes Ayn brought. "Come on, Raya, we need to warm you up," he says, guiding me under the covers.

Then he does something I never expected. He joins me underneath the layers.

Under thick blankets and velvet, the heat is stifling, too much. I try to protest, but he wraps his arms around my waist, holding me in place.

"Where's Dessy?" I ask, so low it's almost a whisper.

"She's home, Raya. In Senna." He says it as if he's sure. As if he knows.

I miss home, I say or whisper or think. I'm not sure.

"I know you do," he says in response. "I know you do."

My eyelids grow heavy until not even my own will or Orion's begging can keep them from claiming the peace they desire.

TWENTY-SIX

Warmth cascades around me, and I can't help but lean into its embrace. All too suddenly, the invisible warmth becomes tangible as hard peaks and valleys press against my back.

I instinctively grind against the sure and stable figure and am met with an all too audible, and not at all imaginary, groan that vibrates in the crook of my neck. The sensation skitters down my body, setting a new heat ablaze deep within my core. Strong hands grip my hip.

I shoot from the bed in a panic. Or at least I try to.

I'm trapped in the sea of a too-large mattress, dark sheets tangled around my legs… and that's when I realize this bed isn't mine and a very bare-chested Orion is lying there with an arrogant smile plastered on his face.

"What the hell are you doing in bed with me?!" I ask, throwing a pillow toward his head.

"No 'thank you for saving my life, Orion'?" he asks, catching the pillow midthrow. "Also, I should point out that *you* were the one grinding against *me*."

"That's not the point, and no, you do not get a thank-you, not when you are naked in bed with me."

"Raya, I'm hardly naked, just lacking a shirt," he says, as if I'm overreacting. "And you had a fever, almost died from poison and hypothermia. I needed to keep you warm."

"You kept me warm, now you may leave."

"Oh no, Raya," he says admonishingly.

He sits up, the covers falling off his body, uncovering his perfectly chiseled abs. I have to actively work not to ogle over him like a starved, lovesick puppy. Scars litter his body, and it takes all the energy I have not to strum my finger over each one, asking him to recount the stories they tell.

"Why the hell were you in the Shifting Wood?"

Yesterday's events come crashing down on me. While most of my memory is a blur, I remember enough. My shoulders sag in realization and embarrassment. Quickly regaining my composure, I cross my arms against my chest.

"I just wanted to go for a walk." I shrug. The lie easily rolls off my tongue. "I didn't realize I ventured that far or what the forest even was. This place doesn't come with a welcome pamphlet."

He chuckles at that, but his eyes are still filled with dread and worry when he responds. "Raya," he says my name like a warning. "I saw the other journal in your room. The next time you go gallivanting on your own, can you please tell someone instead of leaving a cryptic note? Had I arrived a few minutes later, you would've been past the point of healing."

"And if I had my essence, then I wouldn't have been in that position in the first place," I challenge. He only gives me a look that says *in time, Raya*. I roll my eyes at the sentiment. "Well, I guess I'm glad to see that bond of ours definitely works."

"While that may be true, because you were in the Shifting Wood, I couldn't pinpoint your exact location, so transporting to you was impossible. I had to follow the thread between us until it led me to you."

"Well… thank you for healing me," I say.

"You're welcome," he replies, reaching and taking my hand, squeezing once, then dropping his back to the mattress.

Shifting awkwardly on my feet, I ask, "So, is whatever's hiding in the middle of the woods the essence-powered item you're looking for?"

"Possibly," he says slowly, eyes lighting up as if he's just found the treasure of a lifetime. "Why?"

"Because I think I found it."

Orion's eyes grow dark and distant, his voice is cold when he speaks, and I flinch at the sudden change. He doesn't seem to notice my reaction as he asks, "You did?"

"Yeah. It drew me in so easily, I was mesmerized by its essence."

"It must have been a wonder." His voice is softer than before, but his eyes are filled with promise.

I lean in close. "If this is something we need, then what are we waiting for?"

"We'll search again when I'm sure you're fully healed from your last adventure," he says, leaning in just as I did and gently tapping my nose with the tip of his finger.

Such a small, familiar gesture. It almost makes me forget that we're supposed to be keeping our distance, to not give whatever this *thing* is between us anymore power. Which I guess last night's little escapade didn't really help in that regard.

"Fine," I say as I look around the room. My eyes land on a small woven basket resting atop the side table. "What's this?"

"Queen Sarana responded to my letter." Although this is something we should be excited about, his voice has a tinge of curiousness I wasn't expecting.

"Did it come with a note?" I ask, sitting cross-legged on the mattress and pulling the basket into my lap.

"Not exactly." He lifts one of the flat round objects out of the basket. "Just these shells." He knits his brows together in confusion.

I peer inside the shallow ring of the basket. Resting inside are not shells but sand dollars. All of them in different pastel shades.

Reaching in, I pick up a pastel purple one with a full moon painted on the front. There's only one island on this Earth that produces these rare pastel sand dollars.

Memories of Sarana and I flood my mind. Her and I lying in the sun on the feather-soft sand of the beaches. Her hands roaming my body as our tongues danced to the rhythm of the rolling waves, a shimmering rainbow our backdrop.

"She wants to meet at the island of Demiitsch on the night of the full moon," I say, shoving away the memories and placing the sand dollar back in the basket.

"Which is in two days," Orion says quietly as he begins to formulate a plan.

I turn to face him, and a shudder of anxiety courses through me at the realization of what this means.

"We'll need to leave within the hour," he continues, already on the move.

The world seems to spin as I rise from the bed on shaky feet. Hands trembling, I pull on the robe he's left for me at the foot of the bed.

I follow him into the receiving area of his suites as he calls Samson into the room. "Send word to ready my ship in Porton. Let my men know we will be there in a day to sail to

Demiitsch. We'll take the train in from Andres. But please, Samson, we must be discreet."

Samson bows, then walks briskly away to carry out his orders.

"Lady Ayn will help you pack. Meet me in the foyer in an hour."

His words register, but I cannot move. My mind is telling my feet to walk. To leave this room and begin packing. But they disobey. And I continue to stare mindlessly at the prince.

He steps toward me, understanding full well why I hesitate. Taking my shoulders in his hands, he meets my blank gaze. His mouth moves, but this time, I can't hear a word he says.

The only voice I hear is from memories etched in my mind. *Sarana's.*

The only person I see is the one I left behind. *Sarana.*

"Raya," Sarana says.

But how is she saying anything? She's not here. Just a figment of my imagination.

"Raya," the mirage in front of me says again, this time shaking me back to reality.

But it isn't Sarana, it's Orion. And I'm no longer standing but kneeling on the floor. And she's not shaking me, *I'm* shaking. Trembling.

His hands are stern on my shoulders as he rides the waves of shock with me. A steady anchor, ensuring I don't get lost in the sea of my mind.

"I know you haven't seen her in months, and there must be a hurricane of thoughts clouding your mind, but we cannot do this without you. There is no one else I trust more to be at my side."

I hear his words, I swear I do, but they make no sense.

He's only known me for a couple of months. How can he trust me so implicitly? Hell, I can't even trust myself right now.

"How am I going to face her after everything? When I can't even fully explain it myself?" My words are barely more than a whisper.

"You are a warrior. A duchess. And you will face your queen with the grace and power you command." His eyes are filled with all the confidence in the world.

Little by little, I feel that confidence flow into me. Slowly, I nod my head, only half believing my strength, and rise from my knees.

He places a hand on my cheek for a second, which feels more like an eternity, before standing straight, every bit of the determined prince he is, and says, "I'll see you in an hour, Your Grace."

And with that nudge, my legs finally find their strength and make their way to my rooms.

Travel by train takes us about a day. We have a few hours to spare in Porton, so I spend my time in the town similarly to how I spent my time on the train—silently in thought.

I walk the streets, lost in my own world as merchants and townspeople go about their day in the hustle and bustle of the market. A hooded cowl-necked scarf is wrapped tightly around my shoulders, keeping me warm. My guard—Garreth today—trails closely behind.

Only another day until I see Sarana again. I'm not sure

how to feel about this meeting, especially since she's not expecting to see me.

Will she be happy? Will she be angry? Oh, who am I kidding. She'll be furious. She will probably try to plot an escape as soon as she sees me.

But will I go with her if she has one?

I want to, oh how I want to. But I feel there's more here that must be done. An alliance to solidify with the prince that can help bolster his strength in Corath if he truly succeeds in ending this war.

Perhaps I'm thinking a bit too highly of myself, but would Orion even have attempted to reach out to Sarana if I weren't here? It's risky, I know, placing my trust in the enemy prince, but there is so much to gain if this all ends in a peaceful agreement between our two nations.

I do my best to clear my thoughts of what-ifs when an older woman catches my attention.

"My have the spirits cast their light upon you, milady."

Her once dark hair has turned gray—save for a few brown strands still clinging on—and her hands are calloused from years of labor.

She bows in my presence, raising her hands, palms facing up before her.

Garreth stiffens beside me, assessing the situation and surroundings as his grip tightens around his hilt.

"I'm sorry, ma'am, I don't quite understand what you mean," I say, taking one of her hands and helping her to her feet.

"I can sense it, feel their gifts cascading from you. We have waited a long time for you."

I shake my head in confusion. This woman is clearly mistaken.

"Surely you remember," she presses. "But if you don't you will soon."

"I think you have the wrong person." As nicely as I can, I plaster a smile on my face and wish her well.

But when I turn to walk back toward the ship, she grabs my hand, and Garreth steps in between us. I'm not sure if he's trying to protect me from her or her from me, but I place my hand on his shoulder, urging him to relax. The tension that was once there eases, only a fraction, but it eases nonetheless.

The woman returns her focus to me. "Your time to rise is near. When *she* calls upon you, make sure you're ready to answer."

Your time to rise is near... Those words... I have heard those words before.

Then my mind takes me back to months before when I was still in the torturous care of the king. When my mind lost itself in that dark abyss. Where a mysterious voice had echoed those same words. A chill crawls down my spine.

Who is this woman? I don't have time to question her further when a crowd forms, and she's lost from sight.

Garreth pulls me away. Away from the swarming crowd. Away from the babbling old woman. No matter how far we go, I cannot shake her final words from echoing in my mind.

THE ISLAND GREETS us with a cascading pastel rainbow rippling in the shallow waters. A path has been laid from the shore into the forest of palms that tower high above.

A small group of guards walks with us to the meeting

point, the remainder of the troops waiting behind on the ship.

"If we want them to trust us, we must first trust them," he had said when Samson protested. The words not too far from my own mantra when I first arrived in Thestras. Look how far we've come now.

I steal a glance at the prince from the corner of my eye. His expression is stoic, determined as he wills the success of these conversations into existence.

He looks like the epitome of regality and grace in his black gold-embroidered overcoat. He doesn't wear a crown. No collar of state. He doesn't need to. You can feel the power of essence and runes emanating from him. There is no denying who he is or what titles he holds. A true leader born and bred.

Walking next to him, I hold my head high, doing my best to match his confidence. I'm dressed in my battle uniform, donning my signature scaled armor. The delicate tiara on my head is covered in a simple design featuring the crown jewels of both our nations, garnet to represent Corath and diamonds for Promithia. A tribute to the hopeful alliance the prince wishes to make with Sarana, and the faith that our two nations will be brought together. Not by domination, but an alliance.

Two of Sarana's guards stand at the entrance of the tent. They nod to me in acknowledgment but stand firm in their formation. Two of Orion's join them.

Orion enters the tent first, then taking a deep breath, I step inside behind him.

Sarana's face turns rigid when she sees me.

Although her expression does not change, I can tell she is ready to burn this place to the ground if it means she could bring me home. No matter the flood of emotions—

disbelief and shock—I feel seeping from her, she remains composed.

Orion pulls out the chair between him and Samson, and I take the seat, never breaking eye contact with Sarana, who sits opposite me on the round table. A long piece of parchment rests in the center of the table, the wooden surface notched and worn with age. The page is blank, ready to draft the terms of the treaty, spaces for our signatures on the bottom of the paper.

"I wanted to prove to you that what I said in my letters is true," Orion says, claiming the empty seat beside me.

"Showing me my greatest warrior in one piece isn't proof enough that I can trust your word." Her voice is unrelenting ice. "Nonetheless, I am grateful you brought her here as her input is invaluable to Promithia, just as yours is to Corath." She faces me again.

"I hope our two countries only know peace, Your Majesty," I say, my voice sounding more confident than I thought could be possible right now.

Sarana simply nods, never removing her gaze from mine.

Beside me, Orion clears his throat. "Then let us begin."

TWENTY-SEVEN

We sit around the table for hours discussing the terms of the treaty. The lands to be returned to their rightful countries. Prisoners of war to be released. The reestablishment of trade routes. The roles of ambassadors. The dismantling of Orion's grandfather's misogynistic proclamation.

With every word, defense, and rebuttal, we lay the groundwork for the future of our two nations.

I doubt Mattias will ever agree to that last term, to allow women to be treated as equals. A condition that Sarana certainly requested to test Orion's dedication to this cause. But we need to try.

Once we're all agreed, we each sign the bottom of the paper, our signatures and seals branding the parchment in burning solidarity.

"I want to thank you, Queen Sarana, for agreeing to meet with me." Orion's voice slices through the heaviness between us all. "I know this isn't the final treaty. We will need to eventually bring in our advisers and legislators for their input, but I truly hope that we are able to convince my father of the value of this alliance and the peace it will surely bring." He glances between Sarana and me. "I will give you both a few minutes before we leave."

He rises from his seat, bowing before motioning for Samson to leave with him.

Sarana waves a hand, dismissing her own guards as she stands.

Once the tent is cleared, Sarana rushes to me. Planting kisses on every inch of my face, my lips, my neck. She wraps her arms tightly around me as if she can take us away and shatter the runes protecting this armistice.

"Have they done anything to hurt you?" Sarana asks, checking my face for any signs of bruising or malnutrition.

"Sarana, I'm all right. The first couple months in the care of the king were less than pleasant, but I'm much better now." I take her cheek in my hand and wipe away the runaway tear. "How's Dessy?"

Her gaze is bleak, eyes looking away as she shakes her head. "Not well. Leigh has temporary control over your armies, and Orlo has taken a greater role in leading your lands in your absence. She's still learning, but she needs you, Raya."

Hot tears roll down my face at the news.

"Wait, you're not at the king's court?" she asks.

"You think the king would have let his heir take me with him on an adventure?" I laugh, shaking my head as I wipe away the tears under my eyes. "I left Mattias's court almost two months ago now."

"With the prince?" she asks in confusion.

I nod.

"How did you manage that?"

Hesitating, I'm unsure of the right way to tell her this part of the story. Realizing there isn't, I tear the bandage off.

"The prince claimed me during his Birthrite."

The earth rumbles beneath our feet, and the temperature rises around us, her rage boiling from within.

"He did what?" she asks through gritted teeth.

"It hasn't been that bad, Sarana. Better than being under the watch of the king."

"They've brainwashed you into believing that's true. Raya, you are not property to be claimed. You are a person. A fierce, strong warrior. Not something to be owned."

"It's not like that. It sounds terrible, yes, but it's not like that."

"Enlighten me then."

I pace around the tent, telling her everything that happened since I broke through the diminishing bracelet and sent Greva home. Explained how I almost died. The conversations I've been able to overhear. What I learned about Corath's previous king. Orion's plan that's been in place longer than I've been in Corath.

She closes the distance between us and takes my hands in hers, pressing her lips to the backs of them, then pulling me closer.

"Raya, what if this was their plan? To get you to trust them just to tear the notion of peace away."

A question I, too, have asked myself over and over again.

"Before he lessened my diminishing cuff, I thought the same thing. But when my powers returned to me, so did my gift. He speaks the truth, Sarana. Peace is all he cares about."

Her expression softens. She doesn't completely believe me, but she trusts my judgment.

"I still find the tradition of the Birthrite despicable," she says in a hiss.

"On the bright side, my apartments in Thestras are even better than the ones at your court in Arya." I laugh through the comment, but Sarana's deadpan stare and cock of her brow tells me she doesn't see the humor. "Oh, come on, Sarana. We have to learn how to laugh through dark times."

"Why should I, Raya?!" The light hold she has on my hands slowly turns into a tight grip. "Your father was killed, and you were taken from Promithia, from *me*, by these assholes. For what? To be put on show? To be sported around like some prized horse?"

A pang of guilt courses through me. Why did I falter at the voice on the wind? And why does it seem that this invisible force is pulling me down this path?

"I'm sorry, Sarana," I say, looking down.

"Why are you sorry? *You* were the one that was taken." She lifts my chin, so I have no choice but to look into her deep brown eyes.

I wish I could tell her the truth of what happened. How the voice called to me on the wind, knocking into me with a force as ancient as time itself. But she would never believe me, never understand.

"This is your chance, Raya," she says, stroking my jaw with the soft pad of her thumb. "You can leave here with me. I can activate a mirage to disappear once we're off the shoreline. You could come home."

"If I'm here, I can ensure that the treaty is agreed to by the king. And if it's not, I can help the prince win the most important battle of his life."

Her thumb stills against my jaw. "But your people need you home... *I* need you home."

Home. For months, I have thought of nothing more than Promithia. Of Sarana, Dessy, and Leigh. Of Senna and my people.

But as I gaze into her eyes, I realize I don't see home within them anymore. The longing I see in hers isn't matched by my own. I love her and always will. But that love, stolen moments tucked away, isn't enough.

"You know… I helped train some of the newest troops to join the Corathian front. And when I say train, I mean more like prepare them for death. To die with dignity." I scoff at the words. "Those boys barely lasted a few weeks on the battlefield. Half of them are dead, and I'm sure by now that number has risen." I take a step away from her, throwing my arms wide.

"This is bigger than what either of us want," I continue, taking her hands in mine and squeezing in earnest. "Can you not see how this partnership, an alliance with the future King of Corath, will benefit us? Ensuring the prince succeeds will not only end the war peacefully, but we will secure positive futures for both our nations. Ori has been working on a way to end the war, and I intend to help him."

Her expression shifts. Deep concern, passion, and love turn into something else. Something angry, dark, and cold.

"Ori?" she says with a bite. "I didn't realize you were on a nickname basis with *His Highness.*"

Fuck. His nickname rolled off my tongue, as smooth as silk gliding across bodies.

"How long?" she asks.

"Excuse me?" I furrow my brows in confusion.

"How long have you been sleeping with the Prince of Corath?" she spits, fury in her eyes.

I'm stunned silent by her presumptions. My cheeks burn as I try to find the right words to respond.

"Ahhh, you haven't slept with him yet, but by the blush on your cheeks, I can tell you want to," she says, a grin devoid of happiness spreads across her lips as she takes a step closer. "Tell me, my love. Have you kissed? Has he coaxed pleasure from your core using nothing but the tips of his fingers? Has he found the secret to making you sing?"

My blood boils beneath my skin at the audacity of her words.

"Shut your mouth, Sarana!" My voice is frantic, surprising both of us.

I was caught off guard by her comments, but how dare she judge me. The queen who gets to have her cake and eat it too. Spirits forbid I do the same.

"I'm tortured for months, then saved by the prince. So I befriend him to survive, help find a way to end the war for our countries' sakes. Not that it's any of your business, but no, we are not having sex."

"None of my business?" She asks with a chilling laugh that lacks amusement. "You are mine, Raya. You do not belong with some enemy prince who comes up with some half-decent plan for *potential* peace between our nations."

"Your claim on me is about as strong as my claim on you, my Queen. While it's true I am yours, your subject, a royal under your banner, a lover when your husband isn't warming your bed in an effort to produce an heir, or when I'm finally home from the front. I am yours only by action."

"How dare you. We have sworn our love to each other time and time again. Just because the prince saved you doesn't mean he's not using you for his own agenda."

"Of course he's using me for his own agenda!" I yell, exasperated. "I have been using him as well. I need to do my part to make sure he trusts me. But for spirits' sake, look at where this has brought us. Closer to peace. Something our people haven't seen in over three hundred years."

Sarana's rage is erupting into the earth below once more,

but I don't care. I keep on going, sharing my truth no matter how painful it may be.

"So, *Your Majesty*, am I sorry I couldn't be there for you? That I couldn't lead your armies? That I was captured? Of course I am. But if the end of the war, a treaty, and an ally in Corath's future king is the result? Then perhaps those sacrifices, the loss of my father, wasn't all for nothing." The tears roll in streams down my face. "At least what Orion and I are doing could bring this frivolous war to an end. More than what you've ever done sitting high and mighty on your throne."

I can't stop those last words from leaving my lips, my mouth working much too quickly for my mind to catch. But once they're out in the world, I immediately regret them. Her face is pained; the harsh truth slams into her as surely as if the words were my own hand striking against her cheek.

"We were fools to think we can love each other in peace when our paths are so far removed from our desires and wishes," she says, eyes somber. "In truth, we were over before we even began, weren't we?"

"Sarana, we always knew what we could never be. That action was all we could give each other. Our legacies and futures predesigned."

"I just thought it would be enough," she says, a tear rolling down her cheek. Her expression of pain morphs into one of strength and iron as she remembers exactly who she is. A fact I will do well to remember too. "These actions may have expedited a treaty. But if the king signs and there is peace between our two nations once more, then you are to return home to court in Arya immediately after its signing. Rite or no Rite, you are now a high general, a *duchess*, of Promithia, and as such, you belong in our land."

"And here I thought that I—how did you put it—could

claim a future of my own? That I wasn't property to be claimed."

She closes the space between us until I can feel her breath on my cheek, hot and thick with malice. "When the war ends, you *will* return home."

"I can't make any promises," I retort, my stubbornness and pride getting in the way of my own good.

"You have me mistaken. That was not a suggestion." A ruler bidding her citizen to her will. "As your queen, that is my command."

"Your Majesty." I dip down into a deep curtsy, then exit the tent.

A line has been drawn, an irrevocable rift causing a seismic shift between us, from which we will never recover.

TWENTY-EIGHT

My head rests on the cool window as I watch the outside world pass in a blur.

Across from me, the prince watches. Never saying a word. Just sits with me in silence. The same silence I have kept since we left Demiitsch the night before.

The door to our train car opens, and a butler approaches our table. He pours us both a glass of red wine, then swiftly leaves the car without a word.

Orion shifts in his seat, clearly unable to take the quiet any longer.

"What happened?" he asks finally.

"I'd rather not talk about it." I refuse to take my eyes away from the changing views beyond the window.

"I hate seeing you like this. Angry… hurt." He takes my hand that's resting on the table. "Talk to me."

"All you need to worry about is getting your father to agree to the treaty and know that I will be there to assist with any reciprocal fallout," I say, knowing that won't be enough for him.

"Something happened between you and Sarana. I apologize for prying, and I won't press anymore after this, but please know you can lean on me. You can trust me."

Despite my reasoning telling me I shouldn't, I look into his eyes. Seeing them filled with worry and searching my own for answers, I convince myself I can.

"Obviously, our reunion wasn't as joyous as we thought it would be. Although I knew it wasn't going to be entirely pleasant."

"So you argued?"

I nod, taking a sip of wine and allowing the effects of the juices to buzz in my mind.

"What were you arguing about?"

I laugh, knowing there's no better way to share these details. "You."

A flicker crosses his face. Confusion. Surprise. Intrigue. All of the above. "Me? Why were you fighting about me?"

"She thinks we're sleeping together."

His eyes bulge from their sockets. "And why does she believe that?"

"Because I accidentally used your nickname."

He leans back into his seat.

"I was trying to show her you can be trusted. And it just slipped out."

Taking a sip of wine, he shakes his head. "I mean... I guess I can see how that would make her question the depth of our relationship, but it's a stretch to automatically assume sex. Except, we did almost..." he says with a smirk.

"Oh, wipe that look off your face," I say.

With unspoken words, my eyes implore him. *This is exactly why we can't go there.*

He puts his hands up in defeat. *I know,* his own seem to

respond, a twinge of pain resting within, mirroring my expression.

No longer able to bear the monotony of sitting, I rise and pace up and down the aisle of the train car.

"I'm just saying that can't be the only reason you're upset," he says. "You don't seem like the type of person who would care about who knew the partners you may keep."

"I don't." I bite my lip.

"Then what is it?"

"It's funny." I chuckle, though it's far from humorous. "I always thought that whenever Sarana and I eventually had our be-all and end-all conversation about our relationship, I'd be devastated by the closing of our chapter. But I think I knew for a while that we were coming to an end." I sigh and lean against the table across from him. "What really has me reeling is the hypocrisy of her words," I admit.

He faces me, lifting a brow.

"In one sentence, she was saying how I'm not an object to be claimed. Yet, in another, she treats me like I'm exactly that. Commanding me to return home to court when all this is done like I'm nothing more than a thing to be ordered about. The pressures from my father were heavy, but I just never expected her to take the same approach."

"Well, won't you be returning home?" he asks, resting an arm on the table.

"Yes," I say, fiddling with my thumbs.

"Why do I sense a 'but' in there?"

Finally working up the nerve, I share a truth I have only kept in the very far-to-reach corners of my mind. "I'm not sure if I deserve to go home, not when I'm the one who caused my father's death." I hang my head low in shame.

"Raya, that is not true."

"Isn't it?" I meet his gaze, and I don't need to see my reflection to know my eyes are filled with pained defeat. "Frallis was all me. My plan, my strategy. It was supposed to be a perfect trap for Tyrannis, but it just ensured my father's downfall… and my shame."

He takes his hand in mine as I look away, unable to hold the pressing pity of his stare any longer.

"You might have been the one to come up with the strategy behind Frallis, but there is so much out of your control on the battlefield. You couldn't have predicted his death, as surely as you could not have prevented it."

His words make sense, and I hear them, but I can't accept them. My father was coming to save me from my own mistakes. From my own weaknesses.

My fault, my fault, *my fault.*

"I've been thinking a lot about what you asked me a few weeks ago. About what it is I want from life," I say, moving away from the painful topic of my father.

His expression is pained, disappointed that I won't confide in him. But the ache in my chest is too much to bear. I can't talk about it. Not yet. Especially not with him.

"I can't ignore the duties I am bound to as heir to my father's title." I continue. "But since being stuck here, I've realized there's a whole world out there I want to explore. It won't be easy given my position, but traveling and exploring the world, building relationships with international leaders to strengthen Senna and Promithia, will be something I can look forward to, something for *me.*"

Even as I say the words, I realize how preposterous they really are. Just a bunch of wishful dreaming for a life of my own.

"Are you sure I can't convince you to stay here with me?"

"After the treaty is signed, I won't have a choice, but I won't have a reason to stay either," I say, and he flinches at the sting of my words.

"You know, with the Rite, I could make you." He laughs, a deflection. An attempt at a joke, one that I will not entertain.

"You could. But by the spirits, I hope you don't."

He rises from his seat and moves to kneel at my feet, surprising me. He takes my hands in his. Jaw rigid and firm. His eyes fixate on mine, never breaking contact. He digs his way into my soul, grabbing hold. Wishing for me to see the truth. In his words. In him.

"That was a joke, Raya. Poorly timed, I know, but it was." He shakes his head, clearly upset with himself for even trying to joke about using the bond in that way. "With me, you will never be a prisoner. When all this is over, you will be free to make your own decision. The choice will always be yours to make. Not a crowned prince's or a queen's. Only yours."

We stand there for a moment. My hands in his. A prince resting on his knee.

There is one rule for a crowned Prince of Corath. To bow to no one. To submit to no one other than his king.

And here he is. Submitting.

To a person he should consider his enemy. To a person he saved when he should not have. To a person he is allowing a choice when the Rite practically takes that away.

If he wanted me to bend to his will, he could make it so. But he hasn't.

Although I've known I could trust him, something deep in my core projects a shadow of doubt.

Fear.

Of his father, of him, of Corath.

But with just us here, him on his knee, soul gazing into

soul, I can't help but feel we have known each other all our lives. Longer than that if it's even possible. That he and I are connected much deeper than the Rite. We have been brought together by a force of essence and nature we don't quite understand.

TWENTY-NINE

The training fields are quiet save for a few grunts and curses between sparring partners.

I could have sworn I heard a low growl rumble from the woman across from me. Her brows are furrowed, teeth bared, lips drawn up in a wicked smile as we circle around each other, waiting for the other to make the first move.

And then she does, her silver hair flowing around her like billowing smoke. Almost too quick for me to counter.

Almost.

I easily evade her death grip and use her own force to pin her down.

We stare at each other with upturned lips.

Looking down, I find a small blade pointing in between my ribs, just as my own presses against her throat.

Laughing, we help each other up from the muddied ground.

"I have to say, I'm quite surprised to learn that Orion has his own legion," I say as we walk over to the watering station.

Loren, my sparring partner, eyes me quizzically. But just as soon as she does, her face brightens into a wide smile.

"And that he allows all people to join." I reach for a cup of water on the table.

"His Highness definitely skirts expectations. Besides, the Black Brigade would be nothing without *us*." She winks, then takes a hefty sip of water from her canteen.

"My father would have loved your dedication and strength. Your loyalty too. You are all some of the best fighters I have ever encountered. I'm not sure where the prince sends you for your training, but it's sure as hell not in Corath," I say, shaking my head.

If it were, all of Mattias's armies would fight the way the Brigade does, and Promithia would have been lost ages ago. Although I assume his father has no idea his son even has his own personal legion of born and bred killers.

"We were all sent away for months, training in seclusion until we became extensions of death. The training itself is grueling. Those of us standing here are the ones who made it out alive."

I press the rim of my cup to my mouth, a smirk lifting the corner of my lips. "I don't suppose you'd share where this superior training location of yours is?" I ask before taking a gulp of cool liquid.

She takes a step forward, her silken silver hair shining in the sunlight, and whispers in my ear, "Now, if I told you that, I'd have to kill you."

The smile on her face as she leans back against the table and the gleam in her eyes tells me she's joking. But her words are tinged with a seriousness and truth I can't ignore.

"It was worth a shot," I say, simply shrugging, not letting her see my unease.

Off to the side of the training grounds, a man stands at

attention, overseeing each of the fighters. Observing every move and countermove they make. Assessing all their strengths and each of their failures. His rigid face is calculating. No doubt he's weighing the cost of whatever is to come.

Even from this distance, I can see his silver eyes that beg me to inch closer, the certainty in them. Certainty and knowledge that no matter what losses he and his warriors may face in the days to come, their victory—*our* victory— will be worth it.

"That's Xander," Loren says. Her voice breaks me away from my study. "He's our commander."

I look back in his direction with slight surprise, although I'm not sure why I'm shocked. He wears the same black uniform as the rest of the soldiers on the training fields, with nothing to show his rank. But from his stance to his stare, everything about him commands your attention, your respect, your loyalty.

"He looks rather young to be a commander."

"Just like you, General Duchess."

"I suppose so," I manage through a half smile.

Xander has now moved on from studying his Brigade to studying Loren and me. The heat of his silver gaze heavy on my skin.

Ignoring the weight of his stare, I set down my glass of water. "How about another round?"

Loren rolls her eyes. "Aren't you exhausted?"

"Nope. Besides, if your commander over there is going to be watching us, we might as well put on a show." My words are a dare, rolling off my tongue past a scheming smile.

MY HEELS CLICK and clack against the marble floor as I walk down the long hallway. The train of my dress flows behind me with every step I take, a wave of shimmering midnight blue in my wake.

I follow close behind the butler leading me down this long corridor, where suits of armor line the walls on either side. I swear, their heads turn as I walk past them. Every piece of decor, armor, and light fixture seems to bring us back in time, taking us through the decades, centuries, and millennia.

General Mavre is due at some point tomorrow with a small force of his own. Then, the day after, we will be making our way back to Labrynthia. Until then, we are to wait. Sit and stare into the abyss of our bedchambers. But as a naturally restless person, I have been able to do nothing of the sort.

"You will find his grace in here," the man says as he opens two large red doors.

I step into a room I can only describe as a treasure trove of sorts. Walls lined and shelves filled with... *things* on display. Not things, I suppose, but relics. Objects, clothing, and pieces that originate from before the Great Rift.

My eyes aren't sure where to land first as I take in everything before me. Mannequins are dressed in what seems to be old military uniforms. The fabric is made of swatches of different greens and browns to blend into the natural surroundings.

Where's the metal armor? The steel chest plates and helmets? I think to myself. No wonder this species was on its way out when the spirits arrived.

Another section has rows of old metal boxes, fixed with rounded glass screens—*cameras*, as explained by a description card underneath. Apparently, they were used to capture images from moments in time. These *pictures* hang on display on the wall above. Candid images of people walking on busy roads, tall structures in black and white, and colorful landscapes cover the wall. The pictures are faded from time, many with edges burned or torn but preserved by essence and runes.

"It's amazing how one small collection of metal can produce such beautiful creations, isn't it?" someone asks from behind me, a tinge of adoration framing his tone.

I turn to him and release a breath.

Orion leans against a shelf with his hands buried deep in his pockets, sleeves rolled up his muscled forearm, looking more like a carved statue than a real person. Worry lines crease into his forehead. No doubt he's been thinking about the days to come. But the way his eyes light up at the sight of me tells me that I am a welcome distraction.

"How have these objects survived after all this time?" I ask. "Where have you been finding everything?"

"Most of these things—like the cameras and pictures and uniforms—were found a long time ago, when my ancestors started excavating to build Labrynthia. Other items—like the twisting chunks of metal and broken sheets—were found a bit more recently when we started building the new city of Andres."

I look over to the sheet of metal he's referring to. It's green with strange white lettering and faded, the corners and surface covered in rust. Giving up on trying to make sense of what the piece once was, I move to his side.

He locks eyes with me, and that tugging in my core twitches again. The world around us is still trying to pull the two of us together despite how hard I'm trying to keep us apart.

Afraid of what may follow this silence, I clear my throat. "Why this? Why not adopt a different hobby?"

Asking questions is good. Asking questions will keep him talking. Keeping his lips busy talking will prevent them from being busy doing something… else.

A shiver of need and want creeps through my body. And he seems to have noticed as his lips tip up in a smile.

"It's a good distraction from the war. To forget about the horrors we face. But I also enjoy the mystery. The fact that I don't know exactly what I'm dealing with when I'm uncovering a new part of history. When I had more time, I would spend hours down here digging through whatever old books and pictures I could find just to figure out what all these artifacts are."

His eyes light up with boyish charm and wonder as he explains this secret passion of his. Although I will never understand this strange infatuation with old relics, I can appreciate his enthusiasm and desire to learn.

What will become of my belongings, I wonder? The items I have grown to treasure. My amarynthus sword or my amplifier gloves or even my own armor? Will they be on display in museum houses? Or will a distant prince take up a collection, only able to guess what they are or whom they once belonged to?

A shining object glimmers from the corner of my eye. It's resting at the edge of a shelf on the far wall. A flurry of soft whispers sing in my ears. It seems to be calling to me with words I can't quite understand. An ancient language I could never remember.

I gently pick the piece up and let it rest in my palm.

The object that grasped my attention so firmly is nothing more than a bit of amir stone. A translucent rock that tends to shatter like glass when struck a certain way. This one is turquoise and teal with little lines of dark obsidian scattered within.

I lift it up to the light and watch the rays fragment into rainbows and whirling patterns on the ground. A kaleidoscope of runelight swirls around me and dances on the wall. It somehow catches the space between the hanging curtain.

Strange to hang a curtain in a room with no windows, I think to myself.

Setting the stone back in its place, I pull back the thick, burgundy covering, revealing the wall hidden behind it.

My breath hitches when I see what's on display. A mural. Depicting how the earth, as we now know it, came to be. Every color known is used in this painting, and a shimmering hue I've never seen before gives it a life-like quality. Chips are visible on the surface, creating gaps within the visual story. This is probably as old as this new world itself. It's incredible that it's lasted this long.

Of course the story is the same, one known by most, if not all. Earth's tumble toward destruction. The spirits arriving—their plan to destroy the planet to ensure its survival. Their power, foreign to this world at the time, causing the Great Rift and rearranging of the continents.

Even the darker parts of our history are included here: the surviving humans enslaved by the spirits. Until the humans rose up and allied with those of the spirits who wished for them to be free. For spirits and humans to live their lives side by side.

Led by Ach'tella and Ekkheim—two powerful high spirits

—the allied forces secured a future of freedom. A future that resulted in the mixing lines of humans and spirits, creating the new human race. Ach'tella and Ekkheim used their combined power to send all the Abhorrent spirits who wished the humans harm back to their homeland, sacrificing themselves in the process.

Legend says that the pair were lovers. True soulmates in every sense of the word. But they were both partnered with others.

Ach'tella ruled alongside Dane'er—both were the bearers of the Cosmos. Essence that can create and destroy with the power of the sun and stars. They could create galaxies together. Knit together matter to create whatever they wished. Fold time and space to travel between worlds with their people.

On the other hand, Ekkheim and Idris were bound but had a more open relationship. From them derive our Shadow abilities. Reader, Shifter, Empath, and mist-traveling —the ability to walk in the Shadow Plane, the plane between our world and the world the spirits came from.

Artemis and Senta, the high spirits of Nature, were the forces behind the Elementals, Stormnings, and Healers. Their powers, and all those whose power derives from them, have a special relationship with the earth, ensuring its plane can continue to be fruitful.

I've seen these images a million times, but this has something else added to it beyond the orbs depicting Ekkheim and Ach'tella converging their power together. The last scene is one that is typically reserved for those who believe in the prophecies foretold.

Here in Corath and even in Volira, they believe strongly in their faith. In Promithia, we view the tale as folklore. A story to be told, but nothing more.

The last bit, in that same shimmering hue, shows three orbs. Two orbs merging, moving toward a larger circle in the center. I'm not quite sure what it means.

"The mural is beautiful. Where did you find it?"

He walks forward, standing next to me to see the mural in full view.

"My grandfather found it right here, on this wall." He nods to the painted surface in front of us.

Figures.

"You mean, this wasn't brought in from another location? This was already here?" He nods, and I can't stop myself from sucking in a breath in astonishment. "You know, I've never seen a real depiction of the legend before. At least, not that I can remember."

He chuckles, and the sound settles somewhere low in my belly, sending bursts of warmth throughout my body.

"*Legend,*" he repeats. "So you don't believe in the prophecy?"

I simply shrug. "Do I believe that the souls of Ach'tella and Ekkheim still roam the earth, finding the perfect host to save the world from a second devastation? A disaster no one knows anything about?" *When the time to rise is near, the spirits will return.* I shake my head at the outlandish story that has been passed down from generation to generation. But the words are just that, a work of fiction. "Absolutely not."

He shrugs, as if to say "suit yourself," and I chuckle, turning back to inspect the painting.

"It's just incredible how something like this has survived and withstood the test of time."

A smile spreads across his face, washing away the worry that creases his brow. "It is, isn't it? That's the power of essence and runes. Allows us to preserve life, art, history in remarkable ways." His eyes light up with every word he speaks, brightening his features.

I find myself tempted to bring my hand up to his chiseled jaw, to outline the arch of his lips, to push aside the waves of dark hair that tend to cover his tan forehead. But I hold myself back, gripping my hands behind my back, not trusting to leave them at my side.

THIRTY

We arrive too soon at my chambers. The lights on either side of my door illuminate his face, enhancing those worry lines and circles under his eyes.

He's nervous. Not afraid, no. But nervous.

If things go wrong, it's not just his life on the line here. It's all of ours.

I'm greeted again with the urge to raise my palm to his cheek, and this time, I don't fight it. His skin is warm and welcoming against mine, and he presses deeper into my touch. With my other hand, I push that stray lock of hair out of his eyes.

We stand there silent for a moment. His cheek resting on my palm. Our eyes closed, feeling the hum of each other in the silence. There's no need for either of us to say a word.

I try my best to quell his nerves, letting his emotions flow to me. I replace them with hope, trust… love. Doing my best to give him the strength he needs to carry him through the next few days.

He smiles, reaching for my hand. "Thank you, Raya. I needed that."

"I know," I say with a smile. "Goodnight, Orion."

Once inside my rooms, I suck in a deep breath, hoping that's enough to clear my spinning thoughts.

Resting my head against the door, I curse the spirits for fating me to be linked with a person who will surely cause my destruction. A person whom I should run the opposite way from. But for some reason, like the spirits Ach'tella and Ekkheim, I can't seem to pry myself away.

Before another second passes, I open the door and find that he's still there. Staring at me with a look that tells me he never wanted to leave in the first place.

In another moment, we're in each other's arms. Lips locked. Hands trying to touch as much of each other as they can. Because one touch isn't near enough.

He kicks the door closed and pushes me against the wall in one smooth move. Our tongues dance and glide together as if we have all the time in the world to explore. To find the best way to coax moans from our beings, to make each other scream in delight.

He rakes his hands down my body, fumbling over the hem of my skirt. Wasting no time, he dives his fingers between my legs as his mouth claims mine. His fingers circle painfully slow around my clit. He pulls away from me, his lips seconds away from my own, as he watches me come undone with his magical touch.

"That's it, Raya," he whispers against my lips. "Unravel for me."

His words elicit a breathy moan from my chest as he trails kisses from my jaw down to my breast. He nips my nipple through the fabric of my gown before continuing down, down, down.

After gathering my skirt at my hips, he rips away the fabric of my underwear, tossing it behind him before lifting my leg and resting it atop his shoulder. He looks up from where he kneels before me, his finger still circling my sensitive bud.

I've always loved seeing a lover on their knees for me, but him? He is utterly perfect. Eyes driven mad by desire. Swollen lips glistening, tongue swiping across as if he can't wait to dive into the buffet made solely for him.

"You are beautiful," he says, eyes never leaving mine. "Absolutely beautiful."

In an instant, his tongue replaces the pad of his fingers as he licks across my center. I shudder at the sensation. Then his lips close around my clit as he deliciously sucks and licks where I need him the most. Holding my skirt and leg with one hand, he uses the other to reach up, tugging down the top of my dress and freeing my breasts. He pinches the turgid peak in between his fingers, rolling my nipple in time to the rhythm of his tongue.

"Oh, for fuck's sake," I moan, and he hums against me.

Between his expert tongue, the friction of his fingers against the peak of my breast, and the vibrations of his mouth, I'm carried over the edge as wave after wave of release crashes through me. My fingers lace through his hair as his lips ease me through my climax.

He pulls himself back to his feet, and I wrap my leg around his waist, pulling him closer to me. His mouth finds mine again, and the taste of myself on his lips sends a new wave of arousal through me.

As I'm locked in this slow, caressing kiss, realization comes crashing over me. While I will always have love for Sarana—she helped me find beauty in a world of so much bloodshed—I can't help but recognize how this is different, and an understanding dawns on me as to why I felt guilty after my interaction with Orion the night of the Solstice Ball.

It wasn't due to betrayal. It was because of my feelings for the prince that run much deeper than simple lustful attraction. It's driven by hope for what our future could hold. But given our positions, a future for us could never be. Could it?

He covers my mouth, my neck, and spots behind my ear with kisses. Until all of a sudden, he's not.

He pulls back, panting, trying his best to regain all composure while I gaze his way, allowing myself to become completely undone.

But there's a darkness painted in the air between us, uncertainty and… Is that fear I sense from him? Fear of what? Of me? Of us? Of *this*?

Leaning forward, he rests his forehead against mine and whispers, "Is this what you want?"

"What do you mean?" I ask, breathless.

How could he not sense the desire thrumming from me? Desire only for him.

"I know what I want, Raya, but do you? Are you comfortable with this? With me? I have the rune of protection on me, so I'm protected in all ways, though I haven't had a partner in a long time."

I blush at his admission and at his wanting to ensure I'm comfortable. "While it's obviously been months since my last time, I can assure you I am protected as well."

He lifts a brow in question.

"Ayn has been providing me with herbal prevention teas." My blush deepens.

I had asked her to start providing them to me every morning since the winter solstice, just in case. I would prefer the rune, but there was no one here in Thestras that I trusted to administer it. Unfortunately, the one I had before my capture faded as it does every year or so.

"But Orion, I won't push you away." I place my hands on either side of his face and make him return my gaze. "I cannot make promises about what might happen if this war should end, but I want you, Orion."

"I don't need promises, Raya. All I want is this moment with you. When this war ends, we can discuss what this means, what we mean, together."

"Together." I nod in agreement.

With that, he kisses me deeply again, not as feral as before. This kiss is softer, more delicate. Like he's savoring it, unsure if we will have this moment again.

With a wave of my hand, a gust of wind blows the curtains shut, safely hiding us in my quarters. I turn around, moving my hair over my shoulder. He makes quick work of the laces on my dress, and I face him again. After slipping the midnight-blue and silver-specked gown down my body, it falls into a puddle on the floor near my feet.

His body hums with desire as I walk toward him. With every step I take, I use the air around him to ease his clothes off his body, to undress him layer by layer.

First his doublet. Then his tunic. His pants are the last to go. His bared muscles are displayed before me, and his hardened member stands at attention. Throbbing. Ready.

I slide my hand over his chest, down his chiseled arms, committing his being to my memory. He's beautiful. Scars and all. How I want his arms to carry me away.

As if he can hear my thoughts, he lifts me up, and I wrap my legs around his hips. His lips remain fused to mine as he walks us to my bed.

With a playful drop, I land in the middle of my mattress

with a little bounce. He tosses the plush pillows to the floor, and they land with soft thuds.

Bared skin freckled with scars from battle, I let him take me in as I am.

Hovering over me, he slowly begins a trail of soft kisses starting at my ear. Then my neck. Stopping at my breasts, he flicks my nipple with his tongue. After sucking it into his mouth, he releases it with a pop.

A shiver runs down my body.

"I am going to take my time with you," he says, voice gruff and barely more than a whisper.

He makes his way farther south.

"I could do this all day," he says just before his head dips between my legs, his tongue once more devouring my warm center.

I've been so afraid to let myself go completely with him. So tightly wound and always on guard. But in this moment, I can't exactly remember why. Is he my enemy? My ally? My lover? Is he someone I should even consider loving?

I let out a sigh of pleasure and tangle my hands through his hair, ignoring the questions my mind seems pressed to ask. I don't even try to stifle my moans as his tongue takes me over the edge.

He lands a soft kiss on my inner thigh before rising over me, the tip of his cock sliding against my opening.

I suck in a breath between my teeth at the feel of his thickness gliding against my clit, and my eyes roll back at the sensation.

He chuckles at the sight, dragging his lips across my neck, over my chin, before landing at my lips.

With one hand, he braces my hip while lacing the other into my curls.

"Look at me." His voice is as smooth as silk, but his

rolling hips against me never relent. "I want to see your eyes when we join, Raya."

Blinking my eyes back to his, I meet his gaze. A devilish smile plays on his lips as he gently eases into me.

And we both release a breathy moan as one. If the feel of his fingers inside me brought me over the edge, his cock filling me to the brim, this sensation, will absolutely destroy me.

"Raya." He breathes my name like he's saying a prayer. "Raya. Raya. Raya."

I would say his name, or really anything at all, if I could. But his thrusts quicken, push deeper, harder, and I feel that bloom sprouting in the middle of my chest once more. The bud ready to soar.

His lips find mine, mouths colliding as if we're not nearly close enough. My voice finally returns to me just as we both reach our limits, and I scream out a prayer of my own against his lips.

Orion. Orion. "Orion."

THE DUVET and bed sheets are strewn around my room from the hours we spent… not sleeping. We lie together in silence, listening to the rain as it continues to pour. Droplets tap, tap, tapping against the windows.

I glide my fingers over his skin, my mind making a map of his body. They pass over the freckles on his neck, the goose bumps covering his arm, and the lines of scars that scatter across his body.

He's doing the same with me, only not with his fingertips

but with his eyes. He watches my arm rove his skin, scanning my entire being with his gaze.

"Are these from battle?" I ask as my finger traces the scar that travels down his forearm.

He shakes his head slowly, his jaw working as his gaze grows distant and dark. "My father always had a temper, and he thought this was the best way to help me *build character*."

I grit my teeth in anger. "I'm so sorry."

"It was a long time ago." He shrugs.

He doesn't elaborate further, and I don't ask for more information. When he's ready, he will confide.

I nestle into his arms, and he plants small kisses at the nape of my neck and shoulder. He reaches for my waist and pulls me closer to him, grip firm on my hip as if letting go would cause this moment to break apart. Shatter into millions of pieces like the amir stone.

"Careful, dear Prince, if you hold me any tighter, I may break." I laugh, propping my head up with my hand. "What's on your mind?"

"You," he says, taking my hand in his.

"What about me? Other than my talents beyond the battlefield?"

He laughs, and the music of his voice fills the room and my heart with joy. But his laugh is short, and his eyes turn somber as he returns to his original thoughts.

"What thoughts plague your mind?" I ask.

"What will happen if you don't go back to Promithia? If you refuse?"

"Honestly, I don't know. She could have me banished, strip me of my titles and possessions, order my death." Although I'm joking about that last bit, his jaw tightens at that revelation.

"Do you think she would do that? Any of it?"

"I don't think she'd go so far as to kill me, but who knows." I shrug, not really sure how to predict what Sarana will do. No one can. "She was angry the other day, but it would depend on how personally she would take my refusal to return or if she'd just let it go."

He cups my cheek and trails his lips from my forehead to my mouth with soft yet firm kisses.

"Now it's my turn to ask you a question," I say when we part. "How do we know this isn't the Rite making us feel this way? That this is truly us and our own will?"

"The Rite doesn't instill desire, want, or love. It's merely a bond that connects the two subjects. Not only do you belong to me"—he cringes as he says the word *belong*—"but I belong to you just as equally."

"Okay," I say, trying to put the pieces together in my mind. "But how do you know that we're not confusing these feelings of *belonging* that this bond may create with feelings of something else?"

"Before the bond, I had this deep-seated desire to be near you, to protect you. And I knew this was the only way." He runs his hands through my hair, twirling my curls with his fingers. "You will always have a place here with me. No matter the distance between us."

CHAPTER

THIRTY-ONE

The morning air is crisp with dew, and I revel in the soft breeze as it wafts into the bathing chambers.

It's warmer this morning. Much warmer than the days before. The first sign that spring may finally be around the corner.

Or maybe my body is still worked up from last night with the prince. *My prince.*

I definitely shouldn't be calling him mine... But I can call him mine in the safety of my mind. *There's no harm in that, right?*

Hope hangs in the air as heavily as the sun hangs high in the sky. Whether that hope is from Mother Nature changing the seasons to warmer weather or hope for a better future, I can't tell.

Every now and then, Ayn walks into the doorway holding up clothes and outfits I may want to bring with me on our *trip* to Labrynthia.

The rest of my maids will not be joining us on our travels in the coming days. At first, I didn't want any of them coming with us, as I'm unsure what we may face. But Ayn insisted. *"It never hurts to have an extra friend in your corner,"* she had said.

"Why are you packing so early? We still have a few more days," I say as she hurries back into the doorway with another one of my pants and tunic sets.

"No one told you?" she asks.

I raise an eyebrow, clearly confused.

She shakes her head in frustration. "We're leaving today, in a few hours."

"But the Brigade?"

"Has already received their orders and are on their way to Labrynthia."

My body shoots up in response. "When did this happen?"

"This morning," she says and goes back to packing my trunks.

Fuming. Now I am fuming. Why didn't Orion share this information with me? I thought after last night, he finally trusted me. Did he only wish for me to satisfy his *needs*?

The water in the tub begins to boil as I slowly lose control of my temper.

I step out of the basin and rush toward my closet to get dressed.

I didn't realize how easy it would be to go from completely enamored with a person to wanting to rip off their face in a matter of seconds. But here I am, ready to send Orion to the cosmos. Prepared to hand him over to the wrath of Dane'er if I could.

Ayn left to the main rooms of the apartment but now returns to my bedchambers with a gown I haven't seen before. It's a strappy thing made of flowing red satin, leaving little to the imagination.

I immediately start shaking my head. "No, no, no. What exactly am I to accomplish in that thing?" I ask in defiance.

There is no way I will be putting that dress on—which is too generous a word for what it really is.

"You still need to play the part, Raya," she says unflinchingly, expecting and deflecting my rejection with ease. "I need you to try it on to make sure it fits. I thought I would have a few more days to make alterations, but it seems we will need to work with what we've got."

"No." I leave no room for a response as I step into a pair of pants, pull a tunic over my head, then race to Orion's quarters. *Absolutely not.*

The palace halls are hauntingly empty. Just as I have dismissed my maids, Orion has dismissed most of his staff. The Black Brigade that filled these halls not only a day ago have taken their laughs and tales with them, leaving just as quickly as they arrived.

Before I know it, I'm standing in front of the prince's door, which opens before I even have a chance to knock or barge my way through.

Orion isn't shocked in the slightest to see me. In fact, he looks relieved.

He motions for me to come inside, dismissing the guards in his parlor. Samson hangs behind, but one look from Orion has him sauntering out the door as well.

He sends me a soft smile, one strained with his storming thoughts. His stance is rigid, barely moving a muscle.

Something has happened between the moment he left this morning and now. Something that brings the possibility of death too close for comfort. All notion of anger from being left in the dark washes away.

"What happened?" I ask.

"Someone has relayed my plans to my father."

I take a step back, unsure If I heard his words correctly. "Your father knows?"

He nods. "To my knowledge, he doesn't know about the treaty, the meeting that took place with Sarana. Only that I claimed you in order to gain an advantage over him. If he knew the rest, he would've marched an army to our front doors by now."

"Who would have turned on you?"

He looks at me, eyes grave and dark. "Mavre."

Words echo in my mind. Words I thought were flames of dissent.

"There is no way he will ever win."

Dissent, yes. But not from the king. From Orion. That night of the Solstice Ball, Mavre was turning away from Orion's cause and compelling another to do the same.

"Not with the army he has risen. More like a band of misfits than anything else."

The Brigade. He was talking about the Brigade.

My eyes grow wide as the realization settles.

"What is it?" he asks.

So I tell him about the night of the winter solstice. When I overheard Mavre and his companion in the gardens. The words I thought were trying to recruit others to join whatever plot of rebellion was brewing.

"I'm sorry," I say when I'm finally finished. "I should have told you about this sooner."

"It's not your fault." He runs his hands through his hair before turning to stand in front of the window. "I had a feeling he was having doubts for a while now. But it would have been riskier to let him go. We were too far into this. It's why I stopped telling him things, why I kept most parts of the plan to myself."

"Is that why you sent the Brigade ahead?" I ask.

"Yes, Mavre doesn't know I called upon them now. I didn't want them here when he arrived. I don't want any of us here when he arrives."

"So what's the plan?"

He's not facing me, staring out the window, gears grinding in his head. Wondering if he should divulge his plans to me.

"Ori." I walk up behind him, placing my hand on top of his and squeezing.

His thumb grazes softly over my fingers.

"You can trust me," I whisper.

His mind finally relents, shoulders and posture relax as he finally gives in to the wheeling thoughts of his mind.

He turns around to face me, softly tucking a stray twisting curl behind my ear. His eyes bore into mine.

Whatever validation he was looking for, he must have found it. He unravels the plan before me, a roadmap of what's to come. Blueprints of the king's castle emerge in my mind as I analyze every detail, ensuring every hole and pitfall has a fallback plan.

When he's finally through, I can't help but smile.

This plan is madness, but it just might be mad enough to work. Giggles of excitement escape me, but the joy doesn't last long. Not when shouting voices float from the palace grounds and an explosion of essence blasts through the windows, throwing us against the far wall.

We regain our stances as quickly as we can and tunnel the air around us, creating a shield of wind. More explosions rock the foundation, but our shield holds, protecting us from most of the shattering glass and splintering wood.

"I have this, Orion. Burn the plans and hide the treaty," I say.

He catches my gaze for a moment before nodding.

Bracing myself for his departure, I increase the power behind my air shield. Without my enhancer cuffs and the full use of my powers, my veil only works for me. Using my Elemental gifts is my only option.

Before he turns away, he waves his hand over my diminishing cuff. The rest of the runes deactivate, and my essence rushes back to me in a surge of power. The surge reinforces the wall of protection around us, and relief washes over me at the feel of my power fully returned.

"You'll need all your abilities for what's to come," he says, pecking his lips against my cheek, then getting to work.

The shouting is louder than before, and the sound of clanging metal joins the fray outside. Boots thud in the hall just beyond the room as Orion's guards race to join the fight.

I glance back at Orion and see him peering out one of the windows still intact to catch a glimpse at our attackers, although we both have a clue already.

"Shit," he hisses, his lips twisting into a snarl. "It seems my father didn't want to wait for us to go to him after all. We have to leave. Now." He pulls on my arm, tugging me away from my defensive position facing the blown-out windows and door.

"But what about Ayn and Samson?" I do my best to free myself of his grip. To run toward the door, as foolish as it may be, but he pulls me away, deeper into the room.

"They have their orders."

"But—" I protest, and he fixes me with a stern glare.

"They will be fine," he grits out, then focuses his attention on the wall next to his large bed, his hands making the intricate movements to activate whatever hidden runes are embedded into the stones.

As he works to unlock our escape, I run back to his desk to quickly scribble out a note. With my power fully returned,

I transport the message away, hoping it reaches Leigh and Dessy in time.

I return to his side just as he places his palms on the stone surface, and a part of the wall pushes in to reveal a secret passageway.

When he turns to me, his expression is severe, but his words are calm as he cradles my cheeks in his palms. "I know you worry for them; I worry too. But we had a plan in place in case something like this happened, and they will do whatever they can to follow through. Now we need to do the same."

With those words, his lips meet mine in a brash kiss filled with fear. The kiss only lasts a moment, all the time we can afford, before he takes my hand and leads me into the dark passage. He closes the stone door, letting the runes lock back into place.

In the palm of my hand, a ball of flame sparks to life, lighting our way down the winding stone stairwell. Minutes feel like hours as we make our way through the abandoned pathways in the belly of the palace, until light from the outside world bleeds into the tunnel. But when we exit the passageway, we're not alone, and our company is far from friendly.

King Mattias and his men stand around us, circling us completely. There's nowhere else for us to go, and the weight of defeat barrels into me.

"Is *this* part of the plan, Orion?" I whisper as I shift my weight, readying myself for a fight.

His only answer is the tightening of his lips into a thin line.

"Father. Is there any particular reason for your less than pleasant visit?" Orion asks, hands splayed at his side and ready to strike.

"Don't play me for a fool, boy. You think you may be able to sway loyalty, but *I* will always command it."

As I look around the field at the surrounding guards and soldiers, I see Mavre's scheming face among the crowd.

"You are one sad sack of shit, Mavre," I spit at him.

His face barely shifts my way as he says, "That may be true, but look where I am and where you are. At least *I'm* on the winning side."

"But not the right one," I shoot back.

As soon as the words leave my mouth, a hand twists at my throat. I attempt to claw at whoever has me in their grip but end up swatting air as the invisible talons tighten. I look toward the king. His fist is raised and a rune glows brightly on his sleeve.

I try to summon my essence, any bit of it, but my power doesn't respond. I look to the ground around us and see a shimmering film surrounding Orion and me. They've trapped us in a ring that diminishes our abilities.

Orion is yelling beside me, trying his best to help me breathe as I fight unconsciousness. My limbs fail, and he catches me as I fall.

"Release her! You'll kill her!" He pleads to his father.

His features begin to blur and ebb into the surroundings.

"Oh, trust me, I don't plan on killing her yet," Mattias croons. "Not when I've gone through the trouble of securing her a beautiful gift."

And with those words and one last glimpse of hysteria on Orion's face, I fade into darkness.

THIRTY-TWO

The ground is cool and damp beneath my cheek. A blitz of essence whirls in the air around me, the power metallic and electrifying on my tongue.

I'm not alone. Some distance away, chains rattle and tug. Whoever's being held captive, Orion I assume, fights to be free. His begging cries are muffled by something covering his mouth.

It takes a moment for my eyes to adjust to the dim lighting, my temple throbbing as the magic of runes and essence clouds my mind.

Where are we? And how did everything go so fucking wrong?

Boots thud against the stone floor, and a liquid film over the surface splashes as the figure approaches. A hand grips the back of my neck, squeezing painfully as they lift me from the ground. With their touch, my mind unscrambles, and my vision clears. Mattias's dark eyes gleam at me with the closest thing to joy he can accomplish.

"Oh good, you're awake," he says through a sniveling

smile. "And just in time to see my demonstration." With a sneer, he tosses me aside and leaves me scrambling to my knees.

Chains dig into my wrists, binding me to the column at my back. I can't help but watch as he saunters across the room, climbing the few stairs up to the dais. A large block of stone rests at the top, deep grooves etched along its side. Panic overcomes me as my mind races back to my days of torture with the king, and it's like I never left.

But this room isn't merely a torture chamber; it's a place for rituals. The liquid on the ground? Blood.

My stomach roils at the realization.

To the left, Orion stands in chains, fighting and screaming to no avail against the restraints and bit in his mouth. Pure terror blazes in his eyes as he glances between me, his father, and across from him.

I follow his line of sight, and it feels as though I've been sucker punched in the gut. The air around me too thick, too hard to breathe.

Sarana. My queen. My king. Promithia herself.

She stands on the wall opposite Orion with identical chains wrapped around her wrists and ankles. A bruise glistens under her eye, and a trail of blood trickles down her face, a thick cut slashed across her forehead.

I vaguely remember the clearing when Orion and I thought we made it out of the palace, the ring of diminishing runes around us, and Mattias… promising a surprise for me.

Sarana is my gift. He wanted me to find her here. He wanted us to see that he still has a semblance of control. That he knows all.

"You fucking bastard!" I thrash against my chains with all my might, trying desperately to free myself. To run to her aid. To free us all and end this madness once and for all.

But I can't. Too weak from the spell of essence and runes my mind was under. Something either in this room or in these chains is blocking me from accessing my powers yet again.

"Guards!" Mattias ignores me, that maniacal fucking grin still plastered on his scarred face.

I want to smack it off him. To peel back the layers of his malice until there's nothing left but his bones.

From the door behind him, the guards drag a writhing woman covered in grime. Her clothes are tattered and worn, but I can still see the cloud and lightning bolt embroidered on her sleeve, the emblem of Senna torn in half on the left breast of what used to be her tunic. The three stars above it that denote her rank.

"Breena? Breena!" My words are pained as I take in the state of my friend.

She's one of the officers who was taken during the battle before my capture. She's been here, alive, all this time? The others too? And what have I been doing? Playing house with my enemy.

"Let her go!" I'm a writhing mess now, tears streaming down my face as I slam against the chains restraining me.

With every tug and pull, the manacles dig into my skin, and something warm drips down my wrists and over my fists. I'm breaking skin with my struggle, but I don't care.

I watch in horror as Mattias brings her onto the stone slab, lying her down. Panic sets into Breena's eyes as she locks her gaze on mine.

"May we meet again." She mouths the parting words to me.

She knows this is the end for her. I don't want to respond, but I cannot deny her this. I will not.

"May the spirits guide us home," I mouth back, unable to

accept her fate but resigned to the fact that there's nothing I can do to stop whatever is coming next.

The mad king lies his hands flat on the table, speaking in the old language. Slowly, the runes etched into the stone come to life in a sickening red hue. Needle-like blades jut from the surface, pricking deep along her body, and blood pours out, dripping down the table and filling the deeply carved runes with crimson red.

With a knife, he carves runes into Breena's skin, and her cries echo across the stone walls. He slices the blade over his palm and allows his own blood to drip into the wounds, never letting up his chant in the ancient language of the spirits.

In the right hands, blüdcraft and runebinding can be used for good. To search through familial genealogy and detect potential illnesses. To heal sicknesses that often seem incurable. To help enhance one's ability in a more permanent way, within reason. But this is the horrifying result of the practice being used with malice. When the person behind the intent only wishes to cause harm, destruction, pain. Using it to further their agenda.

The blood-filled runes blaze to life with flame, brightening the room. Breena's cries turn into blood-curdling screams as the flames lick across her skin. Slowly, her skin turns to ash, flying off in flakes into the air, metamorphosis following in the path of the flames. The person I once knew, the soldier I had trained with, fades away, and when the flames are gone, a monster remains. One with thick black scales and long, razor-sharp teeth. Its lanky limbs are lined with deadly muscles and claws tipped as sharp as blades.

The beast rises from the table, and a sick understanding washes over me.

I flick my eyes to Orion, and he seems to make the same conclusion I have. The monster that attacked us in Thestras? It looked just like this one. Only now it's stronger and has giant wings jutting from its back.

With steady feet, the figure that used to be Breena—perhaps it still is—rises onto its haunches and sits perched next to the bloody ritual slab.

"Stay," Mattias commands.

She growls, wings twitching with agitation, but obeys the command given.

This is what he's been doing to my comrades? My people?

Then, with dark eyes, he turns his attention to me.

I'm next.

Before the thought has a chance to register, guards are at my side, dragging me by my shackles to the front of the room. With every step they take, I thrash and struggle in their grip. Mattias's eyes seem to delight in the sight, in watching me struggle as I'm dragged to my doom.

Orion and Sarana wreak havoc in their chains, mostly upon themselves as their wrists are rubbed raw, gargling muffled screams accompanying their struggles.

I kick and scratch and buck and do everything I can to loosen the guards' grips on me, but it's no use. Their hold remains strong as they heave my thrashing limbs onto the slab. Every part of my being wants to keep fighting, but the moment my back meets the cool stone of the altar, my whole body relaxes and succumbs to the lull of whatever charm is laced in its runes.

As they walk to whatever dark hole they came from, the guards remove the bits from Orion and Sarana's mouths, allowing their gruff cries to echo throughout the dank chamber.

"Are you out of your mind, Father?!" Orion screams.

"This is insane. Forcing people to… changing them into your slaves, into monsters?!"

"Orion, I'd hardly call them people." Mattias's voice is smooth and calm. Matter of fact.

"This is against the accords. The Council of Nations will—"

"Will what, boy? They won't do a damn thing when we've won this war once and for all." In a moment, Mattias steps through time and space and reappears mere inches away from Orion. "Now let this serve as a lesson to you. Heir or not, you do not take what is not yours and never give away your heart. That's where your weakness lies."

"You are a monster," Orion says.

"And you, my boy, are a damned fool." Mattias's tone is unforgiving as he turns his back on Orion and returns to the dais.

"Why are you doing this?" Sarana asks from where she stands. Voice shaky as each word leaves her mouth. She's growing weaker, but I can sense the defiance emanating from her. "You have me, you've already won."

Mattias ignores her, looking down at me from above, head cocked to the side as he inspects my face. Looking for what? I'm not sure.

He drags his index finger along the ridge of my chin. "The mutts are my infantry, but you will be something so much more, Raya."

He places his hands on the table once more, reciting the ancient words that mean my doom. Those thin blades dig into the skin along my back, and whatever calming lull that paralyzed me before comes undone. A soul-shattering shriek rips from my body as blood pours from the wounds, filling the grooves in the stone with thick crimson.

This is what's fair, isn't it? This gruesome death and end

for me? Repaying the blood I have spilled with blood of my own? The crimson heir, Orion called me. Now I'm meeting an end befitting of the title.

"Take me!" Sarana screams, voice breaking with her plea. "Take me instead!"

"Oh no, Your Majesty. You will have a front-row seat to the destruction of your people. You will watch as the woman you love destroys your home, and then when all is done, she will destroy you."

This warrants another roar from Orion, who is now yanking on the chains with all his might.

With a thin blade, Mattias slices my tunic open, then gets to work carving the runes into my torso, a deep burning following in the blade's wake. Just when I think he's about to slice his palm, as he did with Breena, he draws a small vial from his coat pocket instead. The glass is filled with a dark liquid the consistency of blood, but the color is too dark, near black instead of crimson.

He drips the liquid into the runes etched into my body, and a new wave of searing pain spreads through me, blurring my vision as the runeflames lick across my skin. My screams mix with the roars from Orion and Sarana and echo around the chamber.

Through the haze of pain and blood loss, something stirs from deep within. Despite the flames that grow higher, my skin does not turn to ash. Black flames attempt to spread from the runes on my torso, but for every inch they garner, they draw back by two more. I can't physically fight what is happening—the blades hold me in place—but my body *is*.

A figure, as silver as stars, flickers in the corner of my vision, and I turn my head slightly to see who approaches. The figure is blurry at first, but as it draws nearer, I realize it's a woman. Her features are ancient and gaunt, like the spirits who came before us, and a power thrums around her that is not of this world.

"Who are you?" I ask, but my lips don't move. Is she a Reader too?

I'm here to help, she says, her voice a smooth melody drowning out the chorus of screams.

How can you help me?

She smiles at that but doesn't respond. Instead, she reaches out her hand, and I somehow find the strength through the pain to do the same.

The moment her fingers touch mine, a force erupts from my core. A blast that sends Mattias and his creature flying into the cavern walls. The shackles at my wrists come undone, and my power rushes back to me in full force. With Mattias away from the altar, the ritualistic words suspend, causing the flames to die out and the blades in my back to disappear.

Something about that woman, the ghost of the spirit who somehow saved me, reminds me I am not alone.

Unable to move, still paralyzed with pain, I turn my focus inward, searching for the pathway I know is there. Then I feel the warmth, the welcoming door that connects me to Orion. With a shove, I open it wide, overpowering whatever runes are laid within his manacles.

Orion doesn't miss a beat. Using the surge of power I flood into him, he removes the shackles and transports to his father's side. Mattias doesn't have time to react, still recovering from the force of being blown into the wall, when Orion wraps his arms around him and transports them both away.

Fighting erupts on the other end of the chamber, and before I know it, Ayn and Samson step into view, fending off the king's guards one swipe of a blade at a time. But they're not alone. Fighting by their side is Loren, the brigadier I was training with in Thestras. And beside her is Xander, the fearsome commander of the Black Brigade.

A menacing snarl sounds from beside me. Without its master to hold the reins, the winged monster rises to its full, menacing height, shaking off its tumble into the wall and setting its snakelike eyes on me.

Despite the pain thrumming through my entire being, I heave myself over the edge of the stone slab, rolling a few steps away from the dais and down the short stairs at the front of it.

As I lift myself onto my elbows, Ayn rushes to my aid, but I shake my head. "No. Help Sarana." The words are strained as they leave my mouth.

With a nod, she concedes.

The beast behind me lets out a bellowing roar, fluttering its wings in agitation as it watches its prey scurry away.

Down to the last guard, Samson deals with him while Xander turns my way, eyes focused on the monster currently stalking toward me. He disappears from view as I crawl away from the dais, dragging myself across the blood-slicked floor. But I don't make it far. Whatever energy I had that got me here is quickly fading, and the gargled cries of the beast are the last thing I hear before I succumb to the pain that blinds me.

THIRTY-THREE

"Will she be all right?" Sarana's stern voice says above me, hardened by the evil Mattias has put her through. But a softness rounds out the edges of her tone.

She's worried. Which means I must look like a wreck.

"She'll be fine, just needs a bit more healing." Ayn's words are clipped in concentration.

Ayn? What is she doing here? My memories from the moments before flood to me in bits and spurts.

"Well hurry it up, then. We need to move out of here, now."

I don't recognize the deep timbre of this person's voice, but the rich tones of his words nestle deep within my bones. A comfort I don't expect despite his brash tone.

"I'm going as fast as I can, Xander," Ayn says through gritted teeth. "Not many people knew about this place, given Mattias's secrecy of what he was doing. Besides, now that Orion transported them both to the War Room, the guards aren't going to come down here. We should be safe." Ayn's voice is as calm as a smooth wind.

She's in her element. I can almost hear the gears grinding away as her mind re-maps the plan that has gone terribly awry.

"Well, I don't know about you," I croak, "but I don't feel safe anywhere in this wretched place."

My eyelids flutter open to find all three of them staring down at me.

Three? There should be five.

"Where's Samson and Loren?" I ask, slight panic lacing my voice.

"They're fine, on their way to meet the Brigade," Ayn says, healing the last of the wounds on my abdomen.

"How long have I been out?" I strain to lift myself into a seated position.

Ayn swiftly comes to my aid, sitting me upright and helping me scoot back to lean against the column.

My muscles are screaming, but thanks to Ayn's work, I'm no longer bleeding out.

"Only a few minutes," Sarana answers from beside me, running a comforting hand along my arm.

As each second passes, the zip of my energy restores.

The rigid set of her expression tells me she's still not happy with me. Before she has a chance to object, I pull her into an embrace. She's shaking, and though she resists at first, it only takes a moment for her to wrap her arms around me.

"Sarana?" I break free from her grasp to check her face. The gash on her forehead is already healed, thanks to Ayn. "Why are you here? How did he—?"

"Right after we met in Demiitsch, King Mattias's men sieged our ships on our way back to Promithia." Her voice is strained, telling so much more of the pain he brought upon her.

My heart cracks at the sound.

Dammit, he knew. Even then, he knew.

"Do the rest of the High Court of Generals know of your capture?"

She shakes her head. "I'm not expected back for another day or two. So I doubt they've raised any alarms."

"Don't worry, Sarana. We will get you out of here," I say, taking her hands in mine, my thumb tracing over the diminishing rune bracelet still wrapped around her wrist.

A twisted laugh sounds from deep within her. One with no joy or life. A laugh that sounds like death and defeat.

"Raya… all is lost. We've trusted a prince with no power, no stance. No chance. This brave rescue will be for naught." She gives an apologetic grimace to Ayn and Xander.

But all I can do is shake my head as my mind pieces together the plan I'm sure Orion and the rest of the team have already figured out.

I comb through the details of Orion's original strategy. Ayn mentioned that Orion brought his father to the War Room. If that's the case, then it's only a matter of time until the challenge begins, and we must be ready when it does.

"We won't be here for much longer, Sarana, so you must leave before it starts." The words leave my mouth in shaky breaths as I climb to my feet. "Xander, can you remove the rune bracelet from her wrist?"

The brooding commander of the Black Brigade has been sitting on the steps of the dais, surrounded by chunks of the monster he destroyed protecting me. I swallow down my nausea at the sight of the remains of what used to be a dear friend.

Without hesitation, he nods, and it only takes him a

moment to unravel the woven tendrils of power that lie within the cuff on Sarana's wrist. In an instant, the warmth of her essence floods back to her. Life restored to her being and a ring of gold returns to her irises.

With a wave of my hand, the rest of the sconces blaze to life with light, the flames working quickly to warm the space.

"How are you using your essence?" Sarana asks, watching my every move. "You wear a bracelet as well."

"The prince unraveled the runes on my cuff in Thestras." I glide my bracelet off my wrist with ease and toss it to the ground. "I guess the king and his guards didn't realize it was deactivated before throwing me into the manacles. But those were laced with diminishing runes too, and then the altar? My powers were useless."

"Then how were you able to send that blast into Mattias and the beast?" she asks pointedly, a bit of that venom from our fight in Demiitsch lacing her words.

"I honestly don't know, Sarana," I say, trying to make sense of those last few moments on the altar. "One minute, all I felt was blinding pain, and the next, that woman was there saying she wanted to help me."

"There was no woman there," Sarana says at the same time Xander asks, "What woman?"

Xander whips his head around to face me. He's standing now, his height looming over me, and it's the first time I can really get a good look at him without the fog of pain or distance of a training ring.

I tip my head back just a bit to reach his bright silver eyes, nearly glowing in this dim chamber. His deep brown skin is glistening with sweat from the exertion of fighting, his hair cropped in short coils atop his head, the sides fading to a close shave. His chiseled features are striking and beautiful, and… what did he just say?

"Who did you see?" he asks again.

Oh, right.

"She was more spirit than human, which is impossible. But she said she wanted to help me. When our hands touched, the blast erupted. It was probably a ghost or my imagination. Perhaps I silohed essence and didn't realize?"

He shares a solemn glance with Ayn before nodding, then sits back on the step.

I get a strange sense they're hiding something, but there's no time to ask questions, not when a battle is looming over our heads.

"Ayn, do you have time to escort Sarana to the passageway out of the castle?" I ask, eyes pleading.

"Yes, of course," she says, her red braid gleaming in the dim lighting as she spins away, but I stop her, pulling her into a deep hug.

She's shocked at first, but then her arms relax around me.

"Thank you," I whisper into her ear. "For saving me, for being willing to help my queen."

"You are my friend, Raya. No matter what happens, know I am always on your side." She pulls away, gripping my hands in hers as her green eyes bore into mine.

With a squeeze, she turns toward my queen, who is now standing tall. Sarana's eyes scan to me in a panic, unsure.

I take a step toward her. "There is a clearing beyond the wards," I explain. "You will be able to transport home if you have the strength. If not, wait there, and safety will find you."

"What are you going to do?" she asks. Though her voice isn't filled with worry, the anger in her eyes flickers ever so slightly.

"I will do what I do best," I say with a half-smile.

"Before we leave, I have something for you." Ayn snaps her fingers, and a chest appears at my feet.

"What is this?" I ask.

"A gift from the prince. There's no way in hell he would let you fight without the proper equipment—nor I, for that matter." She nods toward the chest, beckoning me to look at what's inside.

A new set of armor. Glancing down at my tattered tunic, I'm thankful for the change in attire.

The leather pieces are expertly embroidered with runes. The stitching resembles the doublet Orion wore on his birthday. Metal plates coated in black match my signature armor from home. Just from the feel of it, I can tell it's made from tanium steel—a very strong and very rare metal once used to build various types of buildings and structures. It can only be found by excavating ruins of the old world. He must have been planning for this...my participation in this uprising since I was captured. Possibly even before then.

I take a deep breath and start pulling out pieces of the armor. Xander turns around, giving me some privacy as I change into the new set, Ayn helping me when needed.

The leather pants, shoulder, and elbow guards mold comfortably to my body. Bands of runes swirl around my arms and legs, perfectly in line with the contours of my muscles, ready to amplify whatever power I may use. The metal on my chest, back, and arms bends and folds with every movement I make. Boots run thigh high with more black metal and mesh protecting my calves.

I braid back my unruly curls, though not without difficulty with my tangled strands. Ayn is about to assist, but Xander reaches me first, surprising us all.

"May I?" His voice rumbles against my ear.

All I can do is nod.

"Well, aren't you full of surprises?" Ayn huffs, lifting her brows and crossing her arms.

"I have sisters," he responds. The only explanation he deigns to give.

As he delicately weaves the rest of my hair into a series of interwoven braids, I feel a strange sense of comfort in his presence. After a moment, I hand him my leather tie, and he knots the end, returning to his seat on the dais once finished.

Ayn eyes me approvingly. "For all our king's strength, I believe his pride will be his downfall."

"Are you frightened?" I ask.

"Whatever might happen, I've made my peace with it, knowing I'm on the right side of history." She takes a breath and tightens the straps of the bandolier strapped across my chest.

With a nod she turns to leave, checking to ensure the coast is clear as I face Sarana once more.

I pull her into a long embrace, and an uneasy sense of finality lingers in the air around us. No matter the anger that lies between us, my heart still cares for her. I only hope that when I see her again, it will be a new era.

Taking her hand, I place a soft kiss on her wrist. "Goodbye, my Queen."

"Stay alive," she whispers before turning to follow Ayn, disappearing down the dark passageway beyond this cold chamber.

I GRIP my new sword and step far away from Xander to practice a few swings and strikes, getting used to the unworn metal.

He silently watches me, eyes tracking every move I make

before he finally breaks the silence. "What are your thoughts, General of Death?"

"Of my new battle uniform or the events about to occur?" I ask in between swings.

"By the satisfied look on your face, I can guess how you feel about the new armor and sword. I'm asking about the battle to come."

I slide the sword into its sheath, then take a seat by his side. The space between us is smooth and warm, and I ease into the friendly comfort.

"In a normal battle, I know the odds. What's in our favor and what isn't. But this whole plan relies on the will of one person, as opposed to the might of thousands, and I'm just supposed to trust and hope that it will end in our favor. That is not easy for me, especially considering how we got here in the first place."

He takes a moment, pondering his words before responding. "I've been friends with Prince Orion for a long time, have been helping him devise this plan for a better part of the past year now. He could have challenged his father at any point. But it wasn't until he realized you were captured that he really gained the courage to act. It's because of you that we are here."

"But why?" I turn to face him, only to find those silver eyes already locked on me.

"I think you bring him hope." He shrugs while I scoff at the irony.

The Wielder of Death instilling hope? Preposterous.

"Don't look so shocked," he continues. "You do. You bring him hope of the peace this country could have with a proper... treaty." He doesn't dare say the word he wants to. Not wanting to jinx what he hopes will soon become truth. *A proper king.*

"Do you think the rest of this plan will work?" I ask, unsure.

"While things didn't go exactly as predicted, everyone is where they need to be—you're with me, and Orion should be challenging his father any second now. We've made it this far, partly by chance, but I'll take it." Xander's voice is deep and sure when he says, "We just need to be there when all hell breaks loose."

I should be wary around someone new, and I typically am, but being in his presence is… comforting. Like I'm in the company of a long-lost friend who's finally come home, of a person I have known my entire life. It's strange, or at least it should be, but I trust that what he says is true. His faith in Orion. Orion's faith in me.

But there's something strange about the way he speaks about Corath, as if it's not his home.

Just as I'm about to open my mouth to learn more about this comforting stranger, his expression shifts. One second, his silver eyes are on mine. The next, he cocks his head to the side, looking through me instead. His eyes grow distant, as if he is seeing through the lens of someone else.

Then… silence. Not one of sound but of utter stillness courses through the entirety of this chamber and the palace above. It's a heavy thing that presses down on us like a weight. It digs into my skin and skull and mind.

We both shoot to our feet despite the heaviness. Steadying ourselves, readying ourselves for what we know is about to start.

Out of the corner of our eyes, we steal a glance. The only comfort we give each other. No words or nods of confirmation are needed.

Just as Orion warned, a rumbling shakes the stones of the castle. A rattling that is felt throughout the whole of Corath.

The stillness, the killing calm, was Orion's challenge to Mattias. This rumbling is the warning signal to all in the country.

Around us, the wards of the palace come crumbling down as the king, the center of the essence that powers these royal halls, enters the dark abyss with his heir.

The challenge has been accepted.

So begins the Stalemate.

CHAPTER

THIRTY-FOUR

Taking Xander's hand, we transport to the upper levels of the palace. Stepping through space and time, we reappear into a grand room fit for any heir. While the rooms are darker than I would have thought, a stark contrast to Sarana's chambers, I can't say I'm surprised they belong to Orion.

Drapes of deep garnet velvet hide the windows, and the rest of the room is decorated in fabrics of matching jewel tones. The space we're inhabiting may have been made for the heir to dwell, but an overwhelming sense of emptiness rests here. As opposed to Thestras, where life and light are always a staple. Even the land there seems to sing with presence, whereas here it just groans with dread.

Now, a part of the castle once more, we can hear the fighting that inevitably began while we were down below. It's distant. Close enough that we can hear them through the door but far enough away that there are likely no guards nearby, all preoccupied with fighting and bloodshed.

Just to be sure, I use my essence to feel for the minds that may be standing guard. Nothing. Orion warned us that once he and the king entered the Stalemate, they would be encased in a protective dome. But it would be all-out war and chaos as both sides tried to maintain a foothold. As soon as the veiled circle falls, whoever remains victor will either be greeted by further protection of his people or the steel of his enemy. It is our job to ensure we maintain control in the end.

"Ready to travel?" I ask, holding out my hand to take his.

He playfully arches his brow, corners of his lips lifting ever so slightly, then disappears right in front of my eyes.

I'm shocked by the realization that he possesses this ability, *mist-traveling*, and the reminder of how little I actually know about the soldier I'm supposed to trust won't stab me in the back. Despite the shock, I follow suit, joining him in the mists of the Shadows.

Mist-traveling, or traveling for short, allows us to move unseen and undetected by others. Those with essence of the Shadows can access this ability, but few are able to master it.

To visit the Shadow Plane is one thing, but holding oneself in this space is entirely different. The Shadows don't like to have company and work against you, trying to force you out with every step and breath. If, for whatever reason, you can't pull yourself out, they'll swallow you whole. So best not to stay in here too long.

While this ability is useful, I hate the way it makes me feel. Like I'm walking in a daydream. Like a million arms are pulling me this way and that. Like I am something and nothing all at once. The edges of my vision blur to darkness, and reappearing in front of me is Xander, his features muted and dulled by the mists and Shadows, but I can see the smirk still painted on his face as clear as day.

I didn't know you were a Shadow, my mind sends to his.

And now you do, he replies, hand outstretched to the bronzed doorknob.

Our objective: make our way to the king's War Room, where Orion should be. If my memory of the maps and Orion's instructions serve me well, then we are only one floor above and one wing over.

We swiftly move through the doorway and down the halls of the east wing. When we make it to the bridge that connects the east tower to the central building, the zing of clashing blades and clunking armor ruptures through the halls.

Our jogging turns into sprinting, and with every step, the Shadows strain to push me out. I grimace at the sensation of being pulled against my will and curse at the sight of Xander, whose expression is only a calm and focused concentration. No struggling sweat beading down his brown skin or furrowing brows signaling a fight against the Shadow plane. Which means he's either very good at hiding the feeling or he does this often and has trained the Shadows to be comfortable with his presence.

We race across the hall, then down the spiral staircase, flying past the few fighting soldiers as carefully as we can. Despite his height, Xander dances through as if he is one with the wind, a vision of grace.

Down the stairs, we finally enter the long and wide corridor. Black Brigadiers creep their way toward the large doors at the end of the hall—the War Room. Where Orion and Mattias are engaged in a completely different battle all their own.

Xander and I only spare a moment to glance at each other as we duck and spin out of the way of bodies and metal. We give each other a slight nod.

Now. I hear his voice in my mind, a bit strained to my satisfaction.

A grin splays on my lips, one that's met with a vicious sparkle in his eyes. We're released from the Shadows and unleash ourselves upon the chaos ahead.

As I'm thrust into the mortal plane, the vividness of reality comes to life under the brightness of rune and skylights. The clashing of swords against metal rings in my ears, along with the gargled screams of felled soldiers.

I spring into action, propelled forward by the Shadows' eagerness to rid itself of my presence, unsheathing my sword in one second and beheading a King's Guard in the next. Brigadiers around us, worn down by the fighting, find a new sense of urgency and encouragement at the sight of their commander and the Wielder of Death joining them in battle. All cheer with vigor and fright, causing some of the king's soldiers to stumble in response.

"About time you two showed up." Loren's lilting voice floats above the chaos of fighting and cheers in the hall.

Xander and I turn ever so slightly to the sound, never letting up on our defense as we continue to strike down our opponents.

"Someone's mist-traveling abilities are lacking," Xander shouts back in a teasing lilt.

He eases around his familiar companion, face lighting up ever so slightly.

"Oh, shut up." My mouth curls up into a joking sneer. "Lovely to see you again, Loren," I add before the three of us wave off attacks from our enemies.

"Would you three concentrate, please?!" Samson pipes in as his sword pierces the chest of a King's Guard. A spray of blood is splattered on his face, the crimson stark against his pale skin.

And with that, we keep our mouths shut as we focus on our target. The War Room.

From the corner of my eyes, I can see Xander grinning, matching my own fearsome expression. If he's anything like me, he wears the grin of death to appear ruthless, to invoke a bit of fear in his enemies.

Great minds do think alike. His voice purrs in my head. He must have found a small crack in my veil to whisper his way in. *Behind you.*

I turn, ducking low and spinning around toward my foe, driving my sword up as I do so. My blade connects with the soldier's abdomen as Xander swings and beheads the man from above.

As I rise, my companions and the rest of the Brigadiers look to me as I take my stance. With nothing but a nod, they fall into a pointed formation with me at its apex. Xander, Loren, and Samson stand by my side. Step by step, we become a formidable force making our way toward the War Room.

While I know Xander's presence has much to do with the warriors standing at my back, it is because of my strength that these soldiers follow my lead as well. They follow into the belly of the lion's den, not because of the overshadowing figure of my father that always commanded a room and a battlefield, but of the unrestricted power that flows through my veins.

They trust me and my abilities to lead them all into this moment of violence in hopes that days of peace will follow.

And my father would be proud of this moment and my unwavering resolve to persevere and stay true to my beliefs. My eyes water and sting at the thought, but I clear away any notion of emotional upheaval. Not when so much is at stake with this final stand.

One last battle to end the war.

In a matter of minutes, we make it to the large doors. With the power of my wind, flame, and added force from the rune enhancers stitched into the palm of my glove, the doors shatter and explode into the room.

The wood splinters into a thousand pieces, the larger ones finding their marks through many of the king's soldiers. Despite the explosion, the rest of the guards, still well enough to fight, are reforming their defensive positions. We regain our own stances and begin the charge.

The circle, we need to get close to the circle, I whisper to Xander.

You don't need to remind me. I am well aware of the plan.

I send him a mental image of me flipping him off, to which he only replies with a rumble of a laugh.

It's strange to be bantering as though we're old friends. But the feeling I get from his voice grazing against the outskirts of my mind is that of safety and trust, even though I barely know the man.

Strange indeed, I think again as I deflect a soldier's swipe at my head. I gather a swell of air around me, aiming where the soldier stands ahead of me. He stumbles back, and I lunge forward, plunging my sword into his neck. Blood, red and hot, spurts down his armor.

"Can't you just suck the air out of their lungs and call it a day?" Samson calls from a few paces over.

"What's the matter, not having any fun?" Loren chides with a smirk.

With blood splattered on her face and crimson dying her silver hair, she looks every bit the fearsome warrior she is.

I concentrate on clearing a path for the soldiers marching behind us before responding, "If we were on a proper battlefield, perhaps. But in these close quarters and my essence a bit out of practice, I don't want to risk killing us all."

Samson simply nods in reply. "Fine, fighting it is."

Use your essence, Shadowman, I whisper to Xander, grinning.

Who's to say I haven't been? Just as he replies, he ripples into the Shadows, leaving a trail of dead king's men in his path, getting closer and closer to the circle where Orion and Mattias stand.

Following the path Xander laid for us, we make our way deeper into the room.

I see the rippling in the air, and another smile spreads on my face, ready to greet Xander upon his return from the Shadows. *Hmmm, I thought he'd be farther ahead.*

An unease overcomes my senses, but much too late as I'm greeted by a mountain of a man ripping through the Shadows.

My grin is smacked clean off my face as I'm thrown into the far wall.

I crumble to the floor, sharp pain shooting through my lungs with every breath I take. The taste of iron pools in my mouth, but before I can spit the warm liquid out, I'm lifted by the mountain, punched in the gut, then thrown to the ground again. I roll, and amid my pain, I try my best to control the direction of where I land so I'm closer to the circle of protection. To the massive knight, it was the natural course of the tumble he forced me into.

I ignore the yelling of my ribs and lungs and focus all my energy and essence into defense, hoping I'm strong enough to overpower him.

Spitting blood onto the ground, I pull myself into a fighting stance. The tangy copper liquid sits on my tongue, pooling down my chin. Taking a better look, I realize this mountain isn't some random brute in the service of the king.

He is *the* brute. The one with black sharpened teeth. The one who slayed my father right before my eyes. Only now he's taller, muscles bulging beyond the norm. A web of black veins creeps under his skin, and his eyes are completely red, pupils nowhere to be found.

This is what Mattias had planned for me?

Rage fills my core as Tyrannis's malice-stricken eyes stare me down with longing. He wants my death on his hands. *What a glory that would be*, I can almost hear him say.

Unsheathing a blade that was hidden in the leg of my boot, I hold two weapons. A sword in my right, the long dagger in my left.

I ready myself to strike.

He looks at me with an air of indifference. "I thought I might finish you without my weapons," he says with a snarl, his deep voice rumbling in the air around me. "But since you seem to be a nuisance, I guess I'll have to use them. Pity we couldn't play a bit longer." He unsheathes his own sword, a massive thing that looks to be as large as he is.

"Looks like you've had a growth spurt," I spit through gritted teeth, blood spattering out with my words.

"The king gifted me with some *enhancements*." The words drawl out of his mouth with sickening arrogance. "It took us so long to find the right combination of essence and runes. Too bad most of your soldiers died in the testing, except for the mutts. To think, after breaking them all, we could have had a small army. Small but all powerful. This could have been you too."

I tighten my grip on my blades and gather my strength. "It doesn't matter how strong you think you are, nothing will save you."

"Oh, Raya, that is where you're wrong." With the freeing hiss of those words, the serpent strikes the lion.

I WEAVE between my essence and swordplay like they are one and the same. A wicked dance of death and fury.

Where Tyrannis strikes, I block with both blade and wind. Where I attack, he parries with flame.

I try my best to reinforce my veil, but I need to start thinking of another way around him. He seems to have memorized my moves, just as I remembered his habits from months of studying him before our first brawl.

Stop thinking, I hear Xander whisper into my mind. Despite my surprise to hear his voice, I don't falter or stumble. *Your thoughts consume you. Look within and let the essence flow.*

Xander is right. I take a deep breath to center my being. Calm my nerves. Then a thought comes hurling forward. He's expecting me to fail against him. So what if I give him just that?

Throwing my vow to kill him slowly out the door, I switch gears, allowing his next blow to knock the dagger out of my left hand.

I parry a few more strikes before I take another blow to the gut. Whichever ribs evaded damage before have definitely cracked under his pressure now. Grimacing and swallowing my cries of pain, I stumble back, stars flashing across my vision.

My sight clears in time for me to see him shifting his feet. A tell for when he's about to swing high. I duck low, gathering a swell of air behind me to slide on my knees, swiping his thighs with my blade. He roars in anger. The cuts are deep, but with the modifications to his body, I've only sliced through skin, not muscle or tendons.

During his moment of confusion, I rise on the other side of him and swiftly come down on the arm holding his sword, controlling the air above to increase the pressure of my downward force.

Not as smooth a cut as I would like, his skin and bone now thicker and harder than a normal human's anatomy, but it does the job. His sword, hand still clutching the hilt, falls to the ground.

This time, his roar of pain pierces my ears. A rune stitched into the back of his leathers glows a bright amber. I recognize the rune and the power it enhances—veil.

With the force of his veil pushing out, I'm thrown back. I crash into the circle of protection and am forced down to the ground with a shock. My sword and dagger clatter to the ground next to where I lie.

Rallying the air back into my already very damaged lungs, I roll on my side only to be met with a searing pain from my shoulder. The joint is completely dislocated from the socket. Stars cloud my vision, but before I can roll onto my other arm to lift myself up, Tyrannis lifts me by the throat, feet dangling above the ground.

"General of Death," he says with venom, his dark eyes lifeless as they gaze into mine. "It's time to meet yours."

While I strain for air, blood vessels surely popping in my eyes, he watches what he hopes will be my last breath.

Tyrannis might have ended the life of the man who taught me all I know, of the man who did all he could to ensure our family's legacy and the survival of our line. But my father's death will not be in vain, and his retribution will be assured with a new dawn at hand.

I flick a hidden knife from my sleeve. His eyes go wide with confusion, but they quickly grow slick with fear as I allow all the anger and grief and pain from the loss of my father to consume me.

With a slam of my palm to his neck, the dagger, long and sharp, digs deep into his throat.

I think it's time you met yours, I send into his mind.

His grip around my throat slackens, and crimson liquid pools over his lips.

Xander swoops in, catching me and setting me aside just as I'm about to be crushed by Tyrannis's massive frame. His weight drops with a dense thud as he lies face down in the growing pool of his blood.

"Are you all right?" he says, no longer bothering with speaking mind-to-mind.

"I'm fine," I say, strained. "Just a few—" I'm cut off by my own screams.

Xander took my words as distraction enough to set my shoulder back in place. He rips a strip from the bit of tunic that's untucked from his leathers and uses it as a sling for my arm.

"You could've warned me!" I yell, furious.

"It would've hurt more if I did that."

He helps me back to my shaky feet, sword heavy in my right hand. With the rest of the prince's troops still fighting off the dwindling soldiers of the king, we finally have a stronghold in front of the circle of protection.

I just hope that Orion pulls through, and quickly. The last thing we need is for an army to make it here before we can truly win.

Lightheaded, in pain, and down an arm, I take my stance

in front of the dome with Loren, Samson, and Xander at my side. The few soldiers who make it past the lines of Brigadiers are swiftly felled by our blades. I'm swift, well, as swift as one can be when they're injured.

Risking a glance, I look at the prince and king behind me. They stand facing each other, eyes milky white, a filmy glaze over their irises and pupils.

For a moment, I wonder what it's like in the abyss. Do they see each other and know who they're fighting? Or is it a manipulation of memories, twisting and distorting truths with lies until the other one caves?

I steal one more glance at Orion, his dark waves against his forehead. His olive skin, glistening in the glimmer of the dome above him, taut around his arms. Whatever struggle he faces in the abyss, his physical body tries to fight it.

It was only for a moment, but I should have known—I do know—what a few stolen seconds in the middle of battle can cost you.

Just as I'm about to turn and ready my stance again, time seems to still as I hear someone shout from behind me.

Xander? I think. *Why is he screaming my name?*

Then I feel the burning, the numbing pain clouded by adrenaline.

Protruding through my body is a foreign blade. The tip sticks out a few inches, and the hilt digs into my back.

With the last of my strength, I reach with the wind of my essence to size up the soldier who owns the short sword now nestled into my torso, likely piercing my heart. Once I find the body part I'm looking for, I allow the wind to twist with such force that, even through the howling, you cannot ignore the pop of breaking bone it causes.

The soldier falls behind me as someone else takes his

place. Someone who feels like safety. Someone I think I can trust.

Just hold on, Raya, he speaks into my mind in comforting lilts. *Just hold on, amina celas.*

I don't understand those last two words, and I don't have the strength to ask as I fall to the ground. Still looking at Orion and wishing we had just a little more time, I notice another figure falling out of the corner of my eyes.

My body hits the ground at the same time he does.

Xander kneels behind me, keeping me upright, hoping the dagger still inside me will stop the blood flow. It doesn't matter if it's left in or pried out, I am bleeding either way, and my heart won't last much longer.

The atmosphere changes from panic to peace as two rumbles course through the land, signaling the end of the Stalemate. The fighting in the large War Room ceases as everyone turns to bear witness to their king.

I watch through blurred vision as Orion stumbles out of his frozen state with grace. He reaches down and takes the crown from his fallen father's head. Placing it on his own, he turns to face his soldiers. His warriors.

Everyone in the room—the Brigadiers, along with the few of Mattias's guardsmen who remain, realizing they have lost —drops to one knee. Their heads hang low.

The last thing I see before I succumb to the darkness is Orion's panicked eyes as they lock onto mine and my blood pooling around his feet.

THIRTY-FIVE

I open my eyes to find myself in a room of all white. Not a room. An ocean. A sea. An abyss.

Strange. The last time I was here, this place was dark. Black as the deepest night, with not even a speck of starlight to guide my way.

But here, in this place of nothingness, I can see myself. My hands, my feet, my body wrapped in white cloth I do not recognize.

Bare feet pad behind me. I would be alarmed if I didn't know who it was by the way she favors her left foot, the long stride between steps, and the warm power radiating from her.

"Even in death, you must torture me," I say with a smile.

"You aren't dead, Raya," Sarana replies.

I always forget she has this ability. Dreamwalking. A rare power gifted to her from the spirits to travel into a person's mind. Not to manipulate what they perceive, but to meet them wherever they may be in the realm of sleep.

She's finally behind me, her breath warm on the spot just

below my ear. I turn to face her, expecting to find anger in her eyes, but only find worry in them instead.

"How bad is it?" I ask, afraid to know the truth.

The corners of her lips turn up into a grimace that's supposed to be a smile as she places her hand on my cheek. Her warmth radiates through me. "You are healing, but we almost lost you."

The way she says "almost" makes me believe that's a lie. Why she thinks she needs to protect me from the truth, I don't know.

"Come now. That look on your face tells me I didn't entirely make it," I say, trying to be as lighthearted as I can about dying. I mean, what can I do now if it's already happened? "I'm surprised Orion hasn't pulled me back yet," I add in a snort. Half joking. Half not.

A pained look crosses her face. "He tried. But the Stalemate drained him. He could only stop the bleeding, just enough to get you to the healers. Your heart stopped on the way, but they were able to bring you back, luckily."

"Good. Now I can go back to making devious plans." I try to smile, but clearly, Sarana isn't having it. "Sarana, what happened, happened. Nothing can change that. Me being upset or angry won't help. Not when I'm still in... wherever I am."

Despite whatever worries are on her mind, she softens a bit at that.

"I know, Raya." A small smile forms on her lips. "I'll have to thank Ayn for helping me out of the castle. I found the gift you had waiting there."

Leigh. A deep sigh releases from me, filling me with relief.

"Thank the spirits, he made it in time."

"Oh, they sure did. As soon as I walked into the clearing, the last of his soldiers arrived. We were met on the lawn of the palace by a small army. But we held them off until the end of the Stalemate."

"You stayed?" I ask, pride swelling for her and her bravery.

"Of course, I can't have you and Leigh taking all the glory," she says, a hint of jest in her voice. "I laugh, but in truth, you inspired me. You sacrificed yourself for this. For peace. I needed to trust you as much as you trusted in this. I didn't at first, and I failed you in that regard. So, this time, I made sure to follow you into battle. To be honest, it felt good being useful again. To fight alongside my people."

"I'm proud of you, Sarana. And I thank you for trusting in me," I say, taking her hand in mine. I feel so cold compared to her heat. My own personal sun in this cold abyss.

"Ah, before I forget. Leigh is sitting here beside me. He says he owes you a sword, whatever that means." I laugh, never forgetting a debt that one. "And he says to hurry your ass back to the real world."

"I'm not sure I control whatever this is, but I will certainly try."

"Of course you control this, Raya. You just need to be ready to return to us." She gives me a nod of encouragement, then turns as though she's about to walk away.

I tug on her hand, stopping her before she can leave.

"I know I should wait until I'm awake so I can say this to you in person, but the spirits only know how hectic these next few days will be, and I may not get the chance," I start, and she faces me once more.

Her golden-brown eyes bore into mine. They were once filled with love and passion. Although that passion has died, adoration, trust, and care fill them instead.

"I'm sorry. For my hurtful words. For turning my back on you. For putting you in harm's way. I'm sorry for all of it."

Understanding fills the space between us, and she steps toward me once more. "I appreciate your apology, Raya. But because of you, this war has ended, and both Corath and Promithia will know peace. If anything, I'm the one who should apologize. For what I said to you. The accusations, all of it. I have no right to try to control you, especially when it comes from a place of jealousy."

"You have loved me in ways no one else ever could, and for that, I will always have a place in my heart for you, my Queen. But when all this is over and we are home, I hope we can remain friends."

"I know the burden of being tied to a person who can never give you what you truly desire. Commitment. Love that is unconditional." She takes a deep breath. "While we both know I cannot be that person, I hope you find someone who can love you and stand at your side unabashedly. Someone who will be your true partner in every sense of the word. But being your friend, Raya, will be the greatest gift of all," she says, palm holding my cheek.

"If I'm being honest with you, I think I might have found that person," I say in barely more than a whisper. A tear escapes my eye but is wiped away by the tip of her thumb.

"Then why do you not look overcome with joy? What holds you back?" She crooks her finger under my chin, lifting ever so slightly so I have no choice but to look into her sincere eyes.

"Because I'm afraid that what we have isn't real. That it's just the makings of bonds, not fate, that's leading us down this path."

Her gaze softens as she runs her hands down my arms and grips my hands in hers. "My dear Raya, there is only one way to find out. You must be brave, you must be strong."

She kisses me gently on my forehead before turning

away. But before disappearing completely, she looks back over her shoulder. "I sense a great adventure on your horizon. Do not be afraid to chase the stars."

As she fades from this abyss, the pure white light and warmth go with her. My mind drifts back into its healing sleep, readying itself to re-enter the real world.

I can't help but ponder the questions swimming in my head. Questions I am now realizing those around me have asked time and time again. Questions I should have taken care to ask myself before now.

Who will I be if there is no war for me to preside over? No battles to be fought?

I drift off into the abyss once more, dreaming of what a life beyond the war will be like. Of who I will become beyond the soldier.

THIRTY-SIX

"Why isn't she awake yet?" a voice whispers above me.

A sense of desperation hangs on his words, and a tanginess wafts through the air around us.

Fear. That is fear I hear in that voice of velvet dreams.

I've only ever seen fear in his eyes. I never thought it could truly take hold into something much more tangible.

"While her body is fine, her wounds nearly gone, it is her mind that needs more time," Sarana says in a voice that is cool, calm, and sure.

Orion sighs with impatience. "Since I don't have the power to enter her mind, can't you go back and ask her when she thinks she will return?"

"That will only make things worse. I did it once to make sure she was still in there. If I do it again, it will take her mind away from the work it truly needs to do."

"I'm not sure what work her mind needs to do. She has been perfectly fine since entering my care."

A laugh escapes Sarana's lips. "Are you really so blind?

Think of all she has experienced in her life. Both parents dead, before her eyes. From a young age, she was exposed to the casualties of war and bloodshed. And months ago, she was taken as prisoner and tortured by your father, not to mention the trauma she endured in the past few days. She has likely been running on adrenaline all these months. And now that her mind has the time to truly slow down and process all that has happened, it is taking its time to put itself back together. She will wake when she is ready."

"She hasn't been held captive. Not since I saved her from my father."

"*Saved.*" Another dry laugh sounds from deep in her chest. "You tell yourself that, *Majesty,*" Sarana replies with a bite. "But while your cage has wider walls and more freedom than his, the Rite you hold her with is still a cage. Neither of you may want to admit it, but it's the truth."

Heat radiates beside me, but it's not Sarana's warm glow. It's Orion's temper.

Honestly, I would've opened my eyes by now had they not started fighting. As much as I want to return to the world of the living, Sarana's words hold truth. I like the peace of mind I've had in the realm of sleep. The true rest I haven't felt since the rotating nightmares of my parents' death that plague me more than I care to admit.

I don't talk about it often, but that's because I've had other things on my mind to help distract me from the pain of their loss.

"I'll leave you to your brooding. Do fetch me when she wakes." Sarana's hand finds mine, and she pauses.

She knows I'm awake. Half expecting her to tell the prince—now king—and out me, she surprises me by giving my hand a gentle, knowing squeeze before leaving.

Orion takes a deep breath next to me, letting out the air with a sigh.

Before I decide to go back to sleep and never wake, I figure this is as good a time as any for me to finally open my eyes.

When I do, his own are closed. Elbows on my bed and hands clasped against his forehead. One might think he's praying to the spirits, but the way his jaw tenses and the muscles constrict at his temples, it almost looks like he's having a heated conversation with one instead.

"A king in contemplation," I say, my voice hoarse from lack of use. "Someone should come here and paint this moment."

At the sound of my voice, he slowly raises his head from his fists, brows furrowed in disbelief, unsure if what he hears and sees is real.

"I'm surprised *His Majesty* has the time to see to the health of his favorite enemy," I say, playing the best hand of sarcasm I can muster. It's not my best work, but it will do.

A tear makes its escape down his cheek as he springs from his seat in shock, then brings his lips to mine in earnest. Although not completely surprised by the action, I'm still taken aback. Catching his cheek in my palm, I welcome his embrace, matching his longing and relief with my own.

"You will never be my enemy, and I will always have time for you," he says, pressing his forehead against mine.

I can almost hear the words he cannot bear to say. *I thought I lost you.*

He takes my hand before sitting back down in his chair. "The plan was for you to meet Leigh's forces in the clearing."

"You really think I was going to leave everyone when you needed all the help you could get?" I reply as I push myself up to lean against the pillows and metal headboard. My arms and midsection ache from the movement. "Besides, you made me armor for a reason, right? Did you really expect me not to fight?"

"The armor was a precaution." He sighs, his eyes growing somber. "My men told me what you did. How you led them, protected me. The price you would have paid…"

I stop him midsentence. "I would do the same thing a thousand times more if I had to. If it means our people will be at peace, then it was all worth it."

He leans in and kisses me again, but this time, the rush of relief subsides into something more delicate and soft.

"I haven't figured out how to release you from the Rite yet. That power goes beyond me. But I vow you will be relinquished of the hold, in time. I will do everything I can to ensure it."

"Really?" My eyes go wide with… hope. To be free.

While I'm not entirely sure I want to be free of him, I could truly live without this bond looming over us like a cloud about to strike lightning. *We* could truly live.

"Yes, claiming you as my Birthrite wasn't to keep you locked up in a cage or really to claim you at all. Now that my father is gone and the war is over, I don't want there to be any doubt in those intentions."

Throwing my arms around his shoulders, I kiss his cheek as tears stream down my face. My freshly healed wounds pull at the movement, and I hiss at the sharp pain that follows. My joints are stiff and achy from lying in bed for days on end.

I release myself from our embrace, resting back against the plush pillows. "So I guess you didn't need whatever mystical power was resting in the Shifting Wood after all," I say.

"No, I suppose not," Orion replies with a small smile, jaw

ticking as he seems to ponder a thought wiggling in his mind. "But I'm sure we'll venture back there soon enough."

I return a smile of my own, small like his, but I fear it's tinged with a touch of sadness. While I wish to share his optimism for our future adventures together, with the end of the war and impending peace between our two nations, something deep within me knows that those future adventures may never come. Our destinies are forging down different paths.

But instead of rejecting his notion, I swallow the realization, take his hands in mine and squeeze. Nodding my head, I force as much positivity into my smile as I can. A flicker of darkness flashes in his eyes, and I know he sees through my mask.

"So," I start, folding my hands upon my thighs and hoping to change the subject. "What is the king of Corath to do now that peace is here?"

"I have a small group of guards out to retrieve my mother. She may not have committed the crimes of my father, but she was complicit in his terror. I will strip her of her title and keep her in isolation here until the council decides what to do with her." He would decide her fate by council? As if he could hear my thoughts, he shrugs. "I want to ensure her punishment is just. Not the makings of my anger over her actions or love for the mother she used to be. This is the best way."

I shudder at my memories of being tortured by King Mattias and the nights the queen just sat and watched, a devilish smile always on her lips, a twinkle of joy in her eyes.

"And what of Mavre?" I ask, wondering what might have happened to the one who defied Orion and the plan they'd all worked so hard for.

"In a dungeon safe and sound... for now."

Pressing my lips into a thin line, I nod.

A knock sounds at the door and Samson enters. He's dressed in his black leathers and metal armor. Though not unaffected by the battle, a fresh, thin scar skates across his cheek. He sees me, sitting upright and talking, and stops in his tracks.

He gives a bow to Orion and to me before entering.

"Glad to see you're doing much better, General."

General. That's the first time he's called me that. And is that a smile I see playing on his lips? Remembering what he's here for, he turns to the prince—*king.* It will take some time getting used to that title change.

"Your Majesty, the council requests your presence."

"Of course they do." He rolls his eyes and rises from his seat. "I'll have one of the healers come in and check on you. Hopefully, we can move you into your quarters by the time I get back." He leans down and presses his lips to my forehead before following Samson out of the room and into the rest of the castle beyond.

This is only the beginning for Orion. Yes, it's the end of tyranny. Of a king who was more preoccupied with what he could gain by continuing this war rather than preserving the strength of his people. But how many in Corath believed in what Mattias promised? How many, if any, will do their best to defy Orion's rule?

THIRTY-SEVEN

Approved to return to the land of the living, Orion and I make our way through the palace halls to my new rooms—quarters attached to Orion's own. I assume they are meant to be for his betrothed, but seeing as he doesn't have one, he wanted me to be as close to him as possible.

Samson and a few guards follow at our heels. Courtiers stop and bow to their new king, then begin to whisper at the sight of me.

"They're only jealous you are on my arm and not them," Orion whispers in my ear, sensing my shift.

But that blushing smile quickly shifts into a grimace of fear as whispering words of a ghost slither into my mind.

The Wielder of Death doesn't look so deadly to me. The memory of Tyrannis's words crawls up my spine with sharp needles. My back stiffens and mind races with every whisper that passes us.

"If only that were true," I reply, pushing down my growing unease.

We finally arrive at Orion's quarters. The dark room in jewel tones that I saw before with Xander is lighter and airy now that the curtains are drawn back, allowing in the sunshine.

I bask in its warmth as we enter the main sitting room, but my eyes go straight to the group of people sitting around a small table on velveted couches and chaises. Leigh, Sarana, and Loren tip their heads in laughter over a joke we seem to have just missed, filling the room with a harmonious melody. But Dessy, my sweet sister, loses all sense of regal decorum and rushes into my arms, body shuddering as tears stream down her face. It's not long until I follow suit.

"The next time you decide to throw yourself at our enemy, can you at least rely on all of us around you instead of playing the hero all by yourself?" she says, and I can't help but laugh through my tears. "We've been so worried. After Greva came back, near death himself, we thought… we had no idea if…" Then the wave hits her again, with another shudder. "But I got your starbloom and your message."

I pull her head up from my shoulder, forcing her to meet my gaze. "I'm all right. I'm here. I'm alive. And I am not leaving anytime soon," I say, wiping away the tears that continue to fall. I turn to Leigh. "I feared you might not have received my letter in time to meet in the clearing. Thank you for answering my call."

"I will always answer your call, *General*." A wide smile spreads on his face from ear to ear.

"Since when did you become so sentimental?"

He doesn't respond to my teasing. Instead, he stares down at me, love and fear pooling in his eyes. The words he cannot vocalize wrap around my mind. *Since I lost my mentor and then almost lost my best friend.*

"Oh, I almost forgot," he says as Dessy releases me from the hug.

Orion steps in, looping his arm around my waist, becoming my trusty brace once more. Not that I really need one. Thanks to whatever concoctions the healers gave me, I feel as good as new, just a tad sore.

They both eye him and his protective stance.

I send them a shrug, promising the full story later.

Leigh lifts a brow and sends a smirk in response. Always in love with drama.

He brings a long rectangular box over and kneels in front of me, dramatically presenting the gift. "For you, Your Grace. For when I owe a debt, I always pay."

"I thought Sarana was joking when she mentioned you had the sword," I say in shock that he actually brought it here. "Leigh, really, I cannot accept this."

"It's yours, Raya. You won it fair and square."

I shake my head, watching as he sets the long case on the coffee table. "I'd hardly call it fair when I knew it was coming."

While my words are true, a part of me feels guilty for being another reason he succumbed to the allure of gambling.

"Raya, I insist," he says, eyes imploring as he takes my hands in his and gives them a gentle squeeze. This has nothing to do with the silly bet we placed and everything to do with him wanting to show his love for a friend. "Consider it a 'welcome back from the dead' gift."

Finally, I relent. Reaching down to the case, I unclasp the locks on either end. Resting in the center is the sword of gold and diamonds he had made in Volira.

"I can't believe you brought this all the way with you," I say, chuckling in disbelief.

"I had plans to present it to you when we met in the clearing, thought you'd find it funny." He smiles. "I couldn't bring the matching armor though."

"Thank goodness," Loren says, coming around to inspect the sword. "If the armor is anything like the sword, the weight would've held you up."

I close the box, and Leigh sets it down on the table in front of the fireplace.

"You gave us a good scare there, Duchess." Loren steps closer beside me.

"You can't get rid of me that easily," I tease, knocking into her arm with my shoulder.

"I'm glad to hear. Xander will be glad to see you too."

"Where is Shadowman anyway?" I ask.

Loren grins at the nickname. "He's tucked away in some meetings, but you shall see him soon. Although I have been called away, so I just wanted to say goodbye before I departed."

I extend my arm, taking hers in a firm grip, "It was a pleasure meeting you, Loren."

"The pleasure was all mine," she says. "I would say I hope to have the chance to fight at your side again, but I'd like to wait a long while for that."

"Indeed," I say through a laugh.

Loren dismisses herself from the room, off to whatever adventure is calling her.

Sarana steps forward now, looking as stunning as ever in a gown of creamy silk. Taking my hands in hers, she loosens a deep breath. "I'm glad you made your way back to us, Raya."

"Thank you for visiting me. Reminding me there's a life to come back to."

"I know how easy it can be to get lost in your mind." She places a kiss on my forehead.

"Now, how has our country and my region been faring since I've been gone?" I ask, looking at my friends.

"Raya, we can talk about this tomorrow or when we're home," my sister says. "You should rest."

"I swear, if someone tells me to rest one more time, I might lose it. I've done enough resting to last me a lifetime. I think I can handle one conversation to talk about my home. *Our* home." I take Dessy's hand in mine and squeeze.

"Very well," Sarana says, and we all find a seat in the living quarters as Orion leaves us be.

They share all they can on the state of our country and forces. Once I was captured, the kidnapping of our soldiers ceased. Not much has changed. We are still rationing where we can, and goods have been imported as usual from our allies.

Without its ruler, however, Senna has been faring… as expected. I can tell from the added stress lines around Dessy's eyes and the creases in her forehead, all of this has been too much for her to bear on her own.

Strategizing has never been her strong suit, but Orlo and Leigh have been doing all they can to help, getting Senna back on her feet as best as they could manage.

I shared with them the information I was able to glean from King Hesten's journal, from Orion and from Tyrannis, the testing they were conducting on the prisoners of war from our country. Even the seemingly magical item hidden deep in the Shifting Wood in Thestras. Thankfully, Sarana has been working with Orion to bring the remaining prisoners home safely, although not many were left alive.

After several hours, Leigh and Sarana move on to their own agendas, leaving Dessy and me alone in the foreign quarters. We move to the chairs by the windows that overlook the gardens.

The grass and flowers, once clipped and manicured to perfection, are now trampled in some areas from the battling that took place. Large portions of bushes and trees are rooted out of the dirt and tossed aside as if they were little more than twigs. Areas of grass scorched from fire or bolts of lightning.

Courtiers and other visitors here for the coronation swarm the portion of the gardens untouched by the fighting. In the middle of a small, rounded clearing is a canopy and chairs. Sitting in them are the rulers of Valtan and Alwilke. A sight I never thought I'd see.

"I'm sorry," I say, the twinge of guilt coursing through me. "I should've been there—"

"No," Dessy says, eyes closed and head leaning up toward the warm glow of rays shining in through the windows. "Don't apologize."

"But I-I… it's all my fault," I say, eyes filling with tears at the truth I've been avoiding all these months.

And with that release, the words don't stop. I let it all out. Relaying everything that happened on that battlefield outside of Frallis. The call on the wind that caused my distraction. The price our father paid for that mistake.

My actions. My fault. *I killed him. I killed him. I killed him.*

And what's worse? I left my sister behind to clean up the mess I made all on her own.

The weight of the truth hangs heavy in the air between us. For a time, we just sit there, both fighting, and failing, to hold back the tears from our eyes as I unpack the horrors I've been holding all this time, until she wraps her arms around me in a warm embrace.

"Raya, look at me," Dessy says as she slowly unwraps her arms from around me and grips my shoulders.

I reluctantly obey, not wanting her to see the shame I feel.

"You made your decision on the battlefield that day, and Father made his. We all knew the risks, especially Father. What happened after he made the decision to go after you, to try to save you, is not your fault. Whatever called to you that day on the field wanted you to follow it, and look where it has led us. I know these words will not be a magic cure to make you feel better about what occurred, but one day, you will find peace."

She's right. I know she's right. But I fear that one day won't come soon enough.

I nod nonetheless, no matter the ache I feel in my chest.

"I just wish I could have been there for you," I say, wiping a tear from my eye.

"When I found the starbloom you sent? I was overcome with relief to know you were alive. There were so many nights I fell asleep wishing you were home. But luckily Leigh was there to help, filling that hole in your wake." Her glassy eyes look away from me, her cheeks blushing.

I quirk my head at that revelation.

"He's always been a great friend to us, and these past few months, he really held true to that." She fumbles, recovering quickly. But the tinge of pink on her cheeks tells me all I need to know. "Feel free to fill me in on all about you and the prince. I'd love to hear about your real-life enemies-to-lovers, scandalous affair."

I scoff, attempting to blow it off like it's nothing, but she sees right through me. "I wouldn't call it enemies to lovers… Maybe more like allies with an understanding."

And with an intrigued lift of the corner of her lips, it's all the encouragement I need to share the winding and utterly confusing road that is Orion and me.

"He claimed you as his *Birthrite?*" she asks, eyes wide with shock. "I guess that explains the progression of your relationship or whatever it is you two are calling this."

"We just had an… *alignment* of interests," I say and sip my water, wishing it was something stronger. The healers have instructed me to wait to drink alcohol for one more day as their tonics and runes do their job.

"Anyone remotely close to you can sense exactly where your interests align."

At that, I cough up the sip I've just taken. Dessy is still trying to wrap her mind around this turn of events.

"It makes sense now why he has given you chambers connected to his."

"It doesn't quite matter where I'm sleeping right now because in three days' time, I'll be home in Senna with you."

At that, she smiles, but it's one I'm not sure I completely believe.

"And I can't wait for you to come home," she starts. "But I've seen the way you two look at each other. When everything is all said and done, I want you to do what makes you happy. Not what others expect you to do."

I know she's right. It's the realization I made while here in Corath. But hearing her speak those words, validating the warring thoughts in my mind, it warms my soul even more than I could have imagined.

"While I do have feelings for Orion, the truth is I want to go home. To honor our father, lead our region, and find some new adventures along the way. Orion and I have time to figure out what our feelings mean to each other," I say, taking her hand. "But our entire lives revolved around this war. I think it's time for us to learn who we are without that violence shadowing over us. To make some new, happier memories."

She grins at that. "Have I ever told you that you're my favorite sister?"

"I'm your only sister," I say.

She laughs, and the sound echoes in my heart, filling my mind with childhood memories and warmth and light and love.

"I've missed you so much, Dessy."

"I've missed you too."

With my cheek pressed to her hair, the scent of sea breeze and sunshine engulfs my senses, calling me home.

THIRTY-EIGHT

My body begs to sit and rest, but I muster up all my energy to stand tall and as regal as the duchess I am supposed to be. And it's all because of this damn dress.

This masterpiece of a gown is truly a work of art. Made for a warrior. The beads of pearls that hang in loops from my shoulders are reminiscent of the metal scales I wear in battle. A full skirt billows out at my waist with a train meant for royalty. The whole ensemble is a nod to both my skill as a warrior and my duty bound to my home, to Senna.

My only concern is that it looks more like a wedding dress fit for a warrior than what is supposed to be a gown to represent the "Honored," yet another Corathian tradition I don't quite understand. The only thing that comforts me is the presence of Samson, who has been ushered into this room with me just off the Great Hall.

He, too, wears all white, except his ensemble is a near replica of his guard's uniform. One with a bit more pomp and circumstance.

Besides, Orion wouldn't trick me into marriage, especially without my consent. *He wouldn't do that.* I reassure myself before my mind descends into a blitz of worry once more.

He's dragged you here too? A comforting voice whispers in my mind.

I turn around with a wide smile plastered on my face, tears threatening to burn their way through their ducts. The last time I saw Xander, I didn't even really see him. He was cradling me as I lay dying in the War Room. I haven't seen him since then, and I'm kicking myself in the ass for not seeking him out yesterday. I may even be a bit pissed that he hadn't tried to visit me either, but that anger is washed away as I walk over to him in quick strides.

He's dressed in all white as well, matching Samson and me, but the fabric of his doublet is made to look like scales. Two white bands encircle the top of his head. At closer look, I realize they're two serpents, twisting around each other, eyes made of sapphire stones.

Before I second-guess my actions, and he can refuse, I wrap my arms around his waist in a strong embrace. Hesitant, he stumbles back in shock, but eventually, his arms do the same.

I'm glad to see you, his voice echoes in my mind.

His smile warms his stark features, clearly an action he doesn't do very often.

I'm just hurt you didn't come see me. We missed you at my welcoming party, I reply in jest.

But a pained look flashes across his eyes. *I was there every day.*

And now I'm the one in shock.

Of course, the day I was summoned into meetings is when you woke up.

Hurt and pain and regret course through him, threatening to cloud my own senses. I take his hand in mine, allowing him to feel my gratitude.

Thank you, I say. *Thank you for being there for me.*

His features settle once more, and the hurt and pain subside, although the regret is still there, thrumming under the surface of calm.

From the other side of the room, Samson clears his throat. "Why do I feel like I'm being left out of a conversation?"

Xander and I laugh, and it feels strange to hear the sound escape his lips. Just like his smile, the bright sound seems to soften every rigid feature and piece of him that he keeps so tightly guarded.

"Shadowman here prefers silent conversations," I say, facing Samson, who's now leaning against the doorframe.

Xander shrugs. "I'm a quiet guy."

"He speaks," I gasp with mock shock.

"I see the battle has made you two closer?" Suspicion fills Samson's voice.

"Almost dying in someone's arms can do that." I tease, but red heat floods Samson's cheeks.

No doubt he has Orion's heart in mind with his suspicion, but I feel the sting of shame emanate around him, caused by whatever thoughts his mind may have conjured.

Before I can quell his emotions, a knock raps at the door and trumpets blare throughout the palace.

The coronation is about to begin.

THE CROWNING CEREMONY is simple yet beautiful in the way it honors the land and the people. Using dirt from the village Retlas that sits at the heart of Corath, ash from the slumbering volcano Brekka in the north, and water from the fresh springs of the Adriata—the lifeline of Corath with streams that connect to the western coast, the gulf, and the Great River—Orion is decorated in the roots of his country.

With the crown jewels placed upon his head and the vows uttered to and from his people and allies, Orion is crowned King of Corath.

One by one, Orion anoints the new members of his council, and the remaining members swear their fealty to their new king.

I have to stop myself from cheering when it's Ayn's turn to take her vow, a wide maniacal grin no doubt plastered on my face. Though I'm sure there are many Corathians who disagree with this turn of legislature, they do not dare disrupt or protest.

Silence settles throughout the hall as Samson, Xander, and I—the three Honored—step down from the dais and face Orion.

"Samson Graves, Commander of the King's Guard, please step forward." He obeys his king with pride. "You have been a trusted guard in my service, but before that, you were my friend. The road here was not easy, and on many nights, I doubted we would ever see the light at the end of the tunnel. It was your honesty that kept me grounded, your perseverance that pushed us through, and your loyalty that ensured we made it to the other side. For this and so much more, I honor you. Please bend a knee." He obeys once more, and Orion unsheathes his golden sword, a ruby glaring in the hilt.

Tapping the side of the blade on either shoulder, he

continues, "For your bravery and your loyalty, I knight thee. Rise, Sir Samson Graves." Samson rises from his knee, bowing to Orion before taking his place at my side.

"Prince Tobias Xander Sedik of Volira, Commander of the Black Brigade, please step forward."

I forget all restraint as my eyes widen, and I snap my attention to the man who stood to my right.

Did Orion just call him Prince Tobias? Prince Tobias of Volira?!

Sorry I couldn't tell you sooner, but please, I prefer my middle name, Xander whispers into my mind, either sensing my confusion or hearing my thoughts. *Yes, I heard your thoughts, you're practically screaming them at me.*

I am? Shit. I patch my veil back together, hoping he can't penetrate the thick wall of glass now standing between my mind and his.

Apparently, others are just as shocked as I am. Confused glances and whispers begin to scatter around the great room.

Once again, I'm reminded of how little I know of the man. Now I understand why he looked so familiar, why he wears the serpent crown of the Sedik line on his head and dons jewels of sapphire—a Voliran staple. But it also now comes as no shock as to why his parents, the emperors sitting across from Sarana, look less than intrigued to be here.

Xander, Prince Tobias, more or less broke Volira's neutrality by siding himself with Orion. Which is probably why he kept to himself and went by his middle name instead.

"I'm sure it is a shock to many of you that the Black Brigade is not my personal legion of well-trained soldiers, but it is indeed Prince Tobias's." He addresses the whispers running rampant. "Tobias, you and I met a few years ago while traveling. And during that trip, we made a pact, one I never thought I would need to call in but am grateful for.

Because of you, your willingness to fight alongside me for what is right, to help me and my people, my country has been able to ring in a new dawn of peace and prosperity. For that, I will always be grateful."

A darkness ebbs in his eyes as he gazes down at Xander. A look that anyone else would've missed. But the emotion I felt behind it, the words he could not dare say, burned through me. *It's a debt he will gladly repay if there's ever a need.*

"Prince Tobias Xander Sedik, I honor you with a gift of the spirits." Without a thought, a small chest appears in his hands as he steps forward to place it in Xander's outstretched palms. "May you use it wisely."

With a nod of respect, Xander returns beside me.

"Raya Leona Ontaria, Duchess of Senna, High General of Promithia, please step forward."

With a deafening quiet that falls around the room, I take my step toward the dais, all too aware of how loud my heels click against the marble floor. Orion's smile fills me with warmth, and my body responds in recognition of what his lips can do. Heat spreads through my treacherous body, but I do my best to push away those thoughts and concentrate on the words coming from them instead.

"There are many ways a Stalemate can end. No matter which party wins, those who await the victor on the other side could be their undoing or their triumph. Many people believe that as soon as the Stalemate is over and the shudder is felt, all soldiers lay down their weapons and vow their fealty to the new or remaining king. But that is not always the case. We knew we needed support; I knew I needed protection. Because of Raya, along with Samson, Xander, High General Leigh, and Queen Sarana from Promithia, that protection was provided, and I am standing here.

"Raya chose to stay and fight to protect and defend a king

she held no allegiance to. And she did it, not just for me, but for all of you. For all of Corath and Promithia. But that choice had a price. She was gravely injured, a breath away from death. Luckily, along with our healers, I was able to prevent death from taking her." He turns, motioning for me to stand beside him on the dais.

I take his hand and ascend the step, careful not to step on my hem.

"Raya Ontaria, I and all of Corath are deeply grateful for the sacrifice you were willing to make. For this, I honor you. Please hold out your hand."

He removes a small dagger that was hidden in his long coat. A miniature version of the long sword he carries. He first makes a small cut on his hand. Some gasps can be heard in the crowd, but all I can do is watch in daft confusion, ignoring the stinging as he does the same on mine. Before the cuts can heal, he clasps his hand with mine, the slices connect, and I can feel the push from his body. The most raw of the Rite interacting.

"Blood that was once mine, a connection once made, after today will be no longer. Raya Leona Ontaria, I release you from the Birthrite. Your freedom is the honor I bestow. From this day forward, for all of eternity."

As soon as the words are spoken and his hand releases mine, something in me snaps.

I'm speechless, unsure what to say or how I should react.

This is what I wanted. To be free of the Rite. But now that it's here, now that this wish of mine has been granted, I feel... empty.

In a daze, I step off the dais, turn toward Orion, and curtsy in respect, then resume my place between Samson and Xander.

Orion doesn't take his eyes off me, somber expression

matching my own, like he felt it too. The reverberating snap of a taut cord and the emptiness. The hollowness.

I'm not sure when we moved to the seats in the first row, but now we're here and seated. Xander pulls out a handkerchief and wraps my palm in the material. I'm not bleeding too much, most of it has dried, but since I'm wearing white, I'm grateful for his thoughtfulness.

Recomposing himself, King Orion addresses his people for the first time.

"I know you all are looking forward to celebrating. Even saying the word seems so strange after so many years of war, so I will make this short and sweet to not keep you all from the festivities." A few rumbles of laughter echo throughout the chamber. "First and foremost, I want to thank you all for joining me today on this momentous occasion. I know I have made my official oath and vows, but I have one more to make to all of you, to all the people of Corath.

"On this day, I vow to you that I will hear you and listen to your concerns, your grievances, even if you may slander my name. To never send another child into battle, whether it's one we are fighting or aiding. To ensure *all* Corathians can find a place here, no matter how you may identify, who you love, or where you are from. I vow to be your sword and your shield whenever you may need defending. This I do solemnly promise and swear."

To this, all Corathians lift from their seats and take a knee, bowing to their rightful king. The rafters sing and pulse with cries and shouts.

"All hail King Orion, long may he reign."

THIRTY-NINE

"I thought you said there wasn't a way to break the Rite?" I ask, barging into our shared living area. My voice comes out angrier than I intended.

I'm not angry, I try to convince myself. I'm just upset that he didn't warn me.

My maids just finished helping me change out of the coronation gown and into a more comfortable one for this evening's festivities. A cream-colored dress that frames my shape then flares out to the ground from my thighs.

He's sitting on one of the plush couches, still in the gold finery from the ceremony, sans cloak. A raging fire crackles in the hearth.

A gold surcoat lays on the back of the chaise. All he needs to do is change his outer layers, and he's ready for his celebration.

"I never said there wasn't a way. Just that there wasn't a way known to me. But since I knew I had to honor you with a gift, one that's bound by essence and tradition, I took a gamble."

Despite the fact that he should look thrilled now that his sparkling new crown is sitting proudly atop his head. He looks as though he's lost it instead.

"Why didn't you tell me sooner?" I lean against the mantel, crossing my arms over my chest, trying to don an air of indifference to cool my... *frustration*... from lack of knowledge, of course.

His brows furrow as he leans back into the chair, one arm dangling behind the back as the other twirls the glass of sparkling wine in his hand. He takes a swig before placing the glass down. "Because, *Duchess*, I didn't want you to get your hopes up if it didn't work."

"It would've been nice to have a little heads up before being surprised in the middle of the ceremony."

He loosens a breath of a sigh. "I'm sorry. It's tradition that the gift to the Honored is not known until it is given. I couldn't tell you even if I wanted to."

"You could've at least asked me first," I say, surprising myself and Orion, who now looks at me with confusion.

"Asked you if you wanted your freedom from me? You knew this was going to happen. I thought you wanted to no longer be bound?"

I fumble over my words. "Wanting to be asked before being sliced open in front of a crowd doesn't mean I'm not happy to no longer be tied to you, because I am."

He winces at my words, and I find myself wincing along with him.

Giving in, I take a seat beside him and pour myself a glass of champagne from the decanter on the small wooden table.

"If you're happy, then why do you not look it?" he asks, seeing right through me.

I turn to face him, my gaze finding his.

I decide to ignore his question. "How did you know it would work?"

"I didn't. But either way, if it did or didn't work, I wanted the world to see that I released you from the Rite."

I nod, taking a sip from the champagne, getting lost in the tendrils of flame and smoke before me.

He wraps an arm around my shoulder, pulling me closer to him. With a tender kiss, he presses his lips to my temple. "I'm sorry I didn't tell you beforehand. Tradition or not, it involved you, you deserved to know."

"Did you not feel it? The emptiness?" I don't dare look his way, but I can feel his stare against my skin. Can sense the furrow that remains in his brow. "As soon as the bond broke, I just felt this bottomless pit of… I don't know. It might've been in my head. But it felt so real. Even now"

"It wasn't in your head, Raya. I feel it too."

I will myself to look in his direction and find somber eyes gazing into my own.

His brows are no longer furrowed, but his lids begin to lower. "But when used on other people, the Rite is like a living thing that takes up space within us. Once it's gone, it leaves a hole in its wake. By tomorrow, that void should feel whole again."

"Look at us. We should be celebrating your coronation," I say, wiping the tears from under my eyes I didn't realize were there. I pull myself back up to look at him, crown and all. "How does it feel to officially step into your destiny, *Your Majesty?*" The words flow out of my lips in a mocking lilt and a sly smile.

A smile, wide and bright, spreads across his cheeks. "Will you ever address me seriously?"

"In front of your esteemed council and court, yes. But

when it's us, Dessy, Leigh, Samson, or Xander, definitely not."

He cocks his head to the side, brows furrowed as if he's about to ask a question. Instead, he releases a heavy exhale.

"Very well." He kisses my cheek. "Honestly, I feel relieved. The people of Corath needed something to look forward to. I think we all did. But I know that will change, and soon, the full weight of leading a nation will land on my shoulders. I'm just glad to be able to celebrate something out of happiness, not about the war."

We sit in silence for a moment more before he takes my hand and gently pulls me from my seat. Standing in front of the warm fireplace, he wraps his arms around me, and I allow myself to melt within the embrace, head resting against his chest.

"I'm glad you're here, Raya," he says, landing soft kisses into my hair.

My heart flutters from the action… and the realization that this is our first time truly alone since that last night in Thestras.

"I mean it. Having you there today and knowing you will be here for the rest of the celebrations and ceremonies gives me more comfort than you know."

"Anything for you, *my King*." I tease.

Lifting my head off his chest, I lean back to look up at him.

A flash of heat crosses his eyes. Not one of fury but of… something else entirely.

"Say that again," he says, voice deep.

Warmth pools low, awareness sprouting over every inch of my skin.

"What? Anything for you?" I laugh, wanting to drag out

his longing for as long as I can, knowing exactly what he's looking for.

A smile tugs up at the corner of his lips, and a rare dimple comes out to play. But something dark crosses his features, transforming his playful smile into one of pure lust and need. He trails his mouth along the ridge of my jaw to the corners of my lips, grip tightening at my hips. His fingers dig deliciously into my flesh, practically burning through the fabric of the gown.

He shakes his head, the tips of our noses touching. "No," he rumbles, lips almost touching mine. "That last part."

"My King?" I whisper, afraid that if I speak any louder, I may shatter this moment like glass.

He nods, and a shudder courses between the two of us. The anticipation of what I know will happen next throbs at the apex between my thighs.

So I repeat the words again, but this time, it's not a question. Matching his tone and intensity, I let the words fly off the tip of my tongue. "*My King.*"

His lips claim mine with a primal need of desire. He swipes his tongue against the seam of my lips, and I happily oblige, opening for him. Our lips move as one while our hands do all they can to bring each other nearer, because just standing in his embrace isn't enough. I need to feel his arms around me, holding me tight. Need to feel his skin on mine without the barrier of silk and chiffon. But time is not on our side at the moment, not when a garden full of courtiers and visitors are waiting to see Corath's new king.

With a chuckle, I tear my lips away. "They are expecting us. You more than me, but we're expected nonetheless."

His eyes darken with need as he swoops me up into his arms. "Then I suppose we shall make this quick."

Lips reclaiming mine, he carries me into his bedchamber.

As we enter the room, the runelights flicker to life with a dim hue.

He sets me down next to his large bed, fit for a prince who would be king. I can only imagine the monstrosity that is in the king's chambers.

My fingers fumble over the buttons on his doublet. After struggling over the third or fourth button, I let out a growl—or maybe he did, I'm not sure—and just rip the rest of the doublet apart. He pulls his white tunic over his head, and I run my hands over his muscled chest. Rimming the scars that splay across the planes. His skin thrums with the current of his storm under my fingertips.

Without breaking my gaze, I make a trail of kisses and licks and sucks down his pecs, along the side of his abs, down to the V that disappears below his unbuckled trousers. On my knees, my mouth grazes over the bulge in his pants. He pulses at the feel of my lips on him—even through the fabric.

His eyes are still locked on mine despite the spark that tells me his patience is running thin. Pure delight and ravenous pleasure paint his face.

Pulling down his pants, his cock springs out, pulsing and ready before me. I run my tongue from his base to the tip, sucking his length into my mouth.

A sigh of relief and pleasure sounds from above me, and he grips the base of my neck, careful not to mess my perfectly styled hair.

Teasing his head with my tongue, swirling in circles at the tip, I close my lips around him and begin to glide him in and out of my mouth.

"Fuck, Raya."

This time, his head rolls back, and his grip on my neck tightens deliciously. He doesn't force my head, though, allowing me to keep the pace. A part of me yearns for the side of him that I know can be rough, but before I can coax him out, he backs away from my grasp and pulls me up to stand in front of him.

"Turn around," he says with the ferocity of pleasure in his voice.

I obey.

One by one, he frees each button with a light pop. He plants kisses starting from the tip of my lobe, down my neck, and past the length of my back, those kisses turning into soft, pleasurable bites here and there.

My dress falls in waves until it's nothing but a heap of creamy white on the floor. He spins me around to face him once more.

Looking me up and down, his eyes graze over every inch of my battle-worn skin.

"I have never met anyone as beautiful as you, Raya Ontaria," he says before taking my lips again.

The slow burn rips through my body. I need him. I want him. Now.

Sensing my desire, he rumbles with a small laugh that passes from his lips onto mine, settling in the pit of my stomach and sending a new wave tingling through me.

"So impatient." His voice is like velvet, and it wraps around me.

I never want him to let me go.

He lays me down on the bed, then hovers over me as he paints my mouth with his own. The tip of his tongue glides across my lips before connecting with mine again.

Stroking his length, he nestles between my legs as he rubs his tip right down my center, circling the nub of nerves until the pressure builds, builds, builds.

I can't control my eyes as they roll, nor the shudder my body gives in response to the sensation.

"Is this what I do to you, dear Raya?" he says, lips grazing the edge of my ear.

Another shudder runs its course through my body, and all I can do is whimper and nod. I'm on the verge of unraveling just from his touch.

"Send you over the edge before we truly join?"

Unable to take it anymore, I wrap my fingers deep into his black waves, pulling at his strands until a deep moan escapes his lips. "Stop asking questions you already know the answer to, and *fuck me*, Orion." My voice is a force of nature he cannot ignore.

With a deep rumble in his chest and a flash in his eyes of what I can only see as hunger for me, he doesn't hesitate. He guides himself into me in a devastating thrust, and we both cry out in pleasure.

"Harder," I rasp out.

Another flash of fire dances across his eyes. He grips my waist, fingers digging in, and harder he complies.

The world around me begins to blur and ebb. The war, the battling, death, Corath, Promithia… everything disappears from my mind.

Nothing else matters. Not the kingdom I have sworn to protect or the throne he has ascended. It's just him and me, with nothing more than our souls to explore.

Something in the center of my chest wants to reach out for him, but I'm met with an adamant wall. A part of himself he keeps locked away and out of reach, a darkness prowling.

My mind shudders in fear, but I won't shy away from whatever mysteries he buries deep inside.

With every touch, every thrust, every inch of sensitive

skin our eyes devour, I'm not really sure where he begins and I end. I pull him down to me, eyes locked onto mine. We don't dare kiss, don't dare close our eyes, neither of us wanting to miss a second of what may very well be our undoing.

With each release and crash of his hips into me, I feel myself inching closer and closer to the edge. His pace quickens, letting me know he's right there with me, nearly ready to explode.

Pressing his forehead against mine, gaze unbreaking, he reaches down between us and runs his fingers in circles over my sensitive bud. That's all it takes for my body to find the release it's been craving, for my eyes to see stars, and for my lips to cry out his name.

Shortly after, his mouth is on mine as he finds his climax, cock pulsing inside me. I kiss him as if he was the breath my lungs need to breathe. The blood my heart needs to pump.

For the first time since waking, my thoughts aren't of returning home. They're of him. Of this room. Of the feelings beginning to bloom, which I now know are not of the Rite's making, and the memories we could continue to create.

But these wishes are nothing but a dream. While I know deep in my heart I cannot stay, I take refuge in his strong embrace, reveling in what little time we have left.

CHAPTER
FORTY

"Dessy, stop fidgeting," I say through gritted teeth and a smile.

We walk deeper into the garden ball through the glittering crowd.

Eyes roam over us with every step we take. A checkered dance floor has been added in the clearing before the makeshift dais. Guests in elaborate ball gowns and glittering jewels sweep and glide across the floor.

"I can't help it. You know I hate wearing dresses like this," she says, playing with the ends of her sleeves again.

I take her hand in mine as I nod in greeting with a curt smile to a few Lords and Ladies of Corath whom I recognize from Orion's birthday celebration. Although they look much less feral now than when I saw them last. When they clawed their greedy fingers into my cage to get a better glimpse at the late king's prize, then Orion's claim… My breath becomes shaky, throat tightening at the memory.

You are no longer a prisoner. You are no longer caged.

I repeat the mantra, taking a deep breath before resuming

my focus on my sister, who's looking at me with furrowed brows. I give her a reassuring smile.

Dessaray always preferred ball gowns that flowed to the ground. But tonight, Frey and Brien surprised us with matching dresses. While mine is cream-colored, keeping with the theme of dress for the Honored, Dessy's is black as night. Both equally stunning and perfectly complementary. Our curls are twisted into low buns, a few wisps left out to frame our faces, although my tryst with Orion caused a few more wisps to pop out. I opted for a short gold tiara with pearls while a band of gold lies atop her head.

Finally, out of the thick crowd, I pull her aside. "Dessy, you look breathtaking tonight." I lift her chin with the knuckle of my index finger. "So, hold your head up high, relax, and have fun."

She smiles and hesitantly nods when Xander approaches where we stand. His silver eyes meet mine, and I can't help but smile.

"Your *Royal Highness*," I say, dipping in a low curtsy. A small smile tugs at the corner of his lips. "Do forgive me for not regarding you with your appropriate title. To think, I would've died in your arms without knowing who you truly are."

"Glad to see you are feeling much better, *Your Grace*," he says, reaching for my hand and bringing my gloved knuckles to his lips. "My sincerest apologies for the deception, Duchess. You surely know what could have happened if word had spread about the involvement of a Prince of Volira with Corathian affairs." His teasing tone strikes through, playing on the sparkle in his eyes.

Despite his teasing, he speaks true. I do know what could have happened. Volira's neutrality would've been destroyed, and his parents' reputation on the international stage would have been sullied.

"Indeed. Although, I'm still hurt you couldn't trust me." *Shadowman*, I whisper secretly. He flashes a playful smirk in my direction. "Xander, I would like to introduce you to my sister, Lady Dessaray. Dessy, this is Prince Tobias, but he prefers to go by Xander."

"It's a pleasure to meet you," she says, dipping into a low curtsy as he bows. Her eyes flicker to mine for a moment before facing him again. "And thank you for being there for my sister when she was injured."

"No thanks necessary. In truth, I didn't do much. Orion and his healers did most of the work," he says shyly.

"You were there to catch her when she fell and supported her after. That's more than most would do, Your Highness."

He laughs awkwardly. "I have a feeling if I didn't, she would be torturing me in the Shadow realm for the rest of my days."

"Yes, I probably would." I laugh.

"You may call me Xander, by the way, I hate the formalities." He smiles warmly at my sister, then turns to me again. "If you have a moment, I was wondering if you'd like to accompany me for a dance."

"I must find Sarana to hear more about how her meetings went with Orion while I was healing. But I will surely take you up on that offer later this evening. I'm sure Dessy would love to dance with you though."

Dessy gives me a glare as harsh as death, but all I do is smile in return.

Xander nods and stretches out his hand toward her. Off they go into the sea of beautifully dressed guests, flickering lights, and overflowing floral decor.

After a few passes around the grounds, I finally find

Sarana in a sectioned-off area just for the Promithian royals, legislators, and other *esteemed* guests from our land. She stands at a high-top table with Leigh and her husband.

"Your Majesty," I say, giving a slight curtsy before approaching the table. "Your Highness, General." I nod toward the gentlemen beside her.

Davison unsurprisingly dismisses himself in search of more wine.

"Leigh, I feel like I haven't seen you," I remark.

"I was invited to play cards yesterday with some of the lords," he says with a devious grin. "And before you give your famous speech about how gambling is a waste of fortune, I promise luck was on my side."

"Well good for you, at least you won't be leaving this country with more money to owe," I say.

"Ah, but there is always tomorrow." He tries to laugh, but the sound is cut short when I hit him with a glare that he can only take as a warning of caution.

He always feels like he's on top of the world when he wins, which makes the losses that much more unbearable.

"Your Majesty, how did the final deliberations on the treaty go with the advisers?" I ask, turning to Sarana.

Orion didn't give me much detail when I asked yesterday, so I'm hoping she can shed a little bit of light on where we now stand.

"You know how they are, always questioning every little thing, but it actually went quite well. The treaty can officially be signed tomorrow." She takes a sip of champagne from the glass in her hand. "Although it seems congratulations are in order."

"Indeed, this will be a wonderful step to securing a prosperous future for our countries," I say, but instead of her smile reflecting my own, she looks at me with utter confusion.

"Not a congratulations for Promithia, Raya. A congratulations for you."

"Whatever for?" I ask. A nervous laugh bubbles, and my brows furrow as my mind races to guess what she may say.

"Why, for your engagement to King Orion, of course," she says, and a pained look flashes across her face. One that's quickly covered with an expression of concern.

"Congrats, Raya… or should we start calling you 'Your Majesty' now?" Leigh chuckles as he raises his glass in my honor, which only makes me bristle even more. "Although, I'm a little hurt you didn't share that he was thinking of proposing."

"That's because it wasn't a thought," I say through gritted teeth.

My heart's steady beat changes tempo, speeding up to a racing pace, my cheeks warming with my rising anger.

The emotional whiplash of it all hits me like a tidal wave. Not even an hour ago, I was screaming his name in pleasure, a bud of something so much more than simple desire blooming in my chest. But now? I'm ready to scream his name for a whole different reason.

As my anger grows, the earth underneath my feet shifts and trembles in response. For a moment, I fear the spirits have returned to destroy us all, finally enacting their revenge.

Sarana's hand touches mine, sending a wave of warming calm through me, which also settles the trembling plane.

Taking a few deep breaths, I finally compose myself enough to face Sarana and ask, "What on earth makes you think Orion and I are engaged?"

A server walks by, and I swap my empty glass for a fresh one.

"He negotiated that your hand in marriage be a part of the agreement we made. A match that is sure to make the bonds between Promithia and Corath stronger," she says, trying to make the situation sound better than it possibly could. But I see the pained look in her eyes as realization settles in. "I'm sorry, Raya. Considering how close you two have become, I figured you had already discussed the idea, and the only way he would've brought it to me was because you agreed. I would've never said yes if you didn't."

I barely hear her as the world around me blurs. I try to make sense of what Sarana just said. The news she shared that shouldn't *be* news.

While one cage has been lifted, I feel as though new manacles have just been shackled on in its stead. The freedom I was so close to feeling now fading away. Fading so quickly that I wonder if that freedom was ever there. Ever truly mine to begin with.

Foolish, I am so very foolish.

I'm not sure when I walked away from the table, but my legs are now moving through the crowd once more. Wandering with a hazy purpose, I walk until I'm approaching the person I very much don't want to talk to right now but know that I must.

King Orion stands in front of his throne at the bottom of the dais, talking with Kassius. When he sees me, his focus shifts entirely. One of his rare, wide smiles engulfs his face, bringing new life to his expression.

I quickly bow. "Forgive me for intruding, Your Majesty, but I was wondering if I could have a word. It's quite urgent."

There is no smile on my face, no kindness in my voice. The smile that made his features appear as though the sun was shining down on him immediately disappears. Dread hangs heavily in the air. But not the kind that people feel when their lives are in danger.

No, this is dread and worry that I uncovered his scheming secrets to prevent my leaving. Which is surely why he asked for our marriage to be a part of the treaty, because he knows that without it, I would certainly leave Corath. Although, I never had any intentions of leaving him. Together. We were supposed to figure this out *together*.

"There is nothing to forgive, Your Grace. Lord Kassius, we will continue this conversation tomorrow. Enjoy the rest of the evening."

Kassius glowers at me, but Orion's words seem to assuage his fear that I may kill their new king. I guess he still doesn't trust me, and right now, he probably shouldn't.

He holds out his elbow. Ignoring his arm, I lead the way to a private area of the gardens, a veranda hidden by twisting vines and tall bushes. Runelight shines on posts in each corner, and two chairs rest in the center of the space. His royal guard protects the entrances from prying ears and eyes.

"Tell me why on earth Sarana is under the impression that we are to be married?" I demand through gritted teeth.

Unclenching and clenching my hands into fists at my side, I feel the pool of my anger well in the pit of my stomach. There's no hint of surprise or shock on his face. If anything, I taste his disappointment. Disappointed in himself or in the fact that I found out so soon?

"Well, I had toyed with an idea of an ambassadorship, but for someone of your stature, that would never do. You deserve so much more." His eyes look distant, his demeaner somehow shifted.

I'm not even sure if the man in front of me is the same person I shared a bed with, gave a piece of myself to.

"And how do you know what I deserve? What I want, Orion?"

His features seem to soften a bit, but his jaw shifts, like he's fighting his own internal thoughts. Fighting whatever primal part of his nature aims to overthrow his compassion and reason.

"I needed to provide Sarana with something that could benefit her and your country. Having one of Promithia's duchesses become my queen will help solidify the alliance. Show both countries, the world, that we are serious about moving forward in peace."

"Well, what about me, Orion? I'm the one who will have to marry you, not Sarana. You should have at least talked to me first. Asked me if this is something I would want or be comfortable with." My voice is pleading now, and something in him finally breaks.

His hard exterior, whatever shield he had up, crumbles ever so slightly. That fear I felt before finally brims to the surface again.

"I don't know why I didn't come to you first, Raya," he says, closing the distance between us. "I'm sorry."

"Oh, don't give me that bullshit," I say, shaking my head. I pull away from his attempt to wrap me in an embrace, as if that could help the situation now. "You know exactly why you didn't come to me first. Because you were afraid that I'd say no."

"Would you have said yes?" he asks, eyes cold as stone.

"It doesn't matter now. You said we would figure out what we were and what that meant *together*. But instead, you took my choice away *again*. Used your power to get exactly what you wanted at my expense."

"Would marrying me be so bad?" Hurt crosses his face. He looks insulted.

Something sour courses through him, and I do my best to reel in my own emotions. To gain control. I don't want to monitor what he's feeling, no matter the situation he's now put me in.

"Orion, marrying you isn't the issue. It's the fact that my life has been decided for me since the day I was born. For once, I want to feel like I am actually in control of my own future. And I thought you understood that. You freed me from the Birthrite, but now you wish to cage me in another way. Why give me my freedom just to rip it away again?"

He shakes his head, sorrow and regret filling his eyes. "Raya, I—" he starts, but I don't let him finish.

"Don't you dare say you're sorry because we both know you're not. If anything, you're sorry I found out this way, right? Perhaps this is what I get for being *'Sarana's whore,'* your father's pet, and then your property. For not establishing these boundaries before. A clear oversight on my part." I shake my head.

This time, I'm the one who closes the distance between us with precise and angry steps, shoving my finger into his chest with every word I speak.

"When the celebrations are over, I am going home. I told you I had no intention of staying here, and that has not changed, even if my feelings for you have. If you are too much of a coward to address your fear and instead wield your power as king to grant your own wishes, then let me be the first person to deny you of that.

"I refuse. I refuse to marry you. I don't care what you say or what you do. Sarana knows these are not my wishes, so this part of the treaty had better be removed by the time your names are signed tomorrow."

His eyes grow dark, the beast within unleashed and untamed as thunder cracks in the distance. "And if it's not?"

His voice is cold and distant, edged with a challenge. A king viewing his lover as little more than his possession.

"Then I will fight you every step of the way." I turn to walk away, but as I reach the exit of this secret corner of the gardens, I turn to look at him one more time, my words filled with fire and ice. "Your father was right. There is more of him in you, and I see that now."

Without waiting for him to respond, I storm out of the veranda, through the guests, and back into the palace. I enter the first door I see.

The door is barely closed behind me when I finally crumble. The room is dark, but cracks of lightning spear the sky, showering the room in a silver glow with each strike. Orion's power, no doubt, striking in anger.

Whatever strength and resolve I had before in front of Orion has completely dissolved into nothingness as I slink down to the ground. Everything I have been keeping locked and tucked away pours out of me in loud sobs.

The war. The deaths I've caused, my father's own as well. My capture. My torture. The Birthrite. And now this. Every decision that was not my own has led me right into this fate.

I thought that this moment of overwhelm, of replaying every emotion from the past several years, would come when I finally settled at home. It never once crossed my mind that I would break down, here and now, in a country that is not and will never be my home. But it does not surprise me one bit that I was betrayed by someone I trust, someone I should have never trusted to begin with.

A knock sounds at the door, or at least I think it does, but when no one walks in or calls, I ignore it.

I know you're in there, Raya, Xander calls in a whisper.

Startled by his voice in my mind, I scurry to my feet. Wiping the tears away from my face as I head to the door, I restore the veil of protection over my mind, being sure to fill every crack that may have appeared in the invisible wall. However, I'm pretty positive none were there. How does he always find the cracks to let himself inside?

Taking a deep breath, I open the door and allow him into the room.

"Are you following me, Shadowman?" I ask as I walk to the window. Although I try my best to tease, there's no hiding my puffy eyes and tear-stained cheeks.

"I saw you practically doze anyone in your way trying to get inside." He looks at me, probably using his abilities to assess my emotions, or at least as much as he can with the wall I've put up. But he settles on my eyes, not needing to look much farther. He stands right where the moon and runelight pool into the room, meeting the shadows. "I knew something was wrong, so yes, I followed you here."

"Well, nothing is wrong. I'll be fine. Everything will be fine," I say, hardly believing my own words.

"Just because we started our friendship with lies doesn't mean that's how it should continue." His expression softens as he approaches the windowsill, leaning against the opposite end from where I stand. "What happened?"

I start to speak, wanting so desperately to find something clever to say to his remark about our *friendship*. But I find no will inside to argue, tease, or fake a smile. "Orion intends to marry... *me*," I share, not even caring to contemplate whether or not I should trust him. He's bound to find out with the rest of the world tomorrow.

"Considering how close you two are, I would have expected this to be happy news. But you are not happy about this?"

I expect his calm voice and inquisitive nature, his wanting to get to the root of the cause. But what I don't expect is the twitching of his jaw and flaring of his nose. *Is he angry?*

"Maybe if he had asked me before requesting my hand in marriage be a part of the treaty, if he thought my opinion mattered in this situation, I wouldn't be so angry or so unwilling to agree. So no, I am not happy about this."

But then my memory reminds me of who was there to help me off the dais when I stood in shock after Orion severed the Birthrite. It was Xander. So, of course, he's surprised by my reaction.

He searches my eyes for the truth that will inevitably set itself free.

"When he released me from the Rite, it was a shock feeling the tether between us snap. But at the end of it all, I was relieved, happy even. Knowing I could make decisions again without a shadow of a doubt that they were truly mine. Now it's clear what I am to him. What I have always been. A thing to be used over and over again by the people I am supposed to be subservient to."

"You are not a pawn, Raya."

"Aren't I? My entire life revolves around duty and honor and what is expected of me," I say, tears pooling in my eyes. "For once, I want to live *my* life, make choices for myself. I'll deal with the consequences of them later, but I need that. If anyone can understand that, it should have been Orion. Hell, even you should be able to understand that." I push off the windowsill and plop down on one of the nearby chaises.

"Yes, I have my duties and my royal obligations, but being the last in line for the throne means I have a bit more freedom than my older siblings. Although, not without consequence, but I understand well enough." His voice trails closer as he sits beside me on the chair. "You deserve your freedom. He shouldn't have put you in a corner like this, and

I hope he does the right thing and allows you to make that choice."

"I just thought he understood me. I had shared so much with him over the past few months. He knew my struggles with my own path, the control I crave. But with this? It's clear that he either never understood me at all or doesn't care. And that is what really hurts," I say, heart aching and cracking as I share my truth.

Tears fall hot and heavy down my cheeks and Xander hands me a handkerchief.

Not wanting to talk about myself any longer, I decide to change the subject entirely. "If you don't mind me asking, why did you help Orion, especially when your parents didn't want to get involved?" I ask through sniffles.

"As an outsider, I saw what the war was doing to both countries. To the people who fled to us to evade the fight and the toll it took on them. I knew I needed to do what I could to help. After Orion was injured and his father ordered him not to fight, our traveling paths collided. He trusted me then with his true feelings of the war and the future he sought for Corath, and I vowed to help. Because I knew it was the right thing to do. Truly, I felt that if no one else was going to help stop the war that has been waging for too damn long, then at least I could."

"And do your parents understand that choice you made?"

"They will, eventually. Right now, I made them look like fools by going against their wishes. There will be consequences, but I don't care. I know I did the right thing."

"Like what? Force you into exile?" I look up at him again and find his eyes have grown distant. He said he's been having many meetings with his parents. I can only imagine what those conversations have been like for him.

"I don't think they'd go that far, but it's possible." He shrugs.

Now that I'm inspecting his face, I see the weary lines caused by lack of sleep taking shape at the corners of his eyes.

"Well, Shadowman, if you need a place to visit before being welcomed home, we would be delighted to have you as a guest in Senna. Maybe you can teach me how you've mastered mist-traveling."

"It would be an honor," he says, dipping his head in a small bow.

"Oh please, Your Highness, the honor is all mine." I smile, nudging his shoulder with my own. "Thank you, by the way."

"For what?" he asks, genuine curiosity in his eyes.

"For following me. Making sure I'm okay. For being here, really. Looks like I now owe you a life and a supportive ear," I say with a chuckle, but I see no amusement in him when he responds.

"Raya, you owe me absolutely nothing. I'm here because I care. I may not be the most open or talkative person, but that doesn't mean I'm going to let someone in need go without. You needed me then, you needed someone now. I will always be here."

I'm not sure why, but I decide to open my veil, just a sliver. It seems he has done the same, as I feel the tendrils of our abilities collide and intertwine. The warmth of his sincerity engulfs my senses. There's no wall beneath his emotions, nothing there but him and what he is willing to give... himself, his friendship. Something I can sense he doesn't give to everyone freely.

So what makes me so special? Why is this man, someone who prefers his Reader abilities, so ready to entrust me with his friendship?

One thing is for damn certain, I don't think I can so readily give him my trust. That will have to be earned from here on out.

In that moment, something new enters the space between us. Something old, ancient, and powerful. It seems to weave itself within and around Xander, blending in with the warmth I just felt moments ago.

I lock onto his eyes, and I must be going crazy because I swear the silver of his irises swirl like pools of glittering starlight.

Wake up. I hear a pleading voice echo in my mind. The words rattle through me, settling deep into my core.

Come home to me. A chill courses through my body, shaking my bones.

Not this again.

"Did you hear that?" I ask Xander, but he shakes his head, confusion tinging the warmth and old entangled power.

I look around the room, unsure where the words came from. The voice wasn't Xander's. This was something entirely different. Like hearing a voice through a tunnel, through time and fate. And the voice, *that* voice, came from all around me and has nestled its way into the very core of my being.

"What did you hear?" Xander asks, capturing my attention once more.

I look back to him. His eyes are normal again, but the feeling of ancient, raw power still hangs thick in the air between us.

"It must've been the wind," I lie, but force a smile and pry away the shock from my features.

Shaken, I rise from the chaise and head to the door. He silently follows behind me.

"I think I will retire for the night. I shall see you

tomorrow for the final festivities." I bow, then head in the direction of my sister's bedchambers after retrieving a nightgown from my room.

Dessy eventually joins me under the covers, her arms wrapping tightly around me as a new wave of tears pour out in a crescendo. For all my pain and heartache, I can't shake the feeling of those ancient tendrils from my being.

FORTY-ONE

Three daises sit at the head of the room. Xander, Samson, and I stand with Orion in the center. Sarana and Promithian representatives—my sister and Leigh included—are to the left of us. To the right are Xander's parents and the rest of the Voliran dignitaries. A smaller table rests in front of the room, the finalized treaty splayed atop just waiting to be signed.

Sarana clears her throat to speak, congratulating Corath on their new king and the prosperous future that lies ahead.

I'm not paying much attention to what she's saying, lost in my own thoughts, when Orion leans to me and speaks in a barely audible whisper in my ear. "Just so you know, we've changed the stipulation of the engagement. It will be your choice. If you decide not to marry me, there will be no consequences. The treaty will remain intact."

I scoff, only loud enough for him to hear. And apparently Xander, who shifts ever so slightly on his feet and is now watching me from the corner of his eyes.

My words are filled with venom, but I keep my tight

smile plastered on my face for all to see. "I am truly grateful, *Your Majesty*, for giving me a choice. If only you cared enough about that in the first place." I don't dare hold back my malice.

"I'm sorry, Raya. I'm trying."

"Not hard enough."

My eyes dare to spy him out of their corners, and I find a tight smile to match my own on his face. But his eyes. His eyes are filled with dread. Regret slick in the air between us.

Sarana motions for Orion to step forward. "Better run along, you've a treaty to sign," I say before stepping aside with Xander and Samson.

Pen scrapes against parchment, filling the silence that envelops the room as they both take turns signing their names.

After the last swoop of his signature is inked, Orion lifts his feather pen from the paper. The treaty is officially signed.

Peace. Peace at last.

WITHOUT A MOMENT TO SPARE, the feast appears on each of the long dining tables that fill the hall. Chalices are filled to the brim with sparkling wine and carved meats roasted to perfection fill our plates along with a wide assortment of vegetables and imported delicacies from the sea.

I try my best to look as pleasant as I can despite being forced to sit by Orion's side at the center of the room. My only saving grace is Xander, who is seated at my left, the perfect distraction to ensure I don't do anything I would regret... or that would cause an international incident. Like,

I don't know, stabbing Orion's hand with my fork, which I contemplate doing every time he inches his pinky closer to mine during our meal.

But no violence from me tonight. I am keeping my anger at bay with wine… and Xander, who is currently whispering in my mind backstories of the courtiers we happen to spy. Neither of us knows anything about any of these people, but it's fun to make up their histories, imagine the lives they live. It's turned into a bit of a game for us. At this point, I can feel the wine as it courses through my veins, on my way to being sufficiently drunk.

Orion hasn't really noticed us either, or the fact that we appear to be deep in conversation when we haven't physically spoken a word at all. Too busy, too deep in conversation with Samson. Which I suppose is a good thing. If he's talking to him, he won't be able to turn his attention to me.

That woman in the sapphire gown, two tables over from your parents' dais? With the way she eyes you, it seems her husband isn't keeping her satisfied, I say in his mind, my silent words punctuated by a slightly more audible hiccup. *Maybe I'm a bit tipsier than I thought.* If my hiccup wasn't any indication, then my too-free thoughts definitely are.

But Xander doesn't seem to mind. He holds back a laugh as we inconspicuously watch the woman's eyes rove over our table, slowing to a sensual gaze as soon as she spies Xander, waiting for the moment he might return her stare, either by chance or on purpose.

And that is why I am not looking in her direction, he says, taking a sip from his glass of bubbling liquid. *But who's to say her eyes stop on me when they are also very clearly roaming to you as well?*

I risk another glance over. She sends me a playful smirk

as her eyes lock onto mine. A chill of excitement and pleasure crawls down my spine at the realization of what her needs imply.

Well, if you won't indulge, perhaps I might, I whisper back to him as I slightly raise my glass and dip my head in her direction.

Xander's eyes widen in surprise.

What? I ask. *I'm not engaged or married.*

Yet, he counters.

Who's to say I ever will be?

The man next to you might have a say in that, Your Grace. His jaw does that twitching thing again, but I ignore it.

He may be king, but he is not mine. I ignore the irony in those words, considering where Orion and I were yesterday. I down my wine in one big gulp, then motion for a waiter to refill my glass. *And he has* graciously *given me a choice to decide, which I do not accept. So with that, I am still very single and willing to spend my last night in Corath in whatever way I please.*

Are you saying this because you truly want to experience all the delights in the world? Or just to make Orion jealous? he asks, eyeing me skeptically, seeing right through my drunken bravado.

Why did Loren leave early? She mentioned being called away for something, I ask, swiftly changing the course of this discussion.

Thankfully, he doesn't push back. *She had some business to attend to back in Volira.*

Hmmmm, sounds ominous, I reply.

Nothing too serious, I assure you, he says while taking a sip of his sweet wine. *But I will surely let her know you asked after her. I'm sure she will be quick to answer your beckoning call.* His eyebrows wiggle in amusement as I hold back my jaw from dropping.

I think I liked you better when you were brooding in the corner of the training field, I say.

He sends me a wink before looking ahead to the center of the room.

Most of the guests have finished their meals, and the music that fills the hall switches to a more lively pace as guests begin to mingle about the room, taking their chances to wander to the head table and dare a conversation with the *Honored.*

With every person who steps forward and introduces themselves, Xander shifts in his seat, bobbing his knee and tapping his fingers against the table as each new person tries to capture his attention.

I reach under the table and place my palm on his thigh just above his knee, squeezing my fingers gently around the taut muscle. Ever so slightly, he leans in my direction.

After a few moments, his bobbing knee and tapping fingers still as the guests vying for our attention subside and venture on to new sights about the room. With his nerves at ease, I swiftly remove my hand, placing it back into my lap.

Clearing my throat, I take a sip of my freshly refilled wine. *What's the matter, Shadowman? Not having any fun?*

I just hate being the center of attention, and this Honored *crap is putting me right in the spotlight.*

For one in such a state of disarray, the smile on your face and ease of conversation says differently.

You shouldn't judge a book by its cover. I'm sure you've had your fair share of putting on a brave face for appearance's sake, he counters.

Touché, I say, loosening a breath and twirling my glass of wine. *How do you get on at home then? Living in a palace means celebrations like this all the time.*

While being in large crowds and having to talk to people is difficult, it's a bit easier at home, where people I know are in attendance.

You can always forget about socializing and dance the night away. Dancing is always a great way to alleviate the stress of communication.

Ah, yes, and just ruminate over the dance moves and hope I don't blunder.

But you asked me to dance last night? I ask, looking his way.

His gaze is heavy when he replies. *Because I wanted to dance with* you.

I see, I reply, blush heating my cheeks. *A prince who doesn't enjoy the splendor of extravagant balls,* I continue, chuckling into my cup as I take another sip. *Tell me then, what do you do for fun?*

Typically, I prefer a private dinner or a night at my favorite pub with my friends. I enjoy being around my people. I'm more relaxed when I am, he says, brushing his leg against mine.

The action sends a thrilling pulse through me, though I'm not sure why.

Well, you seem pretty relaxed at the present, I retort, reveling in the brush of contact.

Can I be honest? he asks, voice timid as he traces the edges of my mind.

With me? Always.

I feel more at ease with you than I have with anyone else in a very long time.

I'm not sure when my hand inched its way back down to his knee or when I leaned closer to his chair, but I'm not shocked at all when his fingers give mine a friendly squeeze.

My eyes are locked onto his mesmerizing gaze, silver and radiant as ever.

I could get lost in them, and I'm about to when one of Orion's newly appointed advisers, Lord Kassius, bellows out a laugh. His boisterous voice pulls us out of our daze, and we put some distance between us. My hands cool instantly from his missing touch.

To my surprise, despite the music now in full swing, no other guests have taken the dance floor. For some reason, I'm even more surprised when Orion extends his hand to me. I meet his gaze with furrowed brows and an uninterested expression.

Pain flashes across his face at my heated glare, but he doesn't let that deter him. "Would you do me the honor of joining me for a dance?" he asks.

"Actually, Your Majesty, I just agreed to dance with Xander," I say, rising from my seat.

Xander doesn't miss a beat as he rises to meet me, holding out his arm for me to take.

"Apologies, Your Majesty," Xander says. "I am more than happy to have a dance with Raya after you, of course." He dips his head in respect, but Orion takes the hint.

Pressing his lips into a thin line, he steps aside, clearing the way for Xander and me.

A quick waltz replaces the song before, and a few couples join us on the dance floor.

"I hate waltzes," he says, whispering aloud so only I can hear.

It's strange hearing his voice out loud and not echoing in my mind. But it's a welcome change.

"It isn't too late to turn back," I respond as we take our place on the dance floor.

He flashes me a wicked grin, filled with that awful male pride. "I do love a challenge."

"Of course you consider a waltz a challenge. I'm the one doing all the turns."

"Well, I do have to lift you here and there."

"What a trying task," I say with a smirk as we bow to one another.

His hand finds its place at my waist, pulling me in close. His grip is safe and strong as our hands clasp together. As the music begins, so do we, sweeping across the floor in sure strides and graceful twirls.

"I'm surprised you aren't telling me I should be easier on him," I say.

"Why the hell would I do that?" He looks at me then, as best as he can despite our position. "What he did was wrong. And if you are not ready to, you shouldn't *have* to talk to him for his sake. You need to do what's best for yourself."

In that moment, I hear something on the wind of the melody that plays around us. It calls to me, reaches to me like a phantom limb.

Wake up.

My eyes dart to Xander as fear courses through me at those words. The same from the other night when we were in that dark room, the voice of fate that keeps calling on the wind, nestling its way deep in my core and reverberating through my being.

I take a deep breath to calm my nerves.

He just cocks his head to the side, unsure what causes my alarm. He lifts me to the swell of the melody, and as my feet touch the ground, the applause of the crowd greets us.

"You didn't hear that?" I ask.

He simply shakes his head, brows knit, as we fit back together in each other's embrace and allow the music to carry us across the floor. With the strength of his arms leading me through every spin and turn, my shaking hands begin to calm.

You're beginning to scare me, he whispers into my mind, and the music takes on a natural lull.

Resorting back to whispering, I see. I try to tease, but the look on his face is serious. Not in the mood for joking.

No, I'm not in the mood for joking, not when you looked at me as you did last night, like death was mere inches away.

It's not you, if that's any consolation, I say as the tempo picks up once more, and we're back to sweeping the dance floor.

I brace myself as his strong hands make their way to my waist, aware of every place his fingers trail along the bodice of my dress, feeling the heat of his touch through the glittering fabric. He lifts me overhead, then sets me down in another twirl. My heart picks up its pace, and I instinctively take another step closer to him.

If it's not me, then what is it? he implores.

With his gaze locked on mine, our bodies moving as one to the rhythm, all concern and worry fly away on the air of the music around us. Nothing matters. Not the whispering winds of fate. Not the childish drama with Orion. All that matters is the peace I feel with Xander by my side.

His eyes search mine for any answers he may find. But they don't come. Not when shouting from the main hall flows into the ballroom and screams fill the air, drowning out the music.

FORTY-TWO

I'm midspin when I force myself to a halt, facing the main doors of the banquet hall.

Guards quickly work to close the doors, hoping to stall the intruders. Giving everyone in the banquet hall precious moments to find safety.

The muffled shouts grow louder now, and I can sense the panic beyond the doors. The partners on the dance floor fly off, following the masses that press deeper into the room, trying to put as much distance between them, the doors, and whoever may be behind them that will surely mean their death.

A few people, oblivious to what may be happening, stand where they are.

"Get back!" I yell, and Xander motions for them to find safety. Attendants shuffle as many partygoers as they can through the hidden passageways.

I turn back to find Orion being hauled away by Samson, the king fighting his guard every step of the way. I dare another second to find Sarana and her husband being led farther back into the room by Leigh and Dessy, following Samson's lead.

Once I know they are all as safe as they can be, I build my veil of protection—a solid wall separating the intruders from the royals and partygoers behind us. All the guests should be safe, so long as Xander and I don't fall. We won't. We *can't*.

The musicians, spirits bless their souls, continue to play the upbeat waltz despite the screams and shouts around them.

The rest of the guards in the room stand in formation around Xander and me, preparing themselves for who might barge in through those doors.

For a moment, all we hear is silence. But that silence is quickly followed by the doors crashing open.

A group of men barge into the banquet hall, bows and crossbows ready to fire. They're dressed in all black, save for silver brooches fastened to their cloaks—a crest of some sort with swirling bits of metal, a symbol that looks oddly familiar. I can't place where I know it from but will surely never forget.

"For the true King of Corath," they shout in unison and release their weapons, not once noticing the wall of protection separating the crowd and king from their bolts.

I'm sure those arrows are intended for Orion and Sarana and everyone else here who supports the treaty, but the man at the apex fires an arrow straight for Xander. Something unlocks deep within my chest at that realization, and in that moment, when all their arrows fire as one, time seems to stand still—to halt and warp and darken around me.

And through that darkness, a light of silver, matching my gown of starlight, cascades down upon us and fills the room. The light is blaring, blinding, and one by one, the runelights ahead wink out of existence.

With a surge of power, the men who barged into the room with death and vengeance slick on their skin are blown back and slammed onto the marble floor—blood slinking out of their eyes, ears, noses, and mouths. The arrows they fired disintegrate before they have a chance to do any damage.

More screams erupt in the room, the music finally stunned to a halt.

I look up and find a strange figure floating in the air above us. Her eyes glow as bright as the silver hue that surrounds her entire being. Her gown, a halo of light, billows around her.

She reminds me of the depictions of the spirits from paintings with her gaunt cheekbones, slender frame, and long limbs defined with a muscle honed to kill. She looks like…a ghost. A beautiful ghost. Ancient. Powerful. And… I think I know her.

Despite the frightening allure of her being, she looks absolutely breathtaking. Ethereal. As though she could capture the heart and soul of anyone who might cross her path. The power emanating from her is strong enough to decimate worlds…. Or create them.

Then it registers. I *have* seen her before. When Mattias was about to turn me into one of his unbreakable warriors. She was there, protecting me, just as she is protecting all of us now.

She opens her mouth, lips moving quickly, but whatever is happening must be affecting my hearing because I only register half of the words she says. The words that do register flow in my ears in a melodic voice and a dying language. Eldrian. The language of the spirits.

Once more, that bright light pulses through the room, and the men who lie there bleeding and twitching on the floor evaporate into a pile of ash and air.

The light recedes, and I am hurled back, tumbling to the ground, only to be caught by someone's sure and steady arms.

As the silver light fades, runelight flickers back to life around the room. With the threat eliminated, I relinquish my veil, and the guests begin to step forward, closer to where Xander has caught me from my fall. They all share an assorted look of astonishment as they stare at us, at where that ethereal being once stood to destroy the band of bandits.

Xander keeps a hand at my elbow until I'm settled on my feet once more. Orion shouts, fighting Samson as he surges through the crowd, running toward Xander and me, worry and fear etched into his features as if they may never leave. Sarana, Dessy, and Leigh trail behind him. My sister's eyes are wide with reverence.

"Who was that?" I ask Xander, but he shares the same expression as my sister.

Then, one by one, everyone in the room, even the visiting royals standing atop their dais, bend a knee, their heads dipping low.

Whispers fill the room, the ancient language once again filling my ears. A phrase I remember from my lessons long ago. One that is reserved for the return of *the* spirits—Ach'tella and Ekkheim. The ones who will save us all. Again.

"Qœo avantos thina tornejna, Alten Spirit, prokats al'toren." *We've awaited your return, High Spirit. Protector of the realm.*

Orion finally makes his way to where I stand. Hands

outstretched, he takes me from Xander's stabilizing grasp. His grip pinching.

"Are you all right?" he asks, glancing me up and down, eyes brimming with a rapture I do not quite understand. Like a part of him has been waiting for this very moment.

All I can do is nod, ignoring the crowd bowing around us. Chanting those ancient words.

I look at both Xander and Orion, who stand before me. Unable to hide the fear and dread and tinge of panic that laces my voice, I ask again, "Who was that woman?"

They share a look before turning back to me.

"That was you," Xander finally answers.

An ancient voice on the wind shifts around me. *Wake up.*

My vision blurs, mind spinning at the absurdity of it all. Shaking my head, it takes all my will to keep my body from trembling.

"Impossible," I say in disbelief. "I saw her with my own eyes."

Orion tries to explain, but I can't hear what he's saying. A blend of words that attempt to console but confirm the stories we learned as kids. The return of Ach'tella and Ekkheim. The spirits reborn to stop the world's second destruction. Retellings that I grew to believe were *just* stories made to solidify a culture, a religion, a belief.

A story. Nothing more than that.

Wake up.

With every word he speaks, the threads of my sanity slowly unravel. That iron will of strength and resolve melts away as if I'm thrust into a forge.

I back away from him, ripping my hands out of his grasp and wrapping my arms around my waist. Holding myself together with the scrap of sanity I have left.

The ancient wind shifts again. *Come home to me.*

Xander immediately steps forward, gripping my shoulders with his soft but sure hands. I want to look away. I want to keep my eyes shut tight. But with a glide of his finger tipping my chin up, I can't help but return his silver gaze.

He opens his mind to me, replaying his memory of what just occurred like scenes from an enchanted painting.

I see it, clear as day. One moment, I'm standing in front of Xander, looking back at him. In the next, the men barge in, taking aim. Even though the man in front had an arrow aimed at his heart, Xander kept his eyes on me. He knew it was too late, and he spent what he thought were his final moments staring at me instead of trying to save himself.

But he didn't need to. Not when that bright light appeared, coming from… *me?*

The person who lifted into the air on the wind of essence was *me.*

The surge of power came from *me.*

The words, ancient and heavy, flowed from my lips as if the language was second nature, "Me ehr Ach'tella. Me ehr Ach'tella tornejde. Prokadela de hashem toren."

Wake up.

I pull myself out of his memory, shaking my head but staying in his grasp. "But I saw what happened," I say unwilling to believe the memory, my voice as soft as the wind.

Your time to rise is near. Those words from a distant abyss and crowded market echo in my mind.

"That burst of energy must have overpowered you. Ejecting your mind from your body," he says slowly, trying to put the pieces together himself. He removes his hands from my shoulders.

Your time to rise is here.

"From whose power?" I ask, but I already know the answer. I heard the name spoken from my own lips.

I am Ach'tella of the Spirits, reborn. I will protect the keepers of this realm.

As if connected by some invisible force, Orion and Xander bend a knee before me, bowing their heads as one.

ACKNOWLEDGMENTS

This story barreled its way into my mind and very quickly nestled into my heart. What was only supposed to be a quick little fantasy story about a captured warrior trying to find her way back to her life and love, swiftly evolved into an epic world filled with alluring magic, a love-triangle (or two), and an ancient prophecy that even I didn't see coming.

To my editor, Jeanine Harrell, thank you for molding my words and this story into this incredible work of art! I'm so happy to have you on my team and am very grateful for the zoom chats and email chains to help work through the plot!

Essence and Runes wouldn't be anywhere it is today without the help of my wonderful beta readers and brainstorming wizards. Gianna, Merissa, Daphney, Robby, Debbie, and my sensitivity reader Alexia, thank you so much for your insights and for providing such incredible feedback that helped evolve the story to what we are reading today (seriously, the first draft and this one are two completely different adventures!). You gave me the confidence to keep moving forward with this story, and for that I am forever grateful!

Lorissa Padilla, thank you for creating such a BEAUTIFUL cover and for being a wonderful friend on our corner of Bookstagram. You are absolutely incredible and so, so, so talented. Thank you for taking my vision and bringing it to life in a way that's better than I ever could have imagined!

Every fantasy world has to have a map, and I couldn't have asked for a better map maker and friend, Gabriel J. Fanara. Thank you for helping me bring this world to life through your epic design skills (and for being an amazing Dungeon Master).

From Blue Hens to writing buddies, thank you Tory for all your advice, support, and friendship! You have helped make this publishing journey so much easier, and I cannot wait for all the writing sprints to come.

To all my friends and family, thank you for believing in me, in this story, and for listening to me talk about it over and over again the past three years. Now that it's out in the world, you'll get to hear all about the making of book two instead!

My parents have always been my biggest cheerleaders, and during the making of Essence and Runes, their support never wavered! Thank you, Mom, Dad, Rich, Gale, and Sam for everything you have done to support me through this journey. I am so lucky to have you in my corner!

He may be a four-legged furball who will never read this, but he is one of the best writing buddies a gal could ask for. Thank you, Tank. Without you, those late-night writing sessions would have been a whole lot harder.

To my love, my forever alpha reader, Mike: Thank you for always being there to listen to all of my new ideas and "brain blast" moments (even when they made no sense to you). For sitting through my read-aloud sessions and for being there through the ups and downs. There were moments when I just didn't think we would get here, but with your support and enthusiasm, you helped keep me going. Thank you, thank you, thank you. I love you to the stars and moon and back!

Last but certainly not least, to YOU, the reader: Thank you for taking a chance on an indie author and reading this tale. I hope you enjoyed meeting Raya, Orion, and the rest of the cast of *Essence and Runes*.

Adventure awaits!

THE WORLD OF ESSENCE
AND RUNES CONTINUES
WITH BOOK TWO! KEEP
READING FOR A SNEAK
PEEK!

SNEAK PEEK: BOOK 2*
*ELEMENTS MAY CHANGE

I ripple into the Shadows and seek my escape out of the room, evading the guards clearing the debris and bodies from the main hall as I find my way into one of the receiving rooms. My only goal is peace and quiet and to be alone with my racing thoughts as I try to make sense of this horrific dream.

Rippling out of the Shadows, I take a seat on one of the plush velvet couches resting in the center of the room.

A nightmare. This is nothing more than a nightmare. Perhaps I'll wake up and find that I'm still dwelling in a cell, still Mattias's prisoner. A prisoner never saved by Orion, and the war is still raging on.

This is real. A familiar voice echoes in my mind, and I jolt to find Xander standing in the doorway.

His words in my mind are clipped, reserved as if he's unsure whether or not his voice should be there to begin with. Much like how he stands by the doorway, unsure if he should approach whatever it is I am now.

Not because he's afraid of me, but because he views me as

something he cannot simply approach anymore. Something... other. Something sacred.

I shiver at the thought.

I don't want any of this, I whisper to him.

Just because you don't want something doesn't stop it from happening, he replies, and I scoff at the frankness, the realness in his voice. We are no longer bantering, teasing, flirting friends. His voice is formal, guiding. *If what just happened is any indication, the people of this world may bow to their rulers, but they will* worship *you.*

No, they will worship who lies within me. Who I carry.

He shakes his head, in complete disagreement with me. *She may dwell inside you, but it will be you they see as you protect them from what's to come.*

Before I even have a chance to ask what the hell he means, the entourage makes their entrance into the room.

My sister is the first one to approach me, not even hesitating to throw her arms around my shoulders. Sarana follows in a bit more cautiously and takes a seat in the chair across from me.

"I always knew you were special," Leigh says, standing behind Sarana. His hand resting on the hilt of his sword is a stark contrast to the joking lilt of his voice.

Does he really think I would hurt her?

They don't know what to think of you right now, Xander clarifies.

When I pull away from my sister, I realize he has taken a similar stance behind my chair, assessing everyone in the room the same way Leigh and Samson are assessing me.

"So, you're saying you always knew the spirit Ach'tella rested inside me?" I look to Leigh and ask with a playful laugh, at least as playful as I can manage.

"Ach'tella isn't what makes you special. You've accomplished that all on your own," he says with a smile.

Dessy takes a seat at my side as Orion kneels before me. He takes my hands in an assertive grasp. I sense a strange emotion from him, a mixture of amazement and possessiveness, differing from the worry that seems to be plastered on his face. His eyes shift between Xander and me.

"Did you know?" he asks, and I can't hold back the laugh that erupts from my core.

"If I did, her power would've been very useful during the war. It probably would've been over long ago." I do my best to keep my joking up but am quickly losing momentum.

"You know you can tell us if that weren't the case?" His tone takes on an air of curious caring, but his eyes tell me another story. One where he doesn't fully believe me.

I tear my hands away from his, needing a bit more energy to do so than I thought I would. He balls his hands into fists at his side while keeping his eyes locked on mine. A flicker of darkness surges through them.

"Did my confusion and panic afterward not tell you everything you needed to know of my knowledge?"

Xander shifts behind me, and if Orion noticed his protective stance, he made no comment on it. But I see Sarana's eyes dancing between the three of us, questions roving in her mind.

I squint my eyes in her direction. "You're rather quiet, Sarana," I start, and the curiosity within her grows stronger.

With my shift in focus, Orion rises and sits in an armchair to the right.

"I am only wondering about you. How do you feel now?" Despite the questions that rest on the tip of her tongue, her words are sincere, drifting to another topic entirely.

As I replay Xander's memory in my mind, a realization

courses through me of the reason why Ach'tella deployed her power. It was only when I saw that Xander was in danger.

"I feel normal. Whatever old power surged before, it's not at the surface anymore. Like she only came out to protect all of us," I say, shifting in my seat.

Xander shifts again as well. There's more he knows about this whole situation that he's not telling me, either because he doesn't trust me or the others in the room. I assume it's the latter.

"Who were they?" I ask

"A group of men who believe I am not their true king and do not agree with the treaty," Orion says expectantly.

Clearly, he was prepared for this kind of backlash. Whether he knew they would hit this close and this soon tells me he either wasn't prepared enough or he has traitors in his ranks.

"So they would prefer to keep fighting a frivolous war?" I ask, disgusted and dismayed.

"My father promised many people great things if Corath had won the war. Land, positions, titles. Now, with the changes being implemented, I knew there would be some opposition. Samson and I will devise a team to get to the bottom of this attack and the group behind it."

Sarana turns her attention to Xander. "My country is not as grounded in the spiritual teachings of the prophecy, but Volira is."

Not a question, but when I turn to look at Xander he nods.

Sarana continues, "And to my knowledge, you are prepared, to a degree, to support the spirits once they have made their presence known." Xander nods in confirmation again. "Well then, what do you think of this? Of the rise of Ach'tella? Ekkheim is sure to follow. What does this mean for Raya and our world?" she asks, some of that curiosity seeping through, tinged slightly with fear.

"Yes, we've been preparing for the return of the spirits, for either Ach'tella or Ekkheim to appear. But we never knew when that was going to happen or how they would manifest, just that they would." He turns my way, ensuring that whatever follows next is addressed to me. "It's imperative for you to make a connection with the spirit. Should that surge happen again, you want to work together as opposed to her taking control. Since Ach'tella is a Cosmic and her powers are often dictated by emotions, there's a lot of essence that courses through you when she is present. You have to learn how to master her power."

The Cosmic spirits—where Sarana's power of harnessing the sun and stars derives from—were the most powerful beings to have ever existed, with their abilities to create, destroy, and travel between worlds. It's because of them that they even came to Earth in the first place.

"And what could happen if I don't?" I'm not entirely sure I want to hear the answer, but I ask all the same.

"She could destroy you from the inside out," he says with a pained look on his face.

"We will not let that happen." Orion's words spew out like fire through his gritted teeth. Darkness surrounds him, clouding the light and warmth that usually embraces his aura.

"So how do I connect with her? Runes? Meditation? Listening to the song of my essence?" I say, once again resorting to sarcasm.

It's the only way my mind can handle this. There's only so much I can take before I completely lose all my senses.

"You'll have to go to the City of the Spirits," Xander explains. "The Sodari will help train and guide you."

Of course, the Sodari—The keepers of the temples. Fanatics over the history of the spirits—namely Ach'tella and Ekkheim—and what the prophecy means for this world. The City is a few hours' ride from the western border of Volira. I should have known that going home or at least staying home for a time was nothing more than a dream.

"When do you suggest I go?"

"As soon as possible," he says with sorrow in his eyes as he realizes what that means for me. *You may visit your home, but the longer you go without training, the more dangerous it will become for you,* he says the rest in a whisper.

"I need at least two months at home to help my sister prepare for restoration," I say.

"One month," Xander retorts.

"Since when did you become her keeper?" Orion growls.

I shoot him a silencing glare, to which he responds in kind with one of his own.

What is happening to him?

Ignoring him as best I can, I turn back to Xander.

"Fine," I concede, voice hard. Dessy laces her hand in mine. "It's clear we do not have all the answers for what's to come, and I really don't feel like being torn apart from the inside out by a very cranky spirit."

Unable to help myself, I spy Orion sitting still and quiet in his chair as his eyes dig into me, my soul, my very being. A spindly chill of pins creeps up my spine, making the hairs on my arms rise and fear swell within me. That darkness I felt filling him before is all-encompassing now. The typical warmth and breeze and fresh spring that normally emanate from him are completely gone. The light in his eyes is snuffed out, and his lips are pressed into a thin line.

When he realizes I'm watching him, his demeanor changes, his features soften, though not entirely.

He simply nods to all of us, then swiftly exits the room.

THE GUARDS on watch cautiously monitor me as I walk through the halls, lightning streaking through the windows. Some give nods of respect, others just stare wide eyed, unsure if they should protectively follow or stay at their post. None trail behind me, though, nor do they stop and question me as I make my way to the royal rooms that I know far too well. To Orion.

I'm not sure why I walked over here. Perhaps it was the look of pain and anger etched into his expression that haunts me. Perhaps I simply can't let go. And while nothing has changed, I couldn't just leave on such wicked terms.

SIGN UP FOR MY NEWSLETTER TO STAY IN THE KNOW!

ABOUT THE AUTHOR

 Taylor Lynn resides right outside of New York City where she works as a recruiter in the entertainment industry. An avid reader and writer, she has always loved the art of storytelling and hopes to create worlds that immerses readers into the adventure. When she's not writing (or reading), you can find her exploring new restaurants, finding new items to add to her "nerd" collection, binge watching her favorite shows, or spending time with her partner and dog. *Essence and Runes* is her first novel.

Check out her website: www.taylorlynnwrites.com

amazon.com/author/taylynn
goodreads.com/taylorlynnwrites
instagram.com/taylorlynnwrites